GALENA

A NOVEL

NORMAN GUTZMER

Publish Authority

Editor: Janie Mills
Cover Design Lead: Raeghan Rebstock

ISBN 978-1-967213-05-4 (paperback)
ISBN 978-1-967213-04-7 (ebook)
ISBN 978-1-967213-03-0 (hardback)

Published 2025 by Publish Authority,
300 Colonial Center Parkway, Suite 100
Roswell, GA, USA
PublishAuthority.com

Printed in the United States of America

To my longtime, former partners and mentors, who taught me it is possible to practice law seriously and still find time to laugh.

PROLOGUE

Paul Hoffman's Journal June 26, 1988

Stockton was icy winters, layers of clothing and snow pants every day, a coal furnace that made the whole house smell like cinders, streetlights bouncing off the snow beneath my bedroom window, summer nights with so many birds nesting in the trees along Sycamore Street that neighbors would go outside at night and bang on pots and pans to scare them away. It was the dark, waxy limbs of Pete Schamberger's cherry tree next door, and eating unwashed cherries from the highest branches until my stomach hurt. Playing Cowboys and Indians in the backyard, hiding behind the Concord grapevines that divided our yard from our neighbor's. A boy could never wait until the grapes had ripened and turned purple before he started eating them. They demanded to be eaten when they were still green and sour. It was bicycle adventures with sandwiches and bottles of lemonade in our handlebar baskets, riding over dusty roads so far from town that it was easy to get lost. Saturday night baths followed by never-ending Sunday afternoons with most of the town napping. If God rested on the seventh day, so would Stockton. It was the kind of small Midwestern town that could have been painted by Norman Rockwell. It must have had some darkness too, but Rockwell wouldn't have painted that, and I never saw it.

Of course, my memories are the impressions of a child because I was a child when I left. When I go back, my impressions will be different. Towns are like people. They grow up over time. Stockton has probably changed as much as I have. No community stands at parade rest while the whole world around it keeps marching on, not even a little farm town in Illinois. Sometimes, I wonder if I remember Stockton very well. There is a sadness about it that lingers. It nags at me and begs me to go back to see if everything was as I remember it. When I get to Stockton, most of the people will be new and things will be different. Abee's Popcorn Wagon won't sit in front of Herman's Clothing Store. Abee must have died years ago. Summers won't last forever like they used to. The lilac bushes where we lived won't give off the perfume that reminds me of my mother, who used to tend them. Even today, when I smell lilacs, I feel her there with me, hovering over me to tell me everything will be okay.

But the morning sun may still shine through the mist and down onto the dew-covered lawns, making Stockton look like a fairy land. I hope so. I will walk the sidewalks I remember and climb up the water tower hill above Sycamore Street to look down on the town. From the top of the hill, Stockton always looked like the toy village next to the model trains in the department store window at Christmastime.

It will seem odd to be a stranger in the town that was once my home. Few people will remember me or my family. Some things that happen to families are best forgotten. When people first notice me, they will wonder who I am and what brought me. I won't tell them that I'm there to wrap the town around me and see if nightmares ever have endings.

CHAPTER 1

Saturday, July 2, 1988

The drive from Nacogdoches to Texarkana was slow: small towns, narrow roads, and pine woods. Paul wanted it to linger. Spring was turning into summer, and the green woods glistened as morning cut through the heavy air.

For once, there was no hurry. Everything he owned in Houston had been discarded or put into storage. All he brought with him was a laptop computer and a couple of suitcases. Northern Illinois was a long way from East Texas, and there would be time to sort things through. Only two hours out of Houston, and the past twenty years were starting to seem like something Paul had been dreaming. But this was no dream. The smell of pine, the steering wheel vibrating against his palms, and the sun glaring into his eyes from behind the visor made him feel free. And yet, there was an unease and lack of direction in how he felt.

His partners at Schartz, Salazar, and Hoffman, LP, told him he was crazy for leaving a law practice they had worked to build for eight years, especially when it was doing well and they were enjoying the income and security they had earned.

It was hard to argue against that. He couldn't make a convincing case for what he was doing. Sometimes in life, a person does something completely illogical, and this was one of those times in the life of Paul Hoffman.

"You're cutting out on us because you want to visit a podunk town from your childhood? Do we have that right? That's a reason for quitting your law practice? Oh, I almost forgot. You are tired of all the crap you put up with as a lawyer. Since when does that matter? It's always been crap. You are messing up, Paul. You are what we in the legal profession refer to as *"non compos dumbass."* But best of luck to you anyway, pal."

They were right. Lawyers burn out from time to time. It was more than that, though. Law practice had finally brought him some real money, and practicing law was better than a lot of jobs he could have had, but making money had never been a passion for him. He was a good lawyer, willing to work the long hours and willing to accept the poor cases when necessary. But there was always too much crap, too much dealing with clogged-up courts and lawyers who wouldn't give an inch to save a little money for their clients. Lately, every case had turned into World War III. He had handled some of the ugliest cases in the firm, cases which sometimes stretched ethical boundaries to their limits. They had resulted in animosity more than anything else.

Paul had been married once. It was a mistake. His wife had left him when he was a young prosecutor in the district attorney's office. She decided he would never really settle into the marriage. She was right. He thought he might never settle into any marriage, any job, any city, or anything else. Altogether, he had spent two years with the DA's office, six years with a large firm, then eight years in the partnership he had just left. That was the longest he had ever stayed in one place. A law practice is a lot like a marriage. It takes commitment to make it work. He had never found anything or any place that drew real commitment from him.

His last partnership was the best. He liked his partners. Good guys, all of them. They were lawyers he respected. They practiced law as they were taught. It was more than a business to them. They cared about upholding the profession and doing good along the way. There really were some good times, and he would be lying to himself if he said anything different, but he still didn't find a home there. Paul had decided that he was just a solitary person who didn't feel part of anything. Not that there was anything awful about that. He was generally happy by nature. The world needs solitary people, too.

Despite all of their objections to his leaving, Paul thought his partners were as relieved to be free of him as his ex-wife had been. He was a good friend and had been an asset to the firm. But he was moody now and wasn't great to be around. He had been drinking too much and wasn't putting in serious hours. Paul had hit a wall, and he couldn't keep banging his head against it. Leaving might hurt the firm in the short run, but money wasn't a problem for his partners anymore. The firm was solid financially. They had recently won a huge case, which had settled on appeal. It was Paul's case, and it made a lot of money for everyone. They had all helped with it, but it was Paul who had brought the case in and he had been the lead attorney. He made far more money from that single case than he had made altogether in the prior fifteen years of practice. If money buys contentment, then Paul should be really, really content. But he wasn't. He was restless and uneasy. There was nothing he enjoyed and nothing he really wanted. He needed to remedy that, which is why he was driving back to the place where his life had begun. It seemed to be where a person should go to start over.

Before leaving the firm, he had read an article in the *Houston Chronicle* about a study by a group of psychologists at Rice University on the topic of "sudden good fortune." They noted that sudden good fortune often caused severe distress, and sometimes even illness, in people who are out of touch with themselves. People who couldn't handle sudden success tended toward low self-esteem. They never expected or thought that they deserved much out of life, so they felt insecure and frightened when they accomplished something good. *God*, Paul thought. *What a farce life can be! Here are these poor bastards who don't like themselves because they have never accomplished anything. Then they finally score a little success, and it drives them even crazier.*

He thought the article wasn't far off the mark where he was concerned. The long hours he and his partners had worked over the years had paid the bills, but not much else. Then, suddenly, a fat case landed in their office, and they became what the public always thought lawyers were: "well off." Well enough off that he wouldn't have to work again if he didn't feel like it. Oddly, it was pretty much like every other case he had handled. He filed the suit, hired experts, built the case, filed motions, took depositions, and tried it to a jury. A very, very kind jury, as it turned out. The case went up on appeal as expected. Big judgments get appealed. But this judgment didn't have a lot of flies on it. It was solid, and it was resolved with a lot less time and effort than he had expected. He filed his brief, had a couple of hearings, and it settled. It was ridiculous that he could make more money on one case than he had made in years of butting heads with obstinate judges, clients, and lawyers. That kind of thing was supposed to happen to other people. He had always worked hard for what he got.

An old lawyer once told him that every time a lawyer goes to the courthouse, he leaves a part of his soul on the courthouse steps. Paul may have left a few chunks of his soul at the courthouse over the years, and he didn't want to see the inside of a courthouse again for a long time. But that wasn't the cause of his unrest. The problem went to his childhood. He would never sort it out if he didn't return to the place where it had begun. Paul felt empty, and he needed answers.

My God! Here he was, speeding along through the piney forests of East Texas with the top down on his brand-new red

Corvette, feeling sad. What a dope! This was a quest he should be excited about.

When he got to a small town just past Carthage, he stopped for coffee at a Dairy Queen. Every little town in Texas is reputed to have two things: a Dairy Queen and a University of Oklahoma football recruiter. There were some local men sitting around the table next to his. The conversation was about politics and weather. They agreed that the liberals had "ruint the country." And it was dry as hell. On the plus side, the Dallas Cowboys had made some good trades, and this could be the year they would win it all again.

The men wore boots and baseball caps or Stetsons. He never understood why anyone would wear clumsy cowboy boots when work boots are cheaper, lighter, and more comfortable. These guys didn't ride up on horses. They drove up in fancy trucks. But he was sure it made sense to anyone who had grown up here. They would find just as many things wrong with Chicago, where Paul had lived much of his early life. He had heard it said that there is one right place for everyone to live. Well, he needed to find his.

Back on the road, he found himself daydreaming about what Stockton would look like when he got there. Who would he remember? Anyone? A few people still living in Stockton might remember him. But they might not have had a high opinion of his chances in life. His father certainly hadn't distinguished himself. They wouldn't know how Paul had turned out or guess that he had become a lawyer. He hadn't done well in school when he lived in Stockton. And after he left town, he had been in a few jams before he grew up. Stories about him could have filtered back to Stockton. Anyone who remembered him and his family might have written him off as a poor comparison to Stockton's other sons and daughters. He wouldn't have blamed them. But how many of them had accomplished much more than he had? How many of them could afford to piss away a well-paying legal career on nothing more than a whim? How about that?

He may have done a whole lot better than they thought he would.

Paul would not be without work while he was trying to sort out his life in Stockton. Shortly before Paul had left the law firm, his old law school had asked him to write some sections of a book the school was going to publish on Texas tort practice. He was asked to work on the project because he had been the lead attorney on one of the largest tort cases in Texas over the last five years and because he had been a part-time adjunct professor at the school while practicing full-time with his firm. Their goal was to have the book ready to go to print by late fall of 1989. Paul was thrilled about it. He had always liked the study of law more than the practice of it, and he enjoyed writing. The timing for the project was perfect. He would have idle time to fill while he was in Stockton, and he could afford to do the work pro bono. They insisted on paying him, but he planned to donate the money back to the school when he was finished. He wouldn't be sitting around doing nothing while he was renewing his acquaintance with the town and solving an old, painful riddle.

CHAPTER 2

Tuesday, July 5, 1988

Paul spent his first night in Stockton at the only motel there was. It was on the highway on the outskirts of town. The next day, he found a place to stay at Mae Wright's house. It was a large, red-brick, two-story on North Hudson Street, a few blocks from downtown and also a few blocks from the park. Paul could remember walking past the house at the same time Mr. Wright was coming home from his clothing store. Mr. Wright would always tip his hat whenever they met on the sidewalk, and Paul would say hello. He didn't remember speaking to Mr. Wright at any other time. But he did remember selling a fire extinguisher to Mrs. Wright once when he was raising money for a school project. He would ask her if she still had it and if she had ever used it.

Mr. Wright had been dead for some time, and Mrs. Wright now rented out the top story of the house whenever she could. Paul had two large rooms with high ceilings to himself, one for sleeping and one for working. The bathroom was just down the hall, and he had it to himself because the two other upstairs rooms were not rented. Mrs. Wright didn't remember him. When she asked him what his business was in

Stockton and how long he would need the rooms, he said he was working on a local history textbook and that he might be around for several months before he was finished. He was surprised that satisfied her. There couldn't be a lot of people coming to Stockton to work on history books. He should have been able to fabricate a better story than that. He was still a lawyer.

That night, Paul looked through the city directory he found in his room, searching for familiar names. He recognized the names of a few people he had gone to school with. Ann McCool was the editor of the weekly newspaper. He thought he remembered a "Mary" McCool who was a year behind him in school. Maybe it could have been "Ann," not "Mary." Either way, it seemed like an appropriate job for the nosy little girl Paul remembered, assuming it was she. Being a newspaper editor was sort of like being a hallway monitor. She just had to keep her eyes on everyone and everything in town, then tell.

Alvin Preston, who used to pee his pants walking to school on cold days, was a banker and Village mayor. Who would have picked him to make a name for himself in finance and politics? Most of Paul's classmates must have left town. There was little future for most of them in Stockton unless they owned a business, worked at the local cheese factory, or commuted to Galena or Freeport every day.

He also remembered the Walker brothers, Joshua and Nathan. They were identical twins who were law partners in Stockton when Paul was a boy. He recalled stories his mother had told him about them. Their father had been a judge, and their mother had been the county clerk. The boys grew up running all over the courthouse in Galena, watching trials and being tended to by courthouse employees. Their father was a bit of a character. One story that still stuck with him was about an ugly divorce case where the parties were fighting over custody of the children. Judge Walker, emulating Solomon from the Old Testament, had awarded custody of the children to his startled bailiff and had given each parent only alternate weekend visitations. Predictably, the couple settled their dispute quickly and reclaimed the children. It was a great relief to the bailiff, whom his mother had described as "a single gentleman of later years" who spent most of his time at the Main Street Tavern. Joshua and Nathan must still be well-regarded after staying so long in the legal profession. Lawyers were often looked up to in small towns. A far cry from the way people regarded attorneys where Paul had practiced.

Stockton surprised him. It was the same size it was when he had lived there. The town looked as if it hadn't changed much at all. He picked up the *Stockton Herald,* which Mrs. Wright had given him to read, and he thought it could have been written in 1955.

Mrs. Doris Borchardt is recovering from surgery at the Deaconess Hospital in Freeport.

Carl and Doris Schultz are the proud parents of a new baby girl, Marilyn.

The town council met last night to discuss the final preparations for this year's carnival and Danny Frazier, president of the Lion's Club, said the proceeds this year would go to the town for park improvements.

"The Evangelical Church in Elizabeth is holding its Sunday school picnic on July 21st, and all are invited."

That one got him thinking. He doubted any Lutherans or Catholics would be found among the invited. They would have their own Sunday schools and their own darned picnics.

> Mr. and Mrs. Oscar Nagle enjoyed the recent stay of their son, Tom, and his family, who are here from Orlando, Florida, where Tom is stationed with the United States Navy.
>
> Mrs. Martha Keele and Mrs. Frieda Payne, of Galena, hosted a dinner party Saturday night for local business and civic leaders. Vernon Tanksley, Jr., and his wife, Maryanne, were the guests of honor.

Paul wondered who qualified as a "local leader" in Galena and how these ladies got to decide. There could be more than a few pissed-off people in town who were snubbed by the selection committee of two.

The next morning, Paul walked to the park nearby and sat on a wooden bench beside a hickory tree that looked older than Stockton. His head was shaded by the tree, and his legs were soaking up the sun's warmth. It felt good. Spring smelled the same, and the park hadn't changed much. The faces of the children playing on the swings and slides were different. But they were the same swings and slides he used to play on with his friends while his mother watched from beside the hickory tree.

Paul took off his loafers and socks. The sun felt so good on his feet that he rolled his pants legs up above his knees. With the shade receding, he could feel the sunshine on his chest. He pulled his shirt out from his pants and brought it up to his neck, locked his hands behind his head, and leaned the bench backward. With his eyes focused on the clouds, he tried to imagine shapes. There was definitely an arrowhead straight above and a formation that looked like a huge pair of breasts just to the left of the arrowhead. Something was forming behind the smaller of the two breasts, but he couldn't make it out yet. His eyelids grew heavy and then closed. Paul was floating in a hazy dream world somewhere.

"HELLO THERE! You must be Paul Hoffman."

"Jesus Christ! " Paul shouted as the bench tipped over

backward with his weight. Then he was lying on his back, looking up from between his bare legs at a woman who was covering her mouth and laughing.

Her eyes sparkled as she calmly asked, "Are you OK?"

He responded before he had gathered his thoughts. "Fine! I'm fine. Who are you?" he exclaimed in an embarrassed tone. "It tipped over. The bench did, then I fell, is all. Just getting sun here is all. I'm fine."

"The bench tipped over while you were getting sun?" she asked, enjoying his predicament.

Paul regained his composure. He noticed that the voice and the laughing blue eyes belonged to a face that was striking, even if not exactly described as perfect. Her nose was sharper than she might have liked, and her wide smile displayed teeth that were the slightest bit crooked. But her eyes held beauty, and everything came together in a face that was attractive in a way he hadn't seen before. It was a face much prettier than the sum of its parts, and he would remember it when she left.

"Yes, the bench fell over, and my name is Paul Hoffman," he answered. Paul gestured to the bench he was now lying on top of. "I'm getting sun. Would you care to join me?"

"I don't think so."

Paul got slowly to his feet, righted the bench, and offered her a seat.

When he did, Ann could see that he was an inch or two taller than six feet and had a slender but solid build. He had nice brown eyes, short brown hair, and a great smile. This time, she accepted his invitation.

"I'm Ann McCool."

"How did you know my name?"

"Stockton's a small place. Everyone knows you are staying with Mrs. Wright, and I own the paper, so I know everything that goes on here. You're news."

"Great."

"Besides, we went to grade school together. Don't you remember? You were a year ahead of me."

Paul looked at her and smiled. "You look a little different, taller, for one thing. And I am almost sure your name was "Mary," but you probably know better than I do."

Ann laughed, and her eyes once again looked like they had when he had first seen them from his reclining position.

"I was 'Mary' McCool then. I am 'Ann' McCool now. Paul, why are you in Stockton after all this time? I know you must live in Texas. There are Texas license plates on a red Corvette parked in front of Mrs. Wright's, and she doesn't drive a red Corvette."

"I'm on vacation. It was either Stockton or the French Riviera. The Riviera had rain. How long have you owned the paper?"

"About seven years now. My grandfather started the *Stockton Herald* in 1914. When he got old, my father ran it. I used to do odd jobs around the paper when I was in high school. After college, I worked for the newspaper in Freeport for a while. I was married to Gene Thurman. You might remember him. He was two years ahead of you in school. Gene died in 1978, and I moved back and went into partnership with Dad. But now he is gone, and Mom too. So I own it alone."

"I'm very sorry. And I don't remember Gene. But I am sure I would have known him."

"Are you staying long? I didn't think you had any relatives left in Stockton."

"I don't. I'll be here for a while, I think."

"Do you mind if I ask why you decided to vacation in Stockton after leaving so long ago? Aside from the weather in France, that is."

Paul could see the direction this conversation was headed, and it made him uncomfortable. He didn't want to explain himself to everyone he talked to, and least of all, to the *Stockton Herald.*

He smiled. "I don't mind you asking if you don't mind me not answering."

"Sorry. I didn't mean to sound so nosy. Well, I had better get back to the paper. It's still a weekly, and tomorrow is the day."

"Ann, I'm sorry. That sounded rude. Please forgive me. I didn't mean it to sound that way. The answer, I guess, is that I just needed to take some time away from Houston. I can't explain it very well. You were not getting nosy. Now ... I don't want to sound nosy either, but there is something I have to know. How in the world can it be that you were 'Mary' when I knew you, and now you are somebody called 'Ann'? That question could keep me awake at night, wondering."

"Okay. You asked for it. My mother was Mary Ann Cooper, from Richland Center, Wisconsin, when she met my father in college. Richland Center was the birthplace of Ada Lois James, a famous Wisconsin feminist in the early 1900s. Mom idolized her, and it led her to become a schoolteacher because Ada James had been a schoolteacher ... Follow me?"

"Not even close."

"Okay. I'm getting to it. This will get easier. My father's name was Martin McCool. When my mother was pregnant with me, he thought I would be a boy. He insisted I would be named Martin McCool, Jr. My mother, priding herself on being a feminist like Ada Lois James, said that was fine ... but if I turned out to be a girl, I would have to be Mary Ann Cooper. That was just a negotiation position for my mother, of course. My father would not hear of it! He stomped around the house for days. But eventually, he was so convinced I would be a boy that he said she could name me Mary Ann McCool, just like her, if I turned out to be a girl. Which I did."

"I can see that you did. But I also see a problem. There were too many Mary Ann McCools in your family."

"You are correct, Mr. Hoffman! It became a very big problem. As I got older, my mother and I would both answer whenever anyone said 'Mary'. We finally agreed that I would be 'Ann', and she would still be 'Mary' since she had carried the name longer … and it had been her mother's name too. And that is why I am Ann McCool."

Paul was speechless for a moment. Then he looked at her with a straight face. "Well, now it all seems so simple."

They both laughed, and he decided then that Ann McCool, or Mary McCool, or whoever she was, was someone he needed to know.

When Ann stood up to leave, Paul asked her if he might be allowed to stop by the paper some time to browse through old editions.

"Anytime," she answered as she turned away to leave. Then, over her shoulder, she added, "Nice knees."

"Nice ass," Paul replied, then wished, too late, that he had not. Oh, MY GOD! Why am I always a wiseass? She must think I haven't matured since I was twelve.

CHAPTER 3

Thursday, July 14, 1988

Harry Townsend didn't look like a typical fifty-seven-year-old businessman. At six feet three inches tall and two hundred forty pounds, heavily built in the chest and neck, with a mostly bald head and a serious frown, he drew some attention to himself. He dressed most often in tight-fitting short-sleeved shirts and dark wool slacks. If he were a little younger, he would have made an imposing bouncer at a nightclub, and he liked that appearance. People had to take him seriously. Harry could buy silk-suited MBAs, accountants, and lawyers. He had made more money than most of them, and he knew how to make more. He knew something they did not. He knew a man could make any business deal on his own terms if he happened to be the one making all the rules. He made the rules in business, he made them with his family, and he made them in his marriage. As a result, he had gone through three marriages. He had four estranged children. His sisters, his widowed mother, and his older brother would not talk to him, nor would his uncles, aunts, or any other relatives. No rule he made had any purpose other than to take advantage of others for his own selfish benefit. Harry never lost and knew no remorse for how he treated others.

Making his own rules was what he lived for. Educated professionals played by rules laid down by others at fancy business schools, and they were hamstrung by those rules. While they hobbled each other with concepts and "best practices" out of books, Harry crossed the finish line in full stride, looking for the next race. He just needed them to run interference for him with their conference calls, letters, lawsuits, business lunches, ethics, documents, and charts while he swept up all the prizes. Harry had grown up in Cicero. Why, hell, he had spent almost two years in college at DeVry. That was more than he needed, so he left and found a job with Ford Motor Company. He soon pushed his way up to overseeing dealers in the tri-state area, and he learned how to put pressure on the poor bastards. If they were dealers for more than one car company, he made damn sure they sold more Fords than anything else. They cut their margins to sell more Fords if he told them to. Dealers never wanted to see Harry coming for a visit. Eventually, the company got rid of him. There was a limit to how much weeping and gnashing of teeth Harry could cause without getting them sued.

You could say Harry got his master's degree in pushing people around while working for Ford. The big shots could keep their degrees. Let them have their expensive suits and plush offices. When the small fish got in trouble trying to eke out a living, they came to see Harry at his office in a converted convenience store in Cicero. They couldn't afford the big guys, so they went to Harry for help and waited patiently in a shabby reception area on worn vinyl chairs until he was ready to see them. When he allowed them into his even shabbier office, he froze their eyes with his, grabbed their hands in his bear paws, and shook them until they were squeezed bloodless. They knew that this was a man who held some cards and could solve their problems with ready cash or a deal that only Harry could pull together. What they didn't know was that the price for it would be steep, often a piece of their businesses, if their businesses still had any value. Then they worked for him, until they didn't. If, in the end, they made any money, they had Harry to thank for it. If not, well then, they didn't. He had one practice that never changed. He always held out a bargain that would leave something of value for the other guy. But some bargains work out for everyone, and Harry's bargains never did. The one thing Harry didn't have was repeat business.

Harry seldom had much knowledge about the kind of business he was dealing for. Small manufacturing, trucking, landscaping, vending machines, or motels, whatever—it didn't matter. There was really only one kind of business, and that was whatever could make him money. The company he wanted now was a manufacturer of cement pipes like those used for drainage and storm sewers. There were several cement pipe factories in Northern Illinois and Southern Wisconsin, but two of them were larger and better established than the rest. He already controlled one of them, Babson Pipe Company in South Beloit. It was once the biggest, but it had struggled in the 1980s when the recession in the Midwest had stifled new building projects. The plant had fallen into the hands of the founder's son, who unwisely leveraged it, betting on an early upturn in the economy, which hadn't happened. Unfavorable union contracts contributed, but it was the untimely and hugely expensive plant renovations and brand-new equipment that had finally sunk the company. It landed in Chapter 11 bankruptcy, and Chapter 7 was a certainty.

Harry borrowed enough money to bring the company out of reorganization by paying creditors an average of thirty-five cents on the dollar. A number of secured creditors retained liens on equipment they had sold to the plant. But with their claims likely to eventually be crammed down and their liens quashed, they also settled for a relative drop in the bucket. He got it done with just over a million dollars, much of it borrowed from the bank and secured by the shares of stock he acquired. None of it was secured by hard assets of the company. He owned 85 percent of the shares by the time it came out of bankruptcy. Without any company debts, the plant was making a small profit right away. Bigger profits came when the union pulled out after the bankruptcy, and labor costs were reduced. Curt Babson held only the remaining shares of the business his own father had built from nothing. He worked for Harry now, like it or not.

Unlike Babson Pipe Company, Galena Pipe Works had stayed profitable during the downturn. The company had continued by shipping pipes down the Mississippi River by barge to places that were still growing in the early 1980s. Then, when that area went into a slump, the local economy started to improve. Galena Pipe Works hadn't taken on any debt. The company's only problem was the obsolescence of its plant and machinery, which made it hard to compete with the production coming out of Babson. Aside from that, it was doing alright. It was one of Galena's larger employers with a workforce of over eighty employees in a town that had a population of under four thousand.

Harry knew it would cost him a substantial sum to get control of Galena Pipe Works, but it would be worth it. Galena, Illinois, was just a three-hour drive from the suburbs west of Chicago, through rolling farmlands and green hills. The town was historic. It had been the site of a Union Army hospital during the Civil War, and Ulysses Grant had owned a home there, which was now a museum. People came from all over the country to visit the shops and the museum. While the town itself had potential for growth, Galena Pipe Works had also developed a vastly wider market area. The first step in acquiring Galena Pipe Works was to bait a hook for Vernon Tanksley, Jr., and his snooty wife, Maryanne.

Vernon, Jr., enjoyed a comfortable living because of his grandfather, who had founded Galena Pipe Works, and because of his father, Vernon Tanksley, Sr., who had run the company until his death. He lived on inherited family money and from his ownership interest in Galena Pipe Works. Vernon held thirty percent of the shares of the company, which made him the largest single shareholder. His two widowed aunts, Martha Keele, and Frieda Payne, held twenty percent of the shares each. Twenty-two percent of the shares were held by past and present employees, and the remaining eight percent of the shares were scattered among a few small shareholders, including Nathan and Joshua Walker. The Walkers, who owned just one share each, had law offices in both Stockton and Galena. They had represented Vernon, Sr., until his death in 1976 and still represented the company as its attorneys. But Vernon, Jr., who ran the day-to-day operations now as company president, called on them less often than his father had. He seemed to think he didn't need much advice.

———

It was no accident that Harry ran into Vernon and Maryanne Tanksley at their country club in Rockford, which was an hour and a half from Galena and just a little farther from Cicero. Galena didn't have a country club suitable for Maryanne, so the Tanksleys joined one in Rockford, seventy-eight miles away, where she had grown up. Maryanne frequented the club much more than Vernon, who hated the drive. His compensation was having frequent time off from Maryanne. Harry didn't make a practice of going to country clubs at all. He detested them and the "powder puff assholes" who joined them. But business was business, and it was not difficult for him to get an invitation to the club in Rockford so that he could meet Mrs. Tanksley. He had a friend who was a member and who was able to tell him when Vernon and Maryanne had dinner reservations. Harry had met Vernon once before that night. Vernon had heard about the miracle at Babson Pipe Company and was envious. But he hadn't heard of Harry Townsend until Harry had called him a few months before and had invited him to come to South Beloit to see the Babson plant.

When Vernon had gone to South Beloit, he had been impressed with all the new equipment and with Harry's confidential disclosure that the company was making more money than he had ever expected. Vernon also learned that this was just one of Harry's profitable businesses. Harry explained that he made his best deals by merging companies with a similar company he already owned. Then, he feigned complete surprise when Vernon brought up the possibility of a merger between Galena Pipe Works and Babson Pipe Company. One had a bigger and older customer base, while the other had new equipment and a streamlined operation. Harry thought the idea was fantastic. Why, it was a natural! He was embarrassed that he hadn't thought of it himself. Harry said he would run Vernon's idea by his team of lawyers for them to consider. But Vernon had heard nothing from Harry since that visit. So, he was excited to see Harry at his country club and even more thrilled when Harry came over to his table to ask if he might join Vernon and his wife for dinner.

Harry knew all he needed to know about Vernon, and he knew that Maryanne Tanksley was working hard to outspend his income. She was a short, squat woman who tried to overcome that deficiency by employing expensive jewelry the way a Christmas tree employs bulbs and tinsel. It was Maryanne whom Harry was trying to impress at the country club. Vernon was already on the hook. He regaled her with talk about the fabulous return on his investment at Babson and about the wonders of modern plant equipment. He talked about belonging to fancy Chicago clubs, travel to Europe, and friendships with business moguls in New York City. All of it was bullshit. And Maryanne lapped it up. So did Vernon, who loved to see Maryanne impressed with an acquaintance of his.

Harry brought up the idea of a merger again at dinner,

which excited both Vernon and Maryanne. He said the idea had not slipped his mind, but he had been in meetings in New York and had just gotten too busy. Harry had intended to call Vernon, but bumping into him and his lovely wife had turned out to be even better. Harry and Vernon arranged to meet with Harry's lawyer and financial accountant, Bernie Torveski, the following week. To save Vernon from a long drive to Cicero, they agreed to meet in Rockford at the Clock Tower Resort and Conference Center, where they could get a small room to go over financials.

Harry and Mr. Bernie Torveski showed up for the meeting in Rockford wearing business suits, a tight-fitting one on Mr. Torveski, who was not a tall man but a very heavy one. They showed Vernon some "absolutely confidential" financial statements prepared for insiders only and had him sign a non-disclosure agreement. The numbers were astounding, and Vernon could understand the reason for secrecy. Harry's enterprises were bubbling with cash—all of it totally aboveboard and legal. Mr. Torveski, as the company's attorney, assured him of that. However, the financial statements that would be shown to the shareholders at Galena Pipe needed to be less robust. Solid, but not as glowing as the confidential financial information Vernon was privy to.

To make the merger work, Harry would buy the forty percent interest owned by Martha Keele and Frieda Payne, the two shares owned by the Walker brothers, and all of the shares owned by the employees and former employees. That would make Harry the majority owner of Galena Pipe Works, and it would remove four potentially pesky shareholders: Vernon's aunts and the Walkers. After the merger, Harry would hold the majority interest in the new company, which would be called Galena Babson Pipe Company, Inc. Vernon would retain a substantial minority interest. He would be a director with a director's bonus (to please Maryanne), and there would be profit sharing. Vernon and Maryanne would enjoy an even better way of life. Vernon wanted this deal badly. His father had been the one to make all the big business deals, but this one would be all his.

Harry would later find ways to dilute Vernon's interest and eventually take him out completely. But Vernon didn't know that. He just knew he was going to make this deal happen, no matter what it took. The key was to get his aunts and the Walkers to sell out. Then, the other shareholders would follow suit. His aunts shouldn't be a problem. He told Harry not to worry about them. Vernon would make damned sure they sold their stock. As for the Walkers, they would have no desire to stay on with the new company, so they would give up their two shares easily.

CHAPTER 4

Thursday, August 4, 1988

Harry left his office before the sun came up and drove toward the toll road, which would take him to Route 20 and then on to Galena for a meeting with the primary shareholders of Galena Pipe Works. Ten blocks from his office, he detoured and reached under the front seat of his Suburban to pull out a Crossman Model Fifteen Marksman Slingshot. He reached into the ashtray and found a metal ball bearing before he came to a stoplight at the intersection of Clark Street and Oak Avenue. Harry rolled down the window, put the ball bearing into the web of the slingshot, and drew it back. When he released the ball bearing, it flew diagonally across Oak Avenue and smashed through the plate glass window in the front of Delgato Transmission and Exhaust. When the light turned green, Harry drove down Clark Street two more blocks, turned left, and got back on his route. Harry had put a ball bearing through one of Delgato's windows every few months for the past year. Delgato had worked on Harry's Suburban two years before and had messed up the transmission so badly that he had taken it to

AAMCO to get it fixed right—according to Harry. When he refused to pay Delgato for the work, Delgato sued Harry for $1,875.00 in small claims court. Harry's lawyer had pleaded with him to just pay the damned bill, but Harry wouldn't listen. The judge asked the parties to settle the case. But neither would budge an inch toward settlement, no matter what advice they were given. Harry demanded a jury trial. So, the case was given to a jury, which found by the preponderance of the evidence that Harry was an arrogant prick and awarded judgment against him for the original amount of the work done, along with an equal amount for Delgato's attorney's fees. Delgato had been cleaning up glass since about a week after the trial, and Harry's lawyer, Bernie Torveski, never collected his fee from Harry, who threatened to file a grievance if Bernie even dared to hand him a bill. Even though Bernie and Harry had grown up together and were lifelong friends, Bernie was afraid to bill him. He knew Harry very well.

Harry pushed down on the accelerator of his grey-and-white Suburban to keep pace with a tractor-trailer descending the hill they had just climbed. Highway 20 from Stockton to Galena is one of the most scenic stretches of highway in Illinois. Since the time the highway was finished, people had been coming from all over to stand easels along the shoulder of the road and paint the pastoral landscapes below.

Of course, Harry Townsend was no painter, and he didn't give a damn about the scenery. He had been trying to get around a tractor-trailer for the last three miles. Every time he had a chance to pass, the road took a sharp curve, or he came to another hill. Highway 20 was a killer for an impatient driver. It had seen many fatalities over the years. At the top of the crest, the road turned north sharply, and he still couldn't pull out to pass.

He finally saw an opening and started to drift into the left lane. Just then, a shiny red Corvette appeared from nowhere in his rearview mirror and signaled to get by. Harry punched the accelerator to the floor and slid into passing position to block the Corvette. But he left a small strip of road and shoulder between his Suburban and the left guardrail. The driver of the Corvette saw it and shot past before Harry could block him. Harry leaned on his horn and thrust his middle finger at the driver. The driver of the Corvette reached his arm above the open roof and returned the gesture as he took his time passing the tractor-trailer. Harry pulled out again, but now he was in a no-passing zone.

He got to Galena Pipe Works just before noon and toured the plant with Vernon ahead of the meeting on the proposed merger. It was what he had expected to see. An employee from Babson had toured the plant once, and Harry had pumped him endlessly for details. The machinery was a little old but well-maintained. The employees hadn't changed much over the years, and labor relations were good. It wasn't a union shop. Harry saw that Vernon didn't know his way around. He deferred all of Harry's questions to the plant manager, Tommy Schumann, who saw that Harry understood plant operations much better than Vernon. Tommy also knew that Harry had turned Babson Pipe Company around and made it successful. Harry was a first-class entrepreneur, the dynamic kind of businessman he wouldn't mind working for.

Tommy had been at Galena Pipe Works since he had finished college fifteen years earlier. He hadn't planned to be there so long, but he had settled into a marriage and never found a better job. Promotions had come easily for him, and the pay was good. He had gone from trainee to kiln supervisor to plant manager in a short time. Now he felt stuck. He had been there too long and saw no chance to move up. It wasn't what he had gone to college for. The owners had no vision for expanding and modernizing the plant. That could all change if Harry was as impressed by him as he was by Harry. Babson's plant manager was getting old. The possible merger, which Vernon had discussed with him, could open up an opportunity. This had to work. He wouldn't have many more chances, and he was bored as hell at Galena Pipe. Harry could feel Tommy's excitement about this deal going forward. He could recognize ambition, and he knew Tommy was somebody who could be useful to him. So, he had spun a fairy tale about the pipe business being only a small part of Harry's giant enterprises in Chicago, and he had patted Tommy on the shoulders. Finally, thought Tommy, there might be a chance for him to reach his potential.

The proposed merger was as complicated as Harry could make it. His plans were always complicated, and not by accident. This one involved numerous classes of stock, warrants, and purchase options. It was structured to give any remaining Galena Pipe Company shareholders an interest in the successor corporation at the expense of having no control. Harry would be able to bleed off profits to some of his other endeavors through phony supply and management contracts. And he would soon eliminate dividends and directors' bonuses.

Martha and Frieda, Vernon's aunts, were seated in the conference room for the meeting when Harry and Vernon arrived. The sisters were both in their eighties. Frieda was the oldest and more dominant of the sisters. Martha, who was frail in appearance, always deferred to her. Normally, the Walkers, as attorneys for Frieda and Martha and for Galena Pipe Works, would be at all shareholder meetings. But Vernon didn't invite them. He wanted to exert influence on his aunts without the attorneys getting in the way. He and Harry told everyone present that Galena Pipe Works was in trouble. The plant wasn't renovated years ago when it would have cost less to do so, and now, the plant was teetering on obsolescence. It had business now, but that could be lost if they didn't keep up with the times. The capital requirements for staying competitive now were going to be astronomical. None of that was actually true. Babson Pipe Company, they were told, had both the means and the expertise to upgrade the factory and make it the largest pipe manufacturer in the Midwest. The merged company, with combined markets and the efficiencies achieved, would be a natural. Galena Babson Company Pipe, Inc. would benefit from all of that, as would the employees. On the other hand, without a merger, the company would slowly be strangled by its inability to compete with Babson, and it would lose its market share. Babson would prosper either way, but this way, they would all benefit. Vernon, being still a young man with obligations, would have a much more secure future. Harry claimed to understand that change does not come easily to everyone. He would be willing to make a very generous offer to Martha and Frieda to buy their stock if they were not personally interested in the merger at their ages. The merger would mainly help Vernon and the employees.

The concept of a merger was not new to Martha and Frieda. Vernon had discussed it with them after his Rockford meeting with Harry. They understood that it was probably the only thing for the company to do, and it would be best for them to sell their shares and be done with it. They had even mentioned it casually to Josh and Nate Walker, who advised them to go slowly and keep them informed. The Walkers were more than just their lawyers. They were trusted friends of many years.

CHAPTER 5

Monday, August 8, 1988

Nathan and Josh were working from their Galena office today. As he was walking back to the office from the courthouse, Nathan saw a red Corvette pull up next to the Hinkle's Drugstore and saw the driver get out of the car and go inside. Nathan hadn't eaten at the drugstore lunch counter in years. The hot beef sandwiches were too dry, and the salad they put together for lunch was as dull as the druggist. A few green peppers and some mushrooms would make all the difference and would cost only a few cents. But try to explain that to Hinkle. The man had no imagination. Otherwise, he could have had a chain of drugstores. But something drew Nathan into the drugstore today. He took a seat at the counter next to the man with the Corvette and looked at the menu.

"Hello, Mr. Walker," said the girl behind the counter. "Haven't seen you here in a while. Too busy to eat, I'll bet. Where is your brother?"

"In court, where he shouldn't be. What's the special?"

"Meatloaf with gravy."

"Same gravy you put on the hot beef?"

"The same."

"Does it come with your famous salad?"

"Sure does."

"I'll take a hot dog and coffee."

A customer got up to leave. Seeing Nathan at the counter, he stopped to visit for a few minutes. Then Nathan turned his attention to the man seated next to him.

"You're Paul Hoffman, aren't you?"

Paul recognized him as one of the Walkers. But which Walker? People often couldn't tell Josh from Nathan and didn't know whom they were talking to. They were wrong half the time, and the Walkers didn't always correct them. This Walker looked older but not much different than Paul remembered and still in good shape for a man his age. He had the same grin the Walkers shared and looked like a proper lawyer should look, wearing a blue blazer with grey pants, sporting a red-and-blue-striped tie, and shiny black loafers.

"Yes," Paul answered. "I remember you. You're one of the Walkers. But I'm surprised you know who I am."

Nathan extended his hand to Paul, who grasped it firmly. "I'm Nate. Ann McCool told me she met you in the park in Stockton. She said you live in Texas now; you will be here for an undetermined span of time, you have no idea why you are here, you are staying at Mae Wright's, and you drive a red Corvette. That's all she knew."

Paul shook his head. "Boy, is she in the right profession. I don't think she needs a newspaper. She could be the town crier. Actually, I am just in Galena today to get out of the little writing room I have set up where I am staying. I'm working on a book my old law school wants to put out this fall. It's taking most of my time, so I decided to break free today and visit Galena. I remember it from when I was young, and I was always intrigued by its history."

"That's Ann, alright. I'm not sure you know that Josh and I were good friends of your father and mother. You were pretty young when he and your mother died, and you went off to Chicago with your uncle. Josh has some pictures of the four of us. They are lying around somewhere in his office back in Stockton. Normally, we spend the first three days of the week there, then Thursdays and Fridays in Galena. I hope you will stop by the office in Stockton next week to see the pictures and meet Josh."

Paul said he would. They spent the next half hour talking. Paul was amazed at the amount of information Nathan gleaned from him in that time without appearing nosy. By the time they had finished talking, Nathan had been able to track his life from junior high school in Chicago right through the Air Force and law school. He even knew that Paul had quit his firm and wasn't practicing law anymore. He didn't ask what had brought Paul back to Stockton. Paul wondered if Nathan already knew why he had come back.

They shook hands, and then Nathan picked up both checks and headed to the cash register, leaving the almost untouched hot dog on his plate. My God, where did Hinkle get his sausage? It's a shame the man had no vision. Serve a little kraut with better sausage, and the place would be packed for lunch. How much could that cost?

He waited outside the drugstore while Paul got into his car and pulled out in front of a grey-and-white Suburban, which was going faster than it should have been going in downtown Galena. The red-faced driver hit his brakes and blasted his horn. Paul appeared to be waving back at the driver of the Suburban as he sped off.

———

Paul stopped by the Walkers' office in Stockton on Wednesday morning. He had coffee with Nate while Josh was on the telephone. Then they went into Josh's office so that Paul could see the old high school pictures Josh kept near his desk. The school pictures had been taken in 1937. Anyone could pick out the Walkers. It was remarkable how little their faces or expressions had changed with age. Paul had some trouble picking out his father because his father had a worn-out look when Paul had been a child. He remembered his father's pale, drawn face and the sadness in his eyes. Paul didn't recognize it then, but he had seen eyes like that many times since, and the look was unmistakable. They were the eyes of a man waiting to die. In these pictures, his father looked robust and athletic. Most of them were team photos. The Walkers had played basketball with his father, and Stockton's team in those years was outstanding for a small school. His father, at over six feet tall, had been a guard. Nathan and Joshua had both been forwards at five feet ten inches. But they played taller than they were. The twins were good players and very good at confusing their opponents.

They visited for several hours. The talk shifted from stories about Paul's family to news about Stockton and eventually to Paul himself. Surprisingly, he didn't feel uncomfortable talking with them about why he felt it was necessary to retrace his early years. It seemed to make sense to them, although they had trouble with the idea of Paul giving up the practice of law. But they were lawyers from a different time and place. When they talked about law practice, Paul had the feeling that the present hadn't caught up with them yet. Paul felt they might not understand today's adversarial system and didn't seem to get that lawyers were hired to win, and for no other reason. These days, winning doesn't mean being the best legal scholar, the best orator, or a bastion of integrity. Winning means punishing the other side more than the other side punishes you. It means inflicting more misery on them than they inflict on you and your client. Winning means cutting corners and touching both feet down just inside the ethical sidelines before being pushed out of bounds. Practicing law is no different than professional wrestling. When the other lawyer gets a head-hold on you, you find a way to twist his arm behind his back. If he has a good half-nelson, you develop a full-nelson and a sleeper hold. The first side to say "uncle" is the side that loses. That was his experience, and it was the version of the law that he was fleeing while every piece of his soul was still intact.

The Walkers lived in a different world—one where the lawyers and judges all know each other. One where young lawyers hang around the courthouse to socialize with old lawyers and sit in the jury box with their feet up, listening to stories when the jury is out. Paul had tried cases in small towns like that in Texas. He envied lawyers who could just drop by and watch a trial for a bit. How did they make a living? Had they never heard of "billable hours?" That was not to say they were bad lawyers. Quite the contrary. They were some of the sharpest he had met. In a small town, you can't afford to specialize and forget everything else you learned in law school. You have to stay up on everything. No matter. The day will come, Paul thought, when they will find themselves staring at a beast they have never seen before. The Nathans and Joshuas of the legal world were headed for painful extinction and everyone would be the worse for it.

Nathan excused himself to take a telephone call just before the three of them left together for lunch. Frieda Payne wanted to talk to him and his brother about an offer she had to sell her stock before the merger of Galena Pipe Works with another company. She didn't know what to do and didn't want to disappoint her nephew, Vernon, who was anxious to get to an agreement. The Walkers knew something about the merger proposal because she had already mentioned it to them. Vernon had also called them, hoping they would convince Martha and Frieda to sell their stock so the deal could go forward. He told them his aunts were sentimental about the business their father had started. They might not realize what was best for them and the company, but fortunately, they had trusted friends like the Walkers to help them make the right decision.

———

They went to lunch at the only restaurant in Stockton, less than a block away. Paul remembered everything inside the restaurant as clearly as if the clock had been turned back to 1955. The tables still had yellow linoleum tops and stainless-steel legs that matched the countertop and the stools. There wasn't any room left at the counter, so they took a table by the window. There were maroon and gold Stockton High School #1 banners hanging on the walls to celebrate last year's championship football team, and posters were still taped to the window advertising the Stockton Carnival, which had already been held. The hum of conversation paused while everyone acknowledged the Walkers and glanced curiously at Paul. Then they went back to their business, and Paul could hear talk about milk prices and how much rain they needed. Paul didn't know much about farming, but he enjoyed listening about it. He admired farmers for their independence and willingness to take a chance year after year on the elements and prices, sometimes mortgaging family farms that were as much a part of them as their children. They seemed to take things in stride. Small businessmen he had represented in Houston were miserable every time they had a bad quarter or their interest rates went up. But farmers were steady. They complained some, but they joked a lot too, and they had a confident manner about them that Paul respected.

After the waitress had brought water and the day's menu to the table, Nathan began discussing office matters with his brother as if Paul wasn't even around. Someone else might have felt slighted, but Paul recognized it as a compliment. They had passed judgment on him and felt that they could talk freely in his presence about things they would not want everyone to know.

"Frieda called me this morning. I think she and Martha want to sell their interest in the company to let the merger take place, Josh. It's what Vernon wants them to do. Of course, Vernon is not the sharpest knife in the drawer."

"What the hell for, Walker? What did you tell her?"

"I told her she needed to think about it and that she shouldn't do it just to make Vernon happy. I told her we would stop in and see Martha and her next week when we go to Galena."

"You know, Walker, that Vernon always was lighter than a popcorn fart. He wouldn't have a damn thing today if he hadn't been born with it. Frieda should tell Babson Pipe what it can do with its offer, then she ought to get that goofy Vernon away from the business. Guys like that Babson bunch are real jackasses. They think they can come in and buy any business they damn well want and whether you like it or not. Let me tell you what the problem is with guys like that. They don't give a damn about anybody else. And when it comes to money, they don't know how much is enough."

Nathan laughed. "Damn, Josh, how do you know so much about Babson? I asked you the other day, and you didn't know who ran the company, how long it had been in business, or what it owned. Now you even know that they are all jackasses. You've come a long mile in one day."

"Well, I think I'm right about it. The whole damn thing seems funny to me. Vernon doesn't know shit from Shinola, and those Babson guys probably saw that right off. If they pissed on his shoe and told him it was raining, Vernon would go out and buy boots. I think those ladies are going to get taken on this deal."

Nathan turned to Paul. "Paul, I'm sorry we disrupted our lunch to talk about something that could turn into a mess."

"No problem. I know a little about how telephone calls from clients interrupt things."

Nate and Josh explained what was happening with Galena Pipe Works and asked him for his thoughts on it. Paul said that he didn't know enough to have an opinion, but it sounded a little to him like Babson Pipe might be trying to pull a fast one to make this merger. Rather than just laying an offer out on the table for the shareholders to consider, they were going around everyone by picking on these two older women to entice them to sell their stock. It sounded shady to him. He had handled something similar in Houston, and the target company ended up in the middle of a shareholder derivative lawsuit, with a block of shareholders suing management to force a merger. The company had eventually been put into receivership, and everyone got hurt. He and the Walkers agreed that the situation with Babson needed to be brought into the daylight with a shareholder meeting. They told Paul they would love to sit down with him and hear more about the suit he had handled in Houston to see if there was any application to what Galena Pipe was facing.

Before they could move on to another subject, Ann McCool appeared at the corner of the table between the two Walkers.

"Josh, Nate. What are you two old rapscallions up to today? No widows or orphans to toss out of their homes on Wednesdays?"

The Walkers laughed, and Josh invited Ann to join them for lunch. When the waitress came back to take their orders, she asked for coffee and lemon pie. Paul wondered how a dessert eater could stay so slim. He had to diet and exercise to stay in shape, but for some people, it just seemed to be easy.

"Ann," Joshua said, "I believe you two know each other."

"We've met. We even went to school together. He was a year ahead of me. So I sort of know him. Although I must say that Mr. Hoffman is rather mysterious. I don't know a lot about him. Like most people with dark secrets, I expected him to show up with you two one of these days."

Ann was afraid she might have made Paul uncomfortable. But when she smiled at him, he smiled back. She did like something about that smile.

Ann turned to Nathan. "Nate, I hear that the Galena Pipe Works is going to be sold to a new owner. What do you know about that?"

"God almighty!" said Josh, "That rumor is already going to be in the paper. What have I been trying to tell you, Nate?"

Nate gave his brother an exasperated look and responded. "Ann, I'll be honest with you. There may be someone interested in buying Galena Pipe, but there doesn't seem to be much to it. These things come and go. A few years ago, a big company from Des Moines wanted to buy it, but Martha and Frieda didn't have any reason to sell. I doubt if this is any different."

The conversation shifted to Paul and the fact that he had given up practicing law. He didn't say much about that or about why he had come back to Stockton. He said he was just retracing his footsteps. Then he asked her again if he could come by the newspaper office to look at some old papers. Ann said she had been very careful in keeping all of the old newspapers and had transferred most of them to microfilm. She was happy when anyone wanted to look through them. But when she invited Paul to drop by, she almost wanted to tell him not to come because she thought she knew what he was looking for.

Ann took one more stab at prying some information on Galena Pipe Works out of the Walkers but finally gave up when Josh called her the town busybody and launched into one of his lectures on the constitutional right to privacy and exactly what is wrong with the press today. She said goodbye and smiled again at Paul. He was sorry he hadn't gotten off to a better start with her at the park. Paul picked up the check before anyone else could, and he thanked the Walkers for their time. He wanted to go at once to the newspaper office, but he knew he wasn't ready. He had some walking and brooding to do before he faced what had drawn him here. It could wait a little longer.

CHAPTER 6

Monday, November 26, 1956

Ed Hoffman opened his eyes and let the light come in to them from the bedroom window. His head hurt from the booze and his goddamned stump felt like it was on fire. He sat on the edge of the bed and took a few deep breaths before he hopped over to the door on his right leg and put on his bathrobe. It was colder than a whore's heart in the hallway leading to the bathroom. Why the hell couldn't Angie stoke the furnace before leaving in the morning? There was plenty of coal in the bucket. He had to get down to the Ford garage, and he was already late. Mel would be pissed because they were supposed to talk to that regional kid from Chicago who would tell them about the new models and prices. Big deal. The same people would buy their cars this year that always bought them. When the farmers around here had money, they bought Buicks. When they didn't, they bought Chevys or Fords. It didn't take a goddamned regional sales representative from Ford to tell them that. Anyway, Mel wasn't about to fire him. He knew how to run the office and the service department, and he could handle the whole damn business while Mel was gone, which was most of the time these days. God, did his head hurt. He glanced in the mirror and saw that he looked like hell. His eyes were their usual shade of red, and his complexion was chalky. He shaved and combed his hair. Then he sat on the commode and rubbed salve on the stump of his left leg, which ended just below the knee. It didn't look good, and he was afraid he would have to stop wearing his prosthetic for a while if it got worse. He hated that. It was bad enough limping around town on one good leg and a piece of wood. Getting around on crutches with an empty pant leg, looking like the town cripple, was miserable. He could hardly remember what it had been like to have two good legs and not to be looked at and pitied.

It wasn't that way when he first got home from the war. He was a first-class hero, and losing his leg made people appreciate him even more. There wasn't a bar in the county where he could pay for a drink. And the women loved it— even Angie. Now, he was just a sad reminder of what war does to the unlucky people. "Poor Ed. He never had much of a chance after the war, with his leg and all. Not much he could do in town but sell cars if anyone was buying. Hell of a guy before the war. You should have known him then. A different person. Always full of fun. Cocky sometimes, like young boys are, but not any wilder than the Walkers or any of the other boys. Not a bad basketball player, either. If you had known him before the war, you would hardly recognize him now. And poor Angie. And poor little Paul." Poor everybody. It's a tough damned world.

Ed made his way back to the bedroom, strapped on his leg, and put on some green slacks and a short-sleeved white shirt. Then he went down the stairs. When he got to the kitchen, he poured a cup of coffee from the pot Angie had left. It was stale. Ed reached into the cabinet above the stove and pulled out an open bottle of Scotch. He poured some into the coffee and drank it down. Then he made a piece of toast with butter and jam. It didn't taste good, and he tossed half of it into the sink when he left the house. It was only six blocks from the house to the garage. Anyone else could have walked to work, but he had to drive. Walking hurt too much. At least Mel gave him a demonstrator to use. He couldn't have paid for two cars, and Angie had to have her own car to drive to work at the restaurant outside of town on Route 20. When he got to the garage, he saw Mel sitting across his desk from a tall, stocky young man wearing a dark brown leather jacket and a brimmed hat. He couldn't have been much older than twenty-four or twenty-five, but he sat there like a man in charge. Mel seemed to be doing all of the talking. Ed wandered closer to Mel's office door to listen. Mel saw him and asked him to come into the office.

"Ed, I told you to be here at nine o'clock, goddamn it. It's nearly ten. He came out all the way from Chicago, and he's here on time. Just sit down and listen."

Ed took a chair next to the visitor and saw the son of a bitch staring at his bum leg. Mel began talking again, and Ed could tell he was in trouble. Ford wanted to see some changes in the operation and wanted Mel to get a floor plan loan from the bank to increase his inventory. Some of the locals had gone to Freeport to buy Chevys because the Chevy dealer had cars on hand. When Mel ran out of things to say, the visitor just sat there looking at him, waiting for him to go on, as if he hadn't heard anything that was worth the trip from Chicago. Mel was as nervous as Ed had ever seen him, and the awkward periods of silence were not helping. Ed didn't have the patience for this crap. The guy from Ford was just like some of the jerks he had served under in the Marines. He got up abruptly and walked out into the showroom to get a drink of water. Mel frowned but didn't say anything. He was on the hot seat and didn't need to start anything with Ed. The last thing Ed was going to do was toady up to some smart ass from Chicago who was there to tell him how to sell cars to farmers. He stood by the showroom window and watched Nate Walker go into the bakery across the street. Lucky bastard had both of his legs. Of course, he went to college, got married, and never got drafted. Ed thought he had been a damn sight better basketball player than Nate or his brother, but that didn't matter now. They could still go out and shoot baskets. He could hardly stand up, leaning against a window.

Ed glanced through the glass front of Mel's office and saw that Mel was doing all the listening now. He walked over and stood outside the door to hear what was going on. Young Mr. Ford was talking in a low voice with long pauses between each sentence. His eyes were locked on Mel's, and his face showed no emotion as he spoke.

"It's your choice, Mel. You can make this place run like a business, or next time I come out here, it will be to shut the doors. We don't need dealers that don't sell cars. Your service department is shit. You got no inventory. You got no salesman. That drunken, washed-up gimp working for you couldn't sell new assholes to people with hemorrhoids. Now I'm going back to Chicago, and you are going to call me tomorrow to tell me you got some financing and a new salesman. If you can't tell me that, don't even call; just lock the door and send me the key."

He got up from his chair, tipped his hat at Mel, and started to leave the office. Ed met him in the doorway, grabbed the front of his jacket with both hands, and pushed him up against the open door. He spit in Ed's face and broke free. He was a big, husky man. When Ed backed away, he kicked Ed's right leg out from under him. Pain shot up through his body from his stump. The visitor leaned over Ed, grinning at him while he cried out. Mel shoved his way between them and stood there until he smiled at Mel and left the building.

Mel tried to help Ed up. "Christ … I'm sorry, Ed. I'm just so sorry."

CHAPTER 7

Monday, August 15, 1988

Paul woke up with a newfound determination to stay away from anything connected to the practice of law. The last thing he had come to Stockton for was to get himself involved in a controversy over the sale of a concrete pipe factory and end up spending time hanging around a law office, drawn into a problem like those he left behind in Houston. But that was what was happening. He wanted to kick himself for having ever sounded interested. The Walkers had survived in their practice for enough years without his help that they certainly didn't need it now. Before long, Nate would be introducing him to people as an "associate" in the firm. Paul decided it was time to get back on track and go down to the newspaper office to pore through the archives. He had called Ann to see if he could come by that morning. She told him that it would be fine and she would direct him to the rolls of film he needed. He could make copies if he wanted them.

After breakfast, Paul walked downtown to the newspaper building, arriving shortly after Ann had opened the office. He found her making coffee and mumbling aloud about her plans for the day. Ann's schedule was to first pick up advertising copy from the supermarket. There would be weekend specials. Then, she would stop by Ralph Gustavson's garage to find out what he knew about the new Lutheran minister his congregation had called. He was on the call committee and would know more about it than anyone else. Later, she would start writing this week's "What's Happening in Stockton" column so the readers would know who is home, who is in the hospital, who is getting married, and who is enjoying out-of-town guests. She wondered if she should mention that Paul Hoffman was visiting. No, she decided, he had already been seen around town enough for people to know who he was, even though most people wouldn't remember him or his family. Just to have some fun, she could write up something like that and show it to him for his approval. But that would make him feel uncomfortable. She didn't want to feel sorry for Paul but sometimes it was hard not to. She had felt sorry for him sometimes when they were children. Even though they didn't know each other well, she knew he had a troubled home life. And all these years later, Paul Hoffman, the lawyer from the big city, was still a boy who couldn't come to grips with what had happened to him one horrible night in Stockton.

Paul saw a typical small-town newspaper office. The counter and desks were cluttered with paper. There were pictures on the walls showing Stockton as it had been over one hundred years ago. Filing cabinets were lined up against the walls. He wondered how much of what they held had been put there before Ann owned the paper. The smell of fresh coffee was in the air, and he felt welcome when Ann showed him to the file room where the old newspapers and microfilm files were stored. They had a cup of coffee before she showed him how to work the viewer and printer. Then she went back to work and left him alone. He mounted roll after roll of microfilm, looking for anything related to him or his parents. After several hours, he had found enough.

June 10, 1941
Angela Eden to Wed Edward Hoffman

Mr. and Mrs. Samuel Eden of Woodbine have announced the engagement of their daughter, Angela, to Edward Hoffman of Stockton. Miss Eden attended Freeport Beauty School and is a beauty operator in Woodbine. Mr. Hoffman is employed at Galena Pipe Works. The wedding will take place at the Evangelical Church in Woodbine, and the couple will make their home in Stockton.

February 6, 1942
Weddings

The former Angela Eden of Woodbine was married Friday evening to Edward Hoffman of Stockton in the Evangelical Church in Woodbine. The ceremony was conducted by Pastor Harold Schulte and an organ solo was performed by Marie Darsey. Over thirty guests attended the wedding, and a reception was held later at the home of the bride's parents, Mr. and Mrs. Samuel Eden of Woodbine.

September 4, 1942
Four Area Boys to Join Marines

Two young men from Stockton and two young men from Elizabeth are scheduled to be inducted into the US Marine Corps in Chicago next week. The four are Tommy Mellinger and Edward Hoffman of Stockton, and Carl Spiller and Russell Teppe of Elizabeth. After their induction in Chicago, they will be sent to San Diego, California, for their basic training, where they will join several other young men from the area.

January 12, 1943
Soldier and Sailor News

Seaman Bill Simpson of Galena has been transferred to the North Atlantic aboard the Battleship Texas. He had previously enjoyed shore duty at the Norfolk Naval Base in Norfolk, Virginia. Private Edward Hoffman of the United States Marine Corps will return home for furlough Sunday. He will be able to spend two weeks with his wife before being shipped to the South Pacific. Reuben Kendrick of Stockton has been promoted to the rank of Private First Class by the United States Army. He is currently a radio operator and is stationed in London, England.

October 23, 1943
Area Births

A baby boy was born Tuesday at Freeport General Hospital to Corporal and Mrs. Edward Hoffman of Stockton. Corporal Hoffman is now stationed in the South Pacific and will not be able to obtain a furlough for some time to see the new addition to his family. The healthy baby, who weighs eight pounds and ten ounces, will be named Paul.

March 18, 1945
Stockton Marine Wounded in Action

Mrs. Angela Hoffman received word Monday from the United States Marine Corps that her husband, Corporal Edward Hoffman, was wounded in action during the recent fighting in the South Pacific. Corporal Hoffman reportedly lost a portion of his right leg in a mine explosion but has been recovering satisfactorily in a field hospital and is expected to return to the United States in about three months.

November 27, 1956

STOCKTON MAN KILLS WIFE AND SELF IN MURDER-
SUICIDE

Betty Stieffle, of 102 West Sycamore Street, was awakened at 2:00 a.m. Monday to gunshots from the Hoffman house located next door at 104 West Sycamore Street. When she rushed over, she found the doors locked. When she knocked repeatedly on the door, there was no answer. She returned home and called the Hoffmans, but again, there was no answer in spite of the fact that upstairs lights in the house were on. Mrs. Stieffle then immediately telephoned the police department for assistance.

When Stockton Police Chief Everett Perkins arrived, he learned that Ralph Dillon, who lives across the street at 103 West Sycamore Street, had also been awakened by the shots. They found all the doors locked, so they broke down the back door and went in. Upon entering an upstairs bedroom they found Angela Hoffman, age 34 years, lying dead on the floor. She had apparently died from a gunshot wound to her chest. Lying next to her on the floor was her husband, Edward Hoffman, age 36 years, who appeared to have died from a gunshot wound to his temple. The weapon was found next to Mr. Hoffman and the coroner's office has ruled the incident a murder and suicide. The Hoffmans' twelve-year-old son, Paul, was found in the corner of the room, unharmed.

Paul managed to stand up and walk from the microfilm machine to the washroom. He placed both hands on the sides of the sink and looked into the mirror. His face was white, and he could see beads of sweat on his forehead. His mind kept repeating the last sentence in the newspaper article. "The Hoffmans' twelve-year-old son, Paul, was found in the corner of the room, unharmed." Unharmed? Again and again, it went around in his mind. "Found in the corner, *unharmed …*

unharmed … Hoffmans' twelve-year-old son … *unharmed* … found in the corner … *unharmed.*" As if it didn't harm him.

He could see his mother from a small beam of light in the dark room. She was on the floor. "Wake up!" Blood was all over. "Stop the blood! Wake up! Help … Jesus!" Then he saw them both. "Mom, Dad! Wake up! The blood! Stop the blood!"

Paul dropped to the floor, then leaned his head against the corner wall and passed out. He remembered nothing until he felt someone holding him and rocking him gently. He could hear a soft voice saying everything was alright, that he would be alright, that everything would be alright.

Paul sobbed and answered weakly. "It's not alright, Mrs. Stieffle. Nothing is alright. Nothing will ever be alright now."

But it was Ann, this time, who held Paul in her arms after she found him. The sound of something crashing to the floor had startled her, and she had charged into the washroom expecting to find that an object had fallen from the windowsill. Instead, she found Paul huddled in the corner with his face buried in his hands, shaking so violently that she could not quiet him. Gradually, he regained control of himself and asked to be left alone. When Ann read the words on the screen of the microfilm machine, she wasn't surprised. There was only one thing that could have brought him back to Stockton. It was the nightmare he must have relived every night of his life since one night in 1956.

———

Ann had never forgotten the day she first learned what had happened at 104 West Sycamore Street. Her mother had talked to her after breakfast and had told her to take Prospect Avenue to school because something bad had happened at the Hoffmans'. Nobody knew what had taken place, but Paul's parents were both dead and it appeared to be from a shooting. An accident, maybe. There was no danger to anyone now.

Still, it would be better not to walk by their house that morning. Ann disobeyed and took Sycamore Street to school. The police chief's car was parked in front of Paul's house. Everett Perkins, the chief of police, was standing in front of the big white porch talking to some neighbors and local town officials. She crossed the street unnoticed and stood close enough to overhear the conversation—even then, playing the snoop.

"God, I never seen nothing like it. There was blood all over the floor. They must have bled a gallon and she had it still coming out of her chest. Ed wasn't bleeding near so bad. He just had that small entry hole and a damned big exit hole in his forehead. There was brains and blood blown all over the wall and curtains."

"The poor kid. Think what's going through his mind. How is he going to get over a thing like that? Damn, what's he going to do? Who's going to take care of him?"

"He's over to Betty's place right now. Josh Walker said he was going to called Ed's brother in Chicago. Herb will be here later today. Josh told me he'll take Paul. Ain't nobody else to do it."

"Christ, Everett. Why do you suppose he done it?"

"I don't guess we'll ever know."

Ann rewound the film and put it back in the cabinet. Then she walked out front and found Paul standing by the pasting table.

"I'm sorry, Ann. I'm embarrassed. I haven't done that since I was a kid. I used to lay all huddled up in the corner of my room in Chicago when it got really bad. Blocking out all I could. I thought it was under control. I thought that part was behind me. I'm a grown man now. I am forty-four years old!"

"You've got a knot on your forehead from the floor or the wall. Let me put some ice on it."

"No. It's okay. God, I thought you were Mrs. Stieffle for a while. Do you know that? I mean, I really thought you were Mrs. Stieffle. I shouldn't have come back. Shouldn't be here.

But I'm here, and I can't leave. Why the hell can't I just put it away?"

"How could you, Paul? I remember it like it was yesterday, and it didn't even involve me."

He trusted Ann, but he wasn't going to tell her about the images that newspaper article had evoked. He felt sad, but he didn't feel what he thought he should feel. Maybe there was something wrong with him. He just felt anger at the whole damned thing that took his mother's life. And it bothered him that Ann might feel sorry for him. Nothing was worse than being an object of sympathy. He had taken everything that had come his way in life without self-pity and he had nothing to be ashamed of. No one should feel sorry for him. Especially Ann.

CHAPTER 8

Thursday, August 18, 1988

Paul sat in the chair by an open window in his room, getting the night breeze. It was dark now, and the air was cool even though the day had been hot and muggy. He could hear birds settling into the trees for the night, and if he closed his eyes he was home again in his room on Sycamore Street, lying in bed with the sheets drawn up around him, thinking about the breakfast his mother would cook in the morning and planning the next day's adventures. Then the ache came back. He walked over to the table where a telephone book was lying next to the phone. What was the name of the police chief? Perkins. There was no listing for anyone named Perkins in Stockton. He moved on to the listings in Warren. Same thing. Then he found an Everett Perkins listed in Lena. That was him, Everett. That was the police chief's name back then.

Paul picked up the phone and dialed the number. It rang twice before a woman answered.

"Hello," Paul said. "May I speak to Mr. Perkins?"

"Just a minute. I'll get him."

"Hello."

"Hello. Is this Mr. Perkins? Everett Perkins?"

"Yes."

"My name is Paul Hoffman, Mr. Perkins. I used to live in Stockton when I was young. My father was Edward Hoffman. Do you remember him?"

"No. My father probably knew him. He knew everyone in Stockton. He was the chief of police for a while."

"I really would like to talk to your father. Where does he live?"

"Galena, but he can't talk to you. He's mixed up now. Alzheimer's. Sometimes, he gets real agitated over nothing when you try to talk to him. It's not good for him, and it takes hours to get him settled down. We've got him in a rest home where they take good care of him. But he can't remember anything. Well … sometimes he's just fine. Sharp, almost. But it doesn't last long. He just kind of drifts in and out all the time. Doesn't make sense."

"That's got to be hard on you. Can I visit him?"

"Won't do any good."

"I'd like to try. I want to talk to him about my father. He died when I was pretty young, and I never knew him very well. There are very few people left who knew him."

"I'm Dad's guardian because I'm the oldest child. I don't know if anyone should talk to him or not. Might be bad for him. Nate Walker did the guardianship for me. Ask him. If he thinks it's alright, then it's good by me. I just don't want him pestered, you know."

"Thanks. I'll check with Nate. And if I see your father, I'll try not to upset him."

Paul put down the receiver and looked up Ann's number. The phone rang five or six times, and he was ready to hang up by the time she answered.

"Ann. It's Paul Hoffman."

"Hello, Paul Hoffman. I'm sure you have a great reason for getting me out of the shower and I'm curious about what it could be. Excuse me while I get a bathrobe on."

"Don't bother. I can't see a thing. Although I'm getting a little curious now myself. But I called to find out what you know about Everett Perkins?"

"Not much. He used to be the police chief when we were kids. You remember him. He drove around in an old Chevy coupe with a star on the side. I don't think he carried a gun. He's old if he's still alive. God, I'll bet he would be well over ninety."

"He's alive, and he's in a rest home in Galena. I'm going to see him after I've talked to Nate Walker. He's under a guardianship, and his son doesn't want anyone to see him unless Nate clears it. The old guy is senile and blows up easily. I'm sure Nate won't object. He's just being a lawyer, protecting the family."

"I don't get it. Why do you want to see him? What good will it do?"

"I wasn't sure why I had to come back to Stockton. None of it made sense till now. I just knew I had to come back here and look around. Now I have to know why he did it. Why was my father so crazy that he killed my mother and himself? And why didn't he just take me out at the same time? Make a clean sweep of it. He was miserable, but what the hell? Life is miserable. Not everyone goes around killing people. I can't forgive the son of a bitch for what he did to my mother and me, but I am damn sure going to find out what motivated him. Did he hate us that much? What the hell did I do to deserve that kind of a start in life?

"I'm sorry, Ann, I didn't mean to sound so upset. But I'm going to put it to rest, then get the hell away from this town and forget about everyone and everything associated with it."

"Including me?"

"No, Ann! I certainly didn't mean you. I didn't mean that."

"Paul. The town is not the problem. There is nothing wrong with Stockton or the people who live here. They are good people. Don't blame the town for what happened. It's not fair."

"I know. Go to Galena with me tomorrow, Ann. I won't be long at Nate's office or at the rest home. We can stop on the way back and have a picnic on the top of a hill. I'm just a flatlander from down Houston way, you know."

"I can't. We're not all rich Texas lawyers who don't have to work. Some of us are struggling small-town newspaper publishers who have to grind it out every day to pay the light bill. But you wouldn't know about anything like that."

"No. I wouldn't. Sounds terrible, though! I sure am glad it's you and not me."

"Call me when you get back and tell me what you find out. We will picnic another day."

Paul put down the receiver. Out of habit, he reviewed the conversation in his mind, word by word. He wondered if everyone does that or just lawyers. Ann wasn't angry with him. He was sure of that. She was witty and could give and take as well as he could. He might want to cut back a little on the wiseass stuff, though. It could get weary for people sometimes. He could feel himself being drawn to her as someone he could talk to. How long had it been since there was someone he enjoyed talking with the way he enjoyed talking with Ann? How long since he had felt so comfortable with someone that he could let down his guard and just say what he felt like saying? Never. He had never been able to open up to anyone so quickly. He had trained himself not to let on what he was feeling. That made for a good lawyer. Contrary to popular thought, good lawyers listen a lot more than they talk, and when they speak, every word is measured. But with Ann, conversation was so natural he enjoyed opening up. Talking to Ann was like stepping out into the fresh air after a long day in a musty courtroom. It felt good.

Paul slept well and got up early so that he could get to Galena at about the time Nate would open the office. He knew Nate would be there because the Walkers kept office hours in Galena on Thursdays and Fridays. As he was leaving the house, Mrs. Wright called to him from the kitchen and invited him to have some breakfast with her. He could smell pancakes cooking, and he knew that she would have made more than she could eat. She liked company and had asked Paul to join her for breakfast several times before. It would have been rude not to accept, and she was far above average when it came to making pancakes.

She brought over a platter stacked with them. She poured Paul a cup of coffee and then bowed her head for a moment.

"Where are you off to so early? I heard you showering and decided you would need a hearty breakfast for whatever got you up this time of day."

"I'm going to Galena to look around a bit. I may stop off to visit with the Walkers if they have time. I might even drop in to see Everett Perkins. He's in a rest home."

"Really! What on earth would you want with Everett? He must be at least ninety years old. He always was a strange one anyway. Didn't amount to a hill of beans as a chief of police. He couldn't have caught anyone if he tried, and he didn't. Vandals painted up our garage out back one Halloween. We all knew who did it, but old Everett wouldn't even talk to them about it. He said they wouldn't own up to it anyway, so what was the use? Can you believe a policeman like that? We didn't have any crime to speak of in those days, so maybe it didn't matter. He just drove around town in that old Chevrolet coupe the town had as a police car and never put anyone in jail. Nate and Josh were always on the town council in those days, one of them at least, and they saw to it that the town kept Everett on so he would have a job. That was alright, then. It wouldn't be any good today. What did you say you wanted to see Everett for?"

"Oh, I just thought it would be good to talk to an old Midwestern police chief to see what stories he can remember. Those kinds of memories can be priceless when you are working on a history text. They will add color to the book. History can be pretty dull stuff."

Paul finished his pancakes and offered to help Mrs. Wright with the dishes, but she wouldn't hear of it. He had things to do, and she had all day.

———

Once again, he enjoyed the drive to Galena. It was like looking down from an airplane when he got up into the hills. The morning sun was at his back, so it didn't impair his vision. There was a light mist in the air, and the sun cutting through it made the cornfields below a brilliant green. It looked like a patchwork. Green corn. Other fields freshly plowed. This part of Illinois had soil so rich and dark it looked black. There were fenced pastures and small wooded areas. He took his time and pulled over once to appreciate the scenery. Ann should have come with him.

When he got to the Walkers' office, he looked at his watch and realized it was still only seven forty-five. He thought about finding a coffee shop to kill some time until the Walkers arrived. Then he noticed movement inside the office, so he got out of his car and rapped on the door. Nate and Josh were already there.

"Hello, Paul. Pretty morning, isn't it?"

"It really is, Nate. But I didn't think you would be here this early."

"We usually get here around six-thirty. You can't practice law eight hours a day and do it right. Practicing law is like hauling garbage. You've got to get up early to haul everything away. If it sits there, at the end of the day, it gets a little rancid. But I'm not telling you anything you don't know. How about some coffee?"

"Thanks. Sorry to just pop in. You're probably using this time to get organized. I won't stay more than a minute. I understand you are handling a guardianship for the Perkins family. I spoke with Everett Jr. last night, and he told me his father is in a rest home up here. I sure would like a chance to talk to him a bit, and I wonder if you would arrange it for me."

"Hell, I'll take you up there myself. But I can't do it today. What about you, Josh?"

"Damn, Walker. I've got clients coming in all day. And I don't think he can go alone. Everett may not talk to him if one of us isn't there. Did I tell you what happened when his niece went to see him? First, he cussed at her. Then he just shut up like she wasn't even there. And he used to love that girl. She was heartbroken. I don't even know if he'll talk with one of us there. He doesn't make much sense when he does. Everything is confused for him. I don't know why that happens. It's probably something chemical that will be treatable one of these days."

"Let's pick another day to go see Everett," said Nate. "I may have some free time the first of the week, and there isn't much point in your going up there without me. If you've got a little time to kill today, I sure wish you would come with me. I'm trying to help those old widows keep their ox out of a ditch over that merger. You might have some ideas, and you'll enjoy meeting them. Then I'll take you to lunch. A client of ours just opened a little café. I don't know if he is going to make it work. But I told him I would come by and take a look. Josh can dine at Hinkle's Drugstore."

———

It was still early when Nate and Paul got to the house Martha and Frieda shared. It was one of the oldest homes in Galena, a white, three-story Victorian with a huge wraparound front porch. It sat on the top of a hill overlooking the Galena River and the original town, which now consisted of a few streets lined with antique shops and galleries.

Frieda took them to a screened porch at the rear of the

house. Then, she led them on a tour of the garden while Martha put together a tray of coffee and cinnamon rolls. As they walked along the old brick paths, Frieda identified every plant and bush by its common name and by its botanical name. She and Martha had inherited the house from their father, who had been an avid gardener and a successful businessman. Both of the sisters had been widowed early in their marriages, and neither had children. Along with the house and various securities, they had inherited their shares of Galena Pipe Works. Their brother, Vernon Tanksley, Sr., had received the rest of the shares owned by their father. Upon his death, those shares ended up with Vernon, Jr.

After some small talk about happenings in Galena and about what it was like for Paul to live in Texas, Martha finally got to the point.

"Nathan, I don't want to sell my stock to Harry Townsend. At first, I was sure that I would. It seemed like the sensible thing to do. But the more I think about it, the more I don't like the man or trust him. Neither does Frieda. Vernon is anxious to do the merger, and he has implied that if we don't sell our stock then it won't happen, and it will be our fault. Mr. Townsend won't do the merger unless Frieda and I sell him our stock because he wouldn't control the company. Vernon says the price Townsend is offering is more than the shares are worth. He really wants us to do this. Our accountant, Pete Gressett, isn't so sure. But it is not a matter of the money. Townsend could be offering too much or too little. It wouldn't make much difference to us at our age. Pete didn't like Mr. Townsend when he met him either. He says the price might be considered fair or not. It's kind of speculative if there is going to be a merger. Do you think we need to sell out for the sake of everyone else?"

"Do you mean for Vernon's sake?" asked Nathan.

"Heavens, no," said Martha. "Whatever Townsend is offering him won't last long when his wife gets involved. I'm concerned about the town, the employees, and others who depend upon Galena Pipe Works. Vernon says the company won't last if we don't sell. We still have a good amount of business right now. But there hasn't been much construction going on over the last few years, and the plant is becoming old. We haven't had any new customers lately. Babson Pipe Company is getting some of the orders we used to get. Mr. Townsend told Vernon that Babson will put us out of business in a matter of years if we don't sell. We should have had you or Josh in the meeting we had with Mr. Townsend. But it came up when you and Josh were on vacation. That's what Vernon told us, at least. That you were both on vacation and couldn't be at the meeting. Nate, Frieda wants to turn it down, and I think I will go along with her. We just don't like Mr. Harry Townsend very much."

CHAPTER 9

Wednesday, August 24, 1988

Paul and Ann sat on the stoop outside Ann's back door, looking at the night. The sky was clear and they could see the moon through the limbs of the elm trees. Neither of them had planned to spend the day together. It began early in the morning when Paul had stopped by the newspaper office to read more old newspapers and try to reconstruct the years preceding his parents' deaths. He wanted to see if anything he read could shine some light on what happened the night they died. Nothing did. Paul had read almost every paper printed in those final years, but something continued to nag at him, and he couldn't seem to leave it alone. Shortly before noon, Ann had interrupted him to say that she was leaving for a few hours and that he could lock the door behind him when he was ready to go. When he found out that she was driving into Wisconsin to do a story on a small family-owned cheese factory, he invited himself to ride along. It was time to forget the old papers. They were a dead end, leading him nowhere.

Southern Wisconsin is green and beautiful in the summer.

They rolled down the windows and let the wind blow past them as she drove along in no hurry. They stopped once beside a small bridge over a stream just to watch a barn owl they had spotted.

The owner of the factory met them and introduced them to his wife and two sons, who were all hard at work in different stages of making brick cheese. When he referred to them as "Ann McCool and Mr. McCool" from the Stockton paper, Paul flashed a big grin at Ann. She started to correct the mistake but let it go. Later, when Ann started taking pictures inside the factory, she asked Paul to go back to the car to get some film out of her camera bag.

"Yes, dear," Paul had answered, and Ann realized she had made a big mistake in not setting the record straight. When the tour was finished, they were invited inside the house for some pie and coffee. Paul accepted for both of them and cautioned that Ann should have only a small piece of pie because "the little woman is putting on a pound or two around the hips." Ann gave him a look which went unnoticed by everyone but Paul. When it was time to leave, Paul thanked the cheesemaker's wife and told her that he would be a happy man if only "the missus could bake a pie that good." Ann flashed Paul another exasperated look, but Paul smoothed it over by bragging about her wonderful meatloaf. As they pulled out of the driveway, Ann laughed first, to Paul's relief. Then they both started giggling like teenagers. Ann asked Paul over for dinner that evening.

As they sat out on the front stoop, the mood changed. They talked about Ann's marriage, her family, and her work. She was a naturally optimistic person. Bad things rarely brought her down because she stayed caught up in the moment. Her hair looked soft under the light from the stars. Her eyes and her smile seemed incredibly bright to Paul. Their bodies touched as they sat together, and Paul could feel her warmth. Ann led him from the stoop into her bedroom.

When Paul awoke, Ann was curled up in his arms with her back against his chest. She rolled over, smiled at him brightly, and said, "Good morning, Mr. McCool."

CHAPTER 10

Thursday, August 25, 1988

Several times now, Paul had asked Nate to arrange a meeting with Everett Perkins, and each time it had been put off. Paul finally decided to make an end run by mentioning the problem to Josh, who enthusiastically promised to remind Nate. But still, nothing came of it. After a week, Paul realized that it wasn't going to happen. He would get no help from Nate or Josh, but he couldn't get the idea out of his head that he needed to talk to Mr. Perkins. As he drove toward Galena, he thought about the way Josh and Nate had ignored his request. It could be inadvertent, he supposed. Sometimes, they took on a lot more work than they could handle easily. Then, other things got put off. Their clients were used to it and didn't press very hard. Still, he was surprised they hadn't been more responsive to what seemed like a simple favor. He felt bad going to see Mr. Perkins without telling them, but he thought they would understand.

Paul found the rest home without any trouble. He walked up the path to the front porch, where several elderly people sat, rocking on porch swings and visiting. A plump woman about sixty years old, wearing a white nurse's uniform, met him at the door. Paul smiled and said that he had come to see Mr. Perkins and that he had permission from the family and Nathan Walker. She led him inside and down a dark hallway to a small room with an open door. An old man was seated in a wheelchair with his back to the door, facing a window that had been opened to let in the fresh morning air.

"Mr. Perkins?" Paul asked. There was no response, so he asked a little louder.

"Mr. Perkins?"

The wheelchair turned slowly toward him, revealing the slumping figure of the man he had come to see. Perkins looked like a wadded-up blanket with a grey head poking out of the top. His eyes were dull, and his mouth hung open.

"Mr. Perkins," said the nurse, "This is Mr. Hoffman. Nate Walker told him he could come by to visit with you. Isn't that nice?"

"What the hell does he want?"

"He just wants to talk, Mr. Perkins."

"Does he have a cigar? I want a cigar."

"No, Mr. Perkins. You can't have cigars. You know you can't have cigars."

"I want to talk about Stockton," Paul said. "You were the police chief. Do you remember?"

"Who the hell are you? I don't know you. What's your name?"

"Paul Hoffman. My father was Ed Hoffman. Do you remember him?"

"I was a police chief. I don't know you. Who the hell are you and where is my pillow? Twenty-five years a police chief. Get out of my room. Who are you?"

Paul got a pillow off the bed and tucked it in between Mr. Perkins's head and the back of the wheelchair.

"Do you remember Ed Hoffman, Mr. Perkins? He shot himself and my mother, Angela Hoffman. It was a long time ago—1956. Do you remember?"

Mr. Perkins closed his eyes for a few moments, then

opened them, stared at the ceiling, and said nothing for about thirty seconds more before speaking. *"Where's the boy? Mrs. Stieffle, where's the boy?"*

"Here, Mr. Perkins. I'm the boy. I'm Paul. Ed and Angela Hoffman were my parents. You remember, don't you? I'm grown up now. I'm the boy."

Perkins gazed in Paul's direction but seemed to look past him into a disoriented world that belonged just to him and others like him, to points in time and space that had lost their separation. Moments passed before Paul interrupted his vacant stare.

"Why did he do it? Mr. Perkins. Why did my father kill her? Why did he kill himself?"

Perkins shook his head, then looked directly into Paul's eyes and began ranting.

"Can't put him in jail. Josh knows.

"Josh says, don't put him in jail. Can't do it.

"It's over, Ev.

"Nope, can't do that … it's over Josh … can't do nothing.

"Suicide, Ev … murder and suicide plain and simple.

"Murder … Josh … murder, murder.

"Ev. It's done. Herb can stay with me tonight. Herb will take the boy."

Paul trembled. "What did you say, Mr. Perkins? Think back. It wasn't that way. Herb was in Chicago. He came the next day. He didn't spend that night with Josh. Maybe the next night. The night after."

"Josh, you know. You know, Josh.

"It's done, Ev. No good can come."

"Mr. Perkins, what do you mean? He was dead. My father was dead. He couldn't go to jail. He killed himself. First mom, then himself. You don't remember well. It was a long time ago."

"Look, Josh. She was packed. And the boy, too. Should have just left. Not said nothing … Should have just gone."

"Was she leaving, Mr. Perkins? Is that what happened? She was leaving?"

Paul heard the door open behind him and turned to see the nurse who had let him in.

"Mr. Hoffman, you have to leave now. Mr. Perkins is agitated."

"Yes, of course. He is very confused."

CHAPTER 11

Friday, August 26, 1988

Paul's visit to Everett Perkins just raised more questions. The old man clearly didn't know who he was talking to when he got into his rant. Paul wondered how much Mrs. Stieffle might remember about the day his parents died. She had lived right next door and had been a good friend to his mother. She kept him at her home while they waited for Herb to come for him the following day. Ann knew that Mrs. Stieffle was living on a farm outside of town, and she offered to arrange a visit. She would accompany him. So today, Paul walked downtown to the newspaper office to meet Ann. The exercise felt good. He could almost forget that he hadn't slept well since talking to Everett Perkins. Too many memories had gone around in his head. Thoughts of the way his mother's eyes would shine when she played with him and tucked him in at night. She was a great reader. She read to him even when he was able to read some of the easy books for himself. The characters always came alive when she read. He could close his eyes and see them. Sometimes, she would stop reading and make up new stories with the same characters doing different things. He never knew what would happen, only that the ending would be wonderful. Her eyes were sad sometimes, though. She always tried to keep him from looking at her when she cried, but he saw her tears and never forgot them.

He got to the newspaper office at the same time Ann showed up, and he drove Ann's car to the Stieffles' farm while she gave directions. He pulled up in front of a two-story wooden farmhouse with a large screened front porch that must have served several generations of Stieffles. Farms in this part of the country stayed in the family, passed down from father to son to grandson. Mrs. Stieffle was waiting on the porch. Ann had called ahead to let her know they were coming out. She was wearing a loose-fitting flowery blouse and blue slacks. Paul knew that she wouldn't have been seen in public wearing slacks when he was a boy. Ladies in Stockton rarely wore slacks in public back then. It just wasn't done.

Once the greetings were over, Mrs. Stieffle poured them lemonade from a pitcher, and he sat across from her while she exchanged pleasantries with Ann. He could remember her, but he wouldn't have known her if he had seen her on a street in town. After Betty Stieffle's husband died, she lived alone in town for a few years. But her health was poor, and her brother-in-law's son, who had inherited the farm, invited her to move in with his family. He treated her like an aunt.

The conversation finally shifted to Paul, and Mrs. Stieffle told him what a surprise it was for him to show up. It had been so long ago that his family had lived next door in Stockton. She had no idea where he had gone or what he had done. He filled her in about his life, and then she asked him about his uncle, Herb. She wondered if he was still alive and if he had ever married.

"He died in 1975 of a heart attack. I was in Houston then, and I flew back to see him in the hospital, but he was gone by the time I got there. He never married. I guess I was his only real family by then. He was a father to me."

"I always thought he was a nice fellow. He used to come

visit you, sometimes on holidays, and he always brought baskets of fruit. He was in the fruit business there in Chicago as I remember. Though where he would get them oranges in the dead of winter I never did know. Anyway, it was nice for us. Your mother would always fix us up a small basket and bring it over to the house. She was thoughtful like that."

"Herb had a good produce business. I worked for him before school and in the summer. Mrs. Stieffle, sometimes I can't remember my mother very well. What was she like?"

"Lord, she was a pretty one. She went to high school in Stockton, and she was the prettiest girl in school. She drove all the boys crazy. Not stuck-up either. I always thought she could have married one of the Walker boys. They were both sweet on her, and it was clear to most everyone they would turn out good. But she had to have Ed. Nobody else would have done for her but Ed. Not that it seemed like a bad idea at the time. Most of the girls were after him.

"I went to her wedding, and I visited her the day she brought you home from the hospital, just as proud as she could be. She only wished Ed could be there to see his boy, but he was over there in Europe or the Pacific somewhere in the war by then. It wasn't too much longer after that he was wounded and came home. They bought the house next door a while later, about the time Ed went to work at the Ford garage. She was always friendly to us, no matter what else went on."

"What do you mean, no matter what else went on?"

"I just mean she was friendly, is all. Life is hard for all of us sometimes … but she was friendly … is all I meant. Let me pour you some more of that lemonade. I just love lemonade on a summer day. Nothing quenches the thirst like it. Mr. Stieffle used to say a cold can of beer was better, but then I wouldn't know about that, and I'll just stick with the lemonade."

"What about my father? How do you remember him?"

"I never did know him like I knew your mom. He stayed to himself a lot. I don't think his leg ever did give him a day's peace. It's a shame what happened to so many of the boys back then. Mr. Stieffle went into the Army for a while, but he never did leave the country. Stayed in North Carolina most of the war. And thank God for it."

"Was he a drinker, Mrs. Stieffle. Was he mean? Did he abuse my mother?"

"None of us are put here to judge the rest. I suppose he drank some. Angie didn't like to talk about it so much."

"Why did he do it, Mrs. Stieffle?"

"What?"

"Why did he kill her and himself? You knew them both. You were one of the first to the house that night. You found me in the corner. I just want to know why it happened."

"The only one to answer that is dead, Paul. How can any of us know what goes on inside another person's head? It was sad, that's all. Lord, it's getting a bit of a chill on the porch. Must be a wind from the north. We get them once in a while this time of year. Don't last long. Do you want to come inside where it's more comfortable, or do you have some place to get to?"

Paul stood and helped Mrs. Stieffle to her feet.

"No, we really have to get going. Ann is going to show me around some today, and I just wanted to stop by and say hello and see how you are. Thank you for the lemonade. It's a beautiful farm and I sure love the porch."

"Maybe I'll see you again before you go back to Texas. Glad you're doing so well. We don't have a lot of Texas lawyers in Stockton, you know. Better watch out for this one, Ann."

Ann gave Mrs. Stieffle a hug and helped her carry the lemonade pitcher and glasses back into the house. When she met Paul at the Wagoneer for the drive back, she could tell that he was bothered by the way the conversation had ended. He turned to her and spoke. "That chill didn't come from any north wind, Ann. There is something she is not telling us."

CHAPTER 12

1935 -1956

erb couldn't wait to get out of Stockton. His father had worked in the cheese factory all of his life and came home every night smelling like sour milk. He was destined for the same thing if he didn't get out. He dropped out of school when he was sixteen, packed his bags, and caught a bus to Rockford, where he found a grocery store job. He worked there for two years and lived over the store. Most of the money he made was stashed away. His room was free. He ate bruised produce and day-old bread. He didn't spend much on clothing except for a good winter coat, and rarely spent anything for entertainment.

Mr. Meyer, the store owner, had moved to Rockford from Chicago many years before, after he had saved up enough money to go into the grocery business for himself. He had made his money from a fruit stand. He knew more about produce than anyone in town. Herb soaked up everything Mr. Meyer had to teach him, and when he turned nineteen, he left Rockford with enough money to buy a produce stand of his own in Skokie. His was the first stand open in the morning, and the last one closed at night. The produce was always fresh, and he knew how to price it to make it sell. In 1940, he sold the stand, borrowed some money, and bought a small wholesale produce business on the north side of Chicago. While most of the young men around him went off to the service, his flat feet kept him out of the draft, and he continued to build his business. He made all the sales and deliveries himself and soon knew half of the grocers and restaurant owners on the north side.

Business consumed him for a while, and he had little time for anything else. When he finally had some people working for him who could be trusted to run things while he was away, he returned to Stockton for holiday visits. These visits were practically the only social life he had. His brother was dating Angela Eden, a pretty girl a couple of years behind Ed in school. Sometimes, Herb could find a date so they could double. Other times, the three of them just drove around together in Ed's old jalopy until early morning, listening to dance music on the radio coming from the Palmer House in Chicago. Angie loved to listen to the "WLS Barn Dance" on Saturday nights. She and Ed planned a trip to Chicago to stay with Herb and get tickets to it, but the trip never happened. Ed joined the Marines a few years after he finished high school and married Angie before he went to boot camp. It wasn't long before Angie was pregnant. She stayed with her parents while Ed was overseas, and Herb would always stop by to see her when he visited Stockton. It was a chance for her to get out of the house. They would go on short rides to Lena or Warren and maybe stop somewhere for a bite to eat.

Angie was lonely and missed all the fun of being young. They talked about things they would all do after the baby was born and Ed was back home from the war. The baby, Paul, was born before Ed was home. So, when Herb came to visit after that, Angie was too busy being a mother to talk about the things they would do someday.

Ed was wounded in combat, and when he got home,

everything changed for him. He was the town hero for a while, using a cane to help him strut around town in his Marine uniform. His parents were proud. Angie was proud. But a hero can only be a hero for so long, then he has to do something. Ed only wanted to drink, tell war stories, and be flirted with by all the girls while Angie stayed at home with the baby. Herb could see where things were headed, so he offered Ed a job working for him in Chicago. Ed couldn't drive any of the trucks or load any produce, but there was work to do around the office, and he could learn that end of the business. Someday, maybe Ed could even buy a business of his own. All it took was hard work. But Ed was too proud to admit that nobody would hire a cripple other than his own brother. And he wasn't going to spend his life confined to a dingy little office pushing papers around. Not after what he had gone through and what he had done. Didn't Herb know what Ed had sacrificed for his country while Herb was peddling his produce around Chicago and sticking money in the bank?

Angie wanted him to take the job. She wanted him to be able to do something and support the family. There was a terrible fight over it, and Ed told Herb to stay out of their lives. For a short time, Ed worked at the cheese factory in Stockton. But he got fired over a disagreement he had with another employee. He was unemployed for months. Eventually, he got a job at the Ford garage, and he was pumped up over it. He was going to sell so many cars that he and Angie would be building a big house on the edge of town before long. In the meantime, though, they couldn't keep living with her parents. So, Herb loaned them money for a down payment on the house on Sycamore Street, next door to the Stieffles. When Ed got behind on the mortgage, Herb would send Angie some money without Ed knowing it. Then Angie got a job at the diner outside of town. With her salary and tips, Ed's disability pension, and the small salary he earned at the garage, they were able to make ends meet most of the time.

But Ed withdrew more and more from his family. He became mean-spirited, and soon, he was drinking during the day as well as at night after the garage closed. Life had played a dirty trick on him, and he wasn't happy about it. He had been young and strong, a man with prospects, even a hero. It had all been taken away.

He hated limping around the garage doing whatever Mel needed done. He hated living in a house they only bought with the help of a brother who hadn't gone off to war and who hadn't left his chances of having a good life lying on a battlefield. Most of all, he hated Angie, hated her for ignoring it all as if nothing had happened. Something really bad had happened, and it wasn't ever going to go away. It wasn't ever going to get better, and she just expected him to go on. Angie stayed away from him when he drank. She spent a lot of her time next door with nosy Betty Stieffle and usually took Paul with her. Ed thought she should stay home with him. She should be home so that he could tell her how bad it was. Tell her over and over because it would always be bad.

Herb still came out to Stockton on some holidays, though not as often as he had before. He made it a point to talk to Angie whenever he could and to offer help. He didn't hate his brother. He just hated what Ed was doing to himself and his family. Every time he tried to talk to Ed about it, an argument broke out, and Ed told him to stay out of his life. Angie had hinted at leaving Ed once or twice. Herb didn't think she was really planning to leave. It seemed like she was just sounding him out to see what his reaction would be and what he would think of a young wife who would walk out on her crippled husband. He didn't want to encourage her to leave his own brother, but he understood how sad and lonely her life had become, so he made certain she knew that he would not hold it against her if she decided to pull out of the marriage.

In the fall of 1950, he got a letter from her telling him that she couldn't bear living with Ed any longer and that she was leaving. She couldn't stay in Stockton because that would mean seeing him every day and facing everyone in town. Angie had a cousin in Rockford she could stay with while she got started. She was writing to Herb because she didn't want him to find out from anyone else that she had left Ed. Herb called her the next afternoon to assure her that he would support her decision. Then he called Mr. Meyer at the grocery store, where he used to work. He told him that Angie was coming to town looking for a job. Meyer knew a lot of people, and he was never afraid to ask a favor. The next day, Meyer called him back and told him that his nephew, the one who was a doctor, was looking for a receptionist. Just someone to look nice for the people who came to his office and to answer the telephone, maybe do a little office work, but not much. Angie took the job when she got to Rockford. Although it didn't pay much, her living expenses were small, and she began looking for an apartment after she got her first check. Herb took the train to Rockford to see if he could do anything to help her adjust and to thank Meyer. He met her after work and took her and little Paul to dinner. She was proud of her job. It was her first real job other than waiting tables at the diner, and it made her feel independent and worthwhile. But the relief she should have felt at being out of an unhappy situation was swallowed up by the guilt of having left Ed alone. Miserable as the marriage was, it had become a part of his life. What would he have now but his disability and his bitterness? They talked about it at dinner and in the cab on the way back to her cousin's house. When Herb left for the train station that evening, he hoped she would tough it out for her own good and for the sake of Paul, who deserved a happier life.

The next morning, when Angie got to work, Ed was sitting in the waiting room. The doctor had arrived early and, finding Ed standing in the hallway, had let him come in to wait for Angie. She went to the reception desk without speaking. Ed walked over to her desk and stood in front of her.

"Why, Angie? Why did you do this to me? You just left me

a note that you were leaving and telling me where you were going. What was I supposed to tell people? It's all over town now. 'Poor Ed. Can't even keep a wife.'"

Angie put her hands over her eyes and sat at her desk, shivering. Before she was able to compose herself and respond, the first patient of the day arrived for her appointment. Angie asked her to have a seat and paged the doctor to let him know his patient had arrived. Ed said nothing. Soon, other patients began to arrive for their appointments, the telephone started ringing, and Angie was busy. Ed sat in the room looking at Angie and said nothing. When the office closed for the lunch hour, everyone left but Ed and Angie.

"You can't leave me, Angie. You can't just pick up and walk out. It isn't right. What about me? Just because I'm a cripple doesn't mean I don't have feelings—doesn't mean I don't need a wife at home. What did I do so wrong? I lost my leg, that's what. If I had come home from the war whole, you wouldn't be doing this to me."

"Don't, Ed. You can't make me feel guilty. I won't live like that anymore. I can't."

But Angie gave in. She went back with him. Back to the same half-life she had been living because she couldn't let him sink any lower. Ed continued to drink and spend his nights at home alone or at one of the taverns while Angie worked or visited with Betty next door. Paul spent most of his evenings at his friends' houses or just hanging out with older kids at the park.

When Paul was eleven, he got an afternoon paper route delivering the Rockford newspaper, which didn't get to Stockton until just before school was out. That kept him away from the house and gave him some pocket money he could spend at the drugstore on comics and pop. Whenever he could afford it, he would eat at the drugstore lunch counter, and that would keep him from having to go home to eat. There were some nights he was invited to eat with friends, but he always felt funny doing that because he couldn't reciprocate.

On the night his parents died, he was planning to go to a Boy Scout meeting for boys interested in joining the local troop. He had money for his dues and was going to sign up, but when he got to the front door of the scout hall, he changed his mind. The other boys would have their fathers with them, and he would feel funny showing up alone. When he got home, he was happy his mother was there, standing at the kitchen sink in her bathrobe, washing dishes. She gave him a hug and they talked for a little while before he went up the stairs to bed. He heard his father's heavy breathing when he passed his parents' closed bedroom door, so he walked as quietly as he could into the bathroom at the end of the hallway to brush his teeth. He was careful not to make any noise in the bathroom or going from the bathroom to his bedroom. Paul dropped off to sleep almost as soon as he got into bed and slept soundly. But, early in the morning, an explosion down the hall jolted him awake in his dark room. He jumped out of bed and found his way down the dark hallway to his parents' bedroom. He remembered nothing after that until he realized that Mrs. Stieffle was holding him, rocking him in her arms and telling him everything was alright.

Herb showed up the following day to help with funeral arrangements for Ed. He and Paul stayed with his grandparents in the old family home down by the cheese factory. It was where Ed and Herb had grown up. Paul's maternal grandparents took care of all the arrangements for Angela's funeral, which was held in Woodbine. They did not attend Ed's funeral, and none of Ed's relatives attended Angie's funeral, except for Herb and Paul. Ed and Angela were not buried together. Death had finally worked the separation that Angie had wanted so badly. The circumstances had severed all bonds between the in-laws as surely as divorce would have done. The Hoffmans could not be blamed for their son's actions, and there was no open animosity or hostility between the families, but Angie's family would never feel comfortable around the Hoffmans after that, any more than the Hoffmans would ever feel easy in the company of Angie's family.

It was agreed by everyone that it was best for Paul to leave Stockton behind, along with the daily reminders of what had been. The Walkers handled the probate matters and filed a guardianship, making Herb the guardian of Paul's person and estate while he remained a minor.

CHAPTER 13

1956-1972

To say that Herb was not prepared to take on the responsibility of raising a twelve-year-old boy would be an understatement, worthy of a city which, to Paul, was filled with understatements. Chicago was huge. Paul and Ed took the train into Chicago from Stockton with almost all of Paul's belongings in two suitcases. They would have a few other things of his sent to them. Shortly after they had passed through Elgin, the outlying suburbs began, and he couldn't see where one left off and another one started. By the time the porter shouted out, "Next stop, Chicaaaago" he thought he had already been riding through Chicago for at least twenty minutes. They got off at Union Station and took the El from there. When they rode past the loop, he was mesmerized by the skyline, but the other passengers didn't even look that way. It was as if the giant buildings were just in Paul's imagination, and no one else could see them. In time, he realized that the city itself might be huge, but the neighborhoods where everyone lived were small, almost like Stockton. The neighbors knew each other, helped each other, worked together, went to church together, and talked about the same things people in Stockton talked about.

Herb was busy from before dawn until long after nightfall with his produce business. He couldn't stay home with Paul, so Paul went with him. Every morning before school started, Paul would help load the trucks with fresh produce to be delivered before eight o'clock to the restaurants and markets in the area. After school, he would unload shipments of vegetables and fruit, which arrived late in the day, and stack them in the warehouse to be loaded into Herb's trucks the next morning. On Sundays, Herb slept in. The restaurants that were open on Sundays got their last delivery of produce Saturday afternoon, and there were no deliveries to the warehouse until Monday morning. Sunday was the only day Herb had time to spend alone with Paul, and he always tried to make the day one that would teach Paul something about the city while they entertained themselves. When the weather was bad, they took the El to the museums. When the weather was good, they went to the Lincoln Park Zoo or caught a game at Wrigley Field. After they had visited their main attraction for the day, they sometimes stopped off at Maxwell Street for an hour or so before going home. It was an exciting bazaar of street merchants and small shops selling everything imaginable, some of it with questionable origins. Every sale had to be negotiated. The asking price was never paid on Maxwell Street, nor was any first offer ever accepted. Paul loved it. This was considered part of his education in business and life. Herb had learned to deal in the streets, and Paul would learn the same way.

The first time they had gone to Maxwell Street together Herb found a watch he liked at one of the small shops. It was a top-of-the-line Elgin. The shopkeeper wanted fifty dollars for the watch and Herb had offered twenty-five. They haggled over it aggressively, almost to the point of throwing insults. Back and forth they went on the price before finally agreeing on thirty-five dollars and parting on friendly terms.

On the way back, Paul turned to his uncle and started laughing.

"Boy, did you show that guy! A watch like that for thirty-five dollars. He's lucky guys like you don't come by every day, or he would go broke. You really skinned him, didn't you?"

Herb smiled at Paul.

"Wrong, Paul. He would like to see me again because he made money, and I would like to see him again because he let me find his price."

"I don't get it. The price was fifty dollars, and you paid thirty-five dollars."

"No. I think his price was actually thirty-five dollars, or real close to it. If his price was fifty dollars, he wouldn't have sold it to me for thirty-five, and I wouldn't have bought the watch. I found the price, and we both won. My business is a lot like Maxwell Street. My customers negotiate with me for the price of my produce. This summer, you can ride with me on one of the trucks and we'll see which of my customers finds the price and which ones never do."

Then Herb handed the watch to Paul. It was for him all along. And it wasn't even his birthday.

That first summer, Paul spent almost every morning on one of the trucks with Herb or one of the other drivers. When the truck pulled up in front of a market or restaurant each day, the haggling began. Some items were priced in advance, but other prices had to be found. Even produce that had been price-marked in advance was sold at different rates, depending on how well customers found the prices on the other items. Nobody Paul rode with could play the game like Herb, and no one enjoyed it more.

But Paul was still by himself much of the time, and being young with too much time alone was not a good thing. There was a period when he got in trouble with drinking and other juvenile misdeeds. None of it was very serious, but it got him in trouble with the police once or twice when he was seventeen. Fortunately, nothing was bad enough to keep him out of the Air Force when he turned eighteen. He joined in 1962 and never looked back. Paul was lucky. He picked up some college credits while he was still in the service. Then, when he got discharged after coming back from overseas, the GI bill helped him the rest of the way. Eventually, it even helped with law school. He had made Herb proud of him. Nothing could have meant more to Paul than that. The Air Force had taught him discipline, paid for most of his schooling, and it had taught him that he was capable of succeeding if he was willing to put in enough effort.

CHAPTER 14

Tuesday, September 27, 1988

The shareholders' meeting was set for today, September 27th, and Nate would take it upon himself to give Townsend the bad news. He could have done it easily enough by telephone, but the two weeks preceding the meeting had been pure Harry Townsend. Harry had pressed Vernon to call his aunts once or twice each day, trying to sell the offer as the best thing that could happen to them or to the community and telling them over and over that his feelings should be considered. They might be too old to care, but he was not. He needed the merger to take place, and they had no right to ruin things for him and all the other shareholders. Martha and Frieda wavered and called Nate's office constantly to tell him about Vernon's latest effort.

Since Vernon had gotten nowhere with his aunts, Harry came to town himself the day before the meeting to get the aunts in line. He found both ladies home alone in the middle of the day. They invited him in and entertained him in the parlor because that is what one does when one has company, even unwelcome company. Harry tried his best to be charming, but charm had never come easy to him. He told them he had always appreciated the beauty of Galena and hoped that after the merger, he would be able to spend more time there, where people were gentle and cordial like Martha and Frieda. This part of the state felt like home to him. Although he had grown up in Cicero, he had spent some time working for Ford Motor Company, and he used to call on all the Ford dealers in the area. They had been like family to him, wonderful people. He was always happy to help them whenever they had problems, and he missed them all. It was so nice being back in this very special corner of Illinois. There really was no place like it. Frieda had trouble keeping a straight face.

Later, the talk turned to the proposed merger, and he was filled with praise for the business that their father and brother had worked so hard to build. At that point, Martha suggested that she call Nathan because he just happened to be in his Galena office that day and would be happy to come over and discuss the business details better than she and her sister could.

"Not necessary," said Harry. "You ladies have your father's nose for business. I can tell. This is your decision, and your father would want you to make it. He put you and your deceased brother in charge of his company, not Nathan Walker. Now you and your nephew are in control. So it is really up to you to decide what to do."

He explained that to go forward with the sale and the subsequent merger, they could give Vernon their proxies, and they wouldn't have to be bothered by attending any more meetings. He told them that they knew his offer was a good one. Even their accountant had said the tendered price for the shares was fair. Harry had brought proxies with him for them to sign. They could sign them right now and be done. Then Vernon could cast their votes for them.

But Frieda and Martha were not taken in by Harry Townsend. They had known men like him all their lives—men who didn't think women had the intelligence to act for themselves. Well, Harry was wrong. They politely told him that they would go to the meeting themselves to see what everyone else had to say. If they thought selling him their stock after that was best for the employees and Vernon, then they would do it.

Harry was disappointed. He had hoped to get the matter of their stock settled that afternoon, but he still felt confident it would get done the next day. Vernon would pressure them at the meeting, as would Tommy Schumann, who would also be there. They would both argue that the employees needed the merger to have job security. Frieda and Martha wouldn't be able to turn them down. They would sell. Harry spent the night in Galena at a hotel and showed up at the shareholder meeting the following morning.

The meeting was attended by Harry, Vernon, Frieda, Martha, Tommy Schumann, Paul, Nathan, and Joshua. Also, by Jake Sharp, the assistant plant manager, who brought with him signed proxies from all the employees and retirees who held some shares. He would be voting their shares for them.

It was a much shorter meeting than Harry had expected. When Vernon called the meeting to order and explained the purpose for which they had met, Nathan announced that there would be no sale of stock from Frieda and Martha, and they opposed the merger. Vernon objected that there needed to be a vote, and they should talk about it first. Nate said it wasn't a requirement since Frieda and Martha had made their positions clear. However, he told Vernon to go ahead and call the vote, giving everyone a chance to weigh in. Vernon called on Tommy, who said he was anxious for the sale to take place because the company could fail if the merger was not agreed to. Vernon jumped in and said that they had worked really hard on this. It would be unfair for anyone now to withhold their shares to prevent the merger. He didn't mention Frieda and Martha by name, but his meaning was clear. When all discussion had ended, Vernon called for a vote. His two aunts, Josh and Nate, all voted against the merger and said they would not sell their stock. Under the circumstances, Jake Sharp didn't vote the shares he held as proxy. Only Vernon and Tommy voted for the merger. Without the shares of Frieda and Martha, the merger would not work. And they were refusing to sell their shares.

Harry stomped out of the meeting mad as hell, vowing to put Galena Pipe Works out of business. To everyone's surprise, Vernon appeared to go from being angry at his aunts to being angry with Harry. He made a display of practically chasing Harry out the door. Vernon was yelling so loud that everyone could hear him when he told Harry to bring on the competition. It was so out of character for Vernon that Nate and Josh couldn't understand it. Vernon clearly wanted to work with Harry. But that is the opposite of what they were seeing. They supposed that you just can never know people the way you think you do.

CHAPTER 15

Thursday, October 8, 1988

Unfortunately, the scheme didn't end there. Harry didn't let it end. He was not a man to say 'no' to. Between the time the meeting ended and October eighth, Harry contacted both Frieda and Martha by telephone numerous times, insisting that they had verbally agreed to sell their stock when he met them at their home and that they had promised to give their proxies to Vernon. But now they were going back on their word, and he was hurt. He told them that Vernon needed the merger, and everyone would have benefited from it, if not for them. They were being selfish and foolish to rely on their old lawyers who didn't know anything about the business or the modernization of pipe factories. It was not too late to save the deal and help save their company. He told them that Vernon was on his high horse now and was acting as though he could compete with Babson himself. He couldn't. He would fail terribly if he thought he could. Harry was trying to make Vernon a sweet deal because that is how Harry approaches business. Always be more than fair to those you deal with, even if you don't have to be. Harry said that was his motto. Now they were putting everyone at odds with each other and Vernon was going to get things all messed up if the merger didn't happen. It was a shame because Vernon really did want this deal, and he needed it. His loyalty to Frieda and Martha was hurting him. Harry even had his lawyer, Bernie Torveski, call to tell them that they had a legal obligation to follow through with their promise. Of course, there had been no such promise, and both Frieda and Martha told him that.

Frieda finally called Nate to tell him that she and Martha were being bothered by these telephone calls, and Harry was lying about them making him a promise to sell their stock. Nate told them that he knew that was true and even if they had made a promise, it would not have been enforceable. When Nate put down the receiver, he was angry. He didn't get angry often, but when he did, it was wise to stay out of his way. If anything could be said about Nathan and Joshua, it was that they were not to be taken lightly even though they were no longer young men,

On October eighth, Nathan called Harry Townsend in Cicero and let him know that they would be meeting him in his office at around eleven o'clock the following day to iron out some issues from the stockholder's meeting. They arrived on time, along with Paul, and found a crummy-looking office building that was not yet open. They had never taken Harry to be the head of a fancy business empire, but they were still surprised to find him working out of a converted convenience store. They got tired of waiting, so Nate called Harry and asked him if he had misunderstood when they would arrive. Harry told him not to get excited. He was on his way, and he had more important things to do than talk to them about two silly old ladies and a rundown pipe factory. He arrived about an hour later, parked his grey-and-white Suburban in front, and let them in. The Suburban looked familiar to Paul, who had come along just to watch the fireworks. He was sure he had seen it somewhere before. But he would think about that later.

Josh, Nate, and Paul followed Harry into his dingy office. They were not invited to have a seat, but two of them found chairs anyway. Paul chose to stand. He looked around and wondered if there was a beer cooler, a magazine rack, and a counter for the sale of lottery tickets.

"Well," asked Harry, "What exactly is it you guys have to say? It better be that you and those old ladies have wised up and want to sell your stock. If you have anything else to say, then say it and go. I'm a busy man."

Nate answered this way, "Harry, we have all gotten off on the wrong foot, and there is no need for it. It was never our intention, or the intention of Frieda or Martha, to be disrespectful to you or to your offer. They want you to know that. But they are in a different stage of life and are comfortable with the way things are now. They don't know how you misunderstood what they told you about not wanting to sell their stock. But they never intended for you to think they would sell it. They are not trying to negotiate and get you to increase your offer. They just want to keep their shares."

Harry laughed. "That's it? You drove all the way here to tell me that? What the hell is it with you guys?"

Nate spoke. "I'll be frank with you then, Mr. Townsend. I'll put it this way. You made an offer. Your offer was not accepted by our clients. Further discussions about your offer are not welcome. Your telephone calls to our clients are upsetting to them and have put them at odds with their nephew. If you have anything further to bring up about these failed negotiations, you need to have your lawyer contact Joshua or me so that it can be discussed between attorneys. Your lawyers will understand what we are telling you, they will be able to advise you on the laws involving the persistent telephone harassment of two older ladies. Now that about concludes the reason we came. I'm sure you agree that any conversation like this one should be had face-to-face so that no misunderstanding might arise. We feel you are entitled to that respect. That's why we made the trip here rather than trying to discuss it on the telephone. Unless Josh has anything to add, I believe that is all we have to say."

Harry stood up and leaned his massive body over his desk. "Now you listen to me. You don't come in here and threaten me. You dumb bastards mucked up a good thing for everyone and now have the gall to come here and read me the riot act. I think you are full of shit, and you need to get the fuck out of here. I'll bury Galena Pipe Works. What do you think of that, smartass?"

Everyone was quiet until Josh stood, walked up to the desk and stared the bigger man in the eyes. "This is what I think, Harry. Mrs. Payne and Mrs. Keele are not silly old ladies, and if you had been raised with an ounce of respect or decency, you would know better than to talk the way you do and act the way you do. We've covered everything that needs to be covered with you. Today, and for all time. So, we are leaving. But one more thing, which is more to the point. I think somebody should have pounded your empty bald head into the floor a long time ago to see if that could smarten you up a little bit."

Harry blinked. His face turned beet red, but he said nothing. Josh didn't budge. He held his eyes on Harry's and waited for a response. But there wasn't one. Nate and Paul walked to the door while Josh stayed in front of Harry's desk staring him in the face. Nate told Josh it was time to leave, and they all walked out, with Harry standing at his desk. Sometimes, a big bully is just a bully nobody has stood up to. Paul was shocked at how Josh had pulled that off without being beaten half to death by a guy who outweighed him by seventy or eighty pounds. When he got into the car, he expected Nate and Josh to be all wound up, but they acted as if nothing had happened. They were just talking about the traffic going back to Galena and disagreeing about whether or not there was a better route. Frieda and Martha never received another telephone call from Mr. Harry Townsend after that day.

CHAPTER 16

Wednesday, October 12, 1988

Paul had trouble concentrating on his writing and research. The writing project, combined with his time spent with Nate and Josh, had kept him from thinking about the actual reason he had come to Stockton. He was struggling with the thought that Ed's death no longer seemed like a suicide to him. Had someone really killed his father in his parents' bedroom? Who could it have been? Herb? Or some suitor his mother had known? And who would that have been? After talking to Everett Perkins, he was convinced there were people who knew more than they were telling him. Even Betty Stieffle was uncomfortable talking about it. Everett had said enough to make him think that things had been covered up for a long time. He didn't know who had killed Ed, but he didn't think Ed had killed himself.

Still another big question lurked. Why did it happen at all? Why, on that day, did it happen? Why, on November 26, 1956, did Ed Hoffman go home and murder his wife? That is the one thing he still needed to know. He knew Ed was unhappy with life, with his marriage, and with his disability. He was living in a haze of alcohol and self-pity. He was suspicious of

Herb's relationship with Paul's mother, and he may have foreseen losing her. All of that had been true for some time. But what set it off that day? Why that day?

Paul walked downtown to have breakfast, but when he got to the restaurant, he didn't go in. He wasn't hungry anymore. He walked down Front Street to the building that had housed the old Ford dealership when Ed had worked there. It looked about the same as he remembered from the outside. Now, it was an antique and thrift shop, open only on weekends. He remembered the building well. His father had shown him around a few times, and once he had sat behind his father's metal desk in the showroom. But mainly he remembered waving to his father through the plate glass window as he walked down the sidewalk with his friends. It seemed like his father was always there in the window, just looking out into the street. Mel Howard was the dealer he worked for. Paul remembered that because his name had been on the window.

He walked back to his room and picked up the telephone book. There it was. *Mel Howard, 311 Elm Street, 452-8920.* He picked up the telephone and dialed. What would Mel Howard be like? What had his father thought of him? Paul couldn't remember his father talking much about Mr. Howard at home. A woman's voice answered the telephone.

"Hello."

"Hello. Is this Mrs. Howard?"

"Yes."

"Mrs. Howard, my name is Paul Hoffman. I used to live in Stockton when I was a child. My father was Ed Hoffman, and my mother was Angela. I'm visiting here for a while, and I've been talking to some people who knew them. I was young when they died. My father used to work for Mel Howard. Would he be your husband?"

"Mr. Howard died last year. Yes, he was my husband."

"Oh. I'm sorry to hear that. Did you know my parents very well?"

"I knew Angela well, and I knew most of her family. We

talked a lot. Your father ... well, I knew him and his family, but I didn't really have much contact with him. Mel talked about him quite a bit. He always liked him and felt sorry for the bad break he had in life. Mel didn't serve in the war. He had a bad back, and they wouldn't take him. He always thought he owed something to the young men like your father who had suffered in the war. I remember you, too. Your mother brought you over to the house when you were just a cute toddler. I didn't see you very much when you got older and got busy with things."

"I don't want to impose, but would you mind if I stopped by to see you this morning to visit some about my parents?"

"That would be fine. I don't get much company."

Paul walked from his room to Mrs. Howard's house. What a town. To be able to call someone across town and then just walk over to their house and see them a few minutes later was so great. That morning, he had gotten out of bed, walked to the restaurant in the middle of downtown, walked to the west end of the business district to look at the old Ford building, walked back to his room, and was now walking across town to visit Mrs. Howard. And all of that walking was less than the distance he used to jog every morning on the roof of the downtown YMCA in Houston. He forced himself to take his time and enjoy the cool, quiet morning.

He looked at his watch, a habit it would take a long time to break, and realized that he had been on the telephone with Mrs. Howard only ten minutes earlier. That didn't give her much time to prepare for a visitor. But this was Stockton. People were always ready for someone to drop in without warning. That was the way of life in a small farming community, and no one thought of things being any different. Mrs. Howard met him at the door. She had heard him walking up the wooden steps and across the front porch. Her white hair looked as if she had been to the beauty parlor recently, and she was wearing a neat cotton housedress. (That was another thing of the past. Who wore "housedresses" now?) Paul judged her to be between eighty and eighty-five years old. She was plump and slightly bent forward in her back and shoulders, but she was spry and lively as she led him to an old stuffed recliner in the living room. Mel's chair, probably. She had coffee to offer along with some cherry pie baked earlier that morning. The cherries had dropped off her tree in the backyard in June and she had frozen them to use later. She couldn't reach high enough to pick any off the branches anymore. Sometimes, the neighbors picked some and shared them with her, but they were getting old too and hadn't picked any this year. This was not pie you could get at any restaurant, not even in Stockton. It was delicious.

"Mrs. Howard, I was young when my mother and father died. Sometimes, I feel as though I didn't really get a chance to know them very well. My uncle Herb didn't talk about them, and I didn't grow up around other relatives. I made peace with that a long time ago. I'm not the first kid to grow up without parents. But what really has nagged at me forever is why they died. Why it happened. That just won't go away, and the older I get, the more it haunts me. Did your husband talk about it?"

"He did at first. Everyone in town did. Mel felt sorry for your dad and wanted to help him. But maybe I shouldn't have said that."

"Yes. You should have. I don't want to be told a watered-down version that leaves me knowing less than when I came to town, just because that version sounds nicer. I'm here to find out the truth about my parents. Nothing less than the absolute truth is any good to me. Believe me. Nothing you say will hurt me. I already know how the story ended, so I never had an illusion that it was a pretty one."

"Ed was a drunkard, Paul. I mean, after he came back from the war. And he became mean-spirited as time went on. You didn't have to know him very well to know that he was angry at the world and full of pity for himself. I'm not judging him. He couldn't help being that way. Some of the soldiers adjusted, even some who were hurt worse than he was. But he had been a proud young fellow before he left—good-looking and full of himself. Maybe that is what made it so hard for him. When he was a teenager, he strutted around town like the cock-of-the-walk. Some of us joked about it when we saw him. We shouldn't have, and we felt bad about it later. Mel gave him some work washing the cars back then. After he came back from the war, he still played the big shot for a while. Drank with all the local boys and told war stories. Rubbed it into the boys who hadn't gone over. And that didn't set well for long. I think people finally just got a little tired of it. When the party finally ended, and he had to settle down to a job and raise a family, it hit him hard. He wasn't so special. He was just like every other young man with responsibilities, only in his case, it was worse because he had that missing leg and couldn't do as much as others could.

"It was a come-down for him. Mel said he had a lot of physical pain, too. That's why he drank so much. But I couldn't say on that. I just know that Mel gave him a job selling cars because he had lost his job at the cheese factory and no one else offered him anything. I don't think Mel really needed anyone. He had never hired a salesman before. Not that much business in a town like this and most of it just comes in naturally anyway. The farmers always wanted new cars and trucks. Mel didn't need Ed to sell them. He would have sold the same cars and trucks to the same people anyway. But he didn't pay Ed very much, so he could afford to give him a job and let him drive a demonstrator. I think Mel liked having someone around to talk to."

"How did my parents get by?"

"Not too well. At first, Ed didn't want your mother working. Pride again. But it got to where they almost lost the house, and Angela wouldn't stand for it anymore. Mel told me about it. They had some pretty good battles over the subject. Finally, Angela got a job at the café outside of town on Route 20, and she made enough, what with tips and all, to keep things going. I think that hurt Ed really bad. He felt like he was sort of useless. Not that Angela would have wanted him to feel that way. She was a wonderful girl, your mother, and as devoted to Ed as she could be. He just made it impossible for her."

"Are you saying the marriage was in trouble?"

"Lord, yes! Angela wasn't a selfish person, but she was human, and she felt trapped. She told me that once, shortly after Ed started working at the garage. Ed was mean. She didn't deserve that. She felt sorry for him and felt obliged to stick with him. Couldn't really love him, though. Not like she once did. Divorces were looked down on back then. But she would have gotten one eventually. Everyone said it was just a matter of time, and no one would have blamed her a bit."

"Was there someone else?"

"If there was, it was a good secret. That's all I can say. Things like that get noticed pretty fast around here."

"I can imagine."

"She was good friends with the Walker boys, and everyone knew they were both sweet on her in high school, especially Josh. But the Walkers aren't like that. I think they just worried about her and tried to help when they could. Your uncle cared about her, too. He always brought her gifts when he came to visit. That made Ed mad, but he did it anyway. He knew what she was going through and knew how Ed treated her. I think he felt awful about his brother being that way. She was too good to be abused by someone. She could have found someone else if that's what she wanted. She was so pretty and so nice. Only she didn't have anyone like that, at least that I know about."

"Didn't her family help?"

"No. Not that they wouldn't have tried. She just didn't want them to know how bad it was. Always tried to put the best face on it for them so they wouldn't be worried about her. They weren't happy about her marrying Ed to start with."

"So, they just stayed in the dark about what was going on with her?"

"For a while. Then she left one time and took you with her to Rockford. You wouldn't remember that because you were so young. Didn't Herb ever say anything about it?"

"Not that I remember. What happened?"

"Herb helped her, is what I heard. Got her a job and a place to stay. She came back, though. Ed made her feel guilty over it, and she just came back to more of the same thing. If she had left again, it would have been for good. It was when she left and went to Rockford that her folks knew for sure things were bad. But she kept right on acting to them like everything was rosy. What could they do if she denied things were wrong?"

"How did Ed act when she came back?"

"Got drunk a lot. Missed work. Not that it mattered to Mel if he wasn't there. But Mel worried about him when that happened. Ed was embarrassed. He tried to make it so that she had just gone off to visit some friends. Everyone knew better, though, and Ed just got meaner. Mel said that Ed called your uncle Herb and cussed him out real good. Told him not to come around here anymore. He threatened him, is what I heard."

"Did Herb stay away after that?"

"Some. But he came back sometimes. He just stayed out at the motel instead of in town at your place or with your grandparents. He saw you and your mom for a few hours each time, then took the train back the next day without seeing Ed. He always looked in on some of his old friends in town while he was here, so it wouldn't look bad about him being in town. People talk, Paul. But I know he just came to check on you and Angela. I always suspected he gave her some money when he came. He was here the night before it happened."

"You mean the day after it happened. It happened early in the morning on the twenty-fifth. He took the train out to Stockton the following morning."

"No. That's not right. He was here the night before it happened. The twenty-fourth, I guess it must have been. I know because I saw him myself at the bank late in the afternoon. He was in the back office talking with the banker about something. They were close friends. I walked past the office, going to where the safe deposit boxes are, and I noticed him through the open door. He acted kind of funny when I spoke to him. I figured that was because he worried I might say something to Mel, and Mel might tell Ed he was in town. Mel wouldn't have. The reason I still remember all of that is the next day, when I heard what happened, I thought how lucky it was that your uncle Herb was here to look after things right away. After that, everything just seemed to get confusing with so much going on. There were the funerals, then everyone thought you might go to live with your grandparents. But right away, you went off to Chicago to live with your uncle, a bachelor. Everyone thought that was strange, but some other things were too, and I'm afraid there was gossip for a spell."

"What else was kind of strange?"

"The whole thing, in a way. There you were, going off right away with your uncle. And don't get me wrong. Everyone liked Herb. He was a good man. Not everyone would want to take on the responsibility of raising his brother's child. It just surprised folks. Then, there was the autopsy that never really took place. From what I heard, old Doctor Schwartz just kind of waltzed in and pronounced them both dead of gunshot wounds. Then Everett ruled it a murder and a suicide, and the paper reported it that way. Everett doubled as the county coroner back then. Kind of backward, I always thought. But Stockton didn't have anything like this happen before, so it didn't make much sense to pay someone else to act as coroner when Everett was already on the payroll. The thing was that Merle Simmons, the undertaker, told Mel and a few other people that your father was shot from behind, back of the head, not like it said in the paper. He said he couldn't quite figure out how Ed did that. He told Mel he brought that up to Everett, but that Everett was firm on it. Now, I have to say that Merle was an oddball. He always had an outlandish idea about something. So, Mel didn't take it too seriously. After a while, I don't think anyone else did either."

"Did people ever think someone else was involved?"

"I don't think so. Not really. It fit that your father had killed Angela, then himself. He would have done it that night. It's just that nobody could see how he did it if Merle Simmons was right. But Merle, being Merle, he could just have been causing a stir. Why would Perkins make something up? That didn't make any sense either. The caskets were closed, but that didn't surprise anyone under the circumstances."

"What did you mean when you said he would have done it that night?"

"Mel told me about it. The Ford representative from Chicago was at the garage that morning, giving him a hard time. Sales were down, and this young man was trying to throw the fear into Mel, telling him how to run his business and everything. Mel didn't appreciate it much, especially when this fellow told him to cut his costs by getting rid of Ed. But he needed to keep the dealership with Ford, so he had to listen. Truthfully, Ed had cost Mel some sales by making people angry. He was short-tempered and couldn't deal with people very well. Some of the Stockton people had gone over to Freeport to buy cars—Buicks and Chevys, and they told Mel they were sorry about it, but they just didn't like Ed.

"Anyway, at some point this fellow made a crack to Mel about Ed being a cripple, and Ed heard him. When he was leaving, Ed got into a scuffle with him and he kicked Ed's false leg right out from him and left him lying on the floor crying in pain. Mel said he seemed to enjoy it, and he stood over Ed, leering at him until Mel intervened to push him out of the way and help Ed get up. Mel described the whole thing to me. It was terrible. And I think it was the end of Ed. Mel tried to comfort him like you would a little child. Then Ed finally cleaned himself up, left the garage, and headed down to the tavern. That was the last time Mel ever saw him alive. Fortunately, that mean young man left Ford shortly after all of that took place, and Mel didn't have to deal with him anymore. He was glad of it. Mel never liked him. He was a great big, brawny fellow and a bully. After he made Mel fire Ed, Mel really hated him. He held him largely responsible for what Ed did that night. I hope I haven't said too much."

"You haven't, Mrs. Howard. Do you happen to remember the name of the man who gave Ed such a bad time?"

"Oh, my. It was so long ago. I can't remember. Mel talked about him a lot, but for the life of me, I can't recall his name."

"Thank you for having me over. You have been very kind. If you happen to remember the Ford man's name, I would appreciate it if you would let me know. And thank you for the delicious pie."

Mrs. Howard sent half of the pie home with Paul because he liked it so much. He told her he would come by again and pick some of the cherries for her next Summer. They were too good not to end up in one of her pies. But now Paul had even more questions about who had murdered his father.

CHAPTER 17

Wednesday, October 12, 1988

Babson Pipe Company had been approached almost a year earlier by a land developer in Texas named Brock Johnson, who, along with his partner Jimmy Ponder, had formed a venture they were calling Noble Vista Development to build a small subdivision just outside of Amarillo. They had just acquired the land they needed and were lining up contractors and suppliers. They were going to need a substantial number of concrete sewer pipes, but they were having trouble finding a source. Harry Townsend had made a trip down to Amarillo to check out the opportunity and was not impressed. Clearly, these guys were in over their heads. They had no real experience as developers and had a history of business failures and bankruptcies in homebuilding. They seemed shady, and Harry saw it right off. Although Harry was not above working with shady people, these guys were not even good at it. And they were not getting anywhere with the project. Harry saw no benefit in the thing.

He had forgotten all about them until they contacted him again. They told him they had moved the project along somehow to the point that pipes needed to be obtained and buried. They assured Harry that they had all their ducks in a row now and they needed pipe soon. Bullshit. He knew this project would still be a disaster. They obviously couldn't get bank financing at this point. They must be overextended on their credit and behind schedule. Most likely, they had not found any pipe supplier who would take a chance on them. He surmised they had probably been living off their draws from the bank, and things were coming to a head fast. They wouldn't have been calling Harry if things were going as well for them as they tried to let on. Harry still had no interest in Babson selling any pipes to these guys. He was no sucker. But he was stinging from the shareholder meeting in Galena, where his merger offer was rebuffed by those two old ladies and their lawyers. So, he thought again about what he had seen of this project, and it gave him an idea. If he played things right, he might be able to get some use out of the situation. Neither Brock nor Jimmy came across as very bright, and that is why Harry decided to make a return trip to Amarillo. Providence had put these fools back in his life at just the right time.

Harry was angry and more determined than ever to own Galena Pipe Works. He didn't care what he had to do to make that happen. Noble Vista Development looked like the tool he needed if he played everything just right. Brock Johnson and Jimmy Ponder were going down no matter what happened. There was no saving them, but there might be a way to turn their failure to his advantage. So, he went back down to Texas to meet again with Brock and Jimmy. This time, he had a plan.

When they sat down to talk, he was blunt. "Boys let's just put all the bullshit aside. I'm not selling you any pipes. You guys are going to be tits up in less than a year. Nothing is going to stop that. You would love for me to send you some pipes to put in the ground before you go under. My pipes would at least add some value to the project if it goes into Chapter 11 bankruptcy, because you have to have roads and sewer pipes before the project is worth anything. If I sold you the pipes, I would never get paid. I would be screwed, right? Now is that about it? Have we cleared the air?"

Brock knew that you would have to be a lot better than he was to bullshit a guy like Harry. He kind of respected that.

"Okay, Harry. Just for kicks, let's pretend you are right. So then, what brings you here? Why waste time with us? You have something in mind. Lay it out for us."

Harry did just that. He laid out a lot and laid it out in a way that Brock and Jimmy could foresee a payoff for them. They were sure as hell desperate, and just about any idea Harry had to throw at them would have sounded good. Harry had it all figured out.

"Although I am not dumb enough to send you pipes I would never get paid for, I know somebody dumber than me who might. I think I can get you those pipes from another company. You may have to make a payment for the first delivery, because the pipes you will order are not standard. They are to be 'specially manufactured'. In fact, you might not have to pay anything at all if they are dumber than I think. But we can handle it either way.

"What takes place should look like this: delivery of pipe continues for a while without you paying for them. You are in default, but they keep making and shipping pipe for a while because they think you are credit-worthy and because they have shit for brains. All of a sudden, they wake up and decide to press you for their money. But that's when things start going right into the ditch. They run into unexpected problems, and they have to tell you they can't produce the rest of the pipes you need on time. Even though you are, shall we say, 'a tad slow' in paying them, they are in even more trouble than you because they can't produce any more of the specially manufactured pipes that you have to have. That forces you to shut down your project, and it causes you financial damages. Fortunately for you, there are serious penalties for that built into your contract. You have damages much greater than their losses on the pipes they provided. Time marches on. Even if they offer to send substitute pipes they have sitting around, you don't want them. They don't conform to the specs in the contract. When they ask you for the money you owe them for the pipes you already have, you threaten to sue them for non-performance. It is now a "tit for a tat," and they try to negotiate. But they have a poor negotiating position because if they push too hard, they know you will end up in bankruptcy. Then they will have to deal with a bankruptcy trustee who will be pushing your lawsuit against them. It is a damned mess. Eventually, you may end up in some kind of bankruptcy anyway. But even if you do, you will have something to work with. You will have pipes in the ground and a lawsuit against the pipe company you got them from."

"What's your part?"

"For right now, it will be my job to see that they contact you and offer to sell you pipes. That's how it will all start, and I know exactly how to get them to do that. Your role will be to position your company as one that is well-financed, busy as hell with projects, and in high demand. I'm pretty sure you guys can pull that part off since I am not the dummy on the other side."

Brock knew Harry was going to get something out of this scam, and he wanted to know what it was. All Harry would say is that he had no interest in their business and was only looking out for his own. His business was his own business. They didn't need to worry about Harry Townsend. It would all start with a phony contract for pipe between Noble Vista Development and his company, Babson Pipe Company. It would be a very favorable contract to Babson with a significantly inflated price for the pipes and big penalties for failure to perform. It would be the kind of contract that is a dream for a pipe company. But that contract would never come to anything because neither side would ever perform anything under it.

Brock was kind of unsure. "Harry, let me see if I have this

right. We will be signing a fake contract very favorable to you, and neither of us will have any intention of doing anything the contract says we will do. Is that what you are saying?"

"Well, sure. But let's not call it a 'fake.' I don't ever like to use that 'fake' word. It just sounds underhanded. Let's say it is a 'signed contract' that, for all intents and purposes, appears to be binding on all parties but actually is not worth squat. Because neither of us will ever do any of the stuff it talks about. You got that?"

"I guess so. It's not a fake contract. It just isn't worth squat."

Harry headed back to Chicago with the signed contract in his hands. The specs were carefully drawn, a tight delivery time was set, it was properly dated and signed by all parties. And it absolutely wasn't worth squat. He also had an unsigned copy of the contract.

CHAPTER 18

Friday, October 14, 1988.

When Harry had visited Galena Pipe Works in July, he had taken special notice of Tommy Schumann, the plant manager. He could tell that Tommy saw himself as an up-and-comer who was stuck in a job going nowhere. He had gone to college and had ambitions beyond what he was doing. Likewise, Tommy liked what he saw in Harry Townsend, who was no Vernon Tanksley. Vernon was just a guy who inherited a lot of stock in a company he couldn't run. He made decisions that put the company at risk, and he was easily manipulated. Vernon would never learn the business. He would keep making the same mistakes, thinking he was a savvy businessman. Harry, on the other hand, was a sharp guy who knew how to make money. That's the kind of guy he could learn from.

Tommy was excited. He thought a merger of Galena Pipe Works and Babson Pipe Company would be fantastic. He couldn't wait to get home that night to tell his wife what an opportunity this could be. Babson Pipe Company's plant manager was old and ready to retire. That's what Harry had told him. Tommy had a vision of being Harry's right-hand man when the merger took place.

But then came the shareholder meeting and the bad news. The merger was not going to happen. Tommy was going to be stuck at Galena Pipe with a nowhere job and a piddly few shares of almost worthless stock.

He was surprised when, several weeks later, Harry telephoned him to let him know there might still be a job for him at Babson in the future if he could help Harry out a little. Tommy was onboard. This was an opportunity that he was not going to miss. He was tired of settling for less. He and Harry met that weekend at a restaurant in Rockford. Harry told him to hang around Vernon all he could and stay ready to help when Harry needed him. Something good was going to happen if he was patient and willing to help. That had been in early September, and he had not heard from Harry again until Harry got back from Amarillo.

Then Harry filled him in. "Tommy, let's get back to what we talked about in Rockford. You are a sharp guy with a bad deal at Galena Pipe. Those selfish old women are keeping you from advancing the way you need to and they have just about ensured that the little bit of stock you have isn't going to be worth crap. Vernon is an idiot, as we both know. I have an opportunity to offer you, but not until we can get Galena Pipe Works bought so that their customer base opens up to us. Their business is built on loyalty, and loyalty alone won't cut it. At some point, Galena Pipe is going to run into trouble and lose those customers. That is inevitable. The sooner the better, because I think I can make those customers move to us."

Tommy could not agree more. "What do you need? I'm damned tired of Vernon Tanksley, and I am ready to help."

Harry went on to explain that he had a contract from a developer in Texas, which was just too good to be true because it wasn't really true. Harry was going to start bragging it up around Beloit, where Babson is located. He would brag it up around contractors, developers, county managers, bankers, and everyone he knew in Northern Illinois and Southern Wisconsin. He had even thought about bringing the Texas developers up to Beloit for a meeting to show them off. But he wasn't sure they were capable of making the right impression. It would be better not to have to do that if he had Tommy's help. Harry could tell everyone he ran into that they were big developers and were "dripping with West Texas oil money." He would also run down Galena Pipe Works and Vernon Tanksley in particular, letting everyone know that Vernon hadn't gained new business since his father died. He would tell everyone that he was going to put Galena Pipe Works out of business with more contracts like the one he had just made in Texas. Enough businesspeople in Beloit knew people in Galena that word would get back to Vernon, and it would get under his skin. Tommy's job would be to make sure Vernon picked up on the gossip. He should make sure that the talk about Babson's Texas contract gets around the plant in Galena.

The next part was important. Tommy should talk to Vernon about it and tell him that he had talked to someone at Babson who knows all the company information. It was a friend of Tommy's who was getting ready to leave Babson Pipe. Tommy shouldn't divulge who it is, but the insinuation should be that it is probably the Babson plant manager. Then he should tell Vernon that he learned the Texas contract hadn't actually been signed yet by the developer. Harry was still waiting for the signed contract to come in the mail. Tommy should say his contact told him the deal was not locked up. His friend had talked to an engineer who works for the developer about the specifications for the pipe, and the engineer was very open with him. He wasn't sure Babson could fulfill the contract and fulfill it on time. He is uncomfortable with the deal, and the developer is getting uncomfortable too. The engineer told his friend that the developers were first-class businessmen and were quite wealthy. Their banker had told Harry that every bank in the area wanted their business. Harry doesn't know that the developers have reservations now and that they are looking for another company for the pipes. The developers now think the work is overpriced, but they are even willing to live with that if they can get the work done correctly and on time. They regretted the time lost talking to Harry, and they wanted a more reputable pipe company handling the work. Time was running short for them, and they needed to get things underway without a lot more negotiation. The purpose for telling Vernon all of that was to get Vernon to cut in and take the contract from Babson pipe.

It was basically a script for Tommy. Harry told him to remember all of it and tell it to Vernon just that way. Then he went over it again to make sure Tommy had it all down. Tommy didn't get it. Why would Harry want to get Galena Pipe Works a contract to manufacture pipes for somebody in Texas? It was beyond him, but he paid close attention and said he would do it gladly. Harry must know what he was doing, and Tommy certainly wasn't going to question him about it. He would feed every bit of that bullshit to Vernon and make him believe it. Then, he would tell Harry how Vernon reacted.

CHAPTER 19

Thursday, October 27, 1988

arry put on a show around everyone he knew in business who might have a way of spreading gossip to people at Galena Pipe. He bragged all over Beloit about snagging a contract with a bunch of Texans who had more money than sense and popped his buttons, boasting about the sweet deal he had pulled off. People avoided him because, first of all, nobody liked him, but also because they were tired of his caterwauling. As planned, all of it got back to Vernon, and not just through Tommy Schumann. Other people were talking about it too. Vernon was easy to read. Everyone near him could see that he couldn't stand hearing about Harry's Texas contract. It made him look bad. Vernon would love to get a contract like that and wave it in Townsend's face. How would Harry Townsend like it? Vernon made no effort to hide the way he felt about it.

While all of this was raging at Galena Pipe Works, Harry met Tommy in Rockford again. This time, he handed Tommy an unsigned but otherwise complete copy of the phony Noble Vista Development contract. His instructions were to get it to Vernon without letting Vernon know where he got it. Being completely on board, Tommy went to Vernon with the unsigned contract the first chance he got. He said that his contact at Babson had apparently been telling the truth. Harry's fantastic Texas contract hadn't even been signed by the customer. Until it was signed, it was no good. Vernon practically broke into song; he was so excited. He looked it over and told Tommy he had an idea. He had such a great idea! He knew how to screw Harry, and he was going to do it. He asked Tommy whether Galena Pipe could fulfill that contract by the deadline if they jumped in right now without wasting a day getting it into production. And did he think they could beat the price? He wanted Tommy's thoughts. Tommy told him yes. He was damned sure they could do it, do it cheaper, and do it at a profit. They would have to act fast, though. The deadline for producing the pipe was short. Vernon told Tommy he would sleep on it and come up with a plan. He would call the developer after he had figured out what his pitch would be. All the information he needed was on the contract Tommy had given him. That made it almost too easy. Vernon bragged to Tommy about being a pretty good salesman. Harry would crap when he found out Vernon had snatched the deal away from him.

As soon as he left Vernon's office, Tommy called Harry and tipped him off that Noble could expect a call from Vernon the next morning. Tommy couldn't believe how fast Vernon went for it. But Harry wasn't surprised at all. He found the Irish whiskey he kept in his file drawer for special occasions and drank straight from the bottle. Things were working out just the way he planned. All the pieces were coming together. Everyone knew their own involvement in his plan, but not anything about the involvement of the others. Harry was the only one who knew everyone's part in it and how the pieces fit. That was the beauty of it.

He called Brock to let him know he would be getting a

telephone call from Vernon Tanksley at Galena Pipe Works, and this was the guy who would sell him pipes.

———

Vernon picked up the telephone on his desk the very next morning and called Noble Vista Development. He identified himself and his company and asked to speak to Brock Johnson. He was put on hold. Then the receptionist, who was Brock's wife, came back on the line to tell him that Mr. Johnson was in a meeting, but if he wanted to leave his telephone number, Mr. Johnson would call him back when he was free. Later that day, Vernon got a call from Brock Johnson, who was apologetic about not being able to take his call. He said he had been in a meeting with the mayor of Lubbock all morning, along with some county commissioners from Lubbock who were all trying to coax him into starting a huge development there. It would be similar to the Noble Development in Amarillo but much larger. He was inclined to do it. But first things first. They needed to get this Amarillo project finished.

While Vernon was on the telephone with Brock Johnson, Tommy Schumann showed up at his office door holding some plant invoices. Vernon motioned Tommy to come in and be silent. Then he put the call on his speakerphone.

"Mr. Johnson, I am calling you about that very thing. I am calling about your Noble Vista Development project. I'm the president of Galena Pipe Works, the oldest and best-established concrete pipe company in Northern Illinois. You are free to contact anyone in the construction business in this area, and they will give you a high recommendation of our company. I know that you are in contact with Babson Pipe Company in Beloit about furnishing your pipe. I don't run down competitors very often, but I can tell you that people don't say a lot of good things about Babson. I know that you have a tight schedule, and you need to know your supplier can fulfill your needs. We can do that. Mr. Townsend has made no secret of the contract he wants you to sign. He is waving it around all over the place, so I happen to know the terms. Frankly, he is bragging about how he got the best of you guys. I know we can beat the price in that contract and, unlike Babson Pipe Company, we can do it on time."

Brock seemed happy to hear what Vernon was saying. He said he would have to check them out carefully and he would like to get the names of some customers of Galena Pipe. He would normally do more than that in the way of due diligence, but he was in a hurry. If Vernon sent him a better contract than Babson, and if everything he said about his company panned out with his references, he would consider the contract. How soon could he send it? Vernon told him he would get an offer prepared and sent to him right away. He and Tommy started working up a proposal. Vernon was sorry that he didn't have time to check the developers out very well. But Tommy assured him that Harry's people had done all of that thoroughly, according to his source. That was good to hear, but Vernon knew he should do more before sending pipe to a company in Texas, he didn't know much about.

Brock Johnson was supposedly in another meeting with the mayor of Lubbock about starting the project there when Vernon called him again. My God. The mayor of a neighboring city travels out of town to Brock's office just to entice him! That says all you need to know about these guys, Vernon told Tommy. Still, if Vernon made a contract without doing anything more than talking on the phone with the developer, he would open himself up to a bunch of criticism from his aunts and the Walkers. He didn't need that. He was a sharp enough businessman to know that he would look bad entering into a contract without even making an effort to show diligence. So, he decided to call Brock Johnson in the morning and arrange a visit to Amarillo to see the project. He could take the proposed contract with him and get it signed right there.

CHAPTER 20

Friday, October 28, 1988

At nine o'clock the next morning Vernon called Tommy to his office and dialed up Brock Johnson. This time his receptionist, who was now very charming, put him through to Brock immediately.

"Mr. Johnson, this is Vernon Tanksley. How are you?"

"Just fine. Call me Brock. Are you calling about your proposal? Do you have something for us to look at?"

"I do, Brock. But I would really prefer to fly down to Amarillo, meet with you and your partner, and go over it there. That would give us a chance to get to know each other. I would like to get a look at your project. And you might feel more comfortable with our contract if you had a chance to meet me. I can bring along our plant manager so that you can ask him any questions you have. We could fly down tomorrow morning if that would work for you?

"Sounds like a good idea. It could save time if we go with your company. We might still want to see your plant at some point since we have other projects, but it could wait until this one is underway. We need to get pipe in the ground quickly. Just let me know when you will arrive and we will pick you up at the airport ourselves, or send someone to pick you up if we can't get free."

"Great. I will call to give you the flight information. We won't be able to get there until late in the afternoon. We can spend the night in Amarillo and fly back the following day. Can you recommend a hotel?"

"Sure. If I am tied up when you call, give the information to our receptionist. I'll have her line up a hotel for you guys. We'll put you up and take you to dinner. I look forward to meeting you. Jimmy does too."

Vernon hung up the telephone and looked over at Tommy, who was giving him a thumbs-up.

"Damn right, Tommy. I think we might get one over on old Harry. These guys are anxious. I think I sold them. You and I are going down to Amarillo tomorrow. We won't have a lot of time, but it will let us meet these guys and check things out enough to know they are legitimate. I want to be able to say we actually went down there to check them out if the Walkers squawk. We are going to do this. We are going to lock this up, then laugh at Harry Townsend. Wait and see. When I am finished with Noble Vista Development, they will be begging us for a contract. And there will be more down the road."

"Good work, Vernon! I don't know how you pulled this off so fast. It's going to be a challenge, but we can do it. Oh yeah, these boys could have something for us in Lubbock or somewhere else when this is done."

At five o'clock the next morning,, Vernon and Tommy met at the plant and got into Vernon's car for the long drive to Chicago to catch a plane. They got to Amarillo at four-thirty in the afternoon. Vernon wore a blue business suit with a red necktie and shiny black wingtips. Tommy wore a blue blazer with khaki slacks and loafers. That worked for Vernon. Everyone would recognize who the boss was.

By the time they landed in Amarillo, they were exhausted. They gathered up their small bags and made their way out to the greeting area, where they noticed an attractive, well-dressed woman in her late twenties holding a sign with Vernon's name on it. When they came her way, she ran up to meet them. She introduced herself as Brock's wife and his fill-in receptionist whenever his full-time receptionist was unavailable. That was the case today. Brock and Jimmy were tied up in important meetings and regretted that they couldn't be there to pick them up, but she would take them to their hotel. They would have time to rest before Brock and Jimmy took them to dinner. She drove them to a nice hotel that boasted a good restaurant and a popular bar. Then, she checked them in with a credit card and directed them to the elevators.

Brock called at six o'clock and told Vernon that he and Jimmy were downstairs at the bar. They were both of average size and were wearing nice business suits. They looked to be in their early forties. Tommy, who was younger, was six feet two inches tall and the most imposing of the group. They found a table and ordered drinks. Jimmy introduced Tommy to Ziegenbock beer. Vernon had an old-fashioned, and Brock had Scotch and soda. They talked about the usual things people talk about to get acquainted. Brock didn't know much about Galena or its history. Vernon was proud of his hometown and gave Brock the Chamber of Commerce version. Brock and Jimmy filled them in on Amarillo, although they had both grown up in Dallas and had only been there a few years. Brock told them he was being pressured to start a mixed-use development in Lubbock. He really didn't want to work on that until the Amarillo project was finished, but he had a very favorable borrowing line at a Dallas bank and felt pushed to use it before the interest rate lock expired. That is one of the reasons he was rushing the Amarillo project.

After a second round, Brock picked up the tab and left a nice tip for their server. Then they loaded into a shiny new Chevy Suburban with a magnetic door sign that said "Noble Vista Development." Jimmy had rented it for two days and had slapped the magnetic sign on it. But Vernon didn't need to know that. Brock took them to the Big Texan Steak Ranch on Interstate 40 because people from out of town enjoy its Western atmosphere. The restaurant offers a seventy-two-ounce steak for free, but only if it is all eaten in one sitting. None of them took up the challenge.

After dinner, they drove back to the hotel for more drinks, and they didn't break up until after eleven o'clock. Vernon enjoyed the evening and was impressed with Noble Vista Development. Tommy agreed that these guys were first-rate.

They slept in the next morning, and Brock didn't pick them up until after nine-thirty. Unfortunately, that didn't give them much time for a tour of the property that was being developed. They drove out to it and walked around the few streets that had been built. Then they saw how the unbuilt lots and green areas were laid out and saw some trenches dug for sewer pipes. They spent about an hour reviewing the contract at the site. Then they had to get to the airport, so Vernon left the contract with Brock for him to review with his people. Jimmy took them to the airport because Brock had to meet with an engineer. Then they were airborne, headed for Dallas, Chicago, and the long drive home.

The next morning, Vernon got a call from Brock. He had a revision. The contract offered by Babson Pipe had a provision for liquidated damages if the pipes were delayed. Vernon's contract had omitted that clause. Brock had added it back, and he read it to him over the phone. Vernon had seen that in Harry's contract, and he had intentionally left it out of his. It looked too risky. Everything else in the two contracts was the same, other than the price, which was slightly lower in Vernon's contract.

Vernon complained. "Brock, the penalties that the liquidated damages clause calls for are pretty strong. I don't think our attorneys will go for it."

"Well, Vernon," said Brock. "It is there because we have been very clear in telling you how important it is to us that these pipes get here in time. And you have been telling us how sure you are that you can get them built and delivered that fast. Are you saying you have doubts now that you can do it? Because if you have, we need to know it right now."

"Absolutely not. What the hell … just leave it in. We will take it like that."

Brock said he would sign two originals in that case and send them to Vernon by overnight mail. Vernon should sign both of them and return one signed original to Brock. When Vernon got the signed contracts, he did as requested. Then he called Tommy into his office, showed him the signed contract, and told him to get started fast. The deal depended now on getting the pipe out.

Tommy put aside all work not already on a deadline and ran the shop overtime, doing nothing but making pipes for Noble. He paid double-time to employees who agreed to work on Saturdays and through any holidays. The plant was cranking out pipe for Noble faster than Vernon had ever seen it done. In ten days, he already had enough to begin shipments to Amarillo. It was looking like they would be way ahead of schedule.

CHAPTER 21

Monday, January 9, 1989

At seven o'clock Monday morning, just as Nate was coming in the front door at the Stockton law office, the telephone was ringing. He ran over to the receptionist's desk and picked it up.

"Hello, Walker Law Firm; this is Nate."

Vernon Tanksley was on the phone.

"Nate. We have a big problem, and I'm going to need to see you today. Can you come to Galena?"

"What's the problem, Vernon?"

"We had a fire at the plant, and it is shut down. And we have a big contract to deliver on. I don't know how we are going to deal with that. It's on a really tight schedule. I have to go talk to the fire chief, but I will explain it to you as soon as you can get here."

By the time Nate put down the telephone, Josh was coming through the door.

"Good morning, Walker. Glad you could make it. I've been here working since five thirty, as usual. I just got a call from Vernon Tanksley with a problem. Why aren't you ever here when somebody calls with a problem?"

"Because I'm smarter than you. What's Vernon's problem?"

"He didn't talk long but he said they had a fire at the plant, and they are shut down for a while. He wants to talk about a contract they have that they are going to be behind on. That's about all I got out of him. He wants me to meet him at the plant in Galena. Why don't you come with me? If you had anything important to do you would have gotten to work earlier."

Nate and Josh made it to the plant about forty-five minutes later. They tracked down Vernon near the kiln. He was pacing back and forth and shaking his head.

"Vernon. What happened here and how bad is the damage?"

"It's bad. I got a call from the fire department at about three o'clock this morning. It sounds like some kind of gas leak ignited the fire. The kiln is destroyed. It is going to take a couple of months just to get a temporary roof up over it and get the walls rebuilt. The furnace needs to be replaced along with the big doors we open to tip out the pipes."

"How are you going to operate?"

"That's just it. We can build some big pipes out in the yard for culverts and a few other uses, but there is no point in running the machinery inside to pour the sewer and smaller pipes until we have a drying kiln. The green pipes can't set right without the kiln. Those are the pipes we need. We are going to be late on a few things for some of our regular customers, and they will understand. Winter weather has set in, and construction always slows down here when it gets cold. But the big contract in Texas has me scared. It has strict timeframes built in. Those boys have good weather down there, and they are not going to be happy with any delay at all."

"Texas! What contract are you talking about? You don't have customers in Texas."

"Well, I guess I never showed it to you. It's a good

contract. Maybe you should have seen it before we signed, but it's a good contract, and everything was in a big rush. We had to take it in a hurry to keep Harry Townsend from getting it. Let's go to my office and I'll show it to you."

The Walkers went back to Vernon's office and took seats across from his large desk. Vernon had his secretary make two copies of the contract with Noble Vista Development, and he gave them each one to read while he left his office to go talk to Tommy and the fire chief. The fire had been traced back to a partially ruptured gas pipe, which looked like it may have been damaged by something running into it or striking it in some other way. No one working in the area on Saturday had mentioned any kind of mishap that could have caused it. When he got back to his office, the Walkers had finished reading the contract and had taken notes.

Josh spoke first. "Vernon, I don't know how you got yourself into this contract or how much you know about these guys. You have no payments due until all the pipes for the first phase of the contract have been delivered. Has that happened? And you are locked into an extreme deadline with liquidated damages of three thousand five hundred dollars a day for every day you are late on the delivery schedule. That is a serious penalty and unusual in a contract like this. There is not even a *force majeure* clause to protect you in the event of an act of God, or maybe something like this. For Christ's sake, Vernon! That is a standard clause in any contract. WHY would you ever sign this?"

"You haven't met these guys. They are first class. Tommy and I flew down to Amarillo to meet them and look over the project before we signed the contract. They have a lot of business lined up in other parts of Texas, and delivering on this contract sets us up to get some of it. Tommy and I figured out the timetable and we knew for certain we could deliver on time. There shouldn't ever have been any penalties. How the hell was I to know something like this would happen? A fire in the kiln! It has never happened before. You can't just pass up an opportunity like this. Not when Harry already had his paws on it. Yes, we have sent all of the pipe for phase one. So, they owe on that.

"Harry Townsend! How is he involved?"

"He started out negotiating with these guys before we knew about them. The contract we got is almost like one he tried to get them to sign. But they turned him down because they were uncomfortable with him. That's how we got in on it. We saw the opening and took it."

"Vernon," said Nate; this situation is not good. Maybe everything is going to work out but right now, my instincts tell me you may have your tit in a ringer. There need to be two things done without delay. You need to call this guy … Brock Johnson, is it? Let him know where things stand. And since you have already delivered the first phase of pipe you need to ask him where the money is for that. Then I will call Frieda and Martha. They own more of this company than you do, and they need to know what is going on. I assume they haven't seen the contract either, or they would have called us about it."

Nate could tell that Vernon thought he was being scolded. But if this situation turned bad, Nate was just getting loosened up. Vernon pulled out his file on the Noble deal and called Brock to give him the bad news. Brock's receptionist was apparently doing something else because Brock picked up the phone himself.

"Noble Vista Development, Brock speaking."

"Brock, this is Vernon Tanksley. We have run into a bit of a problem with the pipes."

"What kind of a problem? And it had better not be one that will cause a delay."

"Well, unfortunately, Brock, it may. We had a fire at the plant last night. The plant wasn't affected except for the drying kiln. That's where all the green pipes have to go to set up before we take them out and prepare them for shipping. The kiln suffered serious damage. It's unusable, and we can't make any pipes now until it is reconstructed. That will easily take well over a month. We haven't had time to assess all the damage. I'm really sorry about this, but it is completely beyond our control and not our fault. Until today, we were ahead of schedule. You already got the first phase of pipe, but this will cause delay with phase two."

"Now look, Tanksley. We damned sure spelled it out in the very beginning. We cannot stand a delay. We're ready to lay those pipes in the trenches and there is nothing we can do until they are installed. This is one hell of a mess, and you had better figure something out fast."

"I don't know what to say. I mean, we are having a meeting in a half hour to look for a solution, but I just don't know. I will get back to you."

Both parties hung up, and Vernon put his head on the desk and moaned.

Josh couldn't help feeling a little sorry for him. This guy, Brock, wasn't going to be an easy guy to placate and it was all going to be laid on Vernon's desk.

Josh spoke up. "Vernon, Nate called Frieda. She and Martha will be here in a little while. We'll meet with them first so that they are up to date on this; then you need to get Tommy and whoever else knows about production, and let's see if they have any ideas. By the way, you didn't ask him about payment for the pipes they have. He probably has them in the ground already, and you haven't seen the first cent. Next time you talk to him, you need to ask for the money. It sounds like they are in default."

Frieda and Martha arrived at the plant about forty minutes later. After a quick tour of the ruins, Nate directed them into the meeting room where Josh and Vernon were waiting. Josh took the lead in the meeting.

"Ladies, you need to know that the problem here may be even bigger than the physical damage to the plant. The kiln won't be usable for more than a month and maybe much longer than that. Production is going to grind to a halt until it is back in use. Now that would be a problem any time, but right now the company is trying to fulfill a large contract with some people in Texas. Their project is on a very tight schedule. It is borderline whether Galena Pipe could have performed on time even without the fire. Vernon says they would have. And they were a little bit ahead of schedule, so who knows? But with the fire, it is impossible, and the contract is one-sided, on the wrong side. If the pipes are not delivered on time, the buyer has liquidated damages. Their damages are agreed to in advance and don't need anything in the way of proving up or justifying. In this case, it is three thousand, five hundred dollars a day. That could equal or exceed the entire value of the contract. Worse yet, the contract has no protection for the company in the event of unforeseeable or unpreventable interruptions. Like fire, for instance. Galena Pipe has already performed up to the first payment point, meaning these guys already have a lot of pipes and they have yet to pay anything."

Frieda frowned and spoke up. Whenever Frieda frowned, it reminded Josh of his first-grade teacher when one of the kids passed gas. It was always unsettling to him.

"Josh, didn't you or Nate review this contract before it was signed?"

"No. We knew nothing about it. Vernon was in a rush. He saw an opportunity that he thought had to be taken up at once. But that is something to be talked about at another time. Right now, we need to salvage whatever we can from this boondoggle."

Frieda and Martha were stunned. Nothing like this had ever happened when their brother ran the company. And to think that Vernon had gone around Nate and Josh without even showing them the contract! This whole thing could have been avoided. Frieda was not a lawyer, but even she could see this was a dumb contract for anyone to agree to. It was a mistake to let Vernon run the company. When this was over, they probably would need to revisit that decision.

There was a knock on the door, and Tommy stuck his head in. He had Jake Sharp, the assistant plant manager, with him. "Vernon, Jake was here this morning before I was. Do you want to talk to us now, or should we come back later?"

Vernon looked over at Josh, who nodded, so Vernon told them to come in and have seats. The obvious first question everyone had was how the fire had gotten started. Tommy still had nothing definite from the fire department except that everything pointed to a gas pipe by the kiln furnace being damaged in a way that loosened a pipe joint and caused a slow gas leak. The pipe could have been hit by an end-loader or some other piece of rolling stock, or it could have been damaged another way. It may have happened Saturday if it was a very tiny leak that wasn't noticed. They had talked to everyone who had worked any time on Saturday, from the morning tip-out crew to the night cleanup crew. Nobody they talked to had noticed a gas leak, and nobody claimed to have known anything that could have caused damage to the pipe.

Nate wondered about Sunday. "Tommy. I understand there was no work shift on Sunday. Do you know who was at the plant yesterday?"

"Well, I was here. I was here for about twenty minutes late yesterday evening at about nine o'clock or so because I wanted to review the timecards before I turned them over to payroll today. I didn't notice any problems. But I didn't get close to the kiln. Benny Vaughn was the guard on duty when I was here. The only timecards showing time for Sunday were the two cards for the night guards. Benny worked from six o'clock Sunday evening until midnight. Melvin relieved him at midnight and was supposed to get off at six o'clock this morning. He was the only one here when there was an explosion, and the kiln started burning. He called the fire department right away. That was at two-thirty or three in the morning, I believe. I don't know exactly when. I don't think there was anything he could have done, with or without the fire department. Sure as hell he couldn't do anything with a little fire extinguisher. I think a good sprinkler system in the kiln would have helped if we had one. Apparently, we don't, even though I thought we did. The fire chief said it probably would have helped a lot. There would have been some damage, but not nearly so much. The fire wouldn't have spread so fast after the explosion."

Tommy turned to Jake. "You got any ideas on it?"

Jake answered, "Nah. I think you covered anything I would know. I went home Friday night and didn't come back in until this morning. I guess I was the first one here other than Melvin and the whole Galena Fire Department. I don't know anyone who was here between Saturday evening and Monday morning other than you and the guards. I looked at the pipe that may have set off the explosion. I can't tell anything about it. It's pretty well smashed up. I don't know what could have done it. But we sure can't turn out any pipes now. No place we can cure them. We canceled everyone for today. We probably can bring some people in tomorrow to start cleaning up. I'll check with the fire chief about that and tell him to talk to Vernon or the Walkers if he has any questions. They may not be finished with their investigation of the cause."

Nathan had nothing else to ask. "Thanks, fellas. I guess that's all we need right now. But go over the specs in the contract again, and let us know if you see anything that could help. I don't know what I am asking. I don't expect there is anything there to help us. At least we don't see it. But if you have any ideas, let Vernon or us know."

Josh thought it would be a good idea to have Vernon call Brock Johnson again to grovel a bit more and delicately ask if they were ready to pay for the first installment of pipes.

So, Vernon called Brock, who answered on the first ring. "Vernon, have you had your meeting yet? What are you going to do to make this right?"

Vernon took his time answering. "We're still looking for a solution. Nothing like this has ever happened to us before.

Have you laid all the pipe we have shipped? Are there any left you could use now?"

"Yeah, we probably have a pipe or two left, but that's worthless as hell. We are ready to start the second phase and there's not going to be any damned pipe for it. What the hell are we supposed to do Tanksley? We have to get this done on time. I have subs lined up now to go to work. You can't just get them whenever you want them. They are not going to sit around on their asses waiting. You guys have screwed us good."

"I am sorry as hell. I never thought anything like this could happen. We're still trying to figure something out. How long can you wait for the pipe? What extra time can you allow here?"

"None. We have every one of the trenches laid out and dug. Everything now depends on getting pipe into the trenches. You got no time. You have to fix it now. Don't bother me until you can tell me you got pipe on the way in every diameter and length we need."

Vernon did not bring up the subject of payment for the pipes that had been delivered. Neither Nate nor Josh could blame him. Nate told Vernon to sleep on it if that was possible. They would do the same and be back at the plant the next morning.

CHAPTER 22

Tuesday, January 10, 1989

The minute Brock got off the phone with Vernon he called Jimmy into his office, and they had a good laugh.

"Hell, Jimmy. This thing may work out better than we thought. That Harry Townsend! You gotta hand it to the bastard. We got Vernon's balls in a vice now. Who would have figured a fire in their kiln? You don't think Harry could have planned that? Nah. You can't plan something like that. He just figured we would get as much pipe as we could before we had to go Chapter 11 bankruptcy, right? But … he did say that maybe Galena would be having problems that would keep them from furnishing the pipe on time, didn't he? Huh? That makes me uneasy. And I'm still not sure what's in it for him. Let's call him."

Harry picked up the phone right away and seemed to know who was calling. "Hello, Brock. How's life in Texas this wonderful day?"

"We have all the pipes laid for phase one and it looks like we may actually have some pipe left over. And I have not sent a single check. Vernon doesn't know what he is doing. I expected to get calls for money before now. Nothing. Which is fortunate because we don't have any. It's good to have some pipe down in the ground though, no matter where we end up. Anyway, the darndest thing happened up in Galena. They had a fire and can't give me more pipe any time soon. And liquidated damages are going to start piling up day after day after day. We may get all piped in for nothing unless they pull a rabbit out of a hat."

"A fire," said Harry. "Well, I'll be damned! Imagine that. A fire! It goes to show you that good things can happen to good people. I'd say you are set, buddy. Even if Vernon did have a rabbit in his hat, it would just shit on his head."

"Harry, you don't sound surprised."

"A state of shock is what it is. I am in a state of shock. Listen now. I'm going to fly down and see you guys. I don't like talking on the phone. It's too impersonal if you know what I mean. How about I fly down on Wednesday?"

"Let us know your flight number. We'll pick you up at the airport. I've got a good bottle of Balcones Bourbon I have been waiting to open for a special occasion. It looks like we got ourselves one."

Brock put down the phone. "Jimmy, what's in it for this guy? Harry's not Mother Teresa Townsend, just here to serve his fellow man who can't pay for pipe. He is getting something out of this deal."

Harry flew down on Wednesday and met with Brock and Bill Turl, Noble's attorney. Jimmy was not invited to the meeting. Harry wanted a small audience. He told them the fire in the Galena plant was a godsend. But from this point on, there could be questions raised about it, and they should only say that it hurt them just as much as it hurt Galena Pipe because it was setting their project back. After listening for a while, Turl decided that Harry was making him a little uncomfortable, and he wasn't sure he wanted to hear anymore, so he excused himself to go to his office to see a client. A couple of hours later, he came back to Brock's office to join Brock and Harry for drinks. Harry was in an expansive mood. The more he drank, the more he carried on and bragged about how he had put this whole scheme together. Turl heard more than he wanted to and pretended to himself that he hadn't.

CHAPTER 23

Thursday, January 12, 1989

Nate and Josh drove to the Galena office. It was smaller than the office in Stockton, and it had no receptionist, but it was across the street from the Jo Daviess County Courthouse, and that was a convenience. They called Vernon after making coffee. He told them that Jake Sharp had an idea he wanted to talk about. He would bring Jake to their office because he didn't want to talk about it at the plant. Jake had worked at Galena Pipe longer than anyone else. He was fifty-two years old and had been hired by Vernon, Sr.. Jake had been the plant manager when Vernon Sr. died, but that changed when Vernon Jr. took over. He didn't want to keep Jake on as plant manager because he didn't think Jake respected him. Jake knew the company inside and out. He had worked in every department and could run the company better than Vernon. So, Vernon fired him and put Tommy Schumann in his place. When Frieda found out about it, she blew up. She, Martha, and a few minor shareholders together held the controlling interest in the company. Whatever she said was always fine with the others. She was not okay with getting rid of Jake, and she made it clear that Jake would stay or Vernon would go. Vernon was backed into a corner. They finally came to a compromise. Jake would stay as assistant plant manager. He would have a staff position giving him the latitude to get involved in all plant areas. But would not report to Tommy. He would report directly to Vernon. Tommy didn't like it, of course. He was no match for Jake when it came to knowledge of the business.

When Vernon and Jake arrived, they joined the Walkers at the conference table, where Jake spread out some pictures, contract specs, and diagrams.

"I had an idea last night," he said. "We have pipe. Tons of pipe. When construction slows every winter, we keep making common pipe and we stack it in the yard. When business cranks up in the spring, we sell pipe from that inventory while we are making any new pipe ordered with special specs. The common pipe we have is the same pipe Noble had us making. It is identical in size and construction. The only difference is in the joint. Noble, for some reason, ordered pipe with tongue and groove joints rather than bell and spigot. Bell and spigot is what most contractors use around here. It has a rubber gasket that fits against the shoulder or groove of the joint. The joint actually has greater strength, water tightness, and flexibility. I don't know why they didn't order that type of joint. What they ordered is fine. It will work, but it's certainly not a better joint. Maybe their requirements are less stringent because of the climate or something. Some people may think it takes longer to join pipes when you use rubber gaskets. I don't know if that's it or not. Maybe they are just used to tongue and groove down there. But we have almost all the pipe they need in the yard, and the quality is better in my mind because of the joints. They are a tad more expensive because of the gaskets. But we could provide them at the same cost as the pipes they have. Same size, constructed exactly the same way. We could fill most of the order right now from the yard, and by the time those pipes are in the ground, we should have the plant back up."

Josh said, "Damn, Jake! That might be a lifesaver. Only one question. Looking at these diagrams, it seems like if you start with tongue-and-groove, you have to stick with it because the two different kinds of joints won't mesh."

"Well," said Jake. "It is possible to do some things to make them fit, but it takes time, and most people aren't very comfortable with doing that. But that's where I think we may be really lucky. Their project was divided into two phases. Phase one is the pipe they have already laid. I'm convinced we shipped enough pipe for that phase. The subdivision is divided into two sections. So, if they have laid that pipe in section one and they are now starting section two, they can use pipes with different joints since they won't be hooking them together."

Vernon was skeptical. "I don't know. As far as I know, it's not what they ordered and what we were supposed to provide. They are complaining about needing the same pipes for the other section of the subdivision. I don't see it working. I don't see a way out of this thing at all, to be honest with you. The company is in real trouble here. This fire has sunk us. That is what I think."

"Well, personally, I think it's hopeful," Jake said. "But I am not an engineer, and there may be something I don't know. Do we have time to get an opinion from an engineer?"

Nate said they should call Glenn Burton. He was a good construction engineer and a client."

"I'll call Glenn this morning and get the specs to him," said Josh.

Josh telephoned, but Burton was out of his office. He left a message, and Glenn called him back an hour later. Josh told him about the problem the pipe company was having and explained Jake's idea as well as he could. He told Glenn he would have Jake send over copies of the specs and information on the pipes in the yard. Glenn was happy to offer what thoughts he had once he got the information. Jake faxed him everything he needed, and Glenn called Josh later that day. He had gone over all of the pipe specifications Noble Vista

Development had furnished and had even taken the time to go out to the plant to look at the joints on the pipes in the yard. He didn't see any reason why those pipes wouldn't work. Everything but the joints was identical, and he couldn't think of any benefit deriving from the type of joints they had ordered. He did admit that he was an engineer, not a contractor, and he had no knowledge of construction requirements in the Texas Panhandle. It seemed to him that Galena Pipe could install all the rubber gaskets right in the yard and ship them off to Texas to be put in the ground. It was just what Josh and Nathan wanted to hear.

Josh picked up the telephone and dialed Brock Johnson's number in Amarillo. "Mr. Johnson, this is Josh Walker calling for Galena Pipe Works. I'm an attorney for the company, and we have been talking to Vernon Tanksley about the problem caused by the fire at the plant. I've been out to the pipe factory, and I have seen the destruction, so I understand why there is a delay in building any more pipes until the kiln has been repaired. But I may have a solution."

"I hope so," said Brock. "Your people have me in a real jam down here."

"The answer, I believe, is that Galena Pipe Works has an inventory of finished pipes in the yard that are identical to those you ordered in almost every way. The construction is exactly the same, and all the sizes you need are available. Every specification matches except for the type of joints you wanted. I had an engineer go out to look at them and review your specifications. He's a good one, by the way. You may want to check him out and talk to him. I can give you his contact information. He thinks these pipes will do everything you need unless there is some special code down there that affects the joint design. That is something you or your engineers would probably know, but he thinks that would be unusual."

"Mr. Walker, I don't know about any codes or joints. But I know what my engineers specified for the project, and I know that's exactly what I want. If it doesn't meet their specs, I don't want it."

"Maybe you could talk to them, and they could talk to the engineer who inspected the pipes that are ready. There is a good chance these pipes will suit them, and we can resume shipping. Our engineer tells us the bell and spigot joints meet standards he refers to as ASTM C 990. I have no idea what that means, but you probably do. He also says that this type of joint with rubber gaskets is considered by many to be stronger and more flexible. The company would substitute those pipes under the same price structure in the contract. Normally, they would cost a little more because of the work involved in putting on the rubber gaskets, which they would do in Galena to save you having to do it on-site. I will give you the name and phone number of our engineer, and you can have your engineer call him."

"Listen to me, Mr. Walker. I don't think you are listening. We specified the pipes we need for this project, and we won't accept anything other than what we ordered. Is that sinking in?"

"Why not at least talk to your engineer? What do you have to lose?"

"Mr. Walker, unless you have some other brainstorm to lay on me, this conversation is over. The next conversation you have about it will be with our lawyer."

Josh was out of brainstorms, so the conversation ended. He hung up the phone and yelled, "We're dealing with a regular prick here!"

Then he shouted a few other things at a volume that brought Nate into his office.

"Damn, Walker. What are you shouting about? I could have clients in my office. Did you think of that? These walls are like paper. I should have realized I would need some special soundproofing when we built this place."

"I just talked to Brock Johnson in Amarillo. I told him we came up with a solution to their pipe problem, no thanks to

Tommy Schumann, by the way. Tommy and Vernon should have landed on that right away. Tommy is supposed to be the plant manager, and he was involved in this deal from the start. Instead, Jake is the one who told us about the pipe available in the yard. And Vernon didn't like the idea! I still can't figure that out. Vernon should have been the one really supporting it. It's his ass that is on the line. Any possible solution to the problem would be a lifeline to him. I just can't figure that guy out anymore. Anyway, I offered the solution to Brock Johnson on a platter. He should have been falling all over himself with appreciation. Instead, he practically hung up on me."

It is not normal procedure for an attorney to record telephone calls without telling the other party they are being recorded. It raises serious ethical issues. Illinois is a two-party consent state, so you are not even allowed to do it in Illinois. Texas is a one-party consent state. Only one party on the phone needs to know it is being recorded in Texas. So, which state's law applies? Josh thought Illinois law applied most likely. But Josh had recorded his call with Brock anyway. He didn't know what Brock would say, and he wanted Nate to hear it. He told Nate to pull a chair up to the desk so that he could hear the recording played back. Nate gave him grief for breaking the rules, but they wouldn't mention it to anyone and would erase the recording after Nate heard it. It was within the category they called "graveyard," meaning you go to your grave without telling anyone you did it.

Nate listened to the call and had Josh play it again. "You haven't figured it out yet, have you? Those guys don't want a solution. That's not what they are after. Somebody set this whole thing up. Well, I guess not the fire. But someone needs to take a trip and look into this project of theirs. I am telling you, these guys are up to no good. I don't have time to do it, and I don't think Tommy or Vernon could handle the job. We don't want to send either of them. And you couldn't go down there right now without picking a fight. Do you think Paul would go? He's a Texas lawyer, and that makes him perfect."

Josh was skeptical. "In case you haven't noticed, he's tired of practicing law. He told us that right from the start. Nevertheless, we've been taking advantage of him by asking him to discuss the proposed merger with us. I feel bad about it, and I'm going to tell him that. I can't ask him to get involved in this."

Nate said. "Sure. I understand why you would feel bad about asking him to do something he might not want to do. You have always been a sensitive person with unusually tender feelings for a grown man. So, I'll ask him tomorrow."

Josh agreed. "Damn right. I think he'll go for it if you twist his arm."

The next morning, even before Nate had a chance to talk to Paul, Josh found a Federal Express envelope on his desk in the Stockton office. He looked at the mailing label and noticed that the sender was a law firm in Amarillo called Turl, Sevak, and Associates, PC. Brock hadn't wasted any time. He opened the envelope and read the letter quickly. Then he went back through it a second time to make sure he hadn't missed anything important. No surprise. The letter was signed by a Bill Turl, one of the named partners in the firm. It was addressed to Vernon Tanksley, president of Galena Pipe Works, and to Tommy Schumann, the plant manager, but a copy had been sent to Josh by overnight delivery as a courtesy. The letter was direct and left no room for questions. Noble Vista Development wanted written assurances from them both that all pipes ordered would be delivered on time and built exactly to specifications. Should such written assurances not be received in twenty-four hours, Galena Pipe Works would soon be sued in Texas, where the contract was to be performed.

Nate hesitated before trying to telephone Bill Turl. He was convinced that Noble Vista Development had been angling for a lawsuit from the very time of the fire. He just didn't know why. Calling Turl would do nothing to prevent the suit from being filed, but he always wanted to know an opposing attorney as well as possible before it was too late to negotiate. This would be his first chance to learn a little about Bill Turl. So, he would call him.

His first attempt was not successful. Turl was in a meeting and would be tied up until the afternoon. Nate left a message and went on to other things. There was always more to do than he could stay on top of. By the time he finally looked up from his work, Josh was standing in his doorway, asking him to go to lunch. They walked together to the restaurant, and along the way, he filled Josh in on the letter he had received from Texas. When they got to the restaurant, they saw Paul and Ann sitting at a table in the corner and asked to join them. Ann was, as usual, happy to see the Walkers. She wasted no time filling them in on the latest news around town, then sat back, waiting to see what they might be willing to add about the fire at Galena Pipe Works. They added absolutely nothing, just as she had expected. She had already eaten, so she left to go back to her office.

The conversation turned to Paul. Nate and Josh filled him in on everything that had transpired since the fire, including the fact that Galena Pipe Works had not been paid for the pipe Noble had already accepted. They held nothing back. Paul had heard about the fire from Ann, but all he knew was that the plant was shut down for a while. He didn't know anything about a contract with a company in Texas, and it surprised him. There were plenty of pipe companies in Texas. Why did these guys find it necessary to go so far out of state to get pipes?

Nate said, "We got a letter today from a lawyer in Amarillo. Noble Vista Development, the customer buying the pipes, wasn't happy with the solution Jake came up with. It looks like Josh and I might get to try a lawsuit in Texas. Got any tips?"

"Buy boots. I hate the damned things, but it is Texas. Listen, I don't have much to do these days. If you want, I will come over to the office after lunch and read the letter. Maybe

I can be helpful. I have a working knowledge of construction law in Texas."

After lunch, they went to the office, and Josh went over the contract with Paul. Then, they gave him a synopsis of the proposed solution, explaining the two types of joints and telling him what their engineer thought. Finally, they gave him the letter from Noble's lawyer."

Paul took the contract and the letter to an empty office and sat down to work through the information. He looked up Bill Turl and his firm in the Martindale-Hubble directory of attorneys. It was a small firm that looked like it handled mostly civil cases, specializing in personal injury, but probably handling a host of other things that bring in money. Construction law wasn't mentioned in the profile. Paul also called the Texas Secretary of State's office to find out how Noble Vista Development was constituted as an entity. The incorporator was Bill Turl. That is not unusual. Attorneys often act as incorporators when they set up entities for clients. But Turl was also shown as a director of Noble Vista Development, so he had more than just an incidental connection to the company.

When Paul was in law school, he had a bright moot-court partner by the name of Henry Melton, a black law student whose grandfather had been one of the first black judges in Fort Worth. Henry was born and raised in Lubbock, Texas, and his grandfather had encouraged him to become a lawyer. Paul and Henry had stayed in touch over the years. Henry had returned to Lubbock after law school, had spent five years at the DA's office, and now he was on his own in private practice. He enjoyed taking on the bigger firms. Paul looked up his office number and called him. After catching up on each other's lives, Paul asked him if, by any chance, he knew a lawyer in Amarillo by the name of Bill Turl or anything about a company there called Noble Vista Development. Amarillo and Lubbock are just a couple of hours apart, which is considered next-door neighbors in that part of Texas. He told

Henry a little about the development in Amarillo. Henry knew Bill Turl slightly and didn't have an opinion about him. He had run across him in court in Lubbock. He only remembered that he didn't like the client Turl was representing. Not that you can fairly judge a lawyer by whom he represents. He had represented a few he didn't like. But it got him wondering about the client of Turl's that Paul was interested in now. So he told Paul he needed to make a couple of calls, and he would get back to him later in the day.

It didn't take much more than an hour before he called Paul back. Henry had done some work for a builder of custom homes in Lubbock and Amarillo. He called him to see what, if anything, he might know about Noble Vista Development. His client didn't know anything about the development being built in Amarillo because he hadn't done anything there for some time. But he knew a lot about Brock Johnson and Jimmy Ponder. They had been around for a while and didn't have many friends in the building business. They had a reputation for paying their subcontractors and suppliers late or not at all. The projects they started didn't live up to promises. They often pulled out before finishing and left unsold lots nobody wanted. They were known for starting, but not completing, projects. They had been sued in the past for using construction trust funds for personal expenses and had a number of ventures go into bankruptcy. Local banks didn't loan to them. Local suppliers wanted money up front for everything. So, they must have found an out-of-town lender who took some risks and some suppliers who didn't know much about them.

Paul gathered Nate and Josh together and told them everything he had learned from Henry. Nate had to be right. These guys weren't looking for a solution. They probably couldn't finish this project with or without pipes. Now they had someone to sue. The Walkers saw that Paul was getting interested, and they loved it. Cases sometimes hook you. And this one may have landed Paul.

Nate told Paul, "You have been a great help. I don't know how to thank you. We have taken a lot of your time, even asking you your thoughts about the proposed merger. I hope you don't think that Josh and I are trying to get you to practice law again, knowing that you want no more to do with it."

Paul broke out into laughter. "OH, NO. Where would I get that idea? You guys would never do that to another lawyer who is only trying to reform and go straight. God forbid you would leave me a trail of breadcrumbs and good whiskey to get me to follow you until I was trapped."

"You trapped or not?" asked Josh.

"Yeah. I guess so."

"Good. Because we really need you to go somewhere for us. Now look. From today on, we need to start paying you for your time and expenses. This matter involves Texas, where you are licensed. You don't need to be admitted to the bar in Illinois to bill attorney's fees on this. Galena Pipe pays our fees, and they will be paying yours."

Paul said, "Just tell me what you need me to do. When this is over, I can give you a bill. Or I can bill things along the way if you want. But it's not about fees. Something about this is wrong."

CHAPTER 24

Sunday, January 15, 1989

He still didn't believe it. The plane was taking off from O'Hare International, and he was on it. He would have a forty-minute stopover at Dallas/Fort Worth and fly on to Amarillo. Why me? It's like Texas is a foreign country to those guys, and I'm the only guy they know who speaks both English and Texan.

He waited until they reached a cruising altitude and the seatbelt sign was out. Then he leaned his seat all the way back and closed his eyes. What bothered him most was a suspicion he hadn't even shared with the Walkers. He wondered if somehow Harry Townsend was involved in it all. Harry didn't seem like someone who would let a guy like Vernon walk off with a contract he almost had in hand. That didn't add up, and it seemed to him that only Harry had the money to throw into a fight. Harry was obviously a guy who didn't lose often, and he was definitely pissed off over his failed merger plan. That was just speculation, though, and none of it changed the law.

What was the law? What defense would Galena Pipe have

against a breach of contract suit? He needed to try thinking like a lawyer again. *Impossibility of performance* can be a defense to breach of contract. Galena Pipe Works had geared up to fill a special order, and no reason existed to think they would not have performed the contract if the fire hadn't occurred. The unanticipated fire was the sole factor stopping them from completing the contract. A defense? Possibly. But a defense that was made a lot harder by the liquidated damages called for in the contract and the gaping failure of the contract to include a *force majeure* clause. On the plus side, Galena Pipe had offered to mitigate any damage by furnishing suitable pipe from their inventory. And that was a pretty strong defense. All of those legal pros and cons were racing around in his head.

Then why would Noble want to bring a suit they could not win? Why bring it when their project could have been kept on schedule by accepting the substitute pipes Galena Pipe offered? What reason did they have to dirty the water? He couldn't help going back to Harry Townsend. Harry was angry, and maybe he was so angry he wasn't listening to his lawyers. Maybe, win or lose, Harry was determined to put Galena Pipe Works and the Walkers through the grinder in an inconvenient forum, and they would think twice before screwing around with him again. Maybe it was as simple as that. And maybe Harry had some kind of hold on Brock Johnson and Jimmy Ponder.

If so, nothing could be done to stop him. The key now was to take full advantage of the warning to develop as much information as possible to defend the suit. It was late when he got a rental car and checked in at a hotel, so he would have to wait until morning to review real estate records at the courthouse and drive out to the development. He would find out if there was an immediate need for the pipes and whether there was a valid excuse for insisting on the specially fabricated pipe joints.

CHAPTER 25

Monday, January 16, 1989

Paul slept until about six-thirty and had breakfast at the hotel before driving downtown to the county courthouse, which opened at eight o'clock. There he found the county clerk's office and spoke to a deputy clerk in the real estate recording section. It didn't take her long to locate a subdivision platted by Noble Vista Development. She was able to show him exactly how to find the proposed subdivision, which was called Noble Vista Estates. It was a small development with just a few hundred residential lots, divided into two phases. Phases one and two were equal in size. They were separated by a boulevard. He had the clerk check records for restrictive covenants and found that none had been filed. All he had so far was the plat.

From the courthouse, he drove over to the title company that had recorded it. He had made a copy of it at the courthouse, and he brought it with him. He introduced himself to the receptionist and asked if he might visit with an escrow officer who would be familiar with Noble Vista Estates. She invited him to have a seat while she walked into an office with the plat and a business card from his old law firm. After a few minutes, a well-dressed, middle-aged woman came out and introduced herself.

"Hello, Mr. Hoffman. My name is Sylvia Thompson. I am the senior escrow officer. Are you representing Noble Vista Developers?"

Paul answered, "Oh no. I am just here doing some research for a client of mine interested in homebuilding, I was wondering about Noble Vista Estates. The courthouse had a plat and dedication, but no restrictive covenants, and that seemed odd to me."

"Why don't you step into my office, and we can discuss it."

They moved to her office, and after he was seated, she closed the door and sat down at her desk.

"I have to be careful about what I say, Mr. Hoffman. Often, the restrictions are put on record with the plat or shortly after it, though it is not required. But the way Noble Vista Development bought the property is not the way it is generally done here. At this point, Noble Vista Development has no business with us. Maybe with another title company, but I don't know."

"I don't want you to disclose anything proprietary. But I think you could tell me whether you insured title to the property. That would be important for my home builder to know."

"I guess I can tell you this. Noble came to us before they bought the property. Brock Johnson, I think, runs the company. He said they wanted to buy a title policy for the tract they were acquiring. So, we did all the research on it and gave him a title commitment. There were no title problems showing up. But they didn't come back to us to buy the title insurance. The next thing we saw was a recorded deed showing they had purchased the property. So, they took free title research and then bought the land without paying for title insurance. That means we made no money for all our work. And it means that title to the Noble Vista Estates property appears not to have been insured. People sometimes take advantage of the fact that title companies in Texas can't charge for commitments. If they're dishonest and willing to take some chances, they get a commitment showing that the title company has done all the property research. Then, they buy the property and never buy the title policy. It's done most often on rundown properties where there is not much risk. Seldom is it done on a large tract like this. Maybe I have said too much. But it just sits wrong with us when somebody takes our work and, if you pardon the expression, screws us out of our insurance premium."

Paul said, "Don't worry. I had little interest in that property when I came in, anyway. It seems to me most of the building is going on elsewhere. I won't mention to anyone what you have told me. But I really do appreciate your information. It tells me more about who they are than it does about the property they are developing."

Paul left the title company even more certain that Galena Pipe had made a contract with a couple of crooks. He was ready to see Noble Vista Estates. The drive took only about twenty minutes from downtown, and he was unimpressed with the landscape. There were few trees, and the land was as flat as a desk. He passed several subdivisions with nice houses along the way. Further out were some large lots with room for a horse barn or other outbuildings. That area would appeal to people who didn't want to live in the city but still be within easy commuting distance to work, shopping, and the other amenities Amarillo has.

Then he spotted a large billboard advertising Noble Vista Estates, and he pulled off the road to take some pictures. He saw little activity. There was a man standing by a bulldozer that was parked along the side of the road, and there was a parked grader farther up the road from Noble Vista Estates. There was no heavy equipment in place on the development. He could tell that the first phase had some lots being surveyed and staked out. That is where the first installment of pipe was already in the ground. Paul grabbed his camera. There were streets across from where he was, in what would be the second phase. No work had taken place there yet, although there was a surveyor on the site marking out some boundaries. Paul started filming the two phases of the development to show what had been done and what appeared not to have been started. When he looked back, someone was walking up to him. It was the surveyor he had seen.

Paul spoke, "Hello. How are you doing?"

"Alright. How can I help you?"

"Name's Paul Hoffman. The company I work for is shipping some sewer pipe down here, and I just wanted to check things out and see if everything is ready for the pipe. Looks to me like there is quite a way to go for that to happen."

"Hell, yes. We're still laying out streets and lots in this phase."

"Are you a private surveyor? Or an employee of Noble Vista Development?" Paul asked.

The surveyor was friendly. He took off a glove and offered his hand. "I'm Rolly Timmons. I've got a surveying company here. Most of the newer subdivisions around here were laid out by me or my guys."

Paul decided to open up to him. "Rolly, I'll be honest with you. I'm a little surprised. The company I work for got behind making the pipes for this project, and Noble Vista Development is raising hell like they needed them yesterday. Have you worked for these people before?"

"Never have. But they're a long way away from laying pipe in this second phase of the development. Ask Bobby about it. He's the site supervisor, and he's coming this way now."

Paul looked over his shoulder and saw a large man with a hard hat heading toward him. He was the same man Paul had seen standing by a bulldozer when he pulled up.

When he got right up to Paul's side, Paul turned and extended his hand. "Hello. Paul Hoffman's my name. I was just talking to Rolly here about the project. When do you think you will be ready to lay sewer pipe?"

Bobby didn't take Paul's hand. Instead, he put both of his large paws on his sides and glared into Paul's eyes with a burning cigarette dangling from his mouth. Paul had never been easily intimidated. He looked Bobby over from head to foot and decided that Bobby was about thirty years old, about six feet tall, and a whole lot overweight. Paul wasn't intimidated.

Bobby took another step forward. "What do you want?"

"The company I work for is supposed to ship pipes down here, and your bosses are complaining about the pipes being shipped late. It doesn't look to me like you're even close to being ready for them. What do you think?"

"I think you need to get off this land. This is a construction site and it ain't open to the public, in case you ain't figured that out yet."

Paul turned back to Rolly Timmons. "Who is the engineer on the project?"

Rolly glanced first at Bobby and hesitated for a moment, but Paul held his gaze on Rolly's eyes until he spoke. "Brownie Carpenter. He's local."

Bobby put his hand on Paul's shoulder, and Paul slapped it off like it was a bug. He glared right into Bobby's face. There was no mistaking what would happen if Bobby touched him again. The two stared at each other for a long moment, their faces inches apart, and then Paul smiled. "I'd like to stay and chat some more, but it looks like I've got other people to talk to … and I'd say you have to get your ass busy digging some pipe trenches, wouldn't you?"

Bobby stood and scowled while Paul walked off toward his car, stopping now and then to look alongside the dirt road. When he got to his car to leave, he changed his mind, picked up his camera again, and walked back to the entrance to get some more pictures. He pointed the camera at Bobby and asked him to smile, but Bobby did not smile.

Paul drove around Amarillo for a while until he found what he was looking for, which was a residential construction site with sewer pipes lying beside deep trenches. He was no expert, but the pipes certainly looked like the ones he had seen in the yard in Galena. He drove to a hardware store, bought a tape measure, and went back to the site so that he could measure the pipes and pipe joints. After he had measured them carefully and jotted down his figures, he found the contractor in a construction trailer. The contractor was not too busy to talk about the pipes.

He had been in the construction business in the Texas Panhandle for a long time, and the pipes lying outside were the same as those he had always used. They were common pipes, and he had never heard about anyone having pipes manufactured with tongue-and-groove joints. Somebody might be using them, but he didn't know about it. He had driven by Noble Vista Development on his way to the mountains last weekend, and from what he had seen, they were not yet ready to lay pipe.

Paul stopped to pick up some lunch and had a sandwich on the way back to his hotel.

When he got there, he looked up Brownie Carpenter Engineering in the phone book and placed a call. Brownie wasn't in, but his secretary could reach him by beeper, so Paul left the hotel phone number and settled back to wait for a call. By four-thirty, he knew two things. He knew Brownie wasn't going to call him, and he knew he wasn't in the mood to wait. He went back to the phone book and found no residential listing for a Brownie Carpenter. So he called Josh to see if he might have better luck connecting with Brownie. A few minutes later, Josh called Brownie Carpenter Engineers.

"Hello, can I speak to Brownie?"

"Sorry, he's not in now."

"Damn, I was afraid of that. This is Hal Grant. I'm an old friend of Brownie's, here for the night from Oklahoma City. How can I get ahold of Brownie? I got to leave in the morning. Give me his home number. I'll call him there.'

She gave him the number. "You won't get him at home

until real late, though. He and some of the boys are going out for beers. I heard him set it up just before he left. Why don't you meet him there? He'll be at a little bar down off South Tyler Street called The Rodeo Club."

"Yep. That's old Brownie. That's for sure. Thanks."

Josh called Paul back, laughing, and told him where he could find Brownie.

Paul drove by The Rodeo Club twice, looking for a good place to park, just in case he had to leave in a hurry. Near the front door, he saw a white pickup truck with Brownie Carpenter Engineering stenciled on the side. He walked in, found a place at the bar, and ordered a beer while he let his eyes adjust to the darkness. Then he began to look the place over. A typical watering hole. The bar only allowed fifteen or twenty people to sit, and a few more to stand. Smoke drifted out of a large room in the back where he heard loud laughter and the clacking of pool balls. His eyes began to sweep the tables looking for Brownie. He should be easy to pick out from the young cowboys and the dusty construction workers who had stopped off for a cool one before heading home. Paul noticed a man who had to be Brownie. Late middle-aged, gray-haired, and prosperous-looking, but dressed in jeans, work boots, and a brown corduroy western jacket. It had to be him. He was sitting next to "Bobby the bulldozer", Paul's new friend from Noble Vista Estates. He finished his beer, ordered another, and walked over to the table.

"Hey, Bobby! Can I buy you a cold one?"

"I'll be damned!" What are you doing? Following me?"

"Hell, no, Bobby. I just stopped in for some good music. Don't mind if I pull up a chair, do you?"

Paul didn't wait for an answer. He drew up a chair between Bobby and Brownie and leaned forward, smiling at Brownie. "You're Brownie Carpenter, aren't you? Bobby speaks highly of you."

Brownie looked at Bobby, and Bobby nodded at him quickly. Paul barely paused for his breath. "I see Bobby told you about me, too. You know, I stopped by to see Bobby today. I wanted to make sure the trenches were all cut for those special pipes you ordered. I'll be honest here, Brownie. I'm a little concerned. You've got to bury those pipes. You know what I mean. You can't just let them sit up on the ground. I didn't see any trenches, and the roads aren't all in. But, hell, you're the engineer, I guess."

Brownie's face was red. "I'm not going to talk to you. I don't even know who the hell you are, Mister."

Bobby stood up with some effort and walked back to the pool tables, leaving Paul and Brownie alone.

"Look," Paul said, "I'm not here to make you guys mad. I'm just trying to understand why there is all this trouble over the pipes. I came down here for Galena Pipe Works. They have standard sewer pipes just sitting around, ready to be shipped whenever you want them. Brock Johnson says you can't use them because they have bell and spigot joints. But other contractors use those joints right here in Amarillo. So I don't know what the problem is. He says you need pipes with tongue and groove joints, and you need them now, and I don't get that either. The second phase of the project looks like it's just being laid out. What's going on?"

"Son, I'm the engineer on the project, and I know what kind of pipes they ordered. Brock ordered the pipes from Galena, and we're ready for them. Now that's all I've got to say to you about it. If you look over at the front door, you're going to see that you're not welcome here. So if I were you, I would hit the road."

Paul looked up and saw Bobby standing by the door with three rough-looking guys who belonged in this bar more than Paul did. He looked over to the bar and saw that two of the bartenders had been watching. They both shook their heads at him and nodded to the door. It was a clear warning, which he ignored. He finished his beer and left the table. He wasn't going to get any help from Brownie. But enough people were watching by then that he felt safer than he should have. As he passed through the door, he felt a hand on his shoulder, and this time he didn't slap it away. He doubled up his fist, turned, and drove it straight into Bobby's nose. Then it got dark.

When he opened his eyes, he was lying in the parking lot with his legs drawn up to his chest. He could smell the blood and vomit. He got sick and passed out again. The next time he came around, he was lying on his back in the front seat of his rental car. The driver's side window was smashed in, and he was lying on glass. His arms had small cuts. The keys were in the ignition. He slowly sat up and turned on the dome light so that he could look at his face in the mirror. What he saw almost made him throw up again. He checked under the seat for his camera. It was gone. With all the strength he could muster, he reached into his pants pockets and found his wallet and hotel key. God, he had never hurt this badly. He drove back to the hotel in stages, stopping every few miles to clear his head. When he got to his room, he fell on the bed, fully clothed.

CHAPTER 26

Tuesday, January 17, 1989

Paul slept until the telephone woke him at eight-thirty the next morning. It was Nate.

"Paul, did you find Brownie Carpenter?"

"Oh, I sure did".

"Did you find anything out from him?"

Paul told him. "I found a lot out, but not from him. I got into a little disagreement with Brownie and his friends last night. Tell you about it when I get back. I have something else I need to do. If I can get it done today, I will fly back tomorrow and see you Thursday."

"Alright, Paul. See you whenever you get back. Be careful. And thanks again."

Paul filled the bathtub with hot water and soaked for half an hour. Then he got out of the tub and stood in front of the bathroom mirror. There was dried blood from his nose and mouth, and some small glass cuts on his forehead. He had a nasty-looking bruise above his right eye, but all in all, he looked better than he felt. The blood would wash off, and the swelling would go away. His back and ribs hurt him more than anything else. Bobby and his friends had worked them over pretty well, probably with their boots while he was lying on the ground. (He REALLY didn't like cowboy boots. Lucky they weren't wearing spurs.)

After his hot bath, he felt better. He pulled out the phonebook and looked through the list of detective agencies. It was a short list, but each one looked as good as the next. He called Henry Melton in Lubbock, told him what had happened, and asked him if he had ever used an investigator in Amarillo. Henry knew just the guy he needed. Within an hour, Paul received a telephone call from Roger Pace of Pace Investigations, who had worked for Henry in the past. Paul told Roger Pace what he needed and made an appointment for two o'clock. After that, he took a short, restless nap. He got dressed before noon, went out to the parking lot, and swept the broken glass off the front seat of his rental car. Then he drove to a pawn shop he had noticed the day before. The pawn shop owner was also a firearms dealer. He started talking about handgun registration, but let the subject drop when Paul took four one-hundred-dollar bills out of his pocket and put them on the counter. He went to a room in the back of the shop and returned with a revolver. Paul worked the mechanism enough to feel satisfied with it, then bought a box of .38 caliber shells. He had kept a revolver similar to this one in his desk at the law firm in Houston and had occasionally taken it to the pistol range. He wasn't someone who looked for trouble, and the thought of shooting at a real person was not in his plans. But Bobby and his buddies were playing by West Texas rules, and he needed to let them know that the game had risks to both sides. After he left the gun shop, he had a quick lunch and drove downtown to the building where Roger Pace Investigations was located.

Roger Pace in the flesh was not what Paul had expected. He was short, had a slight build, and wore thick glasses. Pace Investigations was a two-man operation. Roger had started it years earlier after leaving the local police department. He and his partner devoted more time these days to the part of the business involved with videotaping depositions in civil suits than they did in true investigations. Nevertheless, Roger Pace had a good camera and a pocket tape recorder. He didn't seem concerned when Paul let him know they would be unwelcome at the place where the pictures were to be taken. Roger could see Paul had suffered a severe beating, and he didn't like it. He asked if the pictures had anything to do with Paul's battered face. Paul told him everything that had happened. In fairness to Roger, he held nothing back. He told Roger exactly what he had in mind, making it clear that he would understand if he did not want to be involved. But Roger's only reservation was that he would just be present on the job site while taking pictures, and no longer than that would take. Whatever happened after he left was a matter for Paul alone. There was more to Roger Pace than what appeared on the surface. Henry Melton had vouched for Paul, and that was enough for Roger. They agreed on a fee for Roger's services, and Paul paid him up front in cash. Fortunately, he had loaded up on cash before leaving Stockton, realizing that it could come in handy.

Roger followed Paul to Noble Vista Estates and parked behind his rental car on the side of the main road. Then, he followed him down to the building site on foot. Bobby was on the bulldozer, but there were no other workers around. Paul pointed out the areas he wanted photographed and Roger clicked away, taking shots from various angles and distances. Paul saw Bobby watching them from across the road between the two subdivision phases. He turned away and listened for Bobby to approach.

Bobby walked up behind Paul, shouting curses and threats. "Who the hell do you think you are screwing around with, you dumbass? I guess you didn't get the message we gave you last night. Maybe you need a refresher."

Paul spun around and put the barrel of his .38 about

twelve inches from Bobby's forehead. Bobby stopped so abruptly that he almost fell backward. Roger got his camera ready and started the tape recorder.

Paul spoke calmly. "Bobby! Good to see you this morning, buddy. I was afraid you might have been out too late last night with old Brownie, but you look just fine. Photogenic really. Better than me, for sure. Get in some of these pictures I want for my album. I want to remember my trip down here and there is no better way to do that than with pictures. This is a real Kodak moment."

Bobby's face turned white. "Put that thing down. What do you want?"

"Bobby, you and some boys beat the hell out of me last night when I walked out of The Rodeo Club. You all hit me, kicked me, and basically beat the crap out of me. Brownie was in on it, even though he didn't throw a punch. You did, though. Who were your friends?"

"I don't know them. Just guys that are tough and hang around there. I can't give you their names. I didn't think it would get that rough, you know?"

"That's bullshit. Why did you smash the windows of my car, jackass? It wasn't enough that you tough guys all attacked me? Are you boys some gang of teenage vandals or something? Why, Bobby?"

"We got carried away. None of it was planned. You showed up, and that's what happened."

Paul didn't really care who the others were. He just wanted Bobby talking about it on tape. Bobby damned sure wanted it that rough. He probably threw more punches and kicks than any of the others, and he certainly had urged the others on. Paul brought his foot up into Bobby's groin as hard as he could, and did it so quickly that Roger almost missed getting a picture of Bobby's face as he exhaled air from his lungs and fell forward on the ground. Paul promised Bobby a nice print.

Then Roger walked around the rest of the site, shooting

another roll of film. When he had finished, he walked back to his car and watched from about a quarter of a mile down the road, where he pulled over and parked. Paul escorted the doubled-over and limping Bobby to the company Blazer, which was parked close to the bulldozer. He stopped a few feet away and fired two rounds into the side of the Blazer where the name "Noble Vista Development" was painted before opening the driver's door and pushing Bobby face down onto the seats.

"I wouldn't look up if I were you, Bobby."

He shot through a side window safely away from where Bobby was lying. Bobby's feet were hanging out of the open door of the Blazer, and they shook when Paul fired the round. Then Paul walked back to his rental car. Before he got in the car, he turned around and noticed that Bobby had lifted his head to look out. Paul shouted at him to give regards to Brownie and to tell him Paul would be looking him up sometime. Then he fired toward the front of the car, far away from Bobby. Bobby ducked back down and stayed down while Paul drove off. Roger waited until Paul was in his car before driving two miles farther down the road, where Paul met him. Paul handed him the pistol through the open car window. Roger handed Paul two rolls of film and an audio tape. Then, they drove off in separate directions. There was no chance Bobby was going to the police. Two bartenders and several people in the bar had witnessed Paul's beating, and the bartenders had tried to warn him about going outside. He might have been killed. And he had Bobby's admission on tape, which also implicated Brownie.

It was still earlier in the day than Paul had expected it to be, so he drove back to the hotel and called the airline to get a flight out that same evening. He checked out and drove to the airport car rental to turn the car back in, explaining that it had been vandalized while he was sleeping. After all, it was vandalism, and he was certainly not awake when it happened. He didn't actually know who had smashed the windows either.

He had taken out the rental insurance, so he filled out the paperwork, signed it, and took a shuttle to the terminal. If insurance didn't cover the damage, he would pay for it himself. He called Nate from the airport to let him know he would be in the next day.

CHAPTER 27

Wednesday, January 18, 1989

Paul met with Nate and Josh early the next morning and told them what he had seen in Amarillo. He had considered not going into the details of what he did to Bobby. But the Walkers needed to know each and every thing that had happened. So they got all the gory details and heard the tape with Bobby admitting the ambush on Paul.

Josh was a bit stunned. "Wow, Paul! I believe I would have called the police and made a report if I were you. You look pretty bad. They might have killed you."

"Yeah. I probably got a little reckless. I was pretty angry at these guys. But I didn't go off on a rampage without thinking it through. With the bartenders as witnesses, along with the tape recording and the film Roger shot, I would have no problem making a case against Bobby, Brownie, and their buddies if they tried to get law enforcement involved. They knew that, so I didn't think they would file a complaint and have the entire story come out. That's not something they would want."

Nate spoke up. "These people probably think they are dealing with some hard citizens now. That may not be a bad thing, but it went a bit farther than just the fact-finding we had in mind … what with the beating and shooting."

Paul didn't feel the need to defend his actions. Nate wasn't there. Paul was the one that got the crap beat out of him, doing them a favor. Maybe he did go a little too far. But he couldn't undo it.

Then Josh jumped in. "Walker, I have always said a lawyer ought to take the quick initiative. Paul could teach you a lesson. If this had been you, you would have dictated a memo, put it in a file, and waited until the matter came up on your tickler before going out and shooting up the place like he did."

Nate took up the banter. "That's called organization. I would have gotten to it."

Josh said, "We've got no argument with what you did, Paul. Nate wasn't being critical. He just feels bad about putting you in the place where that happened. This isn't your fight. We had no business getting you involved and getting you beat up. We feel responsible. On top of that, when Ann McCool finds out what happened, she is going to give all three of us hell."

Paul grinned. "I won't tell her if you don't."

Then Paul told them he had undeveloped film of the project, which showed absolutely no new trenches ready for pipe and no backhoe on-site to even dig the trenches. He also told them about his conversation with the engineer he met at another subdivision under construction. That information pretty well established that the joints Galena was proposing were used commonly in the Amarillo area. They had a lot to work with now.

Nate said, "Galena Pipe Works is being set up for a lawsuit in Amarillo and it's not going to be a friendly one. They would like to intimidate us into some kind of settlement. They've got no intention of ever paying for the pipe. And they want more than that if they can get it. The best thing we can do is let them think that we aren't afraid to color outside the lines if that is how the game is going to be played. I think Paul has already sent that message. And I think they may be wondering how deep they want to get into this."

"I agree with you," said Paul. "But they sure have gone to a lot of trouble for what they hope to get out of it. Something is still missing here. The way Galena Pipe got the contract bothers me. Maybe Noble Vista Development was trying to con Harry out of pipe, but then Galena Pipe stepped in, so they went after them instead? All this for some free pipe? They are a couple of shady small-time operators, so maybe that is all they wanted in the beginning. But they didn't know there would be a fire. Did they just luck into that? I don't know."

Josh had a thought. "We may be giving them too much credit. Let's say they are just screwups. They fail at whatever they do, then they keep doing it. Brock is a promoter and a good bullshitter. So, when they fail, they just go out and raise more money from investors or lenders, screw some more suppliers, and do it all again."

Nate agreed. "Yeah. They stick it to everybody, hoping to get lucky. They buy the land and screw the title company to save a few bucks, and they slow-pay suppliers. They are leveraged up the ass, but if they can just sell a couple of lots to builders, they have something going. That's why they have two phases. Get one up fast and see if a couple of builders or another developer bites. Their plan was to convince Vernon they are as solid as Rockefeller and get him to ship pipes quickly because they are on a deadline. The pipes are in the ground before Vernon thinks about getting paid or filing mechanic's liens. Vernon swallowed everything they fed him. Meeting with the mayor of Lubbock about a project there? Bullshit. In big meetings when Vernon calls? Bullshit. They played him. I see them as small-time operators throwing darts blindfolded, trying to hit the bull's eye. And this time, they nailed it."

Paul thought the same way. "You have it right. Out of nowhere, God sent them a fire, which put Galena in default and now they think they have both free pipe and liquidated damages. They're going to play that card for all it's worth. As long as they can come up with the cash to file a lawsuit, they can create havoc and see if it gets them something. If nothing comes of it they file Chapter 11 bankruptcy and see what they can come out with that way. At least there is some pipe in the ground.

"But how did this thing go from Harry Townsend, of all people, to Galena Pipe Works? Hell of a coincidence. We are still in the dark about something. Harry was bragging all over the place about this Texas contract. Then Vernon gets a copy and steals it out from under him. Vernon's contract is almost word for word the one Harry supposedly had. Harry would never sign a contract like that! He is a lot of things, but he is not that dumb. It's even hard to believe Vernon is that dumb, but I guess the act speaks for itself."

Now that it was certain that Galena Pipe Works was going to be sued, Nate decided to telephone Brock Johnson to see what kind of reaction Paul had stirred up.

"Mr. Johnson, this is Nate Walker. I would like to talk again about those pipes you ordered from Galena Pipe Works."

"There's nothing more to say, Walker. Your guys defaulted. Talk to our lawyer."

"You're nowhere near ready for the pipes, Johnson. What the hell do you think you are pulling? And you haven't paid for the first pipes which are now in the ground. We've seen your project. We have pictures. You do know that don't you?"

Brock hung up. Nate put down his receiver, smiled at Paul, and said, "Mr. Johnson is obviously aware of your visit. My guess is that he is on the phone to Turl right now. I will be getting an angry call from Turl before the morning is over, telling me it's unethical for me to contact his client directly and threatening to file a grievance against me. Then he will tell me that Noble Vista Development is going to sue the shit out of my client. He never would return my calls before. One thing I hate is a lawyer who won't return calls. But now he will."

They didn't have to wait very long. Fifteen minutes later, while Josh and Paul were still in Nate's office, the call came in. Paul and Josh could only hear Nate's side of the conversation.

"Why, Hello, Mr. Turl, I thought I might be hearing from you. I left several messages, you know.

"Mr. Johnson? Yes, I called him. Not much use though. I don't think he has any idea what Harry Townsend is up to, do you?

"Don't make threats, Turl. I don't like it".

"Bobby who? I don't think I know him, but I hope he gets over it. Right in the balls huh? Sounds like he had a pretty rough time."

"Yes, well I look forward to meeting you too."

Nate placed the receiver back into its cradle. He had tossed out Harry's name just on a whim. Nate said Turl acted like he didn't know who Harry Townsend was. But he paused for a revealing moment before denying that he knew him. He obviously was thrown off balance when Harry's name came up. Interesting.

———

Nate complained that he had now been hung up on twice today, and it wasn't even noon yet. It seemed to him he was getting hung up on a lot lately. Josh pointed out several deficiencies in Nate's personality, which were potential causes of that happening to him. Then they headed to the newspaper office to ask Ann for help in developing the film Paul had brought with him. There were no one-hour photo services in Stockton, so if they needed film developed in a hurry, they took it to her.

When they walked in, Ann looked up from the counter where she was helping an older woman fill out a classified advertisement. She barely acknowledged the three of them when they walked into the building. Then, after the customer left, her eyes fixed on Paul's face.

"Hello, Josh. Hello, Nate. Who's your friend? Rocky Balboa?"

Without taking her eyes off Paul, she continued addressing the Walkers. "You may as well tell me what happened. I'll find out anyway. You know I will."

Nate stepped up to field the question. "Paul had a little trouble in Texas, Ann. But he's fine and it wasn't his fault. We can talk about it later. We have some film that we would like to get developed and we don't have time to send it off. Can you help us?"

"I don't suppose this little trouble he got into has anything to do with the reason you asked him to go to Amarillo, does it?"

Nate rolled his eyes. "Well … now that you mention it, yes it could have. He was asking questions around a construction site down there and one of the workers from the site cornered him later and had him beat up. He did nothing to instigate it. He was an innocent party. It just happened. If you have to blame anyone you should probably blame Josh and me."

"Is that right, Paul?"

"Yes. Blame them."

"You weren't trying to be some kind of a troublemaker, were you?"

"Me? Absolutely not. I go out of my way to avoid trouble. And, once again, it's their fault."

"Where did it happen?"

"In The Rodeo Bar, a crummy place full of rednecks and people who don't like me. Well, I say it's crummy. Maybe it's not fair to blame The Rodeo Bar just because I didn't have much fun there. If you ever go there, you may have a completely different experience than I did."

"I don't think I will ever go there. Just give me the film. I'll call you when it's ready."

They had lunch and then walked back to the office. It was

time to wait. Turl would file suit in Amarillo when he was ready. Paul still didn't relish the idea of acting as a lawyer in this or any other matter, but he had become involved and he was tired of waiting for something to happen. Waiting and playing defense had never suited him.

"You should just sue them first," he said.

Josh looked puzzled. "Sue who? Noble Vista Development?"

"Sure. Why not? Sue them here in Jo Daviess County, Illinois."

"Well," Nate responded, "there's the small problem of jurisdiction and venue being in Texas under the terms of the contract."

"So what?" Paul said. "Do it anyway. Come up with some cause of action that will make them come to Galena for hearings. Why not ask that the contract be declared unenforceable because of misrepresentation and fraud in the inducement? If there is no contract, there is no contractual venue for suit. It doesn't matter what the contract says about venue, if the contract is no good. Sue them *quantum meruit* for the value of the pipe already delivered.

"By the way, Josh, you do have the equitable remedy of *quantum meruit* in Illinois, don't you?"

"Sure do," said Josh. "We were *quantum meruit-ing* around here while you Texas lawyers thought Latin was just music from south of the border. So, what you are saying is that the contract gives them the right to have the suit brought in Amarillo. But if the contract is void, then we can sue them here. Have I got that right?"

"Sure. Now, if Turl is smart, he will file a special appearance because he won't want to concede that Noble is subject to the jurisdiction of an Illinois court. He will try to stop the suit dead, but we can argue that they did business here and the Illinois long-arm statute makes them subject to jurisdiction in Illinois. Do they have sufficient contacts with

Illinois to make it stick? That could be tough under the circumstances, and it would be our burden to prove. But what do we have to lose? We might at least get a chance to dance them around a little bit and maybe do some discovery. It's the last thing they would expect. Turl can't gear up for a fight out of state. They could retain local counsel, which would be great because local counsel would work better with you. But Brock probably can't afford it. They already see us as hard bastards and this would really start them wondering what's coming next.

"There is more here than meets the eye. If we sue them here and stir up the water enough, we may find out what we don't know. But I admit that it is kind of a flaky idea. Do you think a local judge would toss it out with no hearing and hold it against you for filing it?"

"Not a chance of that," said Josh. "We could get it in the court we want and might have enough time to jerk Turl around pretty good before he gets it stopped or tries to work something out. The more I think about it, I think it has merit if we can get it past the jurisdiction hurdle. I probably wouldn't have thought of it. And I'm damned sure Nate wouldn't have."

Nate was warming up to the idea, too. "Their reaction might be to file suit in Texas immediately before they are even ready. We could have some more fun trying to get their suit abated until the court here tosses ours out. Who knows? I'm not sure what we can gain by it, but sometimes funny things happen when you take the offensive and shake things up by doing the unexpected. Paul's right. We don't have anything to lose."

Paul shook his head. "One more thing. I can't get over the feeling that Harry Townsend is involved in all of it. Well, maybe not the kicking my ass part. You guys are 100 percent responsible for that. But there is a connection to him and that alone makes me suspicious. If I am right, our lawsuit will smoke him out. We need to be ready for that. One way or another, Harry Townsend will come into our crosshairs after we file this suit. When that happens, we will learn a lot more."

CHAPTER 28

Wednesday, January 18, 1989

Ann called Nate when the prints were dry. He offered to pick them up at the newspaper office, but she insisted on bringing them over because she had something else to talk about. As she began to lock the front door on her way out, she hesitated and walked back inside. She went to a small filing cabinet in the microfilm room, unlocked it, and pulled out a brown envelope. A few minutes later, she left the office again.

Ann thought about what Paul was like when he was a schoolboy. She had seen him only once after his parents died. During his father's funeral, she had stood behind a hedge next to the funeral home so that she could watch people enter and leave without having to stand out in front. There were not many people at the funeral. Paul showed no expression on his face when he came out. People spoke to him, but he just stared back, as if he was trying to make some kind of sense out of them as they passed. He had looked her way once, and she was certain he had seen her. There was no smile. She was not sure he even knew why he was there. There was an emptiness in the way he stared ahead of him while he walked toward the hearse.

Now, as she walked toward Nathan's office, she remembered that young boy. She knew he was still sad. He just hid it. It was time he knew everything. The hurt would never go away otherwise. She knew that, and she would have to make Nate see it. When she got to the Walkers' office, Nate was on the telephone. She waited in the reception area and tried to think of a way to bring the subject up. There was no easy way to do it. Nate came out of his office and greeted Ann with his typical Walker grin—the one that made her feel like part of the family, or at least like someone whom the Walkers regarded as important.

"Hello, Ann. Got the pictures?"

"Right here, Nate, and they came out well. Whoever took them knew how to use a camera."

They walked back to Nathan's office and fanned the photographs out on his desk. Ann didn't know exactly what Nathan was looking for, but she could see that he was pleased. When he came to the picture of Bobby doubled over in pain, Nathan quickly slipped it into his desk drawer, as if she had not already seen it.

"The poor fellow in that picture looks like he is hurt, Nate. What do you suppose happened to him?"

"Well … I can't really say. I will ask Paul about it when I see him."

Ann didn't crack a smile.

"Oh … to me, it looks like someone kicked him in the balls really hard."

Nathan turned a little red, then broke out laughing.

"I think you have analyzed it about right."

With the ice already broken, it was easier now for Ann to bring up the subject she had come to talk about. She sat down in a chair across the desk from Nathan and opened the brown envelope she was carrying.

"There is something else I have analyzed, Nate, and I'd like your opinion on it."

She opened the envelope she had brought with her and handed him copies of the death certificates of Angela Hoffman and Ed Hoffman. Nathan read quickly through both documents and looked at Ann with a puzzled expression.

"Where did you get these, Ann? These are not public records."

"When my father died and I took over the paper, I went through all of the files and records my father had left. There was a small two-drawer filing cabinet that he had always kept locked. I found a key for it on a key chain in his desk. There wasn't anything in the drawer that I thought was confidential, just some old correspondence with other newspaper publishers who had been his friends. But there was also a sealed brown envelope with 'Simmons Funeral Home" printed on it. Without knowing what was in the envelope, I opened it and found the death certificates. Mr. Simmons must have given them to Dad. I can't speculate on why he would have done that. Maybe he just wanted to get something off of his chest. Dad and Mr. Simmons had known each other for a very long time.

"Nate, Angela Hoffman's death certificate says that she died from a gunshot wound to the chest. That is consistent with her having been shot by Ed. But Ed's death certificate says he died from a gunshot wound to the rear of his head. That's not suicide.

"Even as a little girl, I thought there was more to the story. The morning after the shootings, I walked past Paul's house on the way to school, and I stopped for a while to overhear what had happened. Everett Perkins was talking to you and Josh, and I understood him to imply that Mr. Hoffman was shot in the back of the head. Then the newspaper said he had died by suicide. That must have been the information my father was given at the time. I don't think he would have printed that otherwise, but I don't know. He wouldn't have seen the death certificates that soon. The paper said it was suicide, and so did everyone in town, so I didn't say anything to my parents or to anyone else about what I had heard. I was just a kid. I thought I had probably misunderstood. Only I never forgot about it.

"Dad never corrected the story. Neither did Mr. Simmons, Mr. Perkins, you, Josh, or anyone else who knew better.

"After finding the death certificates, I never mentioned them to anyone. There wasn't any reason to. It had happened long ago, and the family wasn't even around anymore. I knew you and everyone else must have had a reason for doing what I am sure you did, so I let it go."

"What is it that you think Josh and Everett and I did, Ann?"

"I think you covered up a murder. I think you told the newspaper and everyone you talked to that Mr. Hoffman had shot himself in the temple after he killed Angela, and I think you told Merle Simmons, the undertaker, to keep quiet about it. The only thing I don't understand is why his death certificate wasn't falsified. You three could have arranged for that, too. I'm sure of it."

Nathan paused for several seconds, looked back down at the death certificates on his desk, then looked at Ann. He smiled, pensively this time, not the Walker grin she had seen when he greeted her in the outer office. Then he reached for the intercom button.

"Josh. I need you to come in here. Now."

Josh walked in a few seconds later. Ann was surprised. Normally, when Nate asked Josh to do something, she expected some good-natured back and forth. Then she understood that the twins communicated on a different level. Josh had known at once that Nathan was serious and that he needed to go to his office without any banter. Nathan didn't have to tell him that. He didn't have to use any particular tone of voice. Josh just knew. He walked in with the same thoughtful expression Nathan was wearing. After he had taken a chair next to Ann, Nathan spoke.

"Ann knows all about Ed Hoffman's death, Josh, or at least she knows Ed didn't kill himself. We're going to tell her everything about it and let her decide what should be done."

Josh nodded his approval.

"She wants to know why Ed's death certificate is correct, and she wants to know why we didn't fix that, too."

Nathan handed Josh the two death certificates, and Josh looked them over before speaking.

He didn't bother asking where she got them. "Everett Perkins called me at about 2:30 in the morning on the day it happened. I had been a friend of Ed's since we were in high school, and I had known Angela most of her life. For some reason, I was probably closer to them than Nate was. Especially Angela, if you want to know. There was always just something about her that I thought was wonderful. Don't get the wrong idea. Nothing ever came of it. It was just a deep friendship. We could talk to each other and tell each other how we felt about things … confide in each other. Aside from Nate, I was probably closer to her than to anyone else I have known. I'm sure it wouldn't have looked good to people in town if they had known how often we talked and what things we talked about. We were both married. It could have been misunderstood, but it wasn't ever wrong. Sometimes we would drive out into the country and have a picnic, or just sit and talk. It was good for both of us and probably good for our marriages, although hers was beyond saving. I don't know if you have ever had that kind of a relationship with anyone. I know it's the only one I've ever had."

As Josh spoke, there was no sense of guilt in his voice. His relationship with Angela had been a good thing, and there was not so much as a hint of embarrassment as he talked about her. Ann was certain that he had loved Angela, but in a way that was not destructive to either of them or to their other relationships.

"Anyway," Josh continued, "Everett called me right away and told me to come over because he knew that Ann and I were close. When I got there, Doctor Schwartz was already examining the bodies. It was the most gruesome thing I had ever seen. It's as close as I have ever come to passing out. Betty Stieffle, from next door, had already taken Paul out of the house. When we had all decided to call it a murder and suicide, Doc Schwartz offered to draw up Ed's death certificate that way, but I wouldn't let him. He had too much to risk and no real reason to do it. Keeping quiet about it was one thing, but falsifying a death certificate is a felony in this state. We took the chance that no one would ever bother looking at the death certificate. Ed didn't have any life insurance, and Everett was the coroner, so he could call it a suicide if he wanted to."

"Did Ed kill Angela?"

"Yes."

"Why?"

Josh paused for a moment before answering as if he were reaching into a compartment of his memory that had been closed for a long time.

"She was leaving him. Herb was already here, waiting for her so that he could take her and Paul to Chicago to start a new life. He was going to help them get settled in; her with a job and apartment, and Paul with school. Ed had gotten meaner lately and more violent. Angela had suffered more in that marriage than anyone should, and the whole town knew it. Ed was abusive to her even before he got drafted. Hit her when they were home. Embarrassed her in public for no reason except meanness. She always made excuses for him. First, it was because he was young and had big plans, but there weren't any good opportunities for him in Stockton. Then it was the war. His wounds. His nightmares. His stress. His alcoholism. The fact is that Ed just wasn't worth a damn if you want to know the truth. He was a cocky bastard in high school and he came back from the war thinking the world owed him a living. Well, life doesn't work like that. After the glory faded, he got a taste of reality and didn't like it, so he took everything out on Angela. I don't think he was ever capable of loving her. She was a possession to him. Something he had that he thought everyone else wanted. And maybe he was right. Herb still loved his brother, but he couldn't change him, and he knew Ed was a danger to Angela and Paul. He had to do something to protect them, both for their sake and Ed's.

"Worse yet, Ed had found out the previous day that he was losing his job. The district man from Ford had told Mel Howard to let him go. I think Ed started drinking that morning. He went home to sleep off some of the booze, then went back out. Of course, Angela and Herb didn't know anything like that was going to happen that day. They had planned everything in advance. When Ed got home after the bars closed, Angela was all packed. Paul was in bed. I guess Angela wanted him to sleep until she got him up to go. Should have waited until Ed was asleep, too. He usually slept for hours after tying on a good drunk. Then she and Paul could have left safely with Herb. Ed probably saw the suitcases and forced her to tell him what was going on. Then he would have become violent. There may or may not have been a scuffle before he got his hands on the pistol he kept in the bedroom. That is something we will never know. But we know he shot and killed her. We know how it ended."

"But Ed didn't kill himself."

"No."

It was quiet for fifteen or twenty seconds while Ann waited. She looked from Josh to Nathan. These were two of the most honest men she had ever known. They were highly regarded lawyers because clients, judges, and other lawyers could put trust in them and everything they said. And yet they had covered up a murder. Ed Hoffman may have been a violent, abusive human being, but he was a human being. And they were lawyers and officers of the court who had not only obstructed justice but had conspired to falsify a coroner's report to hide the fact that there was a murder and a murderer. Herb had been there all along, but they had lied about that, too. They said he was in Chicago when it happened and that he was coming the next day for Paul. Why would Herb need an alibi? Unless, of course, he had killed Ed. Maybe he had seen Ed kill Angela and had somehow managed to kill him with his own gun after a physical struggle. That could have been what happened. If so, he might not be to blame for it. But it was not up to the Walkers and Everett Perkins to decide.

She was overcome with the arrogance of it. Nathan and Joshua Walker, emperors of Jo Daviess County. Even Doc Schwartz had been willing to risk losing his medical license and go to jail to do what they wanted. For the first time since she had known the Walkers, she didn't know if she liked them very much. She almost demanded that they tell her, unambiguously, who shot Ed. She wanted to look them in the eyes and make them say it out loud, in their own words ... but she stopped herself. What would she do then? What could be done about it now? It would only create a firestorm and hurt lots of people. She didn't want to hear it. Then she would be just like them, holding on to a secret she would have to live with. No. She did not want to carry the burden they carried.

"It must be nice to feel like God on Judgment Day. I guess you two pretty much controlled the local justice system in those days. I wonder how much it has changed. Are you planning to tell Paul?"

Nathan answered for them both.

"We told you when Josh came in here that you could decide what should be done. It's your call. You are the closest to Paul. You may want to tell him everything you know, or you may want us to. It's up to you, Ann. You've even got a newspaper to use if you decide to use it. I promise that Josh and I won't hold it against you, no matter what you decide."

Ann got out of her chair and walked out the door without

saying anything. She was hurt by Nathan's comment that she could use her paper to tell everything. They made it sound like she was there for a story, for God's sake. She was there for Paul, and they knew very well, or should know very well, that was why she was there, and she would never do anything to hurt them or Paul or anyone else just for a story.

"Should we have just come out and told it all to her?" Josh asked.

Nate shook his head. "We did the right thing. She knows it wasn't suicide, and she knows we covered that up. That's all she needs to know. It's a lot for her to deal with, and she didn't press us any further about it. But we have known Ann a long time. She's going to think about it and eventually let it go. She knows there is nothing to be done now."

"What about Paul when he asks? He will now. You know he will. Will we tell him? Doesn't he deserve to know?"

"That's the wrong question, Walker. The right question is whether he would want to know. Would you want to know?"

CHAPTER 29

Wednesday, January 18, 1989

Ann went straight home. She had intended to go back to the newspaper to do some work, but now she could think of nothing except what Josh had said. It hardly seemed possible. Not the Walkers. The worst part was that they had put the whole problem right on her shoulders. She had gone to see Nate to get to the bottom of what had happened so that she could lift a cloud from Paul. Now, she had to decide what to tell him, and she wondered what his reaction would be if she told him the things she had learned. How would the revelation affect his relationship with the Walkers? She knew Paul wouldn't tell anyone else about it. He wasn't like that. He wouldn't want Nate and Josh to lose respect.

Could there even be an investigation if people found out? Probably not. She didn't know if things like that were covered by a statute of limitations or if the bar grievance committee would still be interested in something that happened in 1956. But it would serve no purpose now. Whatever happened had happened, and it couldn't be changed. The whole thing had upset her, and she had too many crazy things going on in her head. The only question for her was what she should say to Paul. She had to tell him something. He had come to Stockton to find out what had happened, and he needed answers.

She poured a large glass of wine and drew a hot bath. That usually helped when something was bothering her. She decided to take the cordless telephone with her. It must have been a premonition because the phone rang after she had been in the tub for about five minutes. It was Paul.

"Hello, Ann. I called the newspaper office, but there was no answer. What are you doing home so early on a busy news day in Stockton? Get tired of competing with the big media moguls? Get scooped one time too many by CNN?"

"No. I just needed a bath, which, by the way, you are interrupting."

"Don't stop on my account. I'll be right over. And don't get up. I'll let myself in. Shall I bring my own towel?"

"I've got a better idea. Wait half an hour and come over for drinks and dinner. I could use some company."

"I liked my idea better, but it's your house. See you in thirty minutes."

By the time Paul arrived, Ann had already dressed, started a small roast in the oven, and put on some music. She met Paul at the door and put her arms around him. He held her for a moment and pressed his face against her hair. She smelled clean and fresh with a trace of the perfume she always wore. When she looked up at him, he saw a different Ann McCool than he was used to. This was not the quick-witted, laughing Ann McCool that had become so much a part of him. This Ann McCool was troubled. She led him into the kitchen and mixed him a drink. Then she poured a glass of wine for herself and led him back into the living room. Frank Sinatra's voice came over her CD player, singing "Glad to be Unhappy," and he had to smile at the timing. He had never seen her looking unhappy before. He would have laughed if it hadn't been so obvious that she was serious about her sad mood. Somehow, suffering just didn't fit her. No one he had ever known before had looked so cute in their misery. She said nothing to him. She just sat quietly, leaning on his shoulder. Finally, when he felt he couldn't ignore it any longer, he asked what was bothering her.

"Paul, from the time you got to town, you have been asking questions about your parents and how they died. What will you do when all of your questions have been answered? Will you leave?"

"Is that what's bothering you, Ann? That I'll solve this little mystery and go back to Texas? No. That wouldn't make me leave. It is mainly the thing that brought me here, but I am starting to realize that it is not the only thing. This town is ingrained in me for some reason. I have lived a few places since Herb took me to Chicago. But I'm not sure I ever left Stockton behind. Of course, it has bad memories connected to it. Those are not the only memories, though. It has many happy memories tied to it, too. It would be foolish for me to say that I will never leave. Nobody has a crystal ball. But if I ever have to leave, it won't be because of what I have learned about the night my parents died. And it won't be because I don't like it here. I think Stockton is a very good place to live."

"What have you learned about that night that you didn't know before you came back to Stockton?"

"If you really want to know, I'll tell you. I've learned that my father was a drunkard and a mean son of a bitch who killed my mother. I think she was going to leave him, and that's why he killed her. She may or may not have been in love with someone else. I don't know and I never will. I'll tell you one other thing I know. He didn't kill himself. He killed my mother, and someone else killed him, most likely with his own gun. I just don't know how the hell they got away with it. Everyone covered it up and called it a suicide, but some of the people in town knew better and kept it quiet. Merle Simmons, the undertaker, knew, and he talked to a few people. I am pretty sure by now that my father was shot in the back of the head. Mrs. Howard heard about it, and Everett Perkins knew it all along. And the Walkers damn sure knew it and have been hiding it from me since I got to town. I don't know why, because they are good men. What do you think?"

There it was, the question she couldn't dodge, and she had walked right into it. Now, what would she do? Tell him what Josh had told her? Should she lie and say she had no idea? It was probably too late for that. She should have acted surprised when he told her what he had learned.

"I think you may be right about your father being killed by someone else, but who could it have been?"

"I don't know. Maybe another man in her life. Someone who was in love with her. It could be that my father caught them together, and he shot my mother. Then, the killer managed to get his gun. Somehow, he got behind my father and shot him in the back of the head. Difficult maybe. But how else could it have happened? It's not impossible. Especially since my father was certainly drunk when he got home. That would have made it a lot easier for someone to wrestle the gun away. But why would he have to shoot him once he had control of the gun? He may have been crazy with fury, I suppose. The whole thing is hard for me to picture. What I remember from that night sheds no light on it. Sometimes I start to see something breaking through in my mind, but it fades before I can understand it. You can't imagine how frustrating that is. It makes me have sympathy for Alzheimer's patients, who start to remember something but then can't quite get to it. At any rate, I don't know how else it could have happened. But none of it even makes sense to me, least of all the cover-up."

Ann decided to leave it there.

The topic shifted to his trip to Amarillo. Ann offered her opinion that, based on the welcome he had received on his last trip to Texas, he may want to consider staying in Illinois as much as possible. He described what had happened to him when he began asking questions. Paul was sure Nate and Josh were into something they would need help with. He told her he had nothing on which to base his theory, but he couldn't shake the feeling that Harry Townsend was behind everything that had taken place, and he thought the Walkers felt the same way. Ann cautioned Paul not to sell the Walkers short. They take their time working through things and don't quit. So they usually get to a good outcome.

Later, they found themselves in Ann's bedroom. Paul thought that Ann was the most passionate woman he had ever known, and later he wondered if she had been like that with Gene Thurman when she had been engaged and married to him. And he wondered whether she had been like that with other men. She must have had other lovers, but they had never talked about it. He knew it wouldn't matter to him. That would be unfair. He had been with other women. Paul realized they had never talked about Ann very much at all. He had been so wrapped up in himself since he came to Stockton that he hadn't given much thought to Ann's life. These things he did know. She was a strong, self-reliant woman who was somehow becoming a part of his life, and she cared about him at a depth he had not expected. She was seldom out of his mind. Almost every thought he had was one he wanted to share with her. When he saw something unusual, read something that made his mind race, or heard something that excited him, he wanted her to see it, read it, or hear it. He fell asleep with Ann in his arms and slept peacefully for the first time he could remember since he had come to town.

When he woke up in the morning, Ann was already up. He dressed in the clothes he had thrown on the floor and went downstairs, where he could smell coffee brewing. Ann was sitting at the kitchen table reading yesterday's *Rockford Morning Star*. If she heard him walk into the room, she didn't let on. He walked up behind her, bent down, and kissed her.

"If you want a cup of coffee that badly, you only need to ask."

"It's how I ask."

Ann turned around and kissed him on the mouth. They

came close to going back upstairs before Ann pulled clear and got up to pour his coffee. Paul thought she looked perfect. He followed her to the counter and put his arms around her again.

"If you want coffee, you are going to have to sit down, Mr. Hoffman. I'm not going to have it spilled all over the floor." He took his coffee to the table and picked up the sports page to see if there was any news about where the Cubs might look for some pitching next season. Ann poured him a second cup of coffee and then reopened the subject she had brought up the previous evening.

"Paul, I had a discussion yesterday with Nathan and Josh about your parents. You need to talk to them. And don't be reluctant to push the issue because they are ready to open up. Don't ask me how I know that; just trust me this time. They have been holding back for a lot of reasons. I think they would rather I told you all about it, but I won't. They need to do it. Then I can try to help you sort it out."

"Why didn't you tell me this last night?"

"I wanted to, but I was too confused about what to do. Now I'm not. You can't hear this secondhand, and I can't be the one to tell you. It would be all wrong".

CHAPTER 30

Friday, January 20, 1989

The next morning, Paul joined the Walkers at their office in Galena to start roughing-out the specific allegations of the suit they would file. It would allege that Noble Vista Development refused to pay for the pipe delivered to them, accepted by them, and buried by them. It would state that they are refusing to accept delivery of additional pipe that conforms to the contract. Those actions demonstrated that they had no intentions of ever performing the duties they had under the contract when it was signed. Therefore, the contract was entered into in bad faith and should be voided. Galena Pipe Works should have judgment for the value of the pipe under the theory of *quantum meruit*.

They would also lay out a case of fraudulent inducement. The allegation would be that Noble induced Galena Pipe to enter the contract by fraud because they had no intention of paying for the pipe. They had intentionally benefited by accepting the pipe and not paying its value to the plaintiff. For that reason, it was equitable that they have judgment to recover the value of the pipe along with punitive damages.

All of that sounded nice, but they agreed it could be tossed somewhere along the way on the grounds that an Illinois court lacked jurisdiction over a Texas entity. Even so, it was worth filing. The idea was that it might cause enough trouble and expense for Noble that they would come up with some money to pay for the pipe they got and drop any suit they were planning to file in Texas. Or, as Paul hoped, it might bring out Harry Townsend or anyone else who might be involved in a bigger plot. Paul suggested that they do a little more digging into how Galena got this contract. How did a copy of Harry's proposed contract with Noble really get into Vernon's hands? He was skeptical of Tommy's explanation. Why would anyone at Babson give it to Tommy? Even if it was just a pissed-off employee, wouldn't they find an easier way to get back at their employer than giving a copy of a contract to Galena Pipe Works?

The three lawyers were getting ready to call Vernon and ask him and Tommy to come down to the office to talk more about Harry's unsigned contract when the phone rang. Carl Kraus, the Galena fire chief, asked if he could come right over to discuss the fire. When he showed up, he was accompanied by Fred Bingham, an arson investigator from the Office of the State Fire Marshal (OSFM). They were shocked by the inclusion of an arson investigator. They had thought the cause of the fire was unaccounted for. Probably an accident of some kind. Nothing about an arson investigation had been mentioned, and it never had entered their minds. Carl told them that they had asked Vernon to come to the meeting also. They did not want to talk at the plant because it might cause employees to have questions.

When Vernon arrived, they all sat in the conference room. Carl introduced everyone but Paul to Fred Bingham. Nate made that introduction and told them that Paul was an attorney working with them on the company's behalf, and anything they had to say could be said in Paul's presence. Fred opened up the discussion. Carl had contacted the State Fire Marshal's office because he was stumped about a cause and he was required to report the fire to the state. That is when Fred got involved. He had looked at all of the photos taken by the fire department during their investigation, and he had been to visit the plant with Carl.

Carl had sent the broken section of the gas pipe to the state to be examined in the lab. They had already deduced, after reviewing all the evidence collected on-site, that a leak from the broken section was the cause of the fire. When the pipe got to the lab it was determined that the joint may have been broken with a tool that may have been used in a way that twisted the pipe at its joint. They did find scratches on the pipe from a wrench. Large pipe wrenches were not hard to find. It would have taken someone strong to exert the force necessary to open the joint, even with a heavy pipe wrench.

Among other things, the state lab had done calculations based on the size of the enclosed kiln to determine the volume of air in the kiln. They used the dimensions of the kiln room to calculate the likely direction of the flow of the released gas, together with the rate of flow based on the opening in the pipe. They considered the distance from the pipe to the flame in the kiln furnace, along with a host of other technical factors. Then they came up with an estimate of the amount of time it would have taken for enough gas to have formed around the flame to ignite the explosion and fire. It all sounded like a very complicated calculation, but Fred told them it was done routinely.

Josh asked, "What did they come up with?"

Fred answered, "Now, these estimates are always kind of broad. It's almost impossible to nail the exact time of the leak from mere calculations. But the range they come up with has an eerie way of working out right. In this case, they think that the leak, assuming the opening by the joint was created by one act, would have begun between seven o'clock and ten o'clock Sunday night.

Nate wondered, "Fred, could it have been leaking longer

than that, for instance, when there were still workers at the plant on Saturday?"

"Probably not based on their estimate. Someone would have smelled it if there were enough people around when it was leaking, even a small amount of gas. We need your permission to interview the night security guards and any other employees we think might have helpful information."

They got permission and left with Vernon to set up the interviews. Nate asked Vernon to come back to the office after Carl and Fred got situated. He was gone about forty-five minutes before he got back.

Nate started off the conversation. "Vernon, it looks to us that we are going to be sued by Noble Vista Development. We would like the lawsuit to be filed here in Galena, obviously, but it is likely going to be in Texas. We need to pin down every single piece of information that can help us. This whole thing started with an unsigned copy of Harry's proposed contract. Nothing more would have happened without it showing up. Tell us again how it got to you."

Vernon repeated what he had told them before. He had heard rumors about the contract for some time and had even talked about it with Tommy. Then Tommy got his hands on a copy and brought it to him. Tommy said he had been given it by someone working at Babson Pipe Company. That is all he knew about it.

Josh asked, "Did Tommy tell you who that was or how it came about? We would like to know more about that."

"No. I did ask who it was, but he sort of ignored the question, and I didn't push him. He brought us the contract out of loyalty and probably didn't want to break a confidence. I think he got it from an employee over there who sneaked it out of Harry Townsend's office or something."

"Vernon, I sure don't like hearing that. We are beyond not wanting to break confidences now. We have big trouble here and it began with whoever it was who gave that damned contract copy to Tommy. Please call over there and get Tommy to come here now so we can ask where he got it."

Half an hour later, Tommy walked in and took a seat. Josh thought he looked nervous. Of course, that would be expected under these circumstances, whether he had done anything wrong or not.

Nate spoke first. "Tommy, I don't know how much Vernon has told you, but it looks like the company is going to be sued over this work in Amarillo. These guys were already in default on making payments before the fire, and now we have a dispute over the joints on the pipes we have offered them. They are being damned unreasonable about it, and we can't figure out why. But the whole debacle started with that contract copy you brought to Vernon, not that we are blaming you for it. You were just being helpful. So, who gave you that contract? And how did they happen to have it?"

Tommy was slow to answer. "He found a copy of it at the Babson plant, I guess. And he was not happy with the company. And he just decided to show it to me, I guess."

"Who, Tommy?"

"He gave it to me in secret, Nate. He could lose his job if they found out what he did."

"Tommy, I'm going to be as clear as I can be. We don't give a damn right now what happens to the guy. None of this shit would have landed in our laps if not for him. We have a serious risk here, and we will do whatever it takes to straighten it out. If there is any way we can keep Babson Pipe from finding out who he is or how we got the contract copy, we will do it. But one way or the other, we need to know who it was and how it came to be."

"It was a guy I know who works there. He called me and told me he had a copy of the contract. Then I met him at a bar in South Beloit, and he gave it to me. He just said he found it somewhere."

"He just found it somewhere! Who, Tommy?"

"Well ... it was Norton. Norton Jensing, the plant manager.

But I don't want him getting in trouble. Please don't tell him I told you."

"Okay, Tommy. Now, the fire chief is trying to get more information on the fire. If you can think of anything or anyone who can help him, let us know. We still don't know what started it but we want to find out, so it never happens again."

"Sure, Nate. I'll help him if I can."

Tommy left to go back to the plant. Vernon went with him. As soon as they were out of the building, Paul said, "I don't believe him."

Josh agreed. "He could be lying to protect the guy he really got the contract from. Or he got it from Norton Jensing, who got it from Harry Townsend to give to him. Or he got it straight from Harry? Is that possible?"

"Sure. All of those are possible."

CHAPTER 31

Friday, January 27, 1989

Nathan and Josh worked over the weekend on pleadings for the suit they were filing in Galena, *Galena Pipe Works, Inc., an Illinois Corporation, vs. Noble Vista Development, LLC., a Texas Limited Liability Company*. The suit asked for the contract to be declared void, and it asked for damages equal to the value of the pipe delivered and not paid for. It also asked for exemplary damages as punishment for fraud. Paul had helped Nate and Josh with it, but they did all the drafting of the documents themselves. Illinois Rules of Civil Procedure, as well as local court rules, were different from what he was used to in Texas. He did what he could to research similar cases and lined up a way to get the suit served on Brock Johnson in Amarillo. It wasn't until Thursday afternoon that they were satisfied they were ready to file. Friday morning, Josh walked the Complaint over to the courthouse and filed it. When the paperwork was filed and the summons issued, he returned to the office. Paul and Nate were having coffee when he walked in.

"Well, it's filed. Normally, since I know the other party's attorney, I would call him and let him know what was coming.

And I would fax him a copy of what was filed, just as a courtesy. He might even agree to accept service for the client. But Turl wouldn't recognize a courtesy if he saw one. So, I will just let him hear about it when his client is served. I see you boys don't have anything to do. I guess I am still the one who has to do all the work around here."

"That's how we see it, too, Josh. But lately, you have been letting us down a little. We have been sitting here doing brainwork about the fire while you were over at the courthouse, gabbing with the clerks. Have you given any more thought to how the fire got started?"

"As a matter of fact, Walker, I didn't mention it to Carl Kraus or the arson inspector, but it sure sticks in my mind that Tommy was the only one at the plant between seven o'clock and ten o'clock on the night the gas leak happened. That's a hell of a thought, and I don't like suspecting Tommy of anything that bad. But it sure does bother me. I didn't say anything to the arson guy because I want him to come to whatever conclusions he has on his own. Do you think Tommy would do something like that?"

"Hell yes, Josh. I thought of it as soon as we suspected that he lied to us about how he got the contract. That sure is a big risk for him to take, though. And there would be no reason for him to do that just on his own initiative. It wouldn't help him."

"Okay. Then the question is: Who benefited from the fire?"

Paul spoke up. "I think it comes down to three. Obviously, if it was Tommy who did the dirty work, he had something to gain. Noble certainly had something to gain. And there just has to be something in it for Harry, meaning Babson Pipe Company. But tomorrow is Saturday, and the owner, publisher, and senior reporter of the *Stockton Herald* has invited me over for dinner tonight. So, I am going to leave now and buy a nice bottle of wine to take with me. Then, the weekend will be pretty much devoted to enjoying movies that said newspaper publisher has rented for us to watch on her brand-new VCR. It bothers me that she made all the movie selections. This could be a long weekend. Anyway, we probably won't get service on Brock until Monday. So, I don't think we will hear anything about the suit we filed until next week. If anything comes up, give me a call."

"Josh and I are going up to the lakes in Wisconsin for a couple of days. They don't always see serious fishermen up there, so we decided to teach them the magic of some innovative fly fishing. See you on Monday, Paul. Enjoy the weekend sobbing over romantic movies."

CHAPTER 32

Monday, January 30, 1989

Monday morning, when Brock got to the office, he was served with the Illinois lawsuit, and he called Harry at once. This was not something he had anticipated. He thought any litigation would take place in Amarillo, where Bill Turl would be able to handle it. Bill was on the board of directors of Noble Vista Development, so he had an interest in what happened. But Bill couldn't help him in Illinois. Harry's plan may have gotten Noble Vista Development some pipe in the ground without paying. But now he had an out-of-state lawsuit on his hands. It wasn't supposed to work that way.

"Brock," Harry said, "you worry too damned much. They're just flailing around. Don't know what the hell they are doing. Wait until you see what Galena Pipe Works has coming at them next. I've been waiting for them to make a move. Now we need to get to work. You and Turl need to fly up and meet with me and my lawyer. He'll let you in on what is going to happen and what your part is. He'll tell Turl what to do. Now, just get ahold of Turl and get the two of you on a plane. Meet me up here tomorrow."

Brock picked up the telephone and called Turl. "Bill, this is Brock. Those guys in Galena just sued us, and they did it in Illinois. How the hell can they do that?"

"They can't. The contract says they have to sue us here if they sue us."

"Well, guess what? They sued us there anyway. I called Harry Townsend. This whole thing was his idea. He's not worried. Of course, they didn't sue him. He says he has a lawyer who knows what to do about it. Harry says they have had a plan all along. He wants us to fly up tomorrow, and his lawyer will lay it out and explain our part. He says this is nothing. There is a whole lot more coming at Galena Pipe Works when his lawyer gets things started."

"He's going to explain *our* part? How did *we* get a part in what he has planned next? This is bullshit. Why don't Harry and his lawyer come down here?"

"Because this whole thing was Harry's idea, and we bought into it. Now we need him more than he needs us. I'll book the flights with what we have left on the company credit card. We have to catch an early flight tomorrow."

Brock and Bill flew out of Amarillo on the earliest flight the next morning. Bill complained all the way from Amarillo to Dallas and all the way from Dallas to Chicago. He cursed Harry and Brock for getting him into this. His law partners were going to be pissed. What the hell business does he have going to Chicago for Noble Vista Development? Noble was already behind on attorney's fees.

When they got to O'Hare Airport, they called Harry to tell him they had arrived. Nobody met them at the airport, of course. Harry told them to take a cab to his office. It would be nice if Harry would cover some of these expenses, but there was a fat chance of that. Harry's office looked like a converted 7/11 store. He showed them the kitchen and told them to help themselves to some coffee while he called his lawyer. Bill Turl was surprised they didn't have to drop some money into a box by the coffee maker. Harry, in addition to his other flaws, was also a cheap bastard. An hour later, Bernie Torveski showed up. He was just under six feet tall and must have weighed two hundred seventy-five pounds. He wore a red tracksuit and white sneakers, and he carried a worn-out leather satchel. He introduced himself to Brock and Bill without waiting for Harry to do it and wasted no time getting down to business.

"Harry sent me a copy of this lawsuit over in Jo Daviess County. You need to get something filed on that. I don't want to mess with it. Bill, you don't need to be licensed in Illinois to file a special appearance. You can do that without submitting to jurisdiction in Illinois. It will slow these guys down and give Harry a chance to go after them in Texas. If you need to do more later, I might take it over. I drafted the special appearance for you. You just need to sign the thing, and I will file it for you. Now, you got any questions?"

Bill Turl was caught short by how fast this was going. "I don't know. I have to read it. But if that is all you needed me for, I'm not sure why I am here."

"Don't worry," said Harry. "We are getting to that. Go ahead, Bernie. Tell them the rest."

Bernie obliged. "We haven't been sitting on our asses here. We just wanted to see what they were going to do. We had a lawsuit ready to file in Texas before you guys even got your first pipe from Galena. It will need to be refined to conform to Texas statutes or local court rules, but the cause of action is universal. That won't be your job, Bill. We have another lawyer down there to file the suit. You can read it later on."

Bill felt rushed by this fast talker. "I think I would like to see it now."

"Hold on, pal. We are getting there. What this is … it's a suit for intentional interference in a business relationship, asking for compensatory and punitive damages. It ought to bring a significant judgment if we all work together."

Bill was confused. "I don't get it. What is the basis for it?"

"Well, Bill, this is what happened. Babson Pipe Company, being Harry, had a signed contract with Noble Vista

Development for the manufacture and delivery of a shitload of concrete pipes—specially-made because most people use a different joint than you guys wanted. Then the guys at Galena Pipe Works filched a copy of the contract and decided to undercut Babson. They contacted Brock completely out of the blue and ran down Babson, saying the company was crooked and Harry was, too. Noble shouldn't deal with Harry, they told Brock. It should deal with them because they were more reputable and they could beat Babson's price. Follow me?"

Brock spoke up, "I guess. I mean … you could sort of say that. But Harry knows it wasn't really that way."

"If I may continue … You, Brock, told Vernon Tanksley that you already had a signed contract. But he convinced you that it didn't matter because Babson couldn't fulfill the contract on time, and you couldn't wait for those pipes. You believed him. So, you signed a contract with Galena Pipe Works and not only did they screw Babson Pipe, meaning Harry, but they couldn't even perform the contract right. Now you guys are standing around with your peckers in your hands and no more pipes to finish the job."

Bill got to his feet. "Holy shit! We need to think about this. I mean, let me put it this way. This meeting never happened. I never came up here, but if I did, we didn't talk about this stuff. We just talked, maybe, about whether Babson could legally step in now that Galena is in default. I think that is what this was about. That is the only conversation we had up here if we were here at all. Agreed?"

"Yeah, Bill," said Harry. "That is exactly what it was about if you ever were here. Right, Bernie?"

"I wouldn't have no idea about none of that, Harry. I wasn't here. Now let me continue. We will get this suit filed in Texas right after your special appearance is filed in Galena. I have a lawyer lined up in Lubbock. Lawyers in Amarillo may know each other, so I am using a lawyer out of town for this. Local guys are sometimes too cozy. We couldn't use you, Bill, because you represent Noble Vista Development, and you are on their board. And we are suing Noble Vista Development."

Now Bill and Brock were both on their feet. Brock shouted, "What the hell! YOU ARE SUING US? Are you crazy? What are you suing us for?"

"Venue and jurisdiction. Bill should understand that. If we sue Galena Pipe Works for interference, we might have to sue them in Illinois. We are here, and they are here. It is where the contract copy was stolen and it is where they conspired to interfere. We don't want to take a chance that the suit may end up in Galena. That is their playing field. They know the judges and the juries. And frankly, they are not in love with guys like Harry and me from Chicago. Whereas, Amarillo is where Noble is working on a new development to provide a nice new neighborhood for the community. Brock lives there. Jimmy what's-his-name lives there. You live there. Texas home cooking. We want the venue there."

"Yeah," said Brock. "But I don't like you suing us."

"Brock. We are only suing you to get venue in Texas. Sometime along the way, we dismiss you from the suit. By that time, it's too late for Galena Pipe to remove it to Illinois. Get it?"

Bill was beside himself. "Just exactly what does Noble Vista Development get out of this trainwreck"

Harry answered that with a typical Harry answer. "There is going to be a big judgment against Galena Pipe Works and we will figure all that out when we get closer to it. Lots of money to spread around. Take this paperwork with you and get comfortable with it. Is it too late for you to fly back today? If you need to spend the night, there is a Holiday Inn near here on West Toughie Street. Bernie can drop you off. One more thing. From this point on do not call me from your phone. If you need to talk to me, do it through our lawyer in Lubbock. Bernie will give you his contact information. Or call a telephone number Bernie will give you. And don't call from your phone. Use a public phone or another phone not connected to you."

Brock and Bill were too shocked to even respond. They called a cab and had one in about five minutes. While they waited, Bernie had Bill Turl sign the answer to the Illinois lawsuit so that he could get it filed and mailed to the attorneys for Galena Pipe Works. When they got to O'Hare, they took an afternoon flight to Dallas and a redeye flight back to Amarillo. They felt like they had been run over by a train.

CHAPTER 33

Friday, February 3, 1989

While he had been in Stockton, Paul had been doing more than digging into his past and spending time with the Walkers. He had also been writing and editing the chapters he was compiling for his old law school and consulting with the law school by telephone. He had help from a team of law students in Houston who shipped him all of the research materials he asked for. Lately, though, the interruptions had been significant due to his involvement with the Galena Pipe litigation. There were meetings, filings, and even a trip to Amarillo, Texas, to take a beating. He had not expected any of that when he had first headed to Stockton, and it had gotten him behind on his project. But there was dead time in the Galena Pipe litigation now, while he and the Walkers waited for Noble Vista Development to file a response to the lawsuit in Illinois. So, he got back to work on the law school project. He started on it early every morning and worked into the early evening. Then he started again, first thing the next morning. It kept him occupied, and he enjoyed doing it. Ann even did some proofreading for him from time to time.

Things were fairly quiet around the Walker Law Firm until Tuesday, February 7th, when they received a faxed copy of the answer Turl had filed in their lawsuit against Noble Vista Development. It was exactly what Paul had predicted. It was a special appearance, basically saying: "Hey! We are in Texas, and we are not subject to the jurisdiction of your court. There are no circumstances here that justify jurisdiction over our company. So, please just dismiss this lawsuit, and thank you very much."

Paul helped draft the reply. He argued that Noble Vista Development sought to buy pipes manufactured in Illinois from two different Illinois companies. He asked for an opportunity for discovery, which would establish that Noble had plotted to defraud Galena Pipe Works, an Illinois corporation, by illegally acquiring products that it manufactured entirely in Illinois. He postulated that those actions constituted doing business in the state and that Noble Vista Development had therefore submitted itself to Illinois law under the Illinois long-arm statute. But he admitted to Josh and Nate that it was a stretch. He wasn't sure a judge would find that Noble had sufficient contacts with Illinois to constitute *"doing business"* in the state. Even so, they could ask for a hearing on it and see what happens. If the court just allowed them to have discovery, that would be a big win. The Walkers were comfortable with the judge assigned to the case, and they felt that even if he threw out the suit, he at least wouldn't rule on it in a hurry. If nothing else, they had created some work for Turl. Of course, they were still waiting for Noble Vista Development to sue them in Texas. They were certain that would happen next.

Instead, the Walkers got a surprise the following Monday, when it was Babson Pipe Company who sued them in Texas, not Noble Vista Development. Babson Pipe Company had sued both Galena Pipe Works, Inc., and Noble Vista Development, LLC. Noble had been sued for breach of contract. Galena Pipe Works had been sued for tortious interference with a business relationship. They knew that Brock and Harry probably collaborated on the whole thing, so Noble was probably just sued to get the case tried in Amarillo rather than Galena. Harry could concoct a settlement with Noble and let them out of the suit at some point, then just go after Galena Pipe Works. An Amarillo jury might be inclined to punish the Illinois company for causing all the trouble.

Paul was at the newspaper office that morning when Nate tracked him down to tell him about it. He headed to the law office right away and Ann took advantage of the situation to go with him, smelling a story of some kind.

Nate made copies of the suit for everyone, even Ann since she could get a copy from the courthouse in Texas anyway if she wanted to. Everyone found a place around the conference table to sit down and read it more than once. Then Nate said, "Paul, I think we all see what Harry has done here. But since it is a Texas lawsuit, why don't you lay it out for us?"

"First, though, Ann. Trust me that I am not intending to be rude or to suggest that we don't trust you. You obviously need to put something about this in the paper. Galena Pipe has been sued in Texas, and it is a large employer here. You have no choice. So, unless Paul or Josh disagrees with me, I am fine with you staying here while Paul goes through the pleadings with us and lays out the basis of the claim. But after that, we are going to get into confidential discussions with Galena Pipe, and we should not have anyone else here. There is an important reason. You are not a party to the case or a lawyer in the case. As a third party, you could be made to testify as to our discussions, and there is nothing we could do to keep you from having to testify. That would make us look like very dumb lawyers. Is that okay, Ann?"

"Absolutely. I appreciate being allowed to hear just what

Paul says about the lawsuit. And I will not put anything in the paper without letting you see it first."

"That sounds good. Paul, you are up."

Paul had been taking notes. He looked up and explained. "The tortious interference allegation refers to Harry's claim that Babson had a signed binding contract to make pipes for Noble Vista Development, which Galena Pipe interfered with. Harry alleges that Galena Pipe somehow learned about the contract Babson had, then connived somehow to get a copy of it and stole the contract from Babson. He claims that Babson had already started making the special pipes for Noble. But Galena Pipe contacted Noble and ran down Babson in order to take the business from them. They supposedly called Babson "unreliable" and on the edge of failure, and said that Babson turned out substandard pipes. And supposedly said that Babson was always getting sued by its customers. So, the claim is that Galena Pipe succeeded in stealing the contract, leaving Babson with a lot of specially manufactured pipes it had already made and had ready to ship. Babson claims the pipes had no other market because of the special joints. So, Babson is stuck with them. Babson says it was harmed by the lost profits from the contract, from the value of the pipes it was stuck with, and from the loss of future business Noble had offered them in Lubbock and other cities."

Nate said, "Complete bullshit, but it sounds good. Okay, we need to talk about how we are going to make this lying bastard pay. He is setting this up to hit Galena Pipe with heavy damages. He thinks Amarillo will be a good forum, especially when he drops Noble as a defendant and they get on his side. Brock will lie and support him. The big thing Harry is after is punitive damages. Big ones. He wants to make a jury mad at Galena Pipe and make them anxious to punish an out-of-state company for tricking Noble Vista Development. So finally, we have an answer to the question of what Harry is up to. If he succeeds in getting a big judgment, he can use it to go after

Galena Pipe's assets and maybe negotiate to take it over. Just what he has wanted all along."

To Ann, he said, "I think this is probably where you need to leave us to ourselves. I won't tell you what to write about the suit. But my thinking is that less is better. I would really appreciate seeing what you write before it is in the paper. If you write it up the way the pleadings sound, it makes Galena Pipe look crooked. And that isn't true or fair. We won't try to tie your hands. But maybe we can help you report fairly and honestly without some of the nasty accusations the suit makes."

Ann agreed. After she left, they started brainstorming ideas. Josh spoke first, "Paul, I think the ball is in your court now. We are playing Texas court rules. How long do we have to respond to this?"

"Thirty days. But I always like to respond as quickly as possible. It makes them think I wasn't caught off guard. We should file an answer right off. Then start discovery. We will use interrogatories, requests for admissions, requests for documents and depositions. All of it. This suit was filed by an attorney in Lubbock. I need to call on my friend Henry Melton. He will know something about the Lubbock lawyer Harry is using."

"Tell me a little about Melton, Paul," said Nate. "We may want to retain him as a co-counsel for you. He is closer to Amarillo and could make some appearances for us. It wouldn't be practical for you to be flying back and forth every time they set a hearing. They could wear us down like that."

"I agree, Nate. Let me tell you about Henry. He's smart and not somebody to be intimidated or pushed around. He's one of a handful of Black lawyers in Lubbock. He grew up there, went to school there, and has family and friends there. When we graduated from law school, he wanted to go back home to practice law. But none of the local firms would talk to him. And according to Henry, the DA "already had a Black guy." Henry was persistent, though, and the DA finally gave in. For a while, he had two Black guys. Henry worked there for a couple of years, then did what all new law school graduates are told not to do. He rented an office and hung up a shingle all by himself, with no clients. Dumb thing to do, but Henry made it work. The local lawyers ignored him in the beginning, and the judges treated him as a novelty. Henry was not seasoned in civil practice and wasn't taken seriously. He had no mentors. But he worked twice as hard as anyone else and didn't back down to anyone. Eventually, there were some older lawyers in town who came to respect him for his tenacity. They took him under their wings and made themselves available to him when he was stumped. After a few years, he was accepted. He has had offers to join one of the larger firms, but he has no interest. Henry is at his best against the big firms. Opposing them gets his juices going. He has one or two associates now and has enough business to hire more. If we want to be aggressive and jump on this thing hard and fast, we should fly him up here and see if he is interested. But it is not my money we are playing with."

That is what Nate wanted to hear. "Paul, money for attorneys and court costs is not going to be an issue here. Vernon may cry about revenue because his wife will never know how much is enough. But Galena Pipe Works is still strong financially. Josh and I have learned over the years that trying lawsuits on a shoestring ends up costing more than putting resources into them at the start. Like you said, we need to jump hard and fast. Josh and I have always had *carte blanche* when it comes to these decisions. Frieda and Martha control all of the votes except for Vernon and Tommy, apparently. So we don't need to worry about our client not being able to fund a battle. Can you call him and see if he is interested?"

Paul walked over to the telephone and punched in Henry's number.

"Henry Melton, how can I help you?"

"Henry, it's Paul. How is life in Lubbock these days? Texas Tech find a defense yet?"

"Who needs a defense if you pass the ball four hundred yards every game? How are you, buddy? Wounds all healed?"

"Yup. I'm as beautiful as ever. I called to thank you for setting me up with Roger Pace. He's a stand-up guy."

"Sure is. Maybe not good enough to keep you from getting your ass kicked, but who would be?"

"No argument. The other reason I called you is to see if your outstanding legal skills are available for hire."

"They could be if you can afford me."

"Me? No chance. But we have a client who can. I'm here with two esteemed legal practitioners I seem to have fallen in with. Joshua and Nathan Walker. I'll put them on the speaker so that they can explain this once-in-a-lifetime opportunity to you. Is that okay?"

"I would enjoy talking to them. And I am open to working with you guys as long as it doesn't involve taking a beating like the one you got. I charge extra for that."

During a long conversation, the Walkers and Henry hit it off well, and Henry took a strong interest in the case. He was quite familiar with the lawyer, Jeffery B. Clements, III, who filed the Babson lawsuit against Galena Pipe Works. Clemments had several partners; Henry had fought with them over the years. They were competent and experienced. But they were not choosy about who they represented and were not above filing suits that were more nuisance than substance. He was glad the case was filed in the district court, where Nancy Harris was the presiding judge. Judge Harris was the oldest judge in the county and the most respected. She had been an excellent trial lawyer for twenty-five years before being elected to the bench. That gave her insight into the challenges of the trial lawyers who appeared in front of her. She had seen every underhanded trick a lawyer could play on an opponent and didn't put up with them. Henry had tried a case before her and had found her to be congenial, fair, and respectful to the parties and their lawyers. If you play it straight in her court, you are rewarded for it. If you don't, you regret it. The Walkers agreed to make arrangements for Henry to fly to Chicago on Monday. They would arrange for his airfare and rental car. He would drive to Stockton to meet them. In the meantime, he would send someone to the courthouse to pick up a copy of the court file so he could read it.

CHAPTER 34

Monday, February 13, 1989

Josh and Nate got to the office at six o'clock Monday morning. Just after eight o'clock, Nate got a telephone call from the Galena fire chief, Carl Kraus. He asked if he could come by the office in Stockton with Fred Bingham, the arson investigator. They showed up about forty-five minutes later and took seats in the conference room.

"Nate," Carl said. "The lab work is finished at OSFM. Fred and I have questions about one of the employees over at Galena Pipe. We could discuss Vernon with him, but Vernon is not as open with us as we would like. He seems to have a whole lot on his mind, and the fire isn't foremost from what we can tell. Anyway, you and Josh know those people at the pipe works as well as anyone. Hope you don't mind us asking you some questions."

"Hell no, Carl. We have some thoughts ourselves, and we want to know what you guys are thinking. Who is the employee?"

"Tommy Schumann. From what we know, there were only two people in the plant between seven o'clock and ten o'clock when OSFH thinks the pipe might have been tampered with. One of them was Benny Vaughn, the night watchman. He was not the one who was there when the fire started. But he was there when we think the pipe was damaged to start a slow leak. Tommy was the only other one there during that period. We have trouble seeing Benny Vaughn as someone who would tamper with the pipe to cause a gas leak, not knowing how long it would take to cause an explosion. For all he would know, the whole plant could have blown up while he was still there. We have checked him out, but we don't see anything in his background that makes him a suspect, and we don't know what motive he could have had. Unless, I guess, he was being paid by someone to do it. But even then, he couldn't be sure he would be gone when the blast came. I just can't see that. Can either of you?"

"Not in a million years. Benny is the last guy who would do that. We have known him for years. And Melvin Singer, the guard who relieved him when he went off duty, would not have been there during the time you think the leak was caused. He was there later, when the blast occurred."

"Well, that kind of leaves Tommy Schumann, then, doesn't it? What do you guys think?"

Nate responded. "We don't know Tommy that well. He moved up to plant manager after Vernon Sr. died and Vernon Jr. took over. Vernon was high on him, and I guess he does a pretty good job, but he likes to take a lot of unearned credit, from what I gather. At least that is the reputation he has. I think he is bright enough and young enough to have ambitions. There isn't much of a career path for him at Galena Pipe if that is what he is looking for. But I don't know if a fire in the plant would do anything to help him with that. To be honest, Josh and I have suspicions about him too. Our suspicions don't relate directly to the fire but to a friendly relationship at a competitor company in Beloit. Now, Carl, that is pure speculation on our part, and we have nothing solid to base it on. So, you can't rely on that. All you have to make him the primary suspect is that he could have been there when the gas leak was caused."

"That's right," Carl replied. "He was there during that time span. Why, though? Why, at that time on a Sunday night, was he at the plant? He says he came in late on a Sunday night to pick up timecards. That just seems odd. We talked to the payroll girl, and she said it was unusual. Normally, he turns in the timecards on Friday. We also talked to Melvin and the other guard, Benny. Neither of them can remember Tommy ever coming in on a weekend night before. We want to talk to him again and see how he reacts."

"Carl, I may as well tell you this. The other matter I mentioned that concerns us about Tommy has to do with a contract. There is a lawsuit involved with that contract, and we can't go into much depth with you about it. But generally, the suit revolves around a copy of the contract that belonged to a different company, a competitor. Galena Pipe should not have had a copy of that contract. It belonged to Babson Pipe Company in Beloit. Vernon tells us the copy of that contract, which they should not have had, was brought to him by Tommy. We have confirmed that. Tommy says it was given to him in secret by an employee at Babson Pipe. He didn't want to divulge the name of the employee who gave it to him. We had to press him hard until he came up with the name of Norton Jensing, the plant manager at Babson Pipe. We don't think he was telling the truth. It seemed to us that he was making it up. But we didn't press him further because we didn't want to make him suspicious. When Fred talks to him, it might just shake him up. Fred is an official of the state of Illinois. Lying to Josh and me is one thing. Lying to Fred ups the stakes considerably. That could be helpful. Do you think you might pry into where he got the contract without letting him know we said anything to you about it? It conceivably could be related to the fire. The damage to Galena Pipe's plant could benefit Babson Pipe."

Fred Bingham spoke up for the first time. "It can't hurt to

inquire about the contract since it could be related to the fire. Lying to a state arson investigator in the midst of an arson investigation is a crime. I will give him that information in the form of a standard disclosure, like it is a requirement for me. But arson is still just a theory here. I think it is a good one, but the arson lab isn't going to call it that without more than what they have."

Carl and Fred drove to Galena and interviewed several employees to create the fiction that they were not centering in on Tommy. Then they interviewed Tommy and hinted that it looked like arson, but that was confidential and not many people knew, so he shouldn't mention it to anyone. Tommy stayed pretty cool until they started asking about the contract. Then he was flustered. He asked what that had to do with the fire. They told him it was probably not connected, but they have to comb through everything when they do an investigation into a possible felony. He finally named Norton Jensing again, but said that they shouldn't get into that because it wouldn't have anything to do with a fire, and he had promised Norton he would not tell anyone about it.

After the interview, Carl called Nate to fill him in. "Nate, Schumann was shaken when Fred homed in on the contract. Wow! There is something going on with that. I don't know if it has anything to do with the fire, but I think Tommy is going to have some sleepless nights. Have you thought about contacting this Norton guy to see what he has to say?"

"Wish I could. But I can't because we are involved in litigation with that company, and I can only communicate with their employees through their attorney. We can probably take his deposition when things are farther along in the lawsuit. Thanks for planting that in Tommy's head."

CHAPTER 35

Tuesday, February 21, 1989

enry Melton took the first flight of the day out of
Lubbock, changed planes at DFW, got to Chicago
by nine-thirty, picked up his rental car, and got to
Stockton at one o'clock in the afternoon. Both Walkers
and Paul were in Nate's office when he got there. He was not
what the Walkers had expected. This was the tough fighter
Paul had advertised. They were expecting six feet four inches,
two hundred fifty pounds. But what they got was five feet
seven inches and one hundred forty-five pounds dripping wet,
with horn-rimmed glasses and lenses as thick as a
windowpane. But Henry had a broad smile and a confident
stride—just what the Walkers liked. They often said that they
didn't mind going against the large, imposing lawyers. They
were used to having a step up on the other guy and thought
they didn't have to do a lot to dominate their opponent. It was
the little guys who always scared them. They would nip at you
until you couldn't take it anymore because that's how they
have always lived their lives. Hell yes, thought Josh. God gave
us David to slay Goliath. He was a small Black man with

glasses who had fought his way through everything that had been thrown at him.

Henry had stopped for lunch on the way to Stockton, and they had eaten as well, so they spent time sitting around and getting to know each other. By the end of the day, they might have been friends for years. They covered the broad outlines of the two lawsuits—both the one Henry would assist with in Texas and the suit they would work on in Illinois. Different cases but intertwined. Henry would need to know what was going on in Illinois since some of the same parties and issues were involved in Texas. But they decided to hold off getting deep into strategy until the next day, when they would move to the office in Galena. At six o'clock, they broke off to take him to dinner at the local restaurant and get him checked into his room. Henry noticed that they couldn't get through dinner without people coming up to their table to talk and joke with the Walkers. They were popular around town, and they introduced Paul and him to everyone they talked to. In Henry's mind, that spoke well of them.

The next morning, they met at seven o'clock and drove to Galena. Henry knew nothing about the area, so the Walkers gave him a short tour. He thought the town was a gem, and he vowed to come back with his family someday to explore it thoroughly. The Walkers offered to play hosts if they ever made the trip.

By nine-thirty, they had shown him around the courthouse and were sitting at a table in the law office. They put the Illinois suit aside and concentrated solely on the Texas suit. Everyone had copies of the pleadings. The lawyer shown on the original petition filed by Babson Pipe was Jeffery B. Clements, III. They had discussed him during their telephone conference with Henry before he came to Stockton. But the pleadings Henry had picked up in Amarillo before coming to Stockton included something new. There was a withdrawal of counsel filed by Clements and the substitution of another lawyer. It is unusual for a lawyer to file a lawsuit and ask to be recused from the case before doing anything else. Nothing in the file explained the reason for the recusal. Henry wondered why Clements had asked to be removed from the case. He would make a few calls and see if he could find out anything.

The lawyer representing Babson now was Nolan Shy, also from Lubbock. Henry knew him. They had met at the local bar luncheon. Nolan Shy had been an in-house lawyer for a small payday loan company with offices in several Texas towns, primarily close to military bases. But he had left the company to go into private practice in Lubbock. He seemed like a friendly guy, but Henry didn't think he had developed much of a practice yet. And he didn't think Shy had become a seasoned litigator. He seemed like an odd choice for a case that could get complicated and intense. But sometimes a lawyer wants the business so badly that he doesn't ask a lot of questions. The pleadings had already been drafted and filed before he took over so he hadn't had to do anything yet. They wondered if Shy had a grasp on the facts of the case or if he only knew what he read in the pleadings.

The suit itself was premised on lies if Vernon could be believed. Vernon had no business contacting Noble Vista Development in the first place and he was at fault for doing that. But they believed that he thought the contract with Babson had never been signed. Most likely, Brock had told him that.

It was time they brought Vernon in to meet Henry. It would be cumbersome for them to have to communicate through Nate or Josh.

Josh introduced them to each other. Then he asked, "Have you had time to read this abomination of a pleading that Harry Townsend's lawyer filed? Is there anything to it?"

"Anything to it? No, Josh. Hell, no. Believe me. Yes, I called Brock Johnson, and I wanted to get the deal Harry was trying to get. But Brock told me he did not yet have a deal with Babson. No signed contract. That is what he said, and I had no reason to think he was lying. And I didn't say all those things about Babson Pipe. I may have said we could perform better and beat the price. That's all. This is a crock."

"Vernon, tell us again how you came to know about this contract," said Josh.

"Like I said, Josh. Tommy Schumann brought it to me. He had told me before about Harry Townsend bragging about the sweet contract he had. I heard it from other people, too. Then he brought it to me and said he got it from an employee at Babson. He wouldn't tell me who."

"You say you heard it from other people. Who were they? Think about it."

"Off hand, I know I heard it from Monte Boone. You remember. He worked at the plant for years and retired. In fact, he owns a couple shares of stock. I see him sometimes around town. And I know I heard it from Tony Butler. He owns the company where we buy all of our rebar for the giant pipes. Uh. . . Wally Peterson, where we bank. I talk to him all the time. I can probably come up with some more. I heard it from some others, I think."

"Would you say that Tommy knows all those people?"

"Oh, sure. He has contact with Tony Butler on a regular basis, and he talks to everyone at the bank. He knows Monte Boone, too. Whether he has much contact with him, I don't know."

"Vernon, Babson Pipe Company has been around a long time. Kind of like Galena Pipe Works. I'm sure you or your father must have met many of the people over there. What can you tell us about them?"

Vernon had to think about it. "Honestly, Josh, I never got to know anyone there. Dad knew most of them. He knew Arnold Babson, who built the company up from nothing. Dad liked him and said he ran a good company. When he died and Curt Babson took over, it all came apart. Curt spent it into the ground. That's how Townsend got control of it. I don't know Curt, but I have heard from people that he isn't involved much now, and he hates Townsend but can't do anything about it. He is a minority shareholder, and that is about all."

"What about the plant manager? Who is that?"

"His name is Norton Jensing. He had already been there a long time when Arnold was living. So, he is probably older than Townsend. But I don't think I ever met him."

"Has Tommy ever mentioned him or anyone else at Babson?"

"Not to me. Why?"

"No reason. I just know that sometimes people in the same kind of work get to know each other. Tommy got that contract from somebody, and he wouldn't tell you who it was. Then he said it was Norton Jensing. I guess that's about all we have to ask you. Thanks for coming over."

After Vernon left, Nate said he was going to see if he could get in touch with Monte Boone, Tony Butler, and Wally Peterson. He knew Monte, and he knew the banker, Wally Peterson. Somehow, he would figure out a way to talk to Tony Butler, but that would be a little difficult. What he wanted to know was who told them that Babson had a big order in Texas and that Harry was bragging about it. He surmised it was Tommy.

Next, they got back to the two lawsuits. They may as well get some discovery going. Bill Turl was supposedly handling the suit in Galena. Nate and Josh would oversee that one. They would start working up some discovery requests and motions just to have them ready. Then they would coordinate with Paul and Henry before they hit Noble with anything. It would be good if they cranked things up on that suit at the same time Paul and Henry served a lot of paper on Noble and Babson in the Texas suit. The idea would be to overwhelm Bill Turl. They saw Turl and Brock Johnson as weak links. In the meantime, while they were waiting to get the discovery rolling, they would give Turl a call to talk to him about scheduling the case and give him something to think about.

The real battle would be with Harry Townsend. Nate and

Josh gathered up their paperwork and notes and went back to their offices, leaving Paul and Henry in the conference room to talk about dividing up the work they would be doing. Nate left to go to the bank. He wanted to bump into Wally Peterson and casually ask him how he learned about the Texas business Harry was bragging about. While he was doing that, Josh was going to call Monte Boone to ask him the same thing.

When Nate got to the bank, he wandered around for a while, visiting with friends and keeping an eye out for Wally. Eventually, he walked over to Wally's secretary and asked if Wally was busy. She called him on the intercom, and he told her to send Nate back.

Wally greeted Nate like an old friend. Nate had done work for the bank over the years. "Well, hello, Nate. Good to see you. How is Josh doing?"

"No better, Wally. He is as ornery as ever. I was in the area, so I just stopped by to see if our money was still safe. You do keep it all locked up, I hope."

"Oh, yes, Nate. We post special guards over your and Joshua's money twenty-four hours a day. Not to worry."

They visited about business and family, and then Nate finally got around to what he was there for. Wally had seen the article in the *Stockton Herald* about the lawsuit in Texas, and Nate assured him it was a silly attempt to get out of paying money owed to Galena Pipe.

"It's nonsense, Wally, but these days people file nuisance lawsuits trying to get money in a settlement. That won't happen. By the way, that made me think of something. Vernon Tanksley mentioned to me that you had said something to him a while back about Babson Pipe having this big deal lined up in Texas, and they had been bragging about it."

"I remember. That is what I had heard, and I did mention it to Vernon when I saw him. I didn't know if there was anything to it. I don't know those guys over in South Beloit. I was just telling him what I heard."

"Damn. Those guys must have been doing a whole lot of braying about it if you heard about it way over here in Galena."

"No, not me. The person I heard it from works at Galena Pipe. A young fellow, Tommy Schumann. I know his parents over in Warren. He was here doing some business, and we got talking. He brought it up after I told him I might see him later at the plant. I had a meeting that afternoon with Vernon."

"Huh. I wonder how he knew about it?"

"He didn't say. I figure those guys in the pipe business probably all know each other. It's that way in banking. Hell, I know every banker from Dubuque, Iowa, to Rockford."

"Sure. Same with lawyers. Well, good seeing you again. I need to get back."

While Nate was at the bank, Josh was on the telephone with Monte Boone. Monte had heard about Babson's big Texas deal from Tommy Schumann when he had dropped by the plant to see some of his old friends and to talk to Vernon.

Nate returned to the office and compared notes with Josh. "Interesting, isn't it? Tommy just keeps popping up here. He tells Vernon about the Babson Texas deal, and he tells Wally and Monte at a time when he knows they are going to talk to Vernon. What do you want to bet Tommy ran into Tony Butler when Tony was coming to see Vernon one day? I don't think we even need to call him. There is a pattern."

———

Nate decided to call Bill Turl and see if he might shake him up a little. He called Turl's law office and spoke to the receptionist.

"This is Nate Walker with the Walker Law Firm. May I speak to Bill Turl?"

About thirty seconds later, she put him through.

Bill Turl asked, "Is this Mr. Walker?"

"That's right, and you can call me Nate. It looks like we

will be getting to know each other. I'm just calling to see if we can talk about some scheduling in the Galena Pipe case. Judge Richardson expects the lawyers to work that out informally rather than just sending out discovery notices without any warning. Max was always that way when he was practicing law, too. He's a good judge and respectful. I think you will like him. But do you have local Illinois counsel? You are only licensed in Texas, correct?"

"I don't have local counsel yet. I don't think I need to since I only made a special appearance. An Illinois court has no jurisdiction to start with and I don't know what made you think you could sue my client there."

"Of course, that is why there will be a hearing. Judge Richardson will decide whether he thinks jurisdiction is proper in Illinois. He may say no. Or he may say yes. In that case, you will appeal it. But unless he tosses it out at the first hearing, I think you are going to need local counsel."

"I think you are wasting everyone's time. You ought to concentrate on the suit Babson Pipe has filed in Texas."

"Yes. In fact, we have two Texas litigators retained to work on that one. Paul Hoffman, who is up here with us now. And Henry Melton, out of Lubbock. He thinks he may have met you in Amarillo. But he is not sure. Who are you going to use?"

"Nolan Shy in Lubbock."

"Nolan Shy! Wait. He is representing Babson. They are suing your client! And you are on the board of Noble Vista Development. How can you be using him?"

"No… Umm… I don't mean *we* are using him. I misspoke. Of course not. He is Babson's lawyer. I will represent Noble Vista Development here. I misunderstood you."

"You sure had me going there for a moment. It's not like Noble Vista Development and Babson Pipe are aligned together, right? That would be very strange. Okay, well, you will probably be talking to Paul or Henry about that suit. By the way, do you know how Nolan Shy got involved? Babson started out with Jeffery Clements, then they jumped lawyers right after he had filed the lawsuit for them. That seems really odd."

"Mr. Walker … Nate, I have no idea why Babson changed lawyers or anything about what they are doing in this lawsuit. How would I? Obviously, I can't talk to them directly since they have sued Noble."

"Getting back to the suit up here, Bill, why don't you think about a good time for a hearing on your special appearance, and let me know. My calendar is pretty open. I don't think the docket is crowded, so I think the court will be accommodating. I still think you ought to have local counsel and make your appearance *pro hac vice*." But that is your call."

"Is that it, Mr. Walker?"

"I think so, Bill. I look forward to meeting you."

———

When the workday was over, the four lawyers drove back to Stockton and sat down in the conference room there to pour drinks and "strike a blow for liberty", as the Walkers called it.

Josh talked about what Monte Boone and Wally Peterson had to say. All the gossip about Babson's Texas deal went from Tommy Schumann to them and from them to Vernon. Neither of them heard it from another source. Tommy planted it for Vernon to hear. He was looking worse all the time.

Then Nate told them about his call to Turl. "This deal down in Texas is really suspicious, guys. Listen to this. Noble Vista Development is being sued by Babson and us, right? Turl is Noble's lawyer, and he is on their board of directors. So I asked him, just messing around, who would represent Noble in the Texas suit. He quickly said, 'Nolan Shy.' But that's Babson's lawyer! Shy is suing Noble. He can't sue Noble and represent Noble at the same time! When I caught him at that, he was completely flustered and said he misspoke. He would represent Noble in the case. But he didn't misspeak, and he didn't misunderstand me either. I'm telling you these Noble guys are in bed with Harry Townsend. Babson and Noble are aligned. I don't know how, but they are in cahoots and that's why he thinks of Babson's lawyer as being Noble's lawyer, too."

After they took Henry to dinner, they took him back to his motel. He wanted to get an early start to the airport the next day. They would not see him again on this trip.

CHAPTER 36

Wednesday, March 1, 1989

As soon as he got to the office, Turl called Brock to tell him that Nate Walker had called to talk about scheduling a hearing and discovery in the Illinois case, and Nate had pressed him about not being licensed in Illinois. Turl was tired of this whole thing, which was all the fault of Harry and Brock for making a shady deal. Turl was sorry he had agreed to be a director of the company, and he wanted off the board now. His partners were putting the heat on him. Brock wasn't paying the fees owed to the law firm, and now Turl was spending even more valuable time on the mess.

Brock told him this would be a bad time for him to do that. It would look like he was afraid and was abandoning ship. Besides, he was a director when the whole thing started, so it would do no good to get off the board now. Brock wanted to call Harry to see if he would front some of the fees for Noble, but Harry had told them never to call him. So, he decided they should call Bernie Torveski instead.

When Bill arrived, Brock dialed Bernie's number and put the call on the speakerphone.

"Hello. Who is this?"

"Bernie? Bernie Torveski?"

"Yeah. Who's this?"

"Brock Johnson. Bill Turl is with me on the speakerphone. We need to talk to you and Harry."

"Yeah? Well, I gotta get him out of jail first. The moron!"

"Jail? Did you say you were getting Harry out of jail? Geez! What's he doing in jail?"

"He got caught on one of those private security cameras. The cops came and arrested him for vandalism. So I gotta get down there and bail his ass out. It has to do with shooting some guy's windows out with a slingshot. Apparently more than once."

It got very quiet on the Amarillo side of the call.

"So, anyway, I'll get him out and see if he wants to talk to you. This is piddly shit. I'm thinking maybe we pay the guy a little, and he agrees to a restraining order. Best he can do, probably." Bernie hung up the phone without so much as a goodbye.

Bill Turl got up and began pacing. "Can this shit get any deeper? Let's call Nolan Shy and go talk to him."

When Brock called Nolan Shy's office, he was put on hold. The receptionist came back and told him that Mr. Shy could not talk directly to him since he was on the other side of a lawsuit from his client. But if he was accompanied by his lawyer, he could talk to the lawyer. They made an appointment to meet with him at ten o'clock the next day.

Thursday morning, Brock and Bill arrived at Nolan Shy's office a few minutes early. It wasn't a fancy office. The reception area was small, and the furniture was cheap. The receptionist was a plump, friendly woman in her fifties. She offered them both coffee and brought it to them. After about ten minutes, she led them back to the lawyers' offices. There appeared to be three offices, but one was not being used. The furniture in Nolan's office and in the conference room was not much better than what was in the reception area.

Nolan was a tall, thin man in his late forties, with glasses and a bad combover. They visited briefly, and Bill learned that Shy had opened his office in Lubbock seven years ago because his wife had grown up in Lubbock and her family lived there. Nolan had one associate attorney. It sounded like most of Nolan's work was with car accidents and collections. When they got around to the Babson case, Bill said that Harry Townsend had told him to go through Nolan Shy or Bernie Torveski if he needed anything. He explained that he didn't have much luck talking to Bernie because Bernie was getting Harry out of jail when he called. He had not originally planned on saying that, but he kind of wanted to see Nolan's reaction. It wasn't what he expected. Nolan didn't ask any questions about it. It was almost as if he had not heard what Bill had told him.

Nolan was getting uncomfortable. "You know, Bill, this is a little unusual. No disrespect to Brock, but I'm not used to having the opposing party in the room when I talk to his lawyer."

Bill had to laugh at that. "There is nothing you can say to me that you can't say in front of Brock. Are you even aware that while Brock is the president of Noble, I am on the board of directors? You could say I am an opposing attorney, and I am also the opposing party. How much have you been told about the suit against Noble Vista Development and about our connection to Harry?"

"I don't know anything about that. What do you mean, your connection?"

"What I mean is that we are not really being sued for anything, regardless of what the pleadings say. We are just named as a defendant to establish jurisdiction and venue in Amarillo. Truth is, we are on the same side as you. Down the line, we will be dropped from the suit."

"Oh, yeah? That's sure news to me. When do you think your magical dismissal from the suit will occur?"

"Nolan, like everything else in this screwed-up mess, it will happen when Harry says it should. And I think you need to get straight with Harry Townsend and Mr. Bernie Torveski about what will trigger it to happen."

Now, Nolan was visibly upset. "I don't have a clue what you are talking about. Look, I think we are getting into areas here that a plaintiff's attorney should not be discussing with a defendant's attorney, especially in front of a defendant in the suit. I've never heard of a situation like this in all my time practicing law. This meeting is over."

Bill and Brock just sat there stunned. Finally, Bill spoke up. "If you think you have never heard of THIS situation, you had better buckle your seatbelt, Nolan, because Harry has more surprises for you than Santa on Christmas morning. We can find the door."

Bill and Brock left and picked up one of Nolan's business cards on the way out of the reception area.

"Cheap printing", said Bill.

CHAPTER 37

Saturday, March 4, 1989

Shirley Howard, Mel Howard's widow, called the newspaper office Saturday morning. When Ann answered the phone, she was a little surprised.

"Ann, this is Shirley Howard. My, you must work all the time and take no time off. I didn't really expect to find you at the paper, but I took a chance."

"I do get some downtime, but Dad was always here on Saturday mornings, and I guess I got that from him. How are you?"

"Oh, I'm fine, Ann. The kids and grandkids are coming to town later today, and they will stay until Monday. So it's going to be a real nice weekend for me. I don't mean to bother you with this, but I called you because I know you are friends with that nice young man, Paul Hoffman. He came to talk to me a while back and asked me a question I couldn't answer then. But now something has jogged my memory, and I would like him to know what I remembered. Will you be seeing him soon? If so, I could tell you, and you could pass it along to him. I'm kind of busy getting the house ready for guests."

"Yes, I will probably run into him tonight or tomorrow. I am happy to give him the information."

"Oh, thank you. Well, I was telling him something about a man who was a representative of the Ford Motor Company when Mel was a dealer. He used to drop in on Mel from time to time, and Mel often talked about him. But I couldn't recall the name until I read your news story about that Galena Pipe business in the paper a few weeks ago. It came back to me because someone in the news story happened to have the same name! The name was Harry Townsend. Not the same person, probably, because the one in the story had a pipe company, and the one Mel knew just worked for Ford. I remember the name though, because Mel described that Harry Townsend as a great big, burly guy. And, I shouldn't say this, but I pictured him as hairy. You know, like a hairy ape, because Mel didn't like him. So, that is what I hope you will tell Mr. Hoffman for me. I should have called you when I read the article, but I got busy and forgot about it until this morning."

"You sound certain of the name, Shirley. I will definitely give Mr. Hoffman that information when I see him. I'm sure he will appreciate it. Call me anytime if you remember anything else. And I hope you have a wonderful weekend with your family."

"Thank you, Ann."

By absolute coincidence, Ann was going to be seeing Mr. Hoffman that very evening for a drive to Freeport in a red Corvette and dinner at the only Italian restaurant anywhere near Stockton. Ann waited until they were sipping their wine and waiting for the pasta before telling Paul about the call from Shirley Howard.

"I got a call at the office this morning from Shirley Howard. She said that when she talked with you at her house, you wanted to know the name of the Ford representative who used to call on Mel when he was a Ford dealer."

"Wow. That was nice of her. She couldn't remember it

when I was there, although her memory about the day of the murder was very complete. But names are hard to remember sometimes. Did it just come to her out of the blue?"

"No. What triggered it was the story I printed in the *Herald* a few weeks ago about the Galena Pipe lawsuit. It turns out that the Ford representative had the same name as Harry Townsend. She said that was his name exactly. It all came back when she read the news story. But she did not get around to calling me about it until this morning. See how valuable newspapers are to people? It's a wonder we don't get more credit. Don't you agree?"

Paul hesitated before talking. "Oh, definitely. Not nearly enough credit … Harry Townsend, huh? Well, the name is not so unusual. There must be a lot of people named Harry and a lot of people named Townsend around Chicago. Probably a coincidence, but interesting."

Actually, it was a whole lot more interesting to Paul than he let on.

"Why did you want to know?"

"Oh, you know. I had been talking to people who were around back then and Mel was deceased, so I talked to Shirley. Mel knew Dad about as well as anyone, and Mrs. Howard mentioned that the Ford guy was in the office with Ed and Mel the morning of the deaths. Just curiosity."

CHAPTER 38

Monday, March 6, 1989

Bill Turl hadn't gained anything from the meeting with Nolan Shy. They couldn't just sit by and do nothing. They had to get something filed in the Amarillo lawsuit, the one where they had been sued by Babson Pipe, for God's sake. Harry had promised to dismiss them eventually, but Harry said a lot of things, and Nolan was apparently not in on that strategy. No telling what Harry would do if they didn't answer the suit. They were all supposed to be in this thing together, then Harry sued them and said, "Don't worry." Well, Bill was worried, and Brock was worried.

He had at least filed a special appearance in the Galena Pipe suit, so that would keep Galena Pipe from trying to get a default judgment against Noble. But Nate Walker was pushing him. He needed to get on that case but he wasn't licensed in Illinois. Bernie Torveski was supposed to take that over when he had run out of options. So he needed Bernie to tell him what was going to be done.

He called Brock. Brock hadn't heard from Harry or Bernie or Nolan either. He told Brock he was going to call Bernie again and if he did not talk to him by the afternoon, he was going to file an answer in that suit just to keep Harry from stabbing them in the back and getting a default judgment against Noble for failing to answer the suit.

He telephoned Bernie at nine-thirty and, to his surprise, Bernie answered the phone.

"Yeah? Who's this?"

"Bernie, it's Bill Turl in Amarillo."

"What do ya need, Turl?"

"A couple of things. First, I am going to file a general denial in the suit Babson filed against us in Amarillo. You know, the one where Harry, for God's sake, sued Noble Vista Development, who, if I understand it, he is supposed to be working with."

"Yeah, sure. You could file it. What else?"

"Well, we need to have a strategy session on it. Harry said you would be dismissing us from the suit. When will that be, or what will trigger it?"

"Bill, we gotta make sure we have jurisdiction locked down in Texas before we let you guys out. Galena Pipe objected to jurisdiction when they filed their answer, so we have to wait until the court throws that out. We gotta wait."

"Fine. I still want to know what the whole plan is after that. But right now, the big problem is that I filed the special appearance in the suit up in Galena, then their lawyer called wanting to schedule a hearing. Nate Walker. Do you know him?"

"I know who he is. His brother Joshua is the real hothead, though. He's got a short fuse, that guy. Those guys went to Cicero to meet Harry one day. Harry thought the bastard was going to jump over his desk and attack him! And the guy is half Harry's weight. So, what do you want to do on that case?"

"I think it's time for you to step in. I'm not licensed in Illinois, and it's going to heat up. I don't see how I can do anything when it gets to a hearing or discovery."

"No problem. You can stay on it. I'll send you the Illinois

rule and application for appearing *pro hac vice*. I'll sign as your Illinois verifying attorney, and you can do anything in this one case, just like you were licensed here. The filing fee is just a couple hundred bucks, and it don't take long. Then you can handle the discovery from where you are because you know all about Noble, and your office is close by."

"But I can't physically go to court in Galena for a hearing. It's not practical, and it's expensive."

"We'll figure it out. I gotta go."

"Damn it, Bernie! We need to talk again after you send me the form. By the way, is Harry out of the clink yet? How the hell did he get into something like that?"

"Oh, yeah. Harry is free as a bird. I sprung him and I'll get something worked out there. It was just kind of a business disagreement. Goodbye."

Bill slapped his forehead, "Son of a bitch! It just keeps getting worse. How do I get loose from this? My partners are going to throw me out!"

While Bill Turl was talking to Bernie, who was in Chicago, Henry Melton was talking to Paul, who was in Galena for the day.

"Paul, this is Henry. I have spent some time on this Babson Pipe file. I think we should file requests for admissions and written interrogatories on both opposing parties, then set depositions. The discovery we do on Noble here may actually turn up some things you can use in the Beloit suit."

"Sounds right. What if I start working on the admission requests and interrogatories for Noble? You can take the ones for Babson. One more thing. When the time comes to take Harry Townsend's deposition, it would be best if you took it instead of me. There was an incident many years ago that may have involved him and a close relative of mine. It may not be the same Harry Townsend but the one involved was from the Chicago area, and the age is about right. It could be him. If so, my name being 'Hoffman' and my being from Stockton could spark a memory for him. There would be nothing wrong with me taking his deposition anyway. But he can be a hard case and there is no use handing him something to bitch about. I may give you some detailed questions to ask when the time comes if you don't mind. The questions would be about his employment history. That's always fair game in a deposition, so it shouldn't raise any suspicions."

"No problem with that. I get into those areas routinely in depositions. I think that's all I have for now. Wait, there is one more thing. Remember that we were wondering why Jeffery Clements got out of the case and Nolan Shy got in? Well, I know a couple of lawyers in Amarillo I have done favors for. I called one of them and asked if they could find out anything about it. He called me back and had some information he got confidentially from a girl who works at the district clerk's office. She told him she was there when Clements came in to file his motion to be recused. He was really pissed off. He had just gotten off the phone with a lawyer for Babson up in Chicago. He had a lot of questions for this lawyer, and the guy wouldn't tell him anything. He had talked to his partners about this case, and they were uncomfortable with it already. So, they decided he should demand a really big retainer. When he got the lawyer for Babson on the phone, Clements asked for the big retainer and this lawyer told him to go screw himself. They would pay fees from itemized bills only after the services were rendered. They got into a shouting match, and Clements hung up on the guy. Then, he went right down to the courthouse and filed the motion for withdrawal. There were no objections from the client, so the judge approved it. Then Nolan Shy filed an appearance for Babson."

"Well, that is interesting. Some lawyer Harry has!"

"I'll say. That's all I have to tell you now. We'll talk later."

———

That same day, there was a call from Carl Kraus to Josh Walker.

"Josh, I got a call this morning from Fred Bingham down at OSFM. I can tell you I was surprised. They are not able to call this fire arson just from the physical and circumstantial evidence they have."

"You are kidding. It really sounded to me like they were going the other direction on it. They are saying it was not arson?"

"No, they don't say it wasn't arson. In fact, they were fairly close to logging it that way. But they just couldn't eliminate another cause with positivity. The gas pipe started it for sure. But the wrench scratches on the pipe could have been put there any time before. Maybe somebody had to tinker with it in the past, maybe more than once, and the weakened joint finally opened up. That is unlikely. But they have to rule out every possibility before they call it arson. The pipe was a bit mangled and twisted, but that could have been from the force of the blast and the debris it was buried under. To bring an arson charge, they can't have doubts. Frankly, they probably think it was arson. I do. But it has to be nailed down completely for them to act. So far, it isn't. If you run across anything helpful, let me know."

"I guess I can understand that. To bring an allegation as serious as arson, they should be sure. Especially in a building where another person could be injured or killed—a security guard for instance."

"I'm glad you understand because Fred Bingham is a good guy, and he really did work hard to find arson. I hate to say this, but fire insurance companies sometimes want to hold up claims on these things. They don't always accept the OSFM rulings. They want to know if it is arson and, if so, is it possible the insured is also the arsonist. For example, is Galena Pipe's claim affected by the fact that it is responsible for the act of an employee who started the fire? You know how they like to stretch out claims."

"That's good insight, Carl. I think the employee would be

acting outside of his duties in that case, but if you guys have heard of it then it isn't out of consideration."

He wondered. Is that good news or bad news? Bad, because they can't prove arson. Or is it good because they can't prove arson? That is how confusing this whole thing had become. When Josh got off the phone, he gathered up Nate and Vernon to tell them what Carl had to say. They met in Vernon's office.

Vernon spoke first. "Josh, that may not be the only problem we have on our claim. Intrepid Commercial Insurance Company, our carrier, is asking for a lot of information. They contacted the fire department records office and asked them to check for any infractions or warnings to our company by the local fire inspectors for the last ten years. They found a warning. I was not even aware of this because it was when Dad ran the company. About six months before Dad died, we got written up for not having a sufficient sprinkler system in the kiln area. Apparently, when we expanded the area, we didn't improve the sprinkler system for the additional square footage and furnace upgrade. The board of directors had a meeting on it because of the expense. The other part of the warning had to do with the smoke alarm, which the report said was too weak and didn't go off everywhere in the plant.

"The board decided to do a full study on it before going any further. But Dad was sick, and I don't think he got a study going. Then he died. Everyone thought somebody else must be working on it. The urgency wasn't there like it should have been because our old system was grandfathered in before a new fire ordinance required upgrades. I only wish I had known about it."

"Who was on the board back then, Vernon?"

"Not me. You guys were on the board, but it doesn't look like you were at any of those meetings. Frieda and Martha were on the board. Jake Sharp, because he was the plant manager at the time and had some stock. One employee was selected by the other employees, and one retired employee was picked by the other retired stockholders. None of them held much stock. It was just something nice Dad tried to do. The director's fees for those who were chosen for the board on a rotating basis were a nice thing for them. I don't remember the names, but that information is in the minutes of the meeting. Do we have to give that to them, Josh?"

"We sure may have to. Whatever you do don't destroy anything. Make copies of everything you have. Nate and I need them. Were there ever any more warnings after you took over running the company?"

"No. Absolutely not. I would have done something."

CHAPTER 39

Wednesday, March 15, 1989

Bernie Torveski sent Bill Turl the application forms he needed to appear in the Illinois case as attorney for Noble Vista Development. Bill reluctantly completed the forms and sent them in with the verifying letter from Bernie and a law firm check for two hundred fifty dollars. Just one more expense out of pocket the firm probably would have to eat. He did nothing else in the case, hoping Nate wouldn't either. At least he could now file pleadings and appear for Noble if he had to.

Nate and Josh took note that Bill seemed intent on handling the Illinois lawsuit without an Illinois attorney. It seemed to them that Torveski could handle the case better himself than Turl could. Turl being out of state really gave them an advantage. They would start serving him with some discovery requests soon.

In the meantime, Paul brought the Walkers up to date on the Texas lawsuit. After filing their answer in the Texas suit, he and Henry had a change in plans. They had decided to be unconventional with their discovery. Nolan Shy didn't seem very well versed in litigation, so they jumped a couple steps ahead by going straight to taking Harry's deposition. Normally, they would go through written interrogatories and requests for admissions first. But they had a feeling that putting pressure on quickly might shake Nolan up. It would add to the impression that they were going to play tough and would have the additional benefit of pissing Harry off. So, they scheduled his deposition right off the bat. Henry would be taking the deposition at his office in Lubbock. They set it for March 15th, and thought Nolan would probably argue about the scheduling. They hadn't even given him sufficient notice. But he let it get by him. He knew Harry would have to come down for a deposition sometime since he was the one who chose to file the suit in Texas. So, he may as well get it over with. It would at least give Nolan a chance to meet his client face-to-face.

Today was deposition day. Nolan had expected Bernie Torveski to accompany Harry to the deposition but it looked like Harry didn't want to spend the extra money. Harry might be a confident person, but Nolan would have felt better if Harry's personal attorney were there with him. The deposition took place as scheduled at nine o'clock.

1   HENRY MELTON: Mr. Townsend. My name is Henry

2   Melton, and I am one of the attorneys in this case representing

3   Galena Pipe Works. The court reporter is Belle Peiyper. Your

4   attorney, Mr. Nolan Shy, is also present, as well as Bill Turl,

5   the attorney for Noble Vista Estates. You have been placed

6   under oath, and you need to know that any intentionally

7   false answers you give could make you subject to perjury

8   prosecution. Do you understand that?

9   HARRY TOWNSEND: Yes.

10 HENRY MELTON: Have you given a deposition before?

11 HARRY TOWNSEND: Oh yes.

12 HENRY MELTON: Good. Then you may remember that

13 Ms. Peiyper cannot record gestures, so you must answer all

14 questions clearly and orally in order for her to hear them.

15 If at any time I confuse you with a question and you need

16 clarification to answer it properly, just tell me so I can rephrase

17 it. Do you understand that?

18 HARRY TOWNSEND: Yes.

19 HENRY MELTON: Are you under any degree of stress or

20 taking any kind of medication that could interfere with your

21 understanding of any questions or prevent you from giving

22 truthful answers?

23 HARRY TOWNSEND: No.

24 HENRY MELTON: Then we will begin.

25 **Q**: What is your full legal name?

26 **A**: Harrold Arnold Townsend.

27 **Q**: What are your home address and office address?

28 **A**: Home is 6932 Bellmont Drive, Skokie, Illinois. Office is

29   1800 East Barden Street, Skokie.

30 **Q**: Are you the president and majory shareholder of Babson

31   Pipe Company, Inc.?

32 **A:** Yes.

33 **Q:** Have you ever been convicted of a felony or any crime

34   of moral turpitude?

35 **A:** Not yet.

Henry interjects. "I will take that as a joke. But you may want to clarify your answer if you care to."

36 **A:** Okay then. It's a joke.

Henry began with his history, including his education and employment from the age of eighteen. Nolan Shy questioned the need for that. Henry cited him the rules for depositions. His was not a valid objection. Then he proceeded. That got him to Harry's job at Ford. Just as Paul had suspected, he was the area representative for the dealers in North Central and Northwest Illinois and Southwestern Wisconsin. That would have included the dealership of Mel Howard in all of 1956. From there, the deposition went into a variety of questions about the ownership of Babson Pipe, the year he had bought his interest, and how he had purchased it. He produced a copy of his most recent financial statements in response to the request for production. They went over all of them, then went on to his first contact with Noble Vista Development and the inception of the pipe contract. He identified a copy of the signed contract along with the specs. They discussed the capacity of Babson Pipe for producing the pipes. He provided the names of other customers he had done business with.

They went into detail about his allegations of interference in the contract by Galena Pipe and the breach and/or interference by Noble. He was asked about all of his conversations with Brock or anyone else at Noble about the contract and the alleged breach. They also covered his attempts to buy out Galena Pipe in a merger and his persistence in contacting Frieda and Martha. Harry admitted that he was angry when they turned him down. Henry questioned him about any and all people he had spoken to about the contract who would know it had been signed by all parties, and asked when it was signed. He asked him to itemize his actual damages from the loss of the contract and how many specially made pipes he had on hand. Harry was unable to give an accurate estimate, but he said it was a very large number, and his attorney agreed to supplement that information.

Then Henry went in a different direction, which seemed to catch Harry by surprise.

———

37 **Q:** Mr. Townsend, when was your last meeting with Tommy

38   Schumann?

39 **A:** Who? Tommy who? Who is that?

40 **Q:** He is the plant manager at Galena Pipe Works.

41 **A:** I don't think I know who that is. Tommy Schulmann?

42 **Q:** No. Tommy Schumann. You met him when you toured

43   the Galena Pipe Works plant on August 4th of last year.

44   He was your guide and you spent considerable time

45   talking with him.

46 **A:** If you say so. I don't remember him.

47 **Q:** But you talked to him after that and met with him. I will

48   repeat the question. When did you last talk with Tommy

49   Schumann and when did you last meet with him?

50 **A:** Never.

51 **Q:** Will you clarify that? Is it your sworn testimony today

52   that you have never spoken to or met with Tommy

53   Schumann since August the fourth of last year?

54 **Q:** (Read by court reporter: Is it your sworn testimony

55   today that you have never spoken to or met with Tommy

56   Schumann since August the fourth of last year?)

57 **Q:** Mr. Townsend, do you understand the question?

58 **A:** Yeah.

(At this point, Nolan Shy interrupted and asked to go off the record.)

Nolan Shy: "There is no relevance here, and the question has been asked and answered. I will instruct Mr. Townsend not to answer your question."

Henry Melton: "Texas rules on depositions make no provision for an objection to questions for relevance, and Mr. Townsend has not answered the question. He will answer, or we will recess this deposition until we get a ruling from Judge Harris in the district court where the case is pending. I will also ask for sanctions. So, let's try this again. Ms. Peiyper, will you please read back the prior question?"

59 **Q:** You are instructed to answer the question. Will you do

60   so now?

61 **A:** I don't remember the guy.

62 **Q:** Is it your testimony that you did not meet with Tommy

63   Schumann or have any conversations with him at any

64   time after August 4th of last year?

65 **A:** Yes. That is what I am saying. I don't know the guy.

66 **Q:** Mr. Townsend, Tommy Schumann came into possession

67 of an unsigned copy of your contract with Noble Vista

68 Development. Did you give him that contract copy?

69 **A:** No. I told you I don't even know who the guy is. You

70 don't listen.

71 **Q:** Did you ask any other person to give an unsigned copy

72 of that contract to Tommy Schumann or Vernon Tanksley,

73 or to any other person associated with Galena Pipe Works?

74 **A:** No.

75 **Q:** Do you know a man named Norton Jensing?

76 **A:** Sure. He runs the plant for us. He works for me.

77 **Q:** Are you aware that he gave a copy of that unsigned

78 contract to Tommy Schumann at a bar in South Beloit?

79 **A:** No.

80 **Q:** Did you ask him to deliver an unsigned copy of the Noble

81 Vista contract to Tommy Schumann or anyone else

82 connected with Galena Pipe Works?

83 **A:** No.

84 **Q:** When did you first become aware of the fire in the kiln at

85 Galena Pipe Works?

86 **A:** I don't know. A couple days later, maybe. I don't remember.

87 **Q:** Do you have any knowledge about the cause of that fire?

88 **A:** Hell no! I don't know what you are getting at. What are

89   you getting at? What are you up to here?

90 **Q:** This is your deposition, Mr. Townsend. You don't get to

91   ask the questions. Now, the pipes you claim to have

92   specially manufactured for Noble Vista Development

93   have tongue and groove joints. Is that correct?

94 **A:** That's right. And nobody else buys them like that from

95   me. So I'm stuck with the damned things now.

96 **Q:** How many did you manufacture?

97 **A:** A couple hundred. I didn't go out and count them before

98   coming down here to listen to you.

99 **Q:** Then is it your testimony today that you still have them

100   on hand?

101 **A:** Yeah. Can't sell them.

102 **Q:** Will you allow our representative to view and count

103   those pipes?

104 **A:** What? Hell no! I don't need you guys snooping around

105   my company. Who do you think you are? You can't come

106   barging onto my property.

Once again, they went off the record while the attorneys argued the right for Galena Pipe to inspect the pipes, which Harry's lawsuit claimed resulted in actual damages. Nolan Shy had to give in when Henry said he would take the issue to the judge the next morning. The pleadings in the lawsuit opened the door to an inspection of the plant in Beloit to see the pipes. The judge would order it for sure and would be angry that a hearing about it was even needed. They agreed to schedule an inspection at eleven o'clock, the morning of March seventeenth, just two days after the deposition. Then, they put that agreement on the record. Harry was red in the face. He gave Nolan a look that almost made Henry feel sorry for him.

There were many other areas covered. The deposition lasted over five hours, after which Harry was exhausted and angry at everyone in the room. Henry asked Bill Turl if he had questions for Mr. Townsend. He did not, which seemed odd to Henry since his client was also being sued by Babson Pipe. Of course, Harry already looked like he would physically attack the next person to ask him anything.

Henry informed Harry that he would have a chance to review the deposition transcript and request corrections he or his lawyer thought were necessary. The deposition of Harry Townsend had come to an end.

CHAPTER 40

Wednesday, March 15, 1989

Paul and Henry had never even discussed an inspection of Babson's yard to look for specially manufactured pipes. It wasn't planned. It just came to Henry when he was reviewing the pleadings again before the deposition. Would Harry really make those pipes knowing he might be stuck with them? Henry called Paul right after the deposition and filled him in. They needed to come up with an inspection of Babson's yard in two days. Fortunately, Josh and Nate were in the office. Paul rustled them up, and they all got on the speakerphone with Henry.

Josh was excited. "Good job! Damn. I can't believe we never thought of that! I want to know if those pipes are there. How are we going to do this now?"

"First off," said Nate. "We need to figure out who to send, and they need to be there on time. With traffic, it is hard to tell how much time the trip will take. South Beloit is less than an hour's drive from Stockton in good weather. Whoever goes should leave at eight in the morning. That leaves plenty of time. We need someone who knows pipes and joints. That would be Jake Sharp. He's the one who came up with our offer to send pipes with other joints. Paul, I think you need to be there, don't you?"

"Definitely. I need to be there and stay in touch with Henry in case they give us any trouble. We need to consider the possibility that we will get there and run into excuses if they don't really have the pipes. And I don't think they do."

Henry agreed. "Hey, do you guys have access to a video camera? I think we need a video of the whole inspection. We can get it introduced in court if we need to."

Paul said, "Excellent idea. Nate, do you have one?"

"We do. I'll get it ready. Both you and Jake should learn how to use it. We don't know how this is going to go."

"One other thing," said Paul. "Nolan Shy is no Bernie Torveski. Harry and Nolan must have been caught off guard with this. Bernie would never have agreed to it. It would have been a big fight and probably would have taken motions, hearings, and an attempted appeal. They would have lost at some point but would have tried to stall until they could make some pipes. He is going to be beside himself when he hears about it. There is a chance they will try to go back on the agreement even though it was put on record in the deposition. The deposition hasn't been signed yet or filed with the court. Henry, how fast could you get in touch with Judge Harris if we need her?"

"I don't know. But I can try to put her on notice that we may need her. Hopefully, they won't try to pull anything. Still, I will try to get through to her about it. I just have to be careful here. It can't look like an attempt to lobby her *ex-parte*. Judge Harris isn't going to get into that kind of stuff, nor should she."

Henry got a call through to the judge later that day. He told her briefly that there was an agreement for the inspection on record in the deposition, but the deposition was not yet transcribed, signed, and filed of record in the case. He just wanted the judge to know that if they did not get access to the pipes, he would be asking for an expedited hearing because of the urgency in seeing if the pipes were actually made. If there was a long delay, there might be time to make them before an inspection, and then the truth might not be discoverable. Judge Harris listened and was accommodating. If they did not get access, she would set an emergency hearing and order an inspection if the testimony in court justified it. When Henry got off the phone, he called the court reporter and asked how fast she could draft out the section of the deposition with the inspection agreement and if she could be available to testify at a hearing on short notice. She said she could do both.

Friday morning, Paul and Jake met in Stockton and set out for South Beloit before eight o'clock. When they got to Babson at ten thirty, they went to the main entrance and asked to meet Mr. Townsend. He was not available. They waited until eleven o'clock, and still no Mr. Townsend. Paul made his way to a telephone down the street while Jake waited at the gate. He called Henry, who called Nolan Shy and threatened to call the judge if the gate wasn't opened and Paul was not let in. An hour later, Harry showed up at the gate with Bernie Torveski and Norton Jensing. Jake got out the video camera and started recording.

Paul demanded to see the pipes that were manufactured specially for Noble Vista Development. Bernie told him they would not let them in without a court order. Paul answered that the inspection time and place were put on record in the deposition, and under Texas discovery rules, they must make the inspection available as agreed. Bernie said he was standing in Illinois, not Texas. Paul told him he would be standing in Texas when he got through telling Judge Harris what kind of crap he and Harry were trying to pull. Babson had submitted to Texas law by filing suit in Texas and Texas law damned sure applied to discovery. And so it went, back and forth, getting more heated as the arguing continued.

Bernie told Jake to put down the damned camera, or they would shove it up his ass because pictures and videos were not allowed on the premises. Jake looked at Bernie and laughed.

He kept the recorder going after Paul told him to. Paul let Bernie know that he had already put the judge on notice of the inspection and the possibility of Babson trying something stupid. And he told him that if they were not going to live up to the agreement, Bernie and Harry were a couple of assholes for not giving them notice to save them from making a trip to South Beloit. A fair amount of shouting and gesturing took place after that. Bernie was shaking his fist and Paul was hot enough to take a poke at him if Jake had not intervened. Harry, true to form, had let Bernie fight the battle for him. Still, the gate was never opened. So, Paul and Jake sped off in Paul's bright red Corvette with Texas license plates. Paul stuck a finger out the window as they left, which triggered a memory for Harry. "So … Hoffman is the son of a bitch that gave me the finger when I went to Galena! Twice! And there! He just did it again!"

Paul pulled over at a public phone and called Henry to report what had happened. Henry got Judge Harris on the telephone an hour later. He filled her in and asked for an emergency hearing. The judge told him to fax over an order and she would sign it. Then her office would call Nolan Shy and Bill Turl to tell them about the hearing and fax them signed copies. The hearing was set for her courtroom in Amarillo the following Tuesday. Nolan was ordered to be there along with a representative of Babson Pipe.

When Nolan got the order, he called Bernie and read it to him over the telephone. Bernie called Nolan a stupid ass for letting this thing get out of hand. He could see only one outcome of this hearing. The judge was going to order that an immediate inspection be allowed. And since there were no specially manufactured pipes to show they were now in deep shit territory. He told Nolan to call the judge and advise her it was impossible for anyone from Babson Pipe to be there on Tuesday or any time soon. Nolan didn't want to do that because he was afraid of angering the judge. But Bernie left him no choice.

He was able to reach the judge on the telephone that afternoon, but he got nowhere on his request for an extension because he did not want one for a few days or even a week. He wanted one for several weeks, which the judge was smart enough to see as a ruse. Extension denied. Nolan called Bernie, who cursed him again and hung up the phone. It seemed to Nolan that the lawyer-client relationship was fraying.

At eleven o'clock on the morning of Tuesday, the twenty-first of March, Henry showed up in the chambers of The Honorable Nancy Harris. What followed was one of the most one-sided hearings the judge had ever experienced. For the *movant*, Henry Melton appeared along with Paul Hoffman, who had flown down from Galena. Belle Peiyper, the court reporter, was present to testify. For the respondent, only Nolan Shy showed up. Bill Turl had been given notice of the hearing as attorney for Noble Vista Development. He also announced present to the court but took no part in the proceeding. Henry Melton called Belle Peiyper and Paul Hoffman to the stand as witnesses, one at a time. Ms. Peiyper (name pronounced "Pepper") read her transcript notes and testified that the agreement for the inspection took place in her presence and that it was a part of the deposition. Nolan Shy had no questions. Paul then took the stand. Video equipment had been set up so that the court could view the recording taken at Babson Pipe. The video didn't require much explanation. However, Paul testified about when it was made, where it was made, that he was present when it was made, and that the others present were Harry Townsend, Bernie Torveski, Jake Sharp, and an unnamed security guard working for Babson Pipe. The judge asked Nolan Shy if he had given notice to his client of the scheduled inspection. Nolan said that he had. The judge asked him if he had given his client a copy of the notice of hearing for today. Nolan said that he had. She asked Nolan what excuse his client had for not appearing for the hearing. Nolan said it was not convenient to do so on such short notice. Judge Harris took off her glasses and looked down at Nolan, priming herself to explain the utter insufficiency of his response. She was a large woman with graying hair pulled back from her forehead and plastered down, and she filled her judicial robe almost to overflowing. She was an imposing figure and knew how to unnerve lawyers who disappointed her. But after a few moments of thought, she recessed the hearing for thirty minutes and left the bench to go back to her chambers.

Paul and Henry waited at the counsel table. Just before the judge returned from her chambers, Paul turned to Henry and asked, "The court reporter's name is 'Bell Pepper'?"

Henry looked at him with a straight face and said, "That's right. Her husband is a doctor ... and her brother-in-law is in the Army. Yes ... he IS a sergeant."

They could not control themselves and had barely stopped roaring when the bailiff called the court to order.

The judge asked Henry to please prepare an order for her signature. It should include these things. One: The plaintiff's pleadings in this case for monetary damages incurred for the production of special pipes for Noble Vista Development is struck, with any recovery of those claimed damages denied. Two: Sanctions are hereby imposed against Babson Pipe Company, Plaintiff, for the total of expenses unnecessarily incurred by the Defendant, including attorney's fees and traveling expenses for the inspection and for this hearing. The hearing was over early enough for Paul to have lunch with Henry and get a flight back home that evening.

Henry drafted the order the following day, attaching an itemized accounting of all the expenses incurred by Galena Pipe. He sent a copy to Nolan Shy, who had no objection. The next day, Henry presented it to the judge and the judge signed it. The money sanctions were not really significant in a case like this. The important outcome was the striking of Babson's pleadings for financial loss on the manufactured pipe. Not only did that take away a ground of recovery for Babson Pipe, but it created a presumption that there never were any such pipes manufactured and that Babson had never had an intention to make the pipes. In that case, the contract between Noble and Babson must have been a sham. No business relationship was interfered with if no real business relationship existed. The case Harry had filed against Galena Pipe had been gutted. They could probably move for a dismissal as to Galena Pipe Works, with prejudice for bringing the suit again. But they would wait to see what else Harry had in mind.

CHAPTER 41

Wednesday, March 22, 1989

Wednesday evening, Tommy Schumann got a phone call from Harry Townsend just as he got home from the plant. Harry wanted to know if he had picked up any kind of vibe from Vernon or the others about how they felt all the litigation was going. He assumed that Vernon knew about the disastrous hearing in Amarillo. Tommy told him that nobody there had really opened up to him about it. He thought they were suspicious of him for bringing the contract to Vernon, and maybe about the kiln fire. He was frightened. And the more frightened he was, the more he wondered why he had gotten into this mess. He had a job that paid a decent salary. He was well-treated by the company. Why did he think he needed to commit a crime just to advance his career? Stupid!

Harry told him not to worry because things were going their way, but he would like to see if they could bring this thing to a quick conclusion. Then Tommy would come to work for him. He wanted Tommy to talk to the employees and former employee shareholders and let them know that there is concern about the company and their jobs. They all knew Babson had proposed a merger that had been turned down, and Tommy should tell them that some employees wanted to approach Babson to see if they were still interested. Harry wanted Tommy to get them stirred up. Tommy agreed to try. Nobody wanted to get this over with now more than he. He didn't want to do another thing for Harry, but he was scared, and if all of this could go away by merger, then he would do all he could. Tommy talked to some employees about it and he also talked to a couple retired employees with stock. After talking to him, they were worried and wanted more information about the status of the company. Tommy talked to Vernon.

"Vernon, employees are worried. The ones that are not working don't know how long they can last, and the guys still working think the company is going to fold. There's concern out there, and it is that way with the retired employees with stock, too. I think you need to see if the board of directors will reopen talks with Babson."

Vernon told Tommy that he didn't see any way around having a meeting. Frieda and Martha should know how serious things are. The employees were always their main worry. The directors, employees, and shareholders all deserved to know where things were headed. Maybe they should back off all the lawsuits and make a deal with Harry to do the merger and end all the fighting. Then he approached Josh and Nate. He explained what Tommy had told him and said that under the circumstances they should talk to Frieda and Martha to see if they would change their minds about selling their stock. But Josh and Nate told him they did not want a meeting yet. Things were changing fast. They had a plan that involved some risk, and timing was crucial. They were going to talk to Frieda and Martha and ask them for more time before making any new decisions about their stock. That was not what Vernon wanted to hear, and he made it known to them.

Nate called Frieda later that day and asked if he and Josh could come out to the house to visit with her and Martha. She told them that afternoon would be fine. When they showed up, Paul was with them. Over coffee and rolls, they got down to the reason for the visit.

"Ladies, it's time you were brought completely up to date on the problems at the company. The good news is that we think the litigation with Noble Vista Development and Babson Pipe is going well for us. We have the upper hand right now. Noble is stalled and we have put some real pressure on Babson over their suit. We were able to knock it out, for all intents and purposes, and the judge even ordered sanctions against them. He hit them with a few thousand dollars in costs which they have to pay us for their behavior. But the problem may not end quickly. if we don't take a gamble. There is fear among the employees that they may not have jobs when this is all over. I think many of them want to get this done with by doing the merger. Vernon still seems to want it. too. The fire is another problem. We need to get the kiln back up and running but the insurance company is balking at paying the claim. They dug up information that before Vernon, Sr. died, the fire department issued a warning about the sprinkler system and the alarm system, and they say nothing was done. Vernon says there are minutes of a directors' meeting where those things were discussed. He says it was before his time, and he had no idea there was a question about the sprinkler system or the alarms. He knew absolutely nothing about it. We wanted to talk to you away from Vernon just to see if you remember it the way he does. Do you know if he was made aware of it?

Frieda said she assumed he would have been. "I just remember that we were going to assign somebody to study it and tell us what we needed to do. We wanted to be sure that it was needed since it wasn't actually required by the city, if I remember. Of course, if we had needed it, we would have gotten it done. But then Vernon, Sr. died and everything just changed. Vernon, Jr. should have known about it, I would think. I don't know if we told him or not. But others may have talked to him about it. We assumed the problem had been handled. I think everyone thought the plant was well protected."

"Nate," said Martha. "Frieda is right. I'm not sure Vernon is being honest. But we still don't know what we should do. The company could fail, and all those people could lose jobs."

"We understand the worry," said Josh. "We don't want that. Some of the employees think we should get back into negotiations with Harry Townsend. Get the lawsuits all settled and do the merger. But Josh and I don't trust Townsend. I don't think you do either. He is a crook and is the last person we would want Galena Pipe to ever be associated with. But the pressure is getting strong from the employees, understandably. They want a shareholder meeting to consider the possibilities and report back to them."

"What should we do, Josh? We can't let them down. Or even Vernon, I guess. He seems to be giving in. I'm not sure we have a choice."

"This is what we are asking. Stick with us just a little longer. Let's tell them that the company will still survive this, but we need a little more time to turn things around. In just a few months, there could be some big surprises because there is more happening than they know. We have things in motion that could turn everything on its head. If they hold a bit longer, we think we can get out of this."

Frieda asked, "What are you planning to do, Nate?"

"It's better right now if nobody else knows that. It's not that you would say anything about it. But we're going to do something out of the ordinary and it would be better if you can just trust us and give us some time."

Frieda and Martha had always trusted the Walkers and they still had enough confidence in them to wait. That is what they told Vernon later when he argued with them. He knew he couldn't get past Josh and Nate, so he reluctantly told them he would go along a little longer, but only if something got done fast to solve the problem. He was wearing down from the stress. He said he wasn't crazy about working with Harry, but it was probably the best for everyone. The employees he talked to wouldn't wait long either. If nothing was different in a week or two, the company had to consider a merger or a sale, or they would leave and find work somewhere else.

Josh and Nate really did have a plan. A bold one. They had gotten the impression from Henry that Bill Turl was utterly deflated. Henry was pretty sure Turl wasn't getting paid. Noble was broke. That was obvious. Harry was not helping Bill Turl at all, and Bill could see that Nolan Shy was getting the same runaround he had been getting. Josh and Nate decided it was time to see if they could have a serious talk with Brock Johnson and Bill Turl. So Nate called Turl and proposed that he, Brock, Nate, and Josh all get together to talk about where this fiasco was heading. If Bill and Brock would fly to Dallas and meet with them at a hotel where they could talk in private and completely off the record, Nate and Josh would pick up all of their expenses. The whole works, travel, hotel, and meal charges. Bill and Brock just needed to fly to Dallas to meet with them. Bill told them he would call Brock and get right back to him. Nate and Josh held their breaths until Bill called back and agreed to the plan with the understanding that it would be kept secret from all parties, whether things got worked out or not. There was no way to guarantee that. It would have to be a matter of trust and good faith.

They had picked Monday, March twenty-seventh, for the meeting. Josh and Nate arranged separate rooms for everyone at the Omni in Dallas. They wanted to make sure Turl and Brock had the impression they were well-financed and more reliable to deal with than Harry Townsend, who had gotten them into this mess. The Walkers arrived early in the afternoon of the twenty-seventh and met Bill and Brock after they had checked in. They had leisurely drinks at the bar and then had dinner in the main dining room. Josh and Nate let their personalities and good stories keep things casual. The evening was surprisingly enjoyable. Bill and Brock got a real kick out of the Walkers. And Josh and Nate actually warmed up some to Bill and Brock, even though they couldn't excuse what they had been up to. They decided to put off all business until morning. The next day, they met for breakfast and then moved to a meeting room the hotel had made available.

Josh took the lead. "Now, this is a bit irregular but there are no ethical issues involved here. Neither of us is aligned with Babson Pipe in any of this litigation, at least on paper. Bill, you only represent Noble. We only represent Galena Pipe. Nobody here has an attorney-client relationship with Babson. What we want is to get the cards on the table without months and months of maneuvering because the cards are coming out one way or another. Nate is going to cut through all the pretense that comes with litigation and just plain tell you where things are with us."

"These are the things we think we have learned," Nate began. "Now, please let me go through all of this before you respond. We will do the same for you. That's the nice thing about not being in court. We don't have to argue about it. We can just each tell the other side where we are. There will be no posturing from us, and we hope we can expect the same from you. Otherwise, this would be a waste of time. Then we can decide how to go forward, whether as adversaries in court or some other way.

"First off, there is this. Galena Pipe is well financed. It can sustain all the litigation costs and unemployment claims of its employees. Even an extended loss of revenue is survivable but, of course, not pleasant. We don't think Noble is in the same position. Frankly, we can envision Noble filing a Chapter 11 bankruptcy if this continues much longer. We also think we have the measure of Harry Townsend. He has assets. Babson Pipe has value, and he owns the largest bundle of stock. He can hang around in this thing if we let him. But he isn't going to bail you guys out. Even if he were to hit the jackpot in his suit against us, which he won't, he would give you no part of it. He and his lawyer, Bernie, will hang you guys out to dry. Bernie isn't going to help you in the Illinois suit, Bill. And you guys can't afford to hire Illinois counsel to take it over. Look at how little Bernie is doing for poor Nolan Shy. Bill, you were at the deposition in Lubbock and the hearing in Amarillo, so you know Shy gets no help. But at least Nolan can cut out of this thing, which I expect him to do soon. You can't. You are in too deep. You were used by Harry for one reason. He wants to take over Galena Pipe Works. I'm not sure if you know that or not. Last year, he made an offer to merge Galena Pipe Works with Babson Pipe Company. He would gain the majority share of the stock in the new company through a combination of cash and stock. He tried to sell his merger plan to the shareholders of Galena Pipe. But enough shares voted to stop him. That was in no small part because of Josh and me. Things got ugly on Harry's side when that happened. He harassed some of the older shareholders until we stopped him. Then he concocted a convoluted plan to use you to get back at Galena Pipe. If you had any questions along the way about what was in this for Harry, now you know. It was just about Harry getting his hands on Galena Pipe Works. It was never about you.

"After the shareholders turned him down, he hoped to back us into a corner with his litigation and with the fire, which we will get to later. But he can't. Now he is desperate, and we are afraid he is going to get much more desperate. This is not going to end well for him. He has been caught lying in his pleadings and his deposition about prefabricating special pipes for you. He said under oath that he had a couple hundred of them in his yard. It was a lie, and the district judge in Amarillo knows it. In his sworn deposition, Harry told several more provable lies, which all will come to light. Harry perjured himself multiple times, and poor Nolan let him do it.

"This contract with you was made up, Brock. He never was going to make pipe for you. And you were never going to buy pipe from him. But you know that. What you didn't know when you got into this is that he intended to set up Galena Pipe to "steal the contract" so that he could come after them and force a merger. We don't know what he promised you out of it. Maybe some buried pipe you wouldn't have to pay for. That's not much. But if you thought you would get anything else out of a deal with Harry Townsend, you were wrong. This was always about getting Galena Pipe Works. If that isn't enough of a problem, I'm going to let Josh fill you in on where this is going next."

Josh took over. "This whole scheme of Harry's rested on one thing. Galena Pipe had to get that contract with you. That is where you come in, Brock. You were to sell Noble Vista Development to Vernon. You were to fool him into thinking this would be an opening to other developments you were planning in Texas."

Nate laughed. "Frankly, Brock, Vernon ate it all up, so you get some credit for pulling it off. But not too much. Vernon is an easy mark. Dispute that if you want, but you know it's true. That was the first thing Harry needed, but the final thing he needed was for Galena to fail to perform under the contract. That is where the fire comes in. The fire in the kiln was started intentionally. There is an office of the State of Illinois with arson investigators. It's called OSFM and it is located in Springfield. An experienced arson investigator from OSFM has visited us twice and has sent evidence to the lab in Springfield for evaluation. I can tell you confidentially that he believes it is arson. He knows it started from a tampered gas pipe within a five-hour timeframe at night by a person using a specific pipe wrench. We know who that person was, and it will come to light when the time is right. Off the record again, here is where you come in.

"This whole thing is wound up in conspiracy. Conspiracy to defraud Galena Pipe and conspiracy to force an unwanted merger of Galena Pipe with Babson, and the key to making it work was a conspiracy to commit arson that would make Galena Pipe shut down production and default under its contract with you. The only question now for us, and eventually for others looking into this, is who all of the people are, who were conspirators and to what degree did each of them all conspire. How much did they all know? Did they know about the planned arson?"

Nate paused there to let it sink in. He had gone beyond what he and Josh could prove, but everything they had seen led to it being fact. The question now was whether Bill and Brock would take it in and look for a way out of the mess they knew they were in. One of two things would happen. Either Bill and Brock would tell them they were full of shit and walk out, or they would take some time to think about what they might have to gain by cooperating.

"Now look," Josh said. "We have done all the talking here and you guys deserve your turn. Why don't we break for an hour, and you can have your say. Then we will know if we can work together to find a way to get you out of this and to resolve the problem Galena Pipe is having without this stretching into months, and probably years, of litigation and who knows what else."

Just over an hour and a half later, Bill and Brock came back, and Bill asked them to step into the hall so they could talk there. "Nate, Josh, we don't want you to take this the wrong way. We actually trust you guys. But while you were gone, I went to the hotel desk and asked if they had another meeting room available. I told them this one had too much noise outside. I don't know if they bought the excuse, but they gave us another room. Let's move there and also leave our briefcases at the front desk while we talk. This whole thing is getting a little serious and I just want to eliminate any thought that someone could be listening. I also don't want notes taken now. I hope you are not offended."

"Not at all," said Nate. "You're just being cautious, and I can certainly respect that."

It took them a few minutes to get moved, then Bill Turl took over the meeting. "Let's be clear that if nothing comes of this, we agree that this meeting never took place because that will certainly be my position and Brock's. Having said that, let me throw out a totally pretend scenario just for fun. Let's just say that you are correct about a few things. It may be the case that Brock here, along with Jimmy Ponder, got into an agreement with Harry Townsend to scam Galena Pipe. Noble Vista Development was out of finances and unable to get any lenders to back the development in Amarillo. It was desperate. Harry had no interest in furnishing them with pipe. He only wanted to lure Galena Pipe into making a serious mistake, as you suggested. The plan was that Noble would get enough pipe to finish the first phase of the development before having to pay for any of it. The buried pipe might get a few builders to take lots and keep the deal going a little longer. If not, then it's Chapter 11 time, and nothing is lost. Who knows? Maybe more builders come in then.

"Brock never understood Harry's part of the deal. He didn't ask because he just wanted to get on with it. As time went on, the whole thing went sidewise. There was the plant fire causing Galena's default, the offer by Galena Pipe to cure its default by furnishing pipe with a different joint, and the visit to Amarillo by your ballbuster, Paul Hoffman. By the way, Brock only wanted Paul Hoffman discouraged, not beaten up. Bobby is a hothead, and he got way out of line with that. In the end, though, I have to say your guy got even and then some. Bobby is still shaking and bitching about his sore crotch.

"Brock didn't know about Harry's plan for Galena Pipe. And didn't know anything about arson. He damned sure would not have gone to that extent for a few pipes in the ground. When he first heard about the fire, he thought it was a stroke of good luck. Then Harry got him thinking about the damages he could get by suing Galena Pipe. I bought into it at that point. That is on me. I have regretted it every day since not that it exonerates me or does you any good. As time went on, both Brock and I started questioning the odd coincidence of a fire in the Galena plant at just the right time to cause them to default under the contract. The inkling that it might be anything other than an accident scared the hell out of us and still does. We decided to have a telephone conference to touch base with Harry and see if we could coax any information out of him about the fire. Harry didn't want to go into any detail over the telephone, but he thought it was important enough to come down to Amarillo to talk about it in person. He flew down to see us on the eleventh of January, and while he was there, he spilled the whole story about the fire."

Nate broke in, "Bill, assuming this "pretend scenario" of yours has some relevance to real life, who else knows about it?"

"Nobody knows it except for me, Brock, and a Sony cassette tape containing the voice of Harry Townsend on November ninth, of last year. It was recorded in Brock's office, where Brock, Harry Townsend, and I were having a very relaxed meeting with drinks. We had talked for a while earlier in the day, and Harry had me so concerned that I slipped back to my office to pick up a cassette recorder. When I got back to Brock's office, I turned it on and put it under a credenza while Harry went to the bathroom. Harry, you may have noticed, is a boastful son of a bitch and is proud about how clever he is. He got all full of himself and opened up too much. He told us that he had gotten a Galena Pipe employee to start the fire, and he said it was the same person who had leaked the phony contract to Vernon Tanksley. He was braying about how smart he had been. He probably felt safe telling us about it because he knew that we were up to our asses in the whole dirty business too. It is all on tape."

CHAPTER 42

Thursday, March 27, 1989

While Josh, Nate, Bill, and Brock were busy meeting in Dallas without Harry's knowledge, Harry decided the best way to get this thing behind him wasn't through protracted litigation. He had gotten a taste of that in Texas, and part of his lawsuit against Galena Pipe had been tossed out. There was not enough of the lawsuit left to even think about. He had gotten his ass handed to him by the court and Bernie gave him a lot of shit over letting that happen. He said that if Harry had let him go to Texas, things would have gone differently.

The only thing to do now was to push those old ladies into selling their stock, like it or not. Then, along with the employee stock he knew he could purchase, Harry would own enough stock to control the company. Actually, the timing seemed beneficial to him. Regardless of where all the litigation stood, which was in the shitter, Galena Pipe was practically shut down. It had to be losing money, and very little construction had been done on the new kiln room. Employees had been laid off for months, and they were going to have to start looking for other jobs. The value of the company was less than it had been when he had made his first offer to buy out the controlling shares. And it would only get worse. But if he got it bought, he would move all the work on kiln-dried pipe to Beloit. Then, he could move the yard work from Beloit to Galena. Galena Pipe Works had a lot of customers. It just couldn't get the work done. After merging the companies, he would use the insurance proceeds, in the event there were any, to finish any remaining repairs from the fire. The newly combined company would take off. He would pick up any shares that had been held out and eventually sell the whole thing for a lot of money.

———

When Josh and Nate got back to Galena, they arranged a meeting with Wayne Belcher, the Jo Daviess County state's attorney. They had known Wayne since he was in law school. He grew up in Galena and had run errands for the Walkers when he was in high school. Nate had also been the State's Attorney for the county many years ago and he still knew many of the people in that office. They had a lot to tell Wayne Belcher.

"Wayne," began Nate. "I am going to tell you a story."

He began with Harry Townsend's attempt to buy the controlling shares of Galena Pipe Works. Then he talked about the contract with Noble Vista Development and all the fraud associated with it. He talked about the lawsuits pending in the Illinois circuit court in Galena and the district court in Amarillo. Wayne was fascinated by all of the illegal machinations that had taken place in Harry's attempt to get his hands on the pipe company. Then Nate told him something that really caused him to sit up. He told them the fire that shut down Galena Pipe Works and put so many employees out of work was arson, that it was set at the behest of Harry Townsend, and that they had the evidence to prove it. Wayne Belcher put everything aside. Not only was a serious crime being described but it was one that affected the city of Galena and its citizens. He called two assistant prosecutors into his office and asked his secretary to call the fire chief and see if he was available to come to his office. Nate and Josh repeated all of what they had told Wayne while they waited for Carl Kraus to get there. They had not yet divulged their new evidence of arson, as the conversation was taped by Bill Turl.

When Carl got there, he filled them in on the fire investigation by Fred Bingham at OSFM and on his own investigation. He explained why he and Fred thought the fire was arson and why the OSFM lab had been unable to call it that, even though arson was certainly indicated. When he had finished answering questions, the prosecutors wanted to know what evidence Nate and Josh had that filled in the blanks and made the fire arson.

Josh spoke. "We just got back from meeting with the president of the development, who was in on the initial fraudulent scheme. He and his attorney, who is also a board member of the development company, met us in Dallas. They are over their heads in this thing. The president of the company had never intended more than getting some pipe laid on their property without paying for it, which by itself was bad enough. And the attorney was not involved at all until the fraud was already in motion. Not an honorable thing for the developer, but far and away less serious than what Harry Townsend had in mind with arson. We sensed that they were ready to turn on Harry because he continued to leave them without support after they helped him get the scam started. We were right. At the meeting, the attorney for the developer revealed that they had a tape recording of Harry admitting to having instigated the arson and arranging for a third party to cause the explosion and fire. It was done for self-gain to bring down a rival company and make the shareholders amenable to a buyout."

He went on to explain that the developer might be willing to make a proffer to the state's attorney with some assurances of lenient treatment. The company's attorney would also give testimony, assuming no charges were warranted against him. With regard to the person who started the fire on Harry Townsend's instructions, Nate and Josh needed some time. They thought they knew who it was and thought they could confirm it. If Wayne was comfortable with them doing so, they wanted to talk to that person in their office with the State's Attorney or assistant present to see if he would make an admission. They felt he had been close to doing that before. Wayne could just bring him into the state's attorney's office for questioning about the arson. But he might refuse to answer and then warn Harry. If Josh and Nate did it, he might not panic. He might take their advice to get an attorney and not tip off Harry. Wayne Belcher liked it. If he failed to take the Walkers' advice and he contacted Harry, well then, he probably would have done that anyway. So they would be no worse off. The prosecutors asked Carl if a taped conversation like the one disclosed would be enough to get the state arson investigators to change their determination to arson. He agreed to call Fred Bringham to discuss it, but he thought that piece of evidence would probably be all they needed. And, of course, if the arsonist was identified that would cement it.

The Walkers spent the next afternoon at the plant talking to Vernon about Harry's new offer. Vernon wanted it. It was lower than the original offer, but Vernon thought it was still the best for everyone. They told him his aunts still had no intention of letting Harry Townsend buy their stock. But they wanted Harry to think there was a possible deal in the offing, so they told Vernon to stay in touch with him and just pretend interest in Harry's numbers. That was bad news to Vernon, and he left the conversation fuming. Once again, they were going to screw up the merger! While they were at the plant, they crossed paths with Tommy and asked him to come over to see him the next morning to talk about how the employees were feeling.

When Tommy showed up Nate took him to the conference room where Josh was waiting. They started off talking about what was going on workwise at the plant. What kinds of pipes were they shipping out? How much work had been completed in the kiln room? He told them that only the large culvert pipes were being made and shipped because the kiln still needed a lot of work. They couldn't keep many people busy. They wanted to know if Tommy had been talking to many of the employees or retirees about the situation and if they were getting restless. He told them they were all concerned, but the newer employees were really troubled. Unemployment compensation would run out at some point. Some had started looking for employment somewhere else. Progress on the kiln was too slow.

That opened the door for Nate to talk about the fire. "Tommy, we ran into a problem with getting the kiln repaired because the fire department and arson inspectors had been building a case for calling the fire an arson and they have been slow coming to a conclusion until now. That kept the insurance company from settling the claim. They have finally determined that it was an act of arson, not just an accident. You need to know that the arson investigator will want to talk to you about the fire. And the State's Attorney wants to talk to you about it, too."

They told Tommy the State's Attorney was on his way to the office right then, and they advised him to only listen to what he had to say and not say anything himself. Then he should find an attorney to represent him and work with the state's attorney's office. They asked him if that would be alright and told him again that he should not make any statements. They also told him he was free to leave now if he wanted to. Tommy held his hands in front of his eyes and took a deep breath. Then he agreed to stay and listen.

Wayne Belcher arrived a few minutes later, and Nate

brought him into the room to introduce him to Tommy. Tommy had met him once at a political rally, but Wayne did not recall it.

Nate said, "Tommy. Let me be perfectly clear. You do not need to stay here and talk to us. You are free to leave at any time. You are not in custody. You can also pick up the phone and call your lawyer at any time. But if you stay, you will learn what it is that we think puts you in some legal jeopardy. Do you understand?"

Tommy said he understood and he would stay.

"One more thing, Tommy. My advice to you is just to listen to what we have to say. Do not talk about any of this with us at this point. Do you understand that?"

Tommy said he did.

Then Josh laid out the case against him.

"We won't hold anything back from you because we would like your cooperation. The state fire investigators nailed down the source of the fire, as you may know. It was a gas pipe going to the kiln. A joint was ruptured, and that released the gas, which caused the explosion and the fire. The investigators determined that the pipe had been tampered with. Someone had twisted it with a large pipe wrench to the point that the joint opened just enough to release some gas into the kiln area. They determined that from the markings when they sent the pipe to their lab in Springfield. They were able to pin down the range of time during which the pipe joint was broken. It was a five-hour time span, during which time there were never more than two people inside the plant. You were one, and Benny Vaughn was the other. You were there for a short period of time during that window and you were clear of the building when the fire started. In the minds of the investigators, that narrowed it down to you two, and they felt more inclined to think the person who created the opportunity for the explosion and fire would have been the one who got out before it took place."

Tommy just sat there and listened, stone-faced.

"Nate, do you want to go on from here?"

Nate took over. "Tommy, something recently surfaced that shifts the focus to you as the one who started the fire. Evidence has come to light which establishes that the person who planned the arson did it because he wanted the kiln shut down to halt production at the pipe works. The intent was to put pressure on certain shareholders to sell him their stock so that a merger of companies could occur. That person, as you know, is Harry Townsend. He has perjured himself in a deposition for which it is likely he will face prosecution. There is evidence that the person who actually started the fire was an employee of Galena Pipe, and he was the same employee who gave a copy of an unsigned contract between Babson Pipe Works and Noble Vista Development to Vernon Tanksley. That was you."

Tommy looked as if he was going to be sick. He stood up and walked to the window, leaned against it, and looked outside. Josh thought he might faint, so he ran over and steadied him. When Tommy turned around, he was dripping tears. Josh offered him a handkerchief and took him back to his seat.

Nate said, "Tommy, this is hard for you and for me. I think you are a decent young man who has let someone get him into a lot of trouble and who wishes he had taken time to think and avoid it. But this is where we are, so the goal now is to get the best outcome. Wayne will talk to you now. Again, it is better that you have nothing to say today. You should not speak until after you talk to your lawyer."

Wayne took over. "Tommy. I won't lie to you. I think the case against you is strong. Arson is a second-degree felony in this state, and that is serious. But thank God nobody was hurt or killed in the fire. It was just property damage. A lot of it. But just property, not lives. Had anyone been hurt or killed, this would have been the highest degree of felony, and your options of cooperating for any leniency would be doubtful. Now, understand this. You are not under arrest. You are not in custody, nor have you been. You are now, and have been all along, free to leave whenever you want. You have also been advised to make no statements, and you wisely have not. So far, so good. What I think you should do, and what Josh and Nate want you to do, is keep this information to yourself. Do not mention it to anyone other than a lawyer you retain. In particular, do not under any circumstances mention it to Mr. Townsend. If you understand what I have told you and what Josh and Nate have told you, just nod yes. If you don't know an attorney, Josh or Nate may be able to give you the names of a few lawyers they think could help you. When you see your lawyer, which I think should be tomorrow at the latest, you should tell them everything we told you today and give them any other information they need to represent you. Hold nothing back. Then tell your attorney to call me. I will give you my card when you leave."

Josh took Tommy by the arm and led him to the door with his other arm on Tommy's shoulder. "Tommy, do you have a lawyer you can use?"

Tommy said that he did, and he thanked Josh and Nate for giving him notice of what was going to happen.

CHAPTER 43

Thursday, March 30, 1989

Paul had applied and had been approved to practice in Illinois temporarily, just for the Galena Pipe Works suit against Noble Vista Development. His application to appear in court *pro hac vice* was sponsored by Nate and Josh. Paul's first decision was to depose Harry Townsend, based on how poorly he had done in the Texas deposition. Neither Harry, individually, nor Babson Pipe Company was a party to the Illinois lawsuit. But Harry was as much involved in the case as either of the parties. He was responsible for Galena Pipe entering into their contract with Noble Vista Development. That was more than sufficient cause to subpoena him for a deposition. Paul had learned that Harry was spending a lot of time now at the Babson plant in South Beloit. He prepared a subpoena for Harry's deposition, to be taken in Galena on April the twenty-eighth, and he arranged for a process server to serve Harry at the plant. Harry was served on March twenty-seventh, just as he was getting into his car to drive back to Skokie. He was not a happy man. He called Bernie Torveski.

"Bernie, some jackass just handed me a subpoena to give a

deposition on April twenty-eighth in Galena in that damned Noble suit. How the hell can they do that?"

Bernie was actually caught a little off guard. "Huh, well, I guess they are suggesting that you may have some information about that lawsuit. It doesn't mean they sued you in Illinois."

"Then I am not showing up!"

"You gotta. You're within a reasonable distance of where the deposition is supposed to be taken, and you have been served. There's a shit load of evidence that you had dealings with Noble over the same contract. We could fight about it and maybe stretch it out, but we would lose, sure as hell. It would mean going to Galena for a hearing AND a deposition. So then they would get two cracks at asking you questions, not just one. You ain't real good at that stuff, Harry. It might just get you into real trouble. Who is the lawyer who had you served?"

"Paul Hoffman, it says. I think that's the guy who gives me the finger! At least it's not that sneaky little bastard in Lubbock, Texas. What the hell do I pay you for anyway! You are coming with me to this thing, and I am not paying you for any travel time."

"Yeah. I'm coming, alright. So I can tell you when to shut up."

On the same day Harry was lambasting his lawyer, Nate was making a telephone call to Bill Turl to follow up on their meeting in Dallas.

"Bill, this is Nate. How are things in Amarillo?"

"Things are always good in Amarillo for a Panhandle boy like me. Have you ever been here?"

"No. Maybe Josh and I will make a trip down there someday. The reason I called … and I hope this doesn't sound presumptuous … you guys were very open with us in Dallas, and Josh and I were open with you. Our real problem is with Harry Townsend. None of this mess we are all caught up in would exist if not for him. Sure, Brock and Jimmy broke the rules—maybe in desperation. Who knows? We don't like that.

But right now, it is 'forgive and forget' as far as I am concerned. If Vernon Tanksley hadn't gotten all wound up trying to screw Harry, it would have stopped there. We are not proud of that either. But that aside, this thing is getting ready to blow up. The arson investigators have come down strongly now on arson. And the State's Attorney here is going to get to the bottom of it. The building was occupied when the fire was set, and if the security guard had been injured or killed, this would have been the highest degree of felony. As things stand, it is still first or second degree. It depends on a lot of factors. It has impacted the community because it caused layoffs at the plant. So the state's attorney, being an elected official, is not going to go easy on it."

"Nate, you know Brock wasn't involved in the arson."

"I do. And I don't see this thing coming down as a conspiracy that brings the fraudulent contract in with the arson. I know the State's Attorney well. I have known him since he was in high school, and I kept up with him while he was in law school. He is an honorable guy and a smart prosecutor. I once held the office myself, so I know a little about its workings. This is what I am suggesting. I would like to talk to him to see if he might forgo criminal charges over the Noble Vista Development contract with Galena Pipe. If he made a commitment like that, would you and Brock consider making a proffer to him by phone, followed later by testimony and introduction of the tape recording?"

"What about the litigation over the pipe Noble already has? Honestly, Nate, a judgment against Noble won't get Galena paid for that pipe. You know that's probably true. Vernon didn't file a mechanic's lien on the pipe in time to get a security interest on the pipe under Texas law. Galena has no claim on the pipe itself. They just have a claim for damages against Noble. I can send you the Texas statute on mechanic's liens and I think you will agree. Galena is stuck as far as the pipe goes. They are an unsecured creditor and there is no money. If Noble ends up in bankruptcy, so will the pipe. Your guys will just stand in line with all the other unsecured creditors who show up."

"Bill, I believe you, but I should probably see the Texas statute. It will help if you fax it to me. Josh and I will talk to Vernon and the other large shareholders and explain that it is going to be a loss whatever we do. I think they will go along with dropping litigation against Noble, assuming Noble drops its claim against Galena Pipe and helps us out against Babson."

"I'll talk to Brock and Jimmy. They need to get loose from this bear if they can do it. And you know damned well that I do too. Will you run everything by your district attorney up there? Or I guess it is called State's Attorney in Illinois, huh?"

"I will do it today, Bill. "Yes. What we call a state's attorney in Illinois seems to be the same as your district attorney. He has all the authority he needs to do this."

Nate called Wayne Belcher next. "Wayne, I just got off the phone with Bill Turl in Amarillo. He is the attorney for the developers who got themselves into this mess. He is also on the board of directors. The two owners and officers are Brock Johnson and Jimmy Ponder. Jimmy doesn't know anything helpful. Bill and Brock do. I think there is a way to get a proffer from them with the tape recording."

"What would we have to give them, Nate?"

"It would be this. Noble, being Brock and Jimmy, got into bed with Harry Townsend only to this extent. They were playing a scam on Galena Pipe Works to get a contract for pipe they knew they probably couldn't pay for. If they got sued, they would just file Chapter 11 bankruptcy and see what they could get out of that. In the meantime, the pipe they didn't pay for might help them sell some lots to builders. There was an outside chance things could have worked out well, and they could have paid for the pipe. But it was a crooked deal for sure. I have to tell you this, though. It could never have happened except for the fact that Vernon got greedy. He sneaked his contract in when he thought that

Harry Townsend already had a deal going with these guys. In other words, it's easy to trick a trickster. Vernon did nothing illegal, but what he did was not above-board, or there would not have been a chance for Noble Vista Developers to scam him. So, I think you could consider not going after them on that. These are the guys that can really make your arson case. The case against them is probably harder to make than the arson case is, and not as serious. I think Galena Pipe is even willing to dismiss the civil suit against Noble. There is no money in it anyway."

"How sure are you and Josh that these guys were not implicated in the arson?"

"Quite comfortable about that, Wayne. We have been on this thing for months and have had time to assess who did what. But if they get caught lying to you in the proffer about not having any reason to suspect arson or that they had no knowledge of it or any part in it, the proffer goes away, and you use everything they gave you against them."

"Will they come up here for this?"

"They could, I suppose. But you may want them again for grand jury and for trial. Is there any way you could do this over the phone? That cuts out one trip. Or maybe there would be a chance to get them up for the proffer and to the grand jury the same day? Either of those would probably be most efficient."

"I think I would want to evaluate the proffer before anything. I don't see a problem doing it by phone if we record it, and if I send them a proffer agreement to sign. Tell them that if what you are telling me pans out with their proffer, we have a deal, but only if they will commit to coming up for grand jury if needed and for trial if it goes to trial.

"By the way. Guess who called me this morning? Leo Becker. He said he is representing Tommy Schumann and wants to come talk to me."

Nate laughed. "Leo! Damn, I thought he retired or died."

"No. He moved to Dubuque. He does a little criminal

defense over there and even picks up a thing or two here. He is a lot older than you and Josh, isn't he?"

"Oh, hell yes. He's got to be eighty at least. I always liked Leo. He's one of the good guys. When I was a young state's attorney, he beat me twice. And one of those times, he may have been right. He could be tough. But he is honest and won't play games. He'll do what's best for Tommy. If he thinks he can get Tommy off, he will give you a fight. If you have the evidence for a conviction, he will know that too and work the best deal."

At four o'clock that afternoon, Leo Becker met with Wayne. After spending some time talking about family, friends, and what-all is going on in Galena, they got down to talking about Tommy.

"Wayne, Tommy came to see me because I am a friend of his family. I have known his dad for most of my life. I don't think he is really a bad young man. What he tells me, though, is that Nate and Josh Walker sat down with him and with you and laid out a case that would implicate him in arson at Galena Pipe. He also told me that he was not in custody, that he was told not to say anything, and that you and the Walkers told him to talk only to his lawyer. I appreciate how that was handled.

"I read about that fire, and I know the plant is practically shut down. I've known Nate and Josh longer than I have known you. They're not game players. What they say is what they believe. But that doesn't mean they aren't wrong. How much are you willing to tell me about it?"

"I won't hold back. This is what we know."

Wayne told him the whole story about Noble Vista Developers, Harry Townsend, Babson Pipe Company, the sham contract between Noble and Babson, which was slipped to Vernon, the ruse to get free pipe for Noble, Harry's goal of using subterfuge to take over Galena Pipe, and how the arson fit into Harry's plan. He told Leo that he and the Walkers were sure the developers were only involved in the scam for free pipe, didn't know how that was helping Harry, and didn't have any reason to suspect there would be a fire. He also told him he was getting ready to take a proffer from the principals of Noble Vista Development, who had personal knowledge that Harry set up an employee at Galena Pipe Works to cause the explosion and fire."

"Wow! That is a lot to lay on me! What makes you think it was arson and that the employee was Tommy?"

"A couple of things. First, the physical evidence indicated arson and the information provided by these guys at Noble fills in the blanks. OSFM is now ruling it arson. And they have pinned down the period of time during which the thing had to have been triggered to go off. At that time, the only two people in the entire plant were Tommy and a security guard, Benny Vaughn. Tommy wasn't there when the blast went off. Melvin Singer was, and he called it in. He was the second shift guard who came on duty after Benny. Secondly, there is a tape that we think can be authenticated, in which Harry Townsend is caught admitting to causing a Galena Pipe employee to set off the explosion. And he identifies that employee as the same one he gave a copy of the phony contract to. Tommy was that employee. Nate and Josh questioned him about it sometime back. He admitted it. He claimed the plant manager at Babson Pipe gave it to him. We think that is a lie. We think he came up with that on the spur of the moment, but we haven't had time to check it out. If it is a lie, that looks pretty bad. Even if it is true, Harry may have gone through that person to give it to Tommy."

"Well, I appreciate knowing all that. Do you know what Tommy's motive would have been, though? It seems weak if he had no motive."

"Tommy met Harry when he visited the Galena plant at the time he made an offer to buy out Galena Pipe. Tommy was taken with him. They spent a lot of time together and Harry talked up the new company he would create in the merger and the opportunities it would bring. Harry's plant manager is an older man, close to retirement, and I could see Tommy thinking that was a better opportunity than he had at Galena. Vernon is not a go-getter or manager. Harry comes across as ambitious and successful. We think that was his motive."

"You may have a case against Tommy, or you may not. So far, it sounds circumstantial. It's not like you have an eyewitness. Circumstantial cases can be hard to make. Will you let me see the proffer when you get it?"

"I will, Leo. I'm not hiding the ball on this. But I can tell you that if the evidence pans out the way it looks, I am going to take it to the grand jury. This is very serious. The security guard could have been injured or killed. That would have made it aggravated arson."

They shook hands, and Leo left. He had a lot to think about.

CHAPTER 44

Friday, March 31, 1989

Wayne Belcher met with his lead investigator, Stan Moss, to give him a copy of the sham contract Vernon had been given by Tommy Schumann and to fill him in on the investigation. The plan was for him to talk to Norton Jensing, the Babson Pipe Company plant manager, to find out if he was the person who had given the contract copy to Tommy. Also, to find out if he had any contact at all with Tommy or if he knew of any other people who might have contact with him, including Harry Townsend. It needed to be done without anyone at Babson Pipe knowing that Norton had been contacted by the investigator.

Stan and his partner, Arethia Harrison, drove to Roscoe, Illinois, and pulled up outside the Jensing home. They had searched the motor vehicle records to find his vehicle license number, make of vehicle, and home address. Just after six o'clock that evening, they saw Norton's truck pull into his driveway and watched him go into the house. He was a small, very lean man for someone who came up working in a concrete pipe factory. That is physical work. They waited thirty minutes to let him get settled in, then went to the door and rang the doorbell. A small, gray-haired woman in her sixties answered. She was wearing a bright-yellow dress and slippers. They smiled at her and identified themselves, showing their badges. She seemed concerned when they asked to speak to Mr. Jensing but they assured her they were looking into something that had nothing to do with him. He might just have information that could help them. She returned with her husband, and they again introduced themselves. They told him they were looking into a matter and had some questions he might be able to answer for them. Is there a place they might sit down to talk with him? Or would he rather talk to them outside?

Norton seemed confused but not concerned. He asked them in, took them to the room he used for an office, and sat behind a small table. They sat on a couch across from him.

Stan began, "Mr. Jensing, we need to ask you some questions that relate to your job at Babson Pipe. We don't know that anyone there has done anything wrong. It is just part of an investigation that goes to some matters in Galena. Do you mind if Officer Harrison records this? We are both lousy notetakers. I can't read hers, and she can't read mine."

"I guess not."

"Then, to speed things up, let me just hand you this document to see if you recognize it."

He handed a copy of the contract to Jensing who paused to put on his reading glasses before looking through it carefully.

"I don't think I ever saw this. It looks like a contract between Babson and a company way down in Texas. We didn't ever have a customer down there. Too far away. Looks like nobody signed it. I can see why. Way too far to ship if you ask me."

"That's interesting. Have you ever heard that company mentioned?"

"No. Where did this come from?"

"As a matter of fact, Mr. Jensing, somebody told us that they got the contract from you. That you had given it to them and asked them to keep it a secret."

"What! Who was it that said that? I never did that. I've never even seen it!"

"It was the plant manager at Galena Pipe Works. Do you know him?

"I know who he is. He's a young fellow. I met him at a meeting up in Janesville or somewhere. I can't really remember. It has been several years. Tommy something is his name, I think. Why would he say that?"

"That's just it, Mr. Jensing. We don't know why he would say that unless he was afraid to tell us where he really got it. I can tell you this: the contract has caused a lot of trouble at Galena Pipe Works. Do you know many people there?"

"I used to. I knew Vernon Tanksley. The senior, not his son. His son runs it now. I may have met him back when his dad owned it, but I don't know. Let's see … I did know the old plant manager there. He was a friendly guy and I think he knew the business. Um … Sharp. I don't remember his first name. I remember Sharp because he seemed to be 'sharp.' I can't think of anyone else I know there. Harry Townsend probably does. I heard he was talking to somebody there, getting calls or making them or something. The receptionist mentioned it one day and asked if I knew what was going on."

"What about Curt Babson? I understand he still owns part of your company. Is he active in it?

"Oh no. He has nothing to do with the business. Harry Townsend runs everything. Curt's out of it completely. Maybe he still gets some money, but I wouldn't know. He never really made good decisions, and I think he may be glad to be away from it."

"Well, Mr. Jensing, we really appreciate your time and the information you gave us. Now I have a favor I would like from you. Would you please not mention anything about this to anyone? I mean nothing about the contract or Tommy

Schumann or any of it. To anyone, even Mr. Townsend. It could really jeopardize what we are working on, and it is kind of important."

"Don't worry. I don't talk to Harry Townsend unless I have to. But don't tell that to anyone, please. We don't really get along. That's all I am going to say about it. I just never got comfortable with him. And I won't mention it to anyone else, either. Even Mrs. Jensing. I love her to death but she's a talker. I'll say your visit was about something taken from the plant."

"Thank you, sir. You have been more helpful than you know."

Mr. Jensing showed them out of the house, and they began their drive back to Galena. They were both certain that they had been told the truth. This is not a man who would get involved in something not on the up-and-up.

When they got back to Galena, they went to see Wayne and brought him the tape of the interview along with their report. They played the tape. Wayne asked for their impressions. They both agreed that Mr. Jensing did not give the contract to Tommy Schumann. And they didn't think he would tell Harry about the interview.

True to his promise to Leo Becker about not hiding the ball, Wayne called him Monday and asked him to come to his office so that he could hear something from his investigators. Leo showed up just after lunch and sat down with Wayne, Stan Moss, and Arethia Harrison. They played the tape, and Leo was able to ask the investigators about their visit and quiz them about what Norton Jensing told them. They were experienced investigators, and they were able to sum up Norton Jensing pretty well. He was close to his retirement and had grown children. He had no reason to get involved in anything cagey, especially for a man he didn't like. Leo thought it was time to have a serious chat with Tommy.

Meanwhile, Wayne wanted to set up a call to Bill Turl to get a handle on what he and his client were willing to include in a proffer if leniency or non-prosecution was offered. Wayne had not heard the recording of Harry admitting to setting up the arson. That was key. The recording had to be verifiable and damning. With Nate's help, he arranged a telephone conference with Bill Turl that had some protection for Bill and Brock if they played the tape for Wayne.

"Bill, this is Nate. I am here in Wayne Belcher's office. Wayne is the State's Attorney for this circuit."

"Hello, Nate. Hello, Mr. Belcher. I'm in my office with Brock Johnson and Jimmy Ponder. We're on the speakerphone."

Wayne Belcher spoke first. "You can call me Wayne. Nate has given me a very detailed report of what you and Mr. Johnson told him and Josh in Dallas. Let me summarize the things he told me. First, you guys discussed the contract Noble had with Galena Pipe, and Nate took from that conversation that you had some remorse for how you entered into that contract. Also, it appears that Galena Pipe was a bit underhanded in trying to sneak a contract away from Babson Pipe. All they are interested in now is seeing a prosecution of everyone involved with the arson in Galena, or anyone aware of the plan to commit arson, or anyone who should have been aware of it. That is also my only interest right now as a prosecutor. Second, there appears to be a tape recording in which Harry Townsend admits putting the arson in play in order to injure Galena Pipe Works. And he indicates in the tape that he gave instructions to commit the arson to an employee of Galena Pipe. Does that sound right?"

At that point, they promised each other that this conversation was not being recorded by either side and was not being taken down by a stenographer, whether or not that promise could really be proven.

Bill looked over at Brock, who nodded approval, then he said, "That pretty well sums it up. We did confide all of that. We also made it clear and would testify that Brock got the idea from Harry Townsend. Harry instructed Brock on how he could do this, and he helped pull the wool over Tanksley's eyes. He lured Tanksley to Brock so that Noble Vista Development could take advantage of him. I was not involved at that time and was not aware of what was happening until later. We also will swear that we had absolutely zero knowledge of what Harry was getting out of this. We assumed he had something to gain, but he never let on what it was, nor did he ever mention that arson or any kind of damage would result to Galena Pipe. We had no indication of it and nothing he told us would have led us to think of something like that. Of course, we are not proud that Noble was scheming to get pipe without paying for it."

"As to the tape, Mr. Turl, I would like to hear it. I promise you we are not going to rerecord it from this telephone call. I have to hear it, then I can decide whether I can offer anything in exchange for a proffer from you and Mr. Johnson. Without hearing it I just can't make that assessment."

Bill and Brock agreed, which was really an indication that they had judged the character of Nathan and Joshua favorably and were willing to take a big chance on Wayne being an honest prosecutor. They played the tape. Nate and Wayne were able to hear it through the speakerphone. When they had heard it all twice, there were things Wayne liked. Harry was boastful and clearly enjoying what he was saying. It was also good that the full conversation was recorded. The admission was not just a piece taken out of context but was centered between the beginning and end of a full conversation. And even though he may have had a few drinks he did not sound inebriated. His speech was clear and cogent. And he really laid it out. He had instigated the arson and had done it for personal gain. Motive was established. It was also established that the employee who gave a copy of the unsigned contract to Vernon was the one he conspired with to set the fire. The original tape, of course, would have to be authenticated by the crime lab as not having been altered in any way.

"Mr. Turl," asked Wayne, "have either of you mentioned

to Harry Townsend or anyone else that you have had these conversations with Nate and Josh or that you were going to be in contact with me?"

"No. And we won't. The information we are giving you won't have much value to us if we do that."

"Good. Now, I will tell you this honestly. Mr. Turl, you are an attorney, so I am not telling you anything you don't know. As State's Attorney, my job is to prosecute some of the things it appears Brock and Jimmy may have been involved with. I exclude you from that because I feel that your attorney-client relationship put you in a situation here that limited your options. Galena Pipe seems disinterested in seeing a prosecution of anyone over Noble's actions. I understand there is civil litigation. That has no interest to me. It's for you guys to work out. From a criminal prosecution standpoint, the greater crime is the arson, coupled probably with some counts involving fraud by Harry Townsend. The arson had the potential of killing or injuring a plant guard and anyone else who happened to enter the plant at the wrong time. Thank God that did not happen, but it could have. The explosion and fire also destroyed hundreds of thousands of dollars of property, shut down the operation of a major part of the plant, and put employees out of work.

"So you can understand my priority is the arson. I want to send you a proffer letter. At the moment I can't tell you exactly what we will be offering, but it will be clear in the letter. If you sign the letter I will hold you to it. Any false information or lack of cooperation by any of you will prevent the offer from taking effect. Then, I would have to take another look at the actions of Brock and Jimmy to see if they should be investigated. That is not what we are after. Bill, you understand where I am coming from here. I am not after your clients."

"Wayne, if Brock and Jimmy agree to the proffer letter, what would they be required to do?"

"Good question. I should have covered that. Well, first off, turn over the original tape recording. Then, agree to come here to testify before a grand jury and at trial, if requested. If you have never been to Galena I am sure Josh and Nate will give you the full tour."

"It might be worth it just for that. Those guys are kind of fun to be around. Send us the proffer letter and we will see what it looks like."

"Okay, anything else? Anyone? No? Then I will get a letter into the mail in a day or two."

They ended the call and Nate asked Wayne what he had in mind for an offer. Wayne said that if Galena Pipe wasn't hot to put these guys in jail, then he had higher priorities. Going after them wasn't worth it if they could help him make the arson case. So, he may just as well offer immunity, assuming that sounded reasonable to Nate. It did.

Wayne spent the next day working on the proffer letter. He required that all three, Bill included, provide testimony as to all of the things they had told Josh and Nate in Dallas. That included the culpability of Brock and Jimmy in conspiring with Harry Townsend to defraud Galena Pipe Works. Specifically, the scheme was to use the unsigned contract to trick Vernon into thinking that a contract like that one would provide an entry into numerous lucrative contracts to provide pipe for developments planned for other Texas cities. In fact, no such plans existed. The letter also required them to furnish the original recording of Harry Townsend and to help authenticate it in court. It required that they give testimony as to all of their dealings with him, together with a few other items. It cautioned them that if any of their proffer turned out to be dishonest or deceptive, the agreement was off and all of the information they gave could be used against them in a criminal prosecution. If their proffer was acceptable and not found to be incomplete or false, they would have full immunity in Illinois from prosecution for any act related to the fraud.

Galena Pipe Works, acting through Nate and Josh, also agreed that if Bill, Brock, and Jimmy followed through with their proffer and obtained immunity from prosecution by helping make the case against Harry, they would drop their litigation against Noble Vista Development.

So now the table was almost set. They only needed Tommy Schumann to flip on Harry.

CHAPTER 45

Tuesday, April 4, 1989

Wayne set up the office to take the proffer from Bill Turl, Brock Johnson, and Jimmy Ponder by telephone. The technicians put a recording system in place, and Wayne had a stenographer present to create a transcript. Wayne had two of his Assistant State's Attorneys present as well. Bill read their prepared proffer while Brock and Jimmy listened. When he was finished, Wayne asked several questions, which Bill answered. After all areas had been covered, Wayne asked all three of them, individually, whether the proffer read by Bill and the answers given to Wayne's questions were all true and correct, and if they each agreed to offer that proffer in response to the letter he had sent Bill. They all responded affirmatively.

Wayne told them that the recording of the telephone conversation would be transcribed, along with the stenographer's notes of the call, and would be sent to Bill. They should all review it carefully and contact him if they wanted changes made. When it was final, they should all sign it under oath and return it to him along with the original tape of the conversation with Harry Townsend.

The following Monday, Wayne got back the proffer transcript, which was verified as correct by Bill, Brock, and Jimmy and signed under oath. Along with it was the original recording of Harry talking about the fire. Wayne called Leo Becker and told him that he was welcome to come into his office with Tommy so they could read the proffers and hear the tape recording of the conversation with Harry Townsend. The next day Leo came in with Tommy. They reviewed the proffers and listened twice to the tape while Leo took notes.

When they had finished Wayne told them that he was going to the grand jury with what they had just read and listened to. He told them that other evidence about the fire and about the delivery of the unsigned contract to Vernon Tanksley had already been presented to the grand jury. Wayne made it clear that he would be asking for indictments against both Harry Townsend and Tommy based on the evidence they had. This would be a good opportunity for Tommy to consider making an admission and offering to give testimony against Townsend. Any offer of leniency that might be made would never get better than it would be for the next seven days. After an indictment was handed down, the chance of a favorable plea agreement for Tommy was unlikely.

Leo said he needed time to work on the case. Wayne agreed to keep the option for a plea agreement open until he had an indictment against Tommy. But repeated that the sooner the admission, the better the offer. After indictment, there could still be a plea agreement, but there was no guarantee that he would cut Tommy much slack. Tommy knew what had happened as well as anyone, and there really wasn't a lot for him to think about. He asked Leo to assure him that neither he nor Tommy would be in contact with Harry Townsend and would not reveal to anyone what they had listened to today. If it turned out that either of them talked to Harry or his attorney, all deals were off. Any offer of a plea deal would evaporate, and Wayne would seek an indictment against Tommy for the highest felony he could prove.

Leo and Tommy asked for some privacy. Wayne left the office while they talked together. When he rejoined them, Leo said they would agree not to communicate with Harry or his attorney until the grand jury had finished considering the case.

———

Paul saw Ann most evenings. She peppered him with questions about the writing project he was working on and about the lawsuit that led to him being involved in the project. Soon, she was proofreading for him. Then she got interested in all of the intricacies of tort law and had question after question about it. Before long, he felt like he was teaching torts to a first-year law student who understood legal issues better than some lawyers. The more interested she got in legal principles, the more curious she got about the Galena Pipe litigation. And Ann was the most inquisitive person Paul had ever known. It became a game of "What exactly are you and the Walkers doing for Galena Pipe Works? I need to know all of it." Ann kept trying to pry loose inside information, while Paul kept fighting to keep everything confidential.

"Paul, don't you think a newspaper in Jo Daviess County has at least some responsibility to report fully on lawsuits involving a large employer in Galena?"

"I don't know. What is there to say that will not just get rumors going in Galena? At this point, people know there are lawsuits going on that involve a company in Texas and Galena Pipe."

"You probably don't realize that there are rumors now. Maybe getting facts out there is better than letting rumors run rampant."

Paul knew everything going on with the lawsuits, but he

also knew there was a criminal investigation and a likely grand jury presentation. It would not be good for any of that to be made public. He had spent enough time as a prosecutor to know how all prosecutors feel about protecting criminal investigations. Yet from Ann's perspective it was news that readers would want to know. It was a delicate struggle for him to shut her out of all the things going on behind the scenes. Damn. There was too much stuff happening right now that she couldn't know about, and she would bug him to death about it until it was all over. Passing the buck was Paul's best option if he could pull it off. He would have to set her after the Walkers and get himself off the hook. It would be like setting a hound after hares, but he saw no other choice.

"Ann, I understand. You have every right, even duty, to inquire into any serious matters that could affect the community. Especially when rumors get started. I can only tell you what you already know. There is a lawsuit pending in circuit court in Galena between Galena Pipe Works and Noble Vista Development Company. All the pleadings in that case are public records. You have access to them. You also know that there is litigation in Amarillo, Texas, that involves Galena Pipe. My trip there had a related purpose. I did not go down there just to get my ass kicked. I could do that almost anywhere. Nate and Josh are heading up both of these suits since they are Galena Pipe's longtime lawyers. They are the ones who have to decide what needs to be held back at this point. I will talk to them and see what information they would be willing to share with you and what information needs to be guarded. Sound fair?"

"Oh, sure. That sounds completely fair. Why didn't I think of that? I really love wasting my time pestering those two for information they won't EVER EVER give me, no matter what. You guys are all alike."

CHAPTER 46

Thursday, April 6, 1989

Wayne Belcher had given Leo Becker until such time as there was an indictment to tell him if Tommy was ready to open up and negotiate for leniency. Non-prosecution was out of the question in a case like this. But there was some softening he could do as to the level of the felony he prosecuted and his sentencing recommendation. He already had sufficient information for the grand jury, so he didn't have to have Tommy's testimony. But it sure would be nice. His testimony would cement the case against Harry Townsend. Hopefully, Tommy would see that his best option was to cooperate.

Eighteen members were seated for the grand jury empaneled to consider charges relating to the arson. No fewer than twelve were present on each day the body met. Nine votes would be needed to hand down an indictment. On the first day, they chose a foreman. Wayne briefly introduced his case, telling the jurors what he would prove. Then, he began introducing evidence. He could keep the grand jury impaneled for three months, if necessary, but that was more time than he needed.

———

Meanwhile, Nathan and Josh were trying to make their own case to a tough jury of one, Ann McCool. She was not sold on the idea that she was being given the information she needed to report on the Galena Pipe litigation or on rumors that the litigation was connected to the fire. By now, people were speculating that the fire had been intentionally started. Paul, who was present at this inquisition of Nate and Josh, had at least warned them that Ann would be coming with hard questions. He felt vindicated. It was all he could do for them.

Nate went first. "Ann. You have known Josh and me for a long time, and you know we would not keep anything important from you."

"Hold on, Nate. I think I may be hallucinating. I thought I just heard you saying that you and Josh would never hold anything back from me."

Josh interjected. "You are right, Ann. Nate is being less than forthcoming with you. He is sometimes like that. I think he lacks sufficient understanding of the role of a free press in our society. What he should have said, and what I would have said, by the way, is that there are some things we can tell you and some small, uninteresting, unimportant things we can't. I hope that helps."

"Okay," said Ann. "Now that the comedy is over, here is what I know. Over the course of just the last four months I have become aware of (a) an offer made by Babson Pipe Company to buy the shares of stock of Frieda Payne and Martha Keele which was apparently spurned, (b) a trip by you, Nate, and Paul to Cicero where you threatened to pound either the bald, or the empty, head of a six-foot-four-inch gorilla into the floor, (c) a fire which burned down a good portion of the largest factory in Galena, (d) a trip to Texas by one Paul Hoffman who returned looking like he had been dragged by a horse, (e) a photo of a man who had obviously been kicked or punched in a sensitive area below the belt, (f) a lawsuit filed in Illinois against a company in Texas, (g) a lawsuit filed in Texas against two companies, one of which is in Texas and one of which is in Illinois, (h) a visit to Galena Pipe by an arson investigator from Springfield, (i) a special grand jury just now impaneled in Galena by our state's attorney, and (j) a Houston lawyer, rather cute, cloistered reclusively in Mrs. Wright's house, who gets irritatingly evasive whenever a newspaper owner-editor-reporter asks him a couple of simple damned questions.

"I think the subscribers to the *Stockton Herald* and the cheapskates who don't subscribe but just wait to read it after their subscribing neighbor is done with their copy deserve to know how all of this fits together. Oh yes! There are cheapskates like that in this town and I know who they are."

"Nate," asked Josh. "Do you want to pick it up from here?"

"Ah. . .well, Ann. First of all, Nate and I both subscribe at home. And we have an office subscription. So that is three. Paul should subscribe but he just reads the office copy. Now, as to Galena Pipe, some of this I can tell you, and some I can't. There is some I can tell you a little later, and some of what I may tell you, even then, will be 'graveyard.' We really can't add anything to that at this time. But don't quote me on that."

"Do you have anything to add, Nate?"

"No, I believe you have covered it pretty well."

"Interesting," said Ann, "and after all of that, you still haven't told me one single thing."

"Oh, by the way," Nate said, "did I mention the law firm wants to take out an advertisement in the paper next week? Good for business relations, you know."

"My God, that is the most brazen attempt to bribe a newspaper reporter I have ever heard of! Half-page?"

"I'm thinking a quarter page. What do you think, Josh?"

"Yeah, I was thinking that also. Do you ever try to get ads from any of those lawyers over in Galena, Ann? Or do they just advertise in the *Galena Gazette* there? Because I would try to advertise everywhere in the county if I were them. But that's their loss."

"Damn it! Stop that! Was the fire arson or not?"

"Nate, do you want to pick it up?"

"Sure. Well, is that what people are saying it is, Ann?"

"YES."

"I don't know if anyone knows for sure. You might want to run that one by Carl Kraus, the fire chief."

"I'll tell him you sent me."

"No. You probably wouldn't want to tell him that. It makes it sound like Josh and I are a couple of blabbermouths."

"BLABBERMOUTHS! Well, I guess that ends the interview for today! I thank you for your time, gentlemen and that was a full page, I believe. I'll bill you!"

After Ann left, Josh and Nate smiled at Paul and Josh said, "I think she kind of likes you. But how did she find out about a special grand jury? Boy, she's good."

———

Tommy Schumann had a lot to think about. What the hell had he done? His job at Galena Pipe had been secure, and the salary wasn't bad. He would like more money, of course. Who wouldn't? But mainly, he wanted a position that people respected. He was thirty years old now and hadn't accomplished much. He had a wife and an eight-year-old daughter. He had married his high school girlfriend, Julie, right after he graduated from the University of Wisconsin at Whitewater. There were some sales jobs offered after college, but sales wasn't something he wanted with a child on the way. So, he ended up working in a concrete pipe plant for fifteen years with no hope of advancement.

He had gotten greedy and had seen himself on the business side of things when he met Harry Townsend. Harry was a smart business guy out of Chicago—the real thing. Some day, he wanted to be a big shot like him. Scheming with Townsend about the contract was wrong. But if it led to the merger, it would be good for everyone. The fire was different, but he was already in too deeply to get out. Nobody would be injured by the fire. Neither Benny nor Melvin went anywhere near the kiln on their rounds. The alarm would go off right away, and the sprinklers would all kick in. Melvin would call the fire department, and the fire might even be out when they got there. Damage would be limited. For God's sake, there was no reason it would have been such a disaster! If it just shut things down for a bit and put them behind on the Noble contract, that would make it easier for Harry to pressure Frieda and Martha. Tommy had worked around the kiln long enough to know all of its parts. He thought he could make the fire look like an accident. It would look like inadvertent damage to a gas pipe that had gone unnoticed.

But he was wrong. The fire got completely out of control. Now he had ruined everything. He was going to prison. His wife was a nurse who made enough money on her own that she and his daughter would survive while he was gone. And thank God, her family in Galena could help her out if she was in a jam. He dreaded telling her, but he had to get it off his chest tonight and hold nothing back. He needed to resign from his job, too. Vernon would have no choice but to fire him otherwise. What a damned fool he was!

The next morning, he called his lawyer and made an appointment.

"Mr. Becker, I told my wife last night. I told her what I have done and how bad the trouble is. Today, I am going to see Vernon and resign."

"I'm sorry, Tommy. That may turn out to be the hardest part of everything. Telling your wife about it, then resigning from your job. I wish I could offer you a way out of this that didn't involve making a deal with the State's Attorney. But I have seen enough to know that if we take this to trial, we will lose. If you force a jury trial, punishment will be harsher than what you will suffer if you cooperate. At least you have that option. If Wayne Belcher was really out to get you, he wouldn't make a deal. He could take it to trial, chalk up a nice win for the voters, and hit you with the highest arson penalty. But he is offering you a chance to cooperate and tell the whole story."

"I don't like the idea of ratting out somebody else when I made the wrong decision myself."

"That's charitable of you, Tommy. But let me tell you a little about the guy you will be testifying against. I have been able to check him out with some lawyers in Cook County who know of him. He is a guy who is constantly in litigation, either suing or being sued. He has been investigated numerous times for fraudulent schemes and intimidation, but has never been convicted. He seems to bring disaster everywhere he goes and brings it to everyone he draws close. Harry Townsend is a bad guy, Tommy. Ask yourself this. Would any of this have happened to Galena Pipe if not for Harry Townsend?

"No. Of course not."

"He uses people to do his dirty work for him. Think about it. They end up suffering while he goes on to the next sucker. You are not really a bad guy. But you are a guy who did a very bad thing and will have to pay for it. You will get through it, and you will have learned things about life that not everyone else learns. You are young, and you will get your life back together so that you never again feel what you are feeling today. How did Julie handle it?"

"She cried all night. I did, too. I don't know the last time I ever cried that hard. Our little girl, Tammy, is eight years old, and we put her to bed before we talked. So she doesn't know yet. This morning, she went off to school happy. She will have to know soon, and that breaks my heart. Julie said I should do what you tell me to do. She says I need to admit it and take the consequences. She says she will stand by me and will be here for me forever. I believe her. That helps me do the right thing."

"Then the right thing is for me to call Wayne Belcher and tell him that if he makes an offer you can accept, you will give him your full and honest cooperation, withholding nothing from him about Harry Townsend. Okay?"

"Yes. Call him."

Leo called Wayne and told him it was time to talk. They scheduled that afternoon. It would be just a meeting between Wayne and Leo for now. If there was an offer, Leo would take it back to Tommy. While they were meeting, Tommy would be going to Galena Pipe to resign. He was not giving a reason. Vernon would know the reason anyway.

At two o'clock that afternoon, Leo and Wayne met at Wayne's office. Wayne had an Assistant State's Attorney sit in.

"Well, Leo, what is Tommy going to say?"

"If you are able to make an offer that he and I think is a good offer, he can say a lot. Leo then outlined what Tommy's testimony would include in great detail.

"What about his responsibility? How does he feel about that?

"He's truly remorseful. Not only for what it has done to him and his family, but also for what he did to his employer and for what might have happened to someone caught in the fire. You've known me, Wayne. I'm not trying to blow smoke here. I think he is ashamed of what he did."

"Here is what makes it hard to cut a deal, Leo. Tommy set the fire, and he knew that someone else was in the plant. So, if I am not convinced that he took that carefully into consideration and was confident nobody would get hurt or killed, I couldn't cut a deal. Normally, anyone being in the building would make this an aggravated arson if Tommy knew that person could be in danger. That could be anywhere from six to thirty years. I don't know if I could prove it, but there would be justification to file it."

"I don't think it fits here, and I will tell you why. Tommy knew that the night security guards only make rounds in other parts of the plant and not in the kiln area. That is because the kiln area is supposed to have an elaborate sprinkler system that kicks in at the same time the special kiln fire alarm sounds. That alarm was designed to be heard everywhere in the plant, including every area the security guard would ever be in. At least that was what he and other employees, as well as the security guards, had been told. I'm sure some of them would testify to that. As it turned out, those systems were not working up to the standard they should have been. But Tommy did not know that, nor did any other employees. They are all as surprised as he is by the amount of damage. Tommy swears that he expected a small fire which would be quickly extinguished, even though it would still be harmful enough to disrupt work for a period of time."

"If he comes in and convinces me of it and agrees to cooperate, I will offer simple arson, a lesser felony. And I will recommend the bottom range of three years. I can't do better. That probably gets him out in a year and a half. But I want Harry for the aggravated felony if I can make the case. He is the instigator of all the bad things that have happened, and it was intentional and malicious."

"I will run it past Tommy and let you know what else he can tell me and whether he will take the deal."

When Wayne met with Tommy and took his information, he agreed to offer a Class 2 felony at the very bottom of the range. He also reinforced the importance of keeping his cooperation a secret. He could not talk about it to Harry Townsend or anyone else. That would include broadly friends, relatives, fellow employees, or others who may be giving testimony, such as Jake Sharp, Vernon Tanksley, the night plant guards, and even the fire investigators. Simply put, the fact that he had even talked to the State's Attorney could not get out.

For several weeks, the state's attorney's office had been presenting grand jury testimony and evidence. The Walkers were aware of that and only that. Grand jury testimony and evidence is secret. Grand jurors are sworn to secrecy and State's Attorneys take secrecy seriously. It is a matter of policy. Wayne had not had any communications with the Walkers since the grand jury was called, except to stay posted about the pending civil suits. Knowing that they played into the criminal case, he wanted to stay current on everything that was scheduled in those cases. Nate and Josh agreed. As to what Wayne was doing, they could only speculate and they were as anxious as anyone to know if there had been an indictment signed and, if so, when it would be filed. But Wayne was playing close to the vest.

CHAPTER 47

Friday, April 28. 1989

April twenty-eighth was a gray, winter-looking day. The wind was gusty. The sky was dark and threatening, almost daring you to come outside with a smile on your face or a spring in your step. It was the kind of day that made most people want to go back to bed when they looked outside. It was the kind of day that made school children fake symptoms of cold or flu to fool their parents into letting them stay home. It was the kind of day that makes people angry the moment they step out the door, and the bitter wind slaps them in the face.

There were not many people that Stockton morning who jumped out of bed, stretched, skipped into the bathroom, stripped out of their sleeping attire, jumped into the shower, and broke into song. But there was one. Paul Hoffman was excited. He had been waiting for a long time to have Harry Townsend sitting in front of him, meeting his glare as he methodically took his deposition. Oh, yes! This was a fine, fine day indeed.

The weather was no better in Cicero that morning. It was a little colder, and wind from the lake was just a bit chillier. If all of the citizens of Cicero could have been polled that day, there would have been so few happy people that a benevolent God would have scratched the whole thing and started over. Harry was in such a foul mood that he would not have forgiven God for his failed first attempt at coming up with an acceptable Friday. Even if God had fixed it and made it sunny and warm, that would still not have been enough for Harry since He screwed up the first time.

But God didn't fix the day. It was still cold and crappy. Harry was awake and out of bed by five o'clock that morning. He had to meet Bernie Torveski for a three-hour drive to Galena so that he could have his deposition taken in a lawsuit he was not involved in. It involved only Galena Pipe Works and Noble Vista Development, for Christ's sake. He had intentionally stayed out of that one. He stirred it up for sure and did get those dumbasses in Texas sued. But that was their fault for being so damned stupid. Now, he had to waste his time going to Galena with his lawyer, who, if he had any legal talent, should have gotten him out of it. And if he thought Harry was going to pay attorney's fees for this, then he was as dumb as those Texans. Screw all of them. He knew what it would take to get Galena Pipe, and he wasn't afraid to do it. He didn't originally plan it that way. He made an offer. A good one. When that didn't work, he got Galena Pipe sued in Texas. When that didn't work, he tried harassing the old ladies who were holding out with their stock. Then he burned down half of their plant. And they still think they can refuse him. They can't … not with what was still coming.

This bullshit today was a waste of their time. They already managed to have his deposition taken in Texas by an uppity little lawyer who showed him no respect. It did them no good. His gloves were off now, Vernon's too. First, they would get all the stock the old ladies were holding out. Then he would find some way to go after those smart-assed, small-town lawyers. He would make them all pay for this shit he has to go through. But getting the stock from the old ladies would come first. Too bad it had to be done the hard way, but it was because they had made it that way themselves.

After a cup of coffee and a bowl of cold cereal, Harry got into his Suburban and drove over to Bernie's house to pick him up. Bernie lived in a shithole as far as Harry was concerned. It was a little prewar bungalow that had seen better days, about half a mile from where Al Capone had lived in the twenties. Capone's house had been a lot nicer, of course. Bernie was a chump Harry had known since grade school at Cicero East Elementary. The two of them were bullies even then. Somehow, Bernie had gotten a law degree and passed the bar. In the meantime, Harry was learning how to make money. That's something Bernie never figured out. Both Harry and Bernie had good families growing up. But whereas Harry had alienated his, Bernie still lived with his mother and took care of her. His one attempt at marriage had leaked water from the first day. Bernie moved his poor wife in with his mother, and that was the end of that. Harry just needed Bernie to dirty up this stupid lawsuit, which wasn't going to go anywhere. If it had been serious, Harry would have hired real talent.

After waiting five minutes, Harry laid on the horn. And out ambled Bernie, wearing a trench coat over his business suit, looking wider than he was tall. Harry could swear the car tipped to the right when Bernie slid in.

"Hey, Harry, how's it witchoo?"

"Just wonderful, Bernie. My cup runneth over. I am delighted to be driving on a shitty day to a stupid little town a hundred and fifty miles from here to have some asshole ask me stupid questions because my lawyer couldn't get me out of it."

"Good. I was scared you was going to be in a bad mood."

"Alright, Clarence Darrow. When answering these questions today, is there anything I should avoid saying?"

"Yeah. Don't say nothin' about where Jimmy Hoffa got dumped."

Some genius I got for a lawyer.

And so, the old friends enjoyed a pleasant drive out of Chicagoland and west on old Route 20 to the historic and picturesque city of Galena, Illinois.

———

Prior to the day of the deposition, Wayne had called Paul Hoffman to ask a favor. He told Paul that one of his investigators wanted to have a word with Harry Townsend after the deposition. Paul was going to have Josh sitting with him just because Harry seemed a bit intimidated by him. So, when Paul wrapped up the deposition and began making final remarks for the record, Wayne wanted Josh to leave the room and warn Wayne and the investigator that the session was winding up. Then Paul would go to the door and knock on it to signal Wayne and the investigator to come in. Paul agreed to it and told Josh what his part was. It was going to be a short deposition anyway.

CHAPTER 48

April 28, 1989

The deposition was taken at the courthouse. Harry and Bernie arrived just after ten o'clock. They asked the officer at the door where the deposition would be taken, and he directed them to the right room where a court reporter was already set up. Now they were just waiting for Paul Hoffman, who decided to let them stew for about fifteen minutes before finally walking in with Josh.

Harry gave Josh a look that would have frozen a normal human being. Josh just smiled back, elbowed Paul in the side, and said, "I don't think he likes me."

Paul went through all the preliminaries and made a record of all parties present. He asked Harry if he had ever given a deposition, he asked him if he understood he was under oath and subject to possible perjury penalties if he did not tell the truth, he asked if he was feeling well, and if he was taking any drugs that could affect his ability to understand the questions. He asked all the standard preliminary questions and gave all the basic admonishments. Then he had a copy of the phony contract between Babson and Noble and a copy of the contract between Galena Pipe and Noble, marked as exhibits.

He had a copy of the Lubbock deposition transcript in front of him, which he referred to when asking certain questions that had been covered in that deposition. Harry didn't back off the lies he told under oath in the Lubbock deposition, and now those lies had also been uttered under oath in the state of Illinois. Paul asked about his conversations with Tommy Schumann and got him to deny that there were any. Harry denied asking Tommy to slip a copy of the phony contract to Vernon Tanksley. And he denied asking Tommy to set a fire at the Galena Pipe plant. That question caught Harry by surprise, and Paul could see him getting a little nervous. Bernie was making regular objections to the questions and was beginning to squirm a little himself. Paul noted the objections and then ignored them. Bernie had not expected this line of questioning. He tried to stop the deposition once and threatened to walk out with Harry at his side. Paul told him he would not get far before the judge, sitting in his courtroom right next door, got involved. He told Bernie that the reason he had scheduled the deposition at the courthouse rather than his office was because he anticipated the same kind of monkey business he had run into with the inspection at the South Beloit plant. And Bernie knew how that turned out.

Paul asked Harry if he had ever had a conversation in the presence of Brock Johnson and Bill Turl in which he admitted having an employee of Galena Pipe slip a copy of the phony contract to Vernon. He looked startled and paused to talk to Bernie. Then, he denied ever having had such a conversation. Paul asked if he had ever had a conversation with them in which he admitted being behind the plan to start the fire at Galena Pipe. At that point, Bernie instructed his client not to answer that question or any questions relating to the fire. Paul could tell he was on the verge of telling Harry not to answer any more questions at all, based on his Fifth Amendment right. Paul didn't want that, so he let it pass.

From there, Paul went into Harry's attempt to buy Galena Pipe shares from Vernon's aunts. He asked him to set out the offer he had made first, which Harry did. Then, he asked him to set out the terms of the offer he made after the fire. Harry did that, too. Paul asked Harry how many calls he had made to Vernon's aunts after they had formally declined his offer to buy their stock. Harry could not remember, but he did admit to making more than one call.

The deposition covered several other areas, and there were a few times when they had to go off record so that Paul could admonish Harry to answer his questions and remind Bernie of the deposition rules. But after two hours, he was ready to wrap it up. He informed Harry of his right to review and sign the deposition transcript after it was prepared and asked if he or Bernie had any questions. Bernie made a few threats about how they were going to depose every shareholder of Galena Pipe, including Josh, Nate, the two aunts, as well as Paul himself. Bill Turl had been given notice of the deposition and, of course, had declined to appear on behalf of Noble. Since Bernie had no questions or comments to add, Paul told the reporter that the deposition was over and they were now off the record. While that conversation was going on, Josh had left the room briefly to put Wayne on notice that the deposition was ending. Then he came back into the room, closed the door, and sat down again. Harry and Bernie started to get up. Then Paul said, "We are off the record here, and I want to have a word with Mr. Townsend."

"Yeah," said Harry. "Go ahead. What the hell do you want to say?"

"I just have something on my mind I have been wondering about. You say that you worked for Ford Motor Company back in the 1950s as an area representative to its dealers in Northern Illinois and Southern Wisconsin."

"Yeah, I did. Only it was not just area representative. It was regional manager. There is a big difference. So, what about it?"

"Well, let me test your memory then. Did you call on dealers in Freeport, Stockton, and Galena?"

Now, Harry was getting a little intrigued by all of this. "Sure. What of it?"

"Okay. For instance, take Stockton. Do you remember who the Ford dealer was?"

"Like yesterday. It was this guy, Melvin, something. Ah … Howard. Chubby bald guy. A pushover."

"You think that was the name, okay. Now, let's see how good you are. Do you remember a guy who worked for him who had an artificial leg?"

"Oh, hell yeah! I remember the doofus. Yeah … um … let me think. Yeah, the guy killed himself and his wife. Oh, yeah, I remember that guy. It was Ed, or Eddie, or something. That was it. Ed something or other."

"Congratulations on your memory, Harry. His name was Ed Hoffman. He was a guy who lost his leg in the war. Ed Hoffman was his name. Guess what else, Harry? When he and his wife died, he had a kid. That kid lost both his mother and his father the same day you got his dad fired and kicked him to the floor in the showroom."

"How do you know about all that?"

"I'm that kid, Harry. Ed was my dad."

Harry sat there speechless as Paul's eyes burned into him. Bernie looked down at the table.

Josh sat there absolutely stunned. He knew nothing about this. He had simply expected a deposition. Harry Townsend was the guy who got Ed fired! And Paul just got him to lie under oath in a deposition for a second time. Harry may have to answer for perjury!

After a few moments of silence, Paul went to the door and knocked on it. He expected Wayne Belcher or one of his assistants to be there just to ask Harry some questions. But when the door opened up, Wayne strode in with two armed sheriff's deputies in tow and went straight to Harry.

"Mr. Townsend, my name is Wayne Belcher. I am the State's Attorney for Jo Daviess County. I have with me a warrant for your immediate arrest, and I will hand a copy of that warrant now to your attorney."

He handed the warrant to Bernie, who was dumbstruck. "What is this for? What is he being charged with?"

"He is charged with one count of aggravated arson for participation in the fire which occurred at the Galena Pipe Works plant on the morning of January the ninth of this year and for one count of conspiracy to commit the murder of Mrs. Frieda Payne."

Paul was so shocked he couldn't stay on his feet. He walked to the conference table and sat down. He looked at the door and saw Josh standing there with his mouth open. He was as surprised as Paul.

The deputies cuffed Harry, led him out of the room, and down the stairs with Bernie walking behind, asking what the hell they thought they were doing and when would he see a judge to set bail. They told him that, unfortunately, the judges often leave town early on Fridays to get a jump on the weekend, so it would be Monday at the earliest. Mr. Townsend would have to sit it out in the county jail over the weekend. And their guess was that bail was unlikely anyway, considering the charges. But who were they to say? That would be up to a judge on Monday.

Wayne left the room for five minutes to talk to the deputies, then came back and sat down with Paul and Josh. Nate had picked up on the commotion going on in the courthouse and he saw the deputies leading Harry away in handcuffs, so he joined them in the deposition room. Wayne said he could fill them in now on what had gone on over the past few weeks. He was sorry he couldn't confide in them before, but grand jury secrecy rules prevailed.

Nate said, "Wayne since this involves the arson at the plant and it involves his aunts, should we wait until Vernon can get here to listen?"

"Vernon already has been briefed on it VERY thoroughly. He was arrested at the pipe plant when Paul started the deposition. Vernon had been working with Harry the whole time, playing the innocent dupe who was tricked by Tommy Schumann and Harry into stealing a customer from Babson. But the truth is that he conspired with Harry to get Tommy to set the fire. Harry played them both. Neither of them knew what the other one knew. That was the beauty of it. What Vernon knew that Tommy Schumann did not know was that the sprinkler system was practically useless, as was the alarm system. Carl Kraus had told him about it and had warned him of penalties if he did not get the violation corrected. He told Carl that he was working on it. Vernon had reason to think the whole kiln would burn up, and the fire could spread to the rest of the plant. He also knew there would be a watchman on duty at the plant when it took place."

"But, conspiracy to kill Frieda! What is that about?" asked Josh.

"Funny about that, Josh. Talk about dumb luck. ABSOLUTE DUMB LUCK. We knew that Harry was cautious about talking on the phone. Brock Johnson told us that. But Vernon is not a cautious guy about anything. After Carl told us about Vernon lying about the sprinkler system and alarm system, we were curious and got a warrant to see what calls Vernon was making from his office and his home. One number that kept coming up had a 312 area code — Chicago. It belonged to one of Harry's businesses dealing with rental properties, called "Superior Property Rentals". It was a phone line that ran to his office in Cicero. We didn't think we had enough to get a tap on that line since it wasn't in Harry's name, and Bernie was also a principal of the rental company. That gave Bernie use of the phone line for his own private calls whenever he was at Harry's office, and he is an attorney. There was no reason to suspect Bernie Torveski, and taping a phone he uses could involve other clients who might speak to him on that line. Since it is a little harder to get a judge to sign for a tap when an attorney might be using a phone line, it was easier to just get a tap on Vernon's two phones.

"Sure enough, we picked up on several calls between them. They talked about the fire and whether they thought anything could come back to them on it. They were a little worried about Tommy Schumann, but there would only have been his word that Harry was connected to the fire. The telephone calls made it clear that both Harry and Vernon were behind the arson.

"But then we got the shock of a lifetime when they started talking about getting Frieda out of the way. Harry wanted to have two men he knew of in Chicago kill Frieda in a home burglary. The plan was that with Frieda out of the way, Martha would most likely inherit her stock. Then, with a little urging from Vernon, Martha would sell her own shares and the shares Frieda left her. Probably would sell it cheaply. Vernon said she would have sold her shares already if not for Frieda. Frieda was the insurmountable problem. They figured that if Martha sold, then you and most of the other shareholders would sell, too. You wouldn't want any part of Harry Townsend or the merged company. Harry told Vernon that if the merger didn't get done, he was going to get fired anyway. He said Frieda had let that slip to him when he went to talk to them. She said Vernon was stupid and her brother's shares should never have gone to him to begin with.

At first, Vernon was shocked about the idea of killing anyone, and he resisted it. But he was eventually worn down by Harry. He admitted that he had long suspected that Frieda might get the board to fire him. It was easy to believe what Harry told him. He told Harry that he had hated Frieda ever since she threatened to have him fired once before. That was when he tried to get rid of Jake Sharp, who was the plant manager at the time he took over for his dad. She had forced him to back down in front of everyone, and it was humiliating. She had never shown him the kind of respect she had for his father, and everyone saw that, too. Vernon told Harry that she had always been dismissive of him. He detested her for that and for screwing up the merger. Detested her enough to at last agree with Harry's plan. How many years did the old biddy really have left anyway?

"By the way," said Wayne, "the guys in Chicago who were being solicited for murder have been arrested. After we recorded the calls from Vernon's phone, we finally had enough to get a tap on the phone Harry had been using. So we got those two picked up. But their cases are flimsy. They never acted on it in any way, and they never got any money. They just told Harry over the phone that they would do it. They could always say they were playing Harry along and had no intention of ever carrying out the murder. They might even say they were setting him up to have leverage over him. Just agreeing over the phone may not be enough where there was no overt act. I'm pretty sure they will testify if they get immunity. Nobody wants to give them that, but it might be important testimony. We will have to see.

"But in the cases of Harry and Vernon, it is different. The act was the solicitation itself and the conspiracy to solicit. Harry picked the worst time he could have picked to get loose with his rule about not discussing things on the telephone. The phone calls prove that they performed the act of solicitation of murder for hire, whether they got it done or not. And we have their motive. I don't see us making any good deals with them on either charge, the arson or solicitation. Vernon would flip on Harry in a second, but he doesn't deserve a break. Frieda was his aunt. And Galena Pipe was the company his grandfather started. I am not inclined to negotiate a plea deal with either one of them. These are good cases to take to a jury.

"My God. The looks on all the faces when we entered the room! I felt like Elliot Ness. The reactions ran from pure horror in the case of Harry to absolute disbelief in the cases of Paul, Josh, and Bernie. Well, I should get back to work. It's going to be a busy afternoon."

CHAPTER 49

April 28, 1989 – Same Day

Before Paul, Nate, and Josh even left the courthouse, Nate picked up the phone in the clerk's office and called Ann. She answered after the second ring.

"Ann, this is Nate. I hope I am not bothering you."

"Of course not. Have you decided to finally share a little of your super secret information with the free press, as any good citizen would?"

"I don't know about that. We'll just call this a random tip from an unknown and yet reliable source. You should get over to the state's attorney's office without even taking the time to hang up the phone. And when you get there, you should ask Wayne Belcher about the arrests of one Vernon Tanksley, Jr., of Galena, Illinois, and one Harrold Arnold Townsend, of Cicero, Illinois. You might get a story the wire services will want."

"You are kidding! You are kidding!"

"Nope, I am not."

The next thing Nate heard was a door slamming shut. It took Ann thirty-five minutes to get to Wayne's office in

Galena. Nobody else had picked up on the story yet. It wouldn't take long before they did. But Wayne wanted Ann to have the story first. He had known Ann for a long time, and she had always been honest with him in her reporting. He filled her in on the charges and the arrests. He only held back about the phone taps. That would all come out in court, where there would certainly be challenges. He felt comfortable with the taps, but he didn't want them scrutinized at this point. Nate, Paul, and Josh walked over to the Walkers' Galena office to sit down and digest all that had happened. Lawyers like nothing better than to review things in hindsight and wonder where they went wrong.

"What a day!" said Nate. "Boy, were we ever clueless about Vernon. It makes sense to me now. Something seemed odd about Vernon as time went on. He may have been in the dark at the beginning and didn't know Tommy was working with Harry. But we now know that at some point, he had to have figured it out. By then, Harry was confiding in him. He learned that Harry was working with Brock to set Galena Pipe up to get sued and that Tommy had been involved with Harry in getting him a copy of the phony contract. He even knew that Tommy was going to start the plant fire, even though Tommy thought it was a secret from him. But we didn't suspect any of that.

"It should have bothered us that Vernon knew Harry was harassing his aunts, and he didn't seem to care. That alone should have made Vernon so angry that he would never talk to Harry again. But it didn't. Instead, he increased the pressure on them himself, telling them they had to do exactly what Harry wanted. Why would he side with Harry when he knew by then what kind of a person Harry was? And why, when Jake had a perfect solution to offer to the problem with the pipe joints, did Vernon try to shoot it down? Somehow, all of that eluded us. Three brilliant minds, and we all just thought Vernon was stupid and naïve."

Josh agreed. "Right you are, Walker. We should have suspected Vernon. I fault you for not picking up on it. But, in your defense, you didn't have the key piece of information that Wayne had. Vernon knew all along that the plant was vulnerable to fire, which means Harry probably knew it from him. That may have given Harry the idea of the plant fire to begin with. Carl Kraus, the fire chief, had warned Vernon in person. The fact that the fire was being investigated as arson scared him. He told Harry he was afraid they would start asking him about the warning he had. Wayne said that was in one of the conversations picked up in the phone taps. But we didn't know that. Vernon lied about it. He told us he didn't know about the sprinkler and alarm systems being flawed. He knew the fire would be extensive. If I had known all of it, I would have figured it out. Maybe you and Paul would have, too. But I can't be certain of that."

"Maybe so, Josh. It almost makes me wonder if Paul and I should start listening to what you have to say."

Paul spoke up. "You can, Nate. But I think I will hold off on that. Think about this for a minute, though. It was an amazingly complicated thing. Vernon was playing Tommy. Tommy thought he was playing Vernon. Brock was playing Vernon, or thought he was. And Vernon was playing Frieda, Martha, and us. But Harry was playing everyone. Nobody had all the pieces but Harry. Pretty smart, really."

Nate got serious after that. "Paul, everything is going to drag on now. On the criminal cases, I expect convictions or pleas. Tommy is looking at a couple of years, probably. He will survive and hopefully never do another thing like it. Vernon and Harry are going to get much longer sentences. Solicitation of murder for hire used to have as much as a thirty-year minimum, from what I remember. Maybe not now. But I think that is close. Also, there is restitution. That is probably where we can come in. The restitution to Galena Pipe Works should be huge and could be in the form of Vernon's stock in Galena Pipe Works and maybe Harry's stock in Babson Pipe

Company, at a minimum. One way or another I think Galena Pipe Works will end up owning a pipe plant in Beloit by the time this is over. That's the final irony. It will kind of be a merger. Just without Harry and Vernon. So I think Galena Pipe will be okay. There is enough money now to finish getting the kiln back up and running, with or without insurance money. It won't take much longer. Jake Sharp can take over for Vernon and maybe take that job permanently. It's something we will talk about with the stockholders. But what about you, Paul? How have you come through all of this? What are your plans?"

"I have done a lot of thinking. Ann and I have done some talking, too. I'm comfortable in Stockton. It even feels like home. It's the only place that has ever really felt that way to me. It's been a very long road back. But, yeah, I'm home."

"Will you practice law again?"

"I'm thinking of getting licensed here. Illinois and Texas share reciprocity, so it won't be hard to do. Do either of you know of a small law firm looking for a lawyer who is kind of lazy and doesn't have to make much money?"

"We might suggest the Walker firm, with offices in Stockton and Galena. You seem to fit the firm profile. It has a stellar reputation ... at least among its partners. What do you think of the name Walker and Hoffman?"

"Count me in. But why not Walker, Walker, and Hoffman? Are one of you going somewhere better?"

"No. But we have the same last name and look alike. So if one of us makes somebody angry, they won't know who to ask for when they call."

"Good thinking. But I have to get very serious about something else. And this is the time for it. I need you to open up with the truth about something because I need to settle my mind once and for all. This is hard for me."

Paul paused and then said, "It was me who killed my father ... wasn't it? It was me all along who killed him? Be honest. Did you and Perkins and others protect me? I'm asking because it is finally just starting to come back. But it's still so foggy that I don't know if I can believe it or if it is my imagination playing a mean trick."

Nate and Josh looked at each other until Josh finally spoke. "Yes. Paul. It was you. From what we figured, Ed shot your mother, then dropped the gun and went to her. He was probably standing over her when you ran into the room. You saw her lying there, shot in the chest with blood all over her, dead or dying. In your young life, you had already seen Ed beat your mother more than once. You saw Ed standing over her, and you saw the gun lying on the floor where he had let it fall. On a couple of occasions, you had gone with your father and Perkins to watch them target shoot, and Perkins had let you load and fire his revolver. So, when you picked up Ed's revolver, you knew enough to pull back the hammer, aim, and squeeze the trigger. You fired at Ed from very short range. Probably just a few feet. You couldn't have missed. When Everett Perkins walked into the bedroom, you were lifeless and in complete shock, holding the gun in your lap. In our minds, it was a panicked response. What was to be gained by calling it anything other than suicide, which, in a way, it was. Ed's life ended when he shot Angie the way we saw it. He could never live with that.

"When Perkins tried to talk to you all he got from you was a blank stare. You were practically comatose and didn't know where you were or what had happened. You soon passed out altogether, and old Doctor Schwartz, who showed up soon, had to bring you back around. Betty Stieffle came later. She held you and tried to comfort you. We told her it was murder and suicide, and she believed it. So, we all made a pact, and we lied to protect an innocent young boy who didn't deserve any blame.

"We stayed in touch with Herb to see if you would suddenly have a recollection about what happened. If so, we were going to pass it off as an innocent mistake by Perkins and the rest of us. But that never happened. Years went by, and you adjusted to your new life. Herb was proud of everything you did. He bragged about you every time we talked to him. I thought that was what Angie would have wanted. We thought it had all worked out for the best. Which shows you how little we know.

"We also lied to Ann yesterday when she came to bring us the photos taken in Texas. She figured out that we had covered things up. Ann never stops thinking, as you have probably learned. Before she left the office, we got the feeling that she thought Herb was probably the one who killed Ed. But she never said it and we weren't sure what she was thinking. So we didn't want to bring it up and plant the idea."

Nate took over. "The facts are that Herb was in Stockton when it happened because your mother was planning to leave with him and take you with her to Chicago, where Herb would help her get a new start. Everett had somebody call Josh as soon as he saw the bodies. He had never dealt with anything like that. When Josh figured out what had happened, he called me and had me call Herb at the motel. He could not possibly have been at your house when the shots were fired and be back at the motel when I called him. Herb broke down crying.

"There had been unconfirmed gossip about Herb visiting Angie from time to time and about him helping her when she left Ed and went to Rockford. It wasn't widespread because people in town respected Herb and wouldn't listen to it. It was just a few busybodies. But if word got out that Angie was all packed up to leave town with Herb and then Herb showed up at the murder scene, it could start wild speculation. We didn't know if she had mentioned to anyone that Herb was coming to take you both to Chicago. And people were aware that there was some bad blood between Ed and Herb. I told Herb to stay where he was. I would call him back after I had more information. That is when we all decided what to do. I called Herb back and told him that you had shot Ed after finding your mother dead and seeing him standing over her. I told him that we had trouble holding you responsible for anything that had happened and that we thought we might want to rule it a murder and suicide, leaving you out of it. You had enough to go through. He agreed. But if people knew he was already in town, it might add to speculation that Herb had shot Ed. Then, the truth might have to come out to protect him. It would be better if he just showed up the next day to take you so that there would be no chance of anyone thinking it was anything other than suicide. Betty Stieffle took you to her house and kept you until Herb came for you.

"Perkins sent the gun somewhere for fingerprint comparisons anyway, along with Herb's fingerprints and Ed's. It was just to protect Herb if any questions about him came up later. They identified Eds and an unknown. Herb's prints were not on the gun. Your prints were not taken. When the two spent rounds were recovered, Perkins sent them off to the State Police lab for ballistics, which ended up proving that there was only one gun used. We didn't tell Ann everything. It is up to you to let her know the truth if you want to. But only if you want to. We know what our intentions were at the time, but we don't know if what we did was worse for you than telling the truth right then. Well-intentioned or not, it was probably the dumbest thing Josh and I have ever done. Ann pulled no punches, telling us that we had acted 'like God on Judgment Day.' Ann has a way with words, as you have learned. And she was right. Josh and I let our emotions overcome our thinking. We were beyond furious at Ed for ending Angie's life. We cared so much for Angela that for us, it was like losing a close family member. So, we stepped well over the line to look out for the son she loved. It is the only time in our careers we have ever done anything like that. As time went on, it would have made things even worse for you if we tried to undo it. If it ended up backfiring and causing you more trouble, we hope you can forgive us."

"There is nothing to forgive, Nate. You put your careers at risk for me. Whatever else you may call it, it was incredibly unselfish. I'll tell Ann, and she'll understand completely. After so many years, it eases my mind to finally know the truth. It is going to take a good deal of reflection and self-examination, but it will be alright. I'll tell you something. I was terrified that it might be Herb that did it. That would have broken my heart."

EPILOGUE

December 16, 1989

Paul Hoffman's Journal

Saturday brought Stockton one of those days when the sun is shining on the thin layer of crisp, white snow that crunches under your feet as you walk along the street. I walked up Sycamore Street toward what was once the combined high school and grade school. It burned down to the ground in 1955, and I can still remember the dark smoke filling the sky that Sunday morning. We lived in a white two-story frame house only two blocks from the school, so our home smelled of smoke, our clothing smelled like smoke, and the curtains in my bedroom smelled like smoke. I walked by that house this morning. It looked just the same as when I had lived there with my parents. My mind no longer blocks out what happened in that house on November 27, 1956. In fact, I can remember it all very clearly now. The trauma that had blocked my memory is gone.

But now, what I remember most about that house are the Christmas nights after we got home from the Christmas Eve service with its children's pageant. That is when we opened our Christmas presents. We never waited until Christmas morning. Santa Claus came every year while we were in church. How lucky were we! I remember some Christmas mornings when Ed was in good spirits while we dressed up for church again. My mother would sing carols as she moved around the kitchen, getting everything ready for the Christmas dinner we would enjoy after we got home.

I remember the brand-new sled I got for Christmas only one day before a huge snowstorm that looked like it would bury the whole town before it moved on. When we had storms like that, the city always blocked off Sycamore Street all the way from the water tower hill to Main Street. That opened it up for sledding. I thought my new sled was the fastest on the hill. I would launch myself off a low brick wall with my sled, hit the icy street, and fly past my house, feeling every bump along the way. As I look at the house now, I see that it still has the enclosed front porch. It wasn't enclosed when we moved in. Ed had it enclosed later, with large windows looking onto the street. One Fourth of July, Ed was in a good mood and we were all happy. We had homemade ice cream on that porch while we watched all the cars coming down Sycamore Street from the hill where people had parked to watch the city fireworks display. A once-a-year traffic jam and we had ringside seats to watch it. I remember those things and so many others as I look at that house. All of them wonderful to relive.

I am still renting two rooms from Mrs. Wright, who almost feels like family by now. She has even learned to cook grits in the morning just for me. Soon, I will be moving, though. Ann and I bought a lot not far from the new high school. Marriage is on the horizon. We will start construction on a house in the spring. It won't be large, and it will fit in well with the other homes on the block. The house will have three bedrooms, a large kitchen, dining room, and living room. It will have a double garage and a basement, which is something you don't find in Houston. Ann will use one of the bedrooms as an office. I won't need my own office in the house because I finished the work I was doing on the tort text for my law school. Now, I work out of the Walker and Hoffman Law Firm offices in Stockton and Galena.

Thomas Wolfe wrote that "you can't go home again." I think that could be right in many cases. But there are people who never really left home to begin with, even if they thought they did. We are the lucky ones.

ACKNOWLEDGMENTS

I owe thanks to many people who helped me through the process of preparing this book for publication.

Frank Eastland at Publish Authority walked me through the entire process and struggled to teach me something about book publishing. I am grateful to him and his fine team. Thanks also to Janie Mills at Alliance Book Editing, LLC, for her patience and to Raeghan Rebstock at Raeghan Designs for the wonderful book cover and website design.

The following people generously spent time reviewing my earliest drafts, finding my many mistakes, and providing encouragement and feedback: Gary Cappallo, Joanna Gutzmer, David Gutzmer, Armin Gutzmer, John Lawyer, and Rick Schubert. And, of course, thanks are owed to Dianne Gutzmer for showing patience to a husband who spends too much of his time writing things. None of them are responsible for any inaccurate depictions of the towns and cities, legalities, or other matters found in the novel. Those things are ALL mine.

The historic city of Galena, Illinois, is the backdrop for much of the novel, along with the village of Stockton, Illinois. Stockton is a special town in a special county where I was fortunate to live as a young boy. In the novel, Paul Hoffman had it right when he said, "Stockton is a very good place to live."

ABOUT THE AUTHOR

Norman Gutzmer is a Texas Lawyer with a background in private practice and experience as an underwriting attorney in the title insurance industry. He began life in Stockton, Illinois, a small farming village in northern Illinois, about twenty-nine miles east of Galena, Illinois, in Jo Daviess County, the setting for "Galena.". Somehow, he found himself years later living in Houston, Texas, where an overwhelming desire to try private law practice eventually led him to gather his surprised, yet gracious, wife and children and move them to Amarillo, Texas, where he practiced law until retirement. He now lives in Grand Prairie, Texas, and happily divides his time between his family, his dog, and writing stories.

For more about the author, click the QR Code below or visit his website at NormanQugzmer.com.

THANK YOU FOR READING

If you enjoyed *Galena*, we invite you to leave a review and share your thoughts and reactions online and with friends and family.

www.ingramcontent.com/pod-product-compliance
Lightning Source LLC
Chambersburg PA
CBHW070619300726
48975CB00006B/1866